ABOUT THE AUTHOR

TIM DAVYS is a pseudonym. He is the author of
Amberville, *Lanceheim*, and *Tourquai*, the first
three books in the Mollisan Town quartet, and
lives in Sweden, where he is currently working on
the last Mollisan Town novel—*Yok*.

LANCEHEIM

ALSO BY TIM DAVYS

Amberville

Tourquai

LANCEHEIM

A NOVEL

TIM DAVYS

HARPER ● PERENNIAL

NEW YORK • LONDON • TORONTO • SYDNEY • NEW DELHI • AUCKLAND

HARPER ● PERENNIAL

First published in Swedish in 2008 by Albert Bonniers Förlag.

A hardcover edition of this book was published in 2010 by Harper-Collins Publishers.

HarperCollins books may be purchased for educational, business, or sales promotional use. For information please write: Special Markets Department, HarperCollins Publishers, 10 East 53rd Street, New York, NY 10022.

First Harper Perennial edition published 2011.

Translated by Paul Norlen

Designed by Renato Stanisic

Library of Congress Cataloging-in-Publication Data is available upon request.

ISBN 978-0-06-179744-6

11 12 13 14 15   OV/RRD   10 9 8 7 6 5 4 3 2 1

LANCEHEIM

REUBEN WALRUS 1

Reuben Walrus was too restless to sit down at first. He wanted to get back to his waiting philharmonic, and he could not get the offending note out of his head. Starting rehearsals without having the symphony finished was madness, but there was no other alternative. Now he thought that possibly that note, the one he could sense but not place, was the key to completion. This increased his impatience.

He paced nervously back and forth until his legs got tired and he sat down. He refused to accept that age had made him tired and stiff, that the years had passed faster and faster after sixty. The chair was hard and ugly, and stood alone in the windowless corridor.

Along with the other institutions, the hospitals—including St. Andrews—bought artworks to keep the artists of Mollisan Town alive. On the walls in these gloomy culverts, abstract explosions of gaudy colors hung next to delicate sepia-toned twilight landscapes. Most were competent, but there were even one or two that showed talent. The solitary chair that was the sole extent of the waiting area for the hearing center was beneath such a find, a small watercolor depicting a naked cow. Reuben did not recognize the cow, and she was probably no one special, simply one of the artist's models. Discovering talent in such an unexpected place gave Reuben hope. A good omen. Perhaps this might be a shorter visit than he had feared. At the next moment a nurse showed up in the corridor. Reuben smiled.

"Finally a little company," he said. "Do you come here often?"

The nurse, a llama in the customary white nurse's uniform, looked up from her papers with surprise.

"Are you joking, Mr. Walrus?" she asked.

The llama was apparently not the easily approachable type.

"Absolutely not," he replied. "I mean it. If you come here often, I intend to get sick more often. If you want me to be healthy, we'll have to see each other somewhere else."

Taken aback, the llama observed the broadly smiling Reuben Walrus. She stood like that a long time, just staring. At last she said with disgust in her voice, "Shame on you, old animal."

And he could not refrain from snorting out an amused little laugh as he tugged with pleasure on his mustache. She sniffed, turned around, and asked him in a formal tone of voice to follow her. In her ice-cold wake he followed through the winding halls of the hospital.

He remembered having been one flight up when he left his samples at the hearing center the week before, in a corridor whose walls were pale turquoise. Now the nurse led him to a door that was light yellow. She knocked and opened without waiting for an answer. Behind the large desk, to Reuben's astonishment, sat an older female swan. It was not Reuben's doctor.

The consulting room was similar to the one he recalled

from last time. There were rows of cabinets on the walls, in the corner the sterile examination cot, and everywhere supplies of terrifying instruments gleaming in the harsh light from the ceiling lamps.

"Excuse me," he said, from where he remained standing a few steps inside the door, "but I think there's been a mistake. I was supposed to meet Dr. . . . Dr. . . . another doctor?"

Reuben fell silent. He did not remember the name of the previous doctor. The swan on the other side of the desk got up. She was a few heads taller than him, and she extended her wing.

"Margot Swan," she introduced herself, and he took her wing and shook it. "I am a great admirer, Mr. Walrus."

"Call me Reuben," said Reuben, sitting down on the chair in front of the desk. "Dr. Swan, I am here to see—"

"I have taken over your case, Mr. Walrus."

My case? thought Reuben. What case? He had been worried that the earaches were a premonition of an unpleasant influenza. He was here to get pills, some antibiotics that might keep the bacteria away; he did not have time to be confined to bed. He was not a *case*.

Reuben loathed hospitals. This was Father's fault, and it was not the only thing he had on his conscience. What might Reuben have become with a different upbringing, if the Deliverymen had transported him to a different home? The question ran like a theme through Reuben Walrus's life; it stood in the way of all relationships he initiated.

Reuben never called him anything other than Father. The Chauffeurs had fetched him seven years ago, as of April. They came in the evening one Sunday when Reuben by chance was having dinner at home with his parents. He had seen them through the window in the dining room, seen the red pickup park at the sidewalk, and all he had felt was an exhausting happiness, as if he had reached the finish line after running his whole life.

When the door closed behind Father, Mother collapsed onto the kitchen table, weeping bitter tears. Reuben knew that deep inside she felt just as great a relief as he did. Their consciences were their audience as they played out this scene. He took her in his arms, and they promised to support one another in the difficult loss. They promised to pray as often as Father would have wished, and they promised to always honor his memory. The Chauffeurs—the ones who drive up in their red pickups and fetch the old and worn-out stuffed animals from this earthly life—would take Father to Paradise, and only our faith set limits on how marvelous it would be.

Reuben felt strangely empty when he went home later that evening. The panic did not seize him until the middle of the night. It was as if someone had vacuumed the oxygen out of the bedroom. He woke up with a jerk; it felt as if he were suffocating.

It was too late.

The words echoed in his head. It was too late. All the things he should have asked, all the things he needed to say: Now it was too late. He dragged himself out of bed and into the bathroom, where he filled the sink with hot water and breathed in the vapors with a towel over his head. The water rose so high that his mustache got wet, and all he could think was this: It was too late to pay back.

"To start with," said Margot Swan, "we must take a few more samples. We found out a great deal from the tests last week, but we didn't really know what we were looking for. Now we know better. Now it will be easier, when we know better."

Reuben heard what she said, but he was still not certain. More samples? Above Dr. Swan's desk was a window, and outside was a cramped courtyard squeezed between two gloomy St. Andrews buildings. In the windows opposite the blinds were half pulled, and the impression was irregular and disharmonious.

"And before I've got all the results, I suggest that we be very, very cautious about making any definite diagnosis."

"That sounds reasonable," said Reuben.

My father, he thought, did not believe in hospitals or doctors. If you didn't show respect to Magnus, illnesses were a punishment that you were forced to endure. All the punishments of Magnus were just and necessary. If your faith was sufficiently pure and strong, you went through life healthy and proud.

Early one morning the summer Reuben turned seven, he and Father got into the family's old Volga and drove to St. Andrews Hospital under a light blue sky broken up by thousands of fluffy clouds. The aches in his right ear had kept Reuben up the whole night, and Mother had consoled him as best she could. She was the one who forced Father to take the cub to the hospital; the night watch had given her courage to make an ultimatum. But Father did it against his will, against his better judgment. In the car, whose compartment smelled of vinyl and strawberries, he explained to his son that now Mother would see. The doctors could not perform miracles, it served no purpose to seek help; it was not a matter of diagnoses or medicines but rather of trust in Magnus and the willingness to meet the fate staked out long ago for each and every one of us.

Father's words cut like knives in Reuben's aching ears. His voice was hard and evil, dry and strangely breathless. Reuben remembered how the clearing summer sky seemed to roll past high above the car, like a colorful cloth someone was pulling along. In the corner of his eye he saw Father's wrinkled nose and transverse eyebrows. Again and again he came back to the same thing, saying that now Mother would see.

They parked outside the main entrance to the hospital. At that time the entrance was on the north side, and it was considerably more magnificent than the automatic glass doors that are there today. Reuben had no distinct memory of how they registered or how they found the waiting room, but he recalled that there was already a llama sitting there with a duckling whose head was bleeding. And Reuben had this heretical thought: that Magnus must have been extremely angry at that duck to want to wallop him on the head.

Reuben believed in Magnus. With a father who constantly forced the family toward prayers and meditation, reverence and reading of the Proclamations, the thought of not believing in Magnus was impossible. The first time Reuben encountered an atheist was in high school. It was a shock. It was as if someone were to maintain that, somewhere beyond the forests, there was life equally important to that of stuffed animals.

Then, at the age of seven in the hospital waiting room with an ear infection, Reuben's faith was unconditional. But he believed in a different way than Father, and there was nothing more terrifying than the thought that Father would expose him. Reuben's Magnus was nice. Reuben's Magnus did not involve himself in the lives of stuffed animals, but instead watched over them at a distance. What Reuben's Magnus thought and wanted could not be read in the Proclamations; Reuben knew that, at any rate. And Magnus understood that Reuben was good and nice, even if there were mistakes sometimes.

Father stood up as if shot from a cannon when Reuben's name was called out and it was their turn. He took Reuben by the fin and dragged him through the waiting room. He was in a hurry.

"Now you'll see," whispered Father as they stepped into the examining room.

Margot Swan spoke for a long time about how a diagnosis might change, how complicated it was to be absolutely certain. She spoke about the difficulties of evaluating test results that were influenced by outside circumstances, circumstances that often delayed the correct conclusions. Swan spoke with a steady voice, she used few technical terms, and she was careful to get Walrus's hummed assent before she began the next sentence. She sat stiffly on her chair at the desk, back straight, and her long, white neck extended from the collar of the well-ironed coat. It appeared to be made of porcelain. In contrast to all the whiteness, her beak shone bright red.

"Have you ever heard of Drexler's syndrome?" asked Margot Swan.

Reuben Walrus shook his head. It was strange, he thought, how hard it was for him to concentrate on what she was saying, how easy it was to glide back in thought to the day when he had sat with Father in a room not much different than this one. The memory was strong enough to shut out the present.

"Haven't you ever heard of Drexler's syndrome?"

He had neither heard nor wanted to hear about any syndrome. He wanted antibiotics to keep the infection in check a few more days. He shook his head and the bright red beak began, after a considered pause, to move again. Reuben tried to listen, but all he heard was Father's voice.

"There's nothing wrong with the cub."

The doctor raised his gaze from his papers with surprise and observed Father.

"But you came here anyway?" he asked.

"I have an earache," said Reuben.

He was ashamed. For the first time in his life he was ashamed of his father. This would happen to him more and more often, the older he got.

"He says that he has an earache?" the doctor said to Father.

It was a question, and Father shrugged his shoulders.

The doctor asked Reuben to come over and sit on a little stool. Reuben did as he was told, and the doctor looked in his ear and in his throat and wrote a few brief notes on a piece of paper on the desk. After a few minutes the examination was over.

"The cub has an ear infection," the doctor observed. "I am prescribing penicillin and eardrops."

He turned to Reuben and smiled.

"For external and internal use, so we're attacking on two fronts," he said in a conspiratorial tone.

Reuben smiled back and studiously continued to avoid Father's gaze. And if it could have ended there, if Father and Reuben had got up and left then, the memory of this first visit to the doctor would probably have faded.

"In the ear," explained Margot Swan, "are auditory hair cells. Simply stated, you might say that it is thanks to the hair cells that we can hear. Sometimes these cells are subject to attack. With repeated ear infections, or if the ear is subjected to extreme strain over a long period, high volumes for example, the hair cells can die."

Father had waited for this moment. He explained to the doctor that there would not be a need for any tablets, because the pains would go away when Magnus willed it. Father spoke in a loud, unctuous voice, as much to Reuben as to the doctor. He stood up and raised his paw toward the doctor's desk and said that Magnus was good.

"Shouldn't we let Magnus devote himself to more important matters?" the doctor answered. "So the medicines can help Reuben get healthy?"

This was a mistake. Reuben swallowed a large clump of anxiety and looked down at the floor. The doctor was making a big mistake. You didn't joke about Magnus like that. The gray linoleum floor under the stool began to spin.

"Hair cells that die cannot be reproduced," Margot Swan continued. "What happens is that the fewer cells you have left, the smaller the decibel range you can perceive. It's a matter of range, the highest and lowest tones. But you already know that, of course."

Reuben nodded. He nodded to confirm to Margot Swan that he had understood and to remind Father that forbearance was also a virtue.

"Do you think," roared Father, "that you can decide what the Lord Magnus should devote himself to?"

The paw that was pointing at the desk was now aimed right at the doctor's face.

"Do you think," roared Father, "that you have the right to reduce a punishment that our almighty Magnus has pronounced? Do you think perhaps . . . that you are the equal of Magnus?"

The doctor finally realized what he was up against. Reuben looked down at the floor and put his fins over his ears. He did not want to hear. It could hurt as much as it wanted.

"Drexler's syndrome," said Margot Swan to the old composer, who again refused to lift his gaze from the floor, "is a disease around which I have devoted the greater part of my life to doing research. Drexler's syndrome means that the hair cells in the ear die without apparent reason. The course of the disease is often very . . . aggressive. Sometimes it only affects hair cells, sometimes the hair cells are only the beginning."

I prefer pain, thought Reuben, I prefer pain to this. And he got up and left Father and the doctor in the examining room. He sat down on one of the chairs in the waiting

room, where he could still hear Father telling off the blas-
phemous doctor, and there and then he decided never to
return to a hospital again. Fifteen minutes later Father came
out of the consultation room. His cheeks were red, his eyes
were large, and he was breathing heavily.

"Now we're leaving," he said triumphantly.

Reuben did not recall how they managed to find their
way out.

"You have Drexler's syndrome," said Margot Swan. "As
I said earlier, there is of course a slight possibility that I
am mistaken, which is why we are continuing to take samples, but . . . I advise you to read as much as you can about
the disease before the next time we meet, then I will try
to answer any questions you have. Judging by what I see
today—and once again, more is required to determine this
beyond all doubt, but from what I know at this point—it's
a matter of about three weeks. Then your hearing is going
to . . . be extremely limited, if not . . ."

Reuben Walrus did not know what Margot Swan was
talking about. He could not for the life of him recall the
name of the syndrome. And he would not recall how he
managed to find his way out of the hospital this time either.

WOLF DIAZ 1

Straight out I will confess, at the risk of making myself more ridiculous than I ought to, that the tip of my pen does not even quiver when I describe my cubhood as an idyll. That is how I recall it, as a long series of uneventful days in the secure community that was Das Vorschutz, a few kilometers outside Lanceheim's eastern city limits. Before I begin tiring the reader with recollections from those days of happiness, I will only assure you that I am familiar with many of the well-trodden paths on which I now embark. Humility—hindsight's faithful squire—taps me on the shoulder and reminds me of the hundreds of capably authored depictions of cubbish delight, of the joy and excitement of discovery. I do not wish to promote myself at anyone else's expense, but because the surroundings of my cubhood happen to coincide with his, I am of the opinion that this will nonetheless be of some general interest. So, I beg you, put up with the following pages; they will later prove to be significant.

. . . .

My family and I lived in a forest glade that had been cleared many generations ago just for us, for our profession, and for our kind. On soil that was soft as moss, fertile from humus, and carefully tended by expert and sensitive paws, five timbered two-story houses had been built in a perfect circle: large buildings that seemed to be growing up under their straw roofs. These were dwellings of dark, hewn lumber, just as broad as they were tall. The houses surrounded a round lawn where I played ball for the first time, where I split a seam for the first time, and where I fell in love for the first time.

Every beaver that is delivered to Mollisan Town is invited, when he or she reaches that age, to become one of the forest guards in Das Vorschutz. Many are thereby called, but few are chosen. At the time when I was growing up, the tamers of the great forest were named Hans Beaver, Jonas Beaver, Anders Beaver, Sven Beaver, and Karl Beaver. Each one of them had taken a bird as a wife, and to this day I do not know whether that was only by chance.

My father, Karl, was responsible for the trees. He was a hard gnawer who would rather punish than woo and who sought companionship with his colleagues rather than with his family. My mother was a dreamer, a nightingale, the charming Carolyn. She lived in a world of her own; I think it became more wonderful with each passing year. When she was not at the school or in the kitchen, she spent most of her time in a small room on the upper floor where she sewed curtains and coverings for the couch and armchair from the same rough, white cotton cloth where pink hollyhocks grew and blossomed. She sat at her desk and looked out the window at the massive trees that, ancient and wise, rose up around the glade and protected us from the sun and rain. During the Evening Storm their dense crowns sang to us, and in the breeze during the day the leaves whispered a song whose melody Mother knew.

When Father showed up down in the glade, Mother quickly got up and hurried down to the kitchen to prepare dinner. I kept to the lower floor, in the living room or at the kitchen table, where I sat reading my books. In passing, Mother mumbled the same thing every day.

"Today I know that Papa is going to like the food."

But not one single time did I hear Father comment on Mother's cooking.

I loved Mother's fragile smile and her beautiful voice, and there was nothing I wanted more than to protect and take care of her. She might look at me with a questioning expression, as if she wondered for a moment who I was, before her gaze was veiled again and she withdrew back into her own, inner life. She taught me not to exaggerate the significance of the gestures, words, and expressions that a female shows the world; it is what goes on in her soul that is decisive.

And what did I really think of my father?

I realize that in the above description observant readers may detect a certain antipathy between the lines. The reply to the question just posed is that there were occasions when Father's impulsiveness and aggression coincided in the perfect, cross-ruled system of coordinates that was his spiritual life, and then he was a stuffed animal that you were compelled to fear. Nonetheless I loved him and admired him as if he were the wisest, most remarkable stuffed animal in all of Mollisan Town. For to get an appreciative glance from Father, I was prepared to climb up in the beech tree at Heimat without a ladder or run naked through the thistle field east of Pal's Ravine. Naturally Father would have punished me severely if I had done either of these foolish pranks. He was an animal who set scientific reason and religious veneration above all; he viewed everything else with skepticism.

. . . .

That the trees fell to my father Karl Beaver's lot was completely natural to all who knew him. His character was easy to compare to a tree's: tough and ancient, but strong and confident of victory. The few times when I was growing up that Father showed a sensitive, verging on raw, side were when he was forced to fell any of his stately friends, for he knew them all as individuals. If he had shown me or Mother the same consideration, he would have—according to Father's way of seeing things—betrayed himself and revealed a weakness that a model father ought not to show an impressionable son.

He would leave us early in the morning, along with the other beavers, and did not come home until dinnertime. He participated in all the ceremonies and activities that were part of our isolated miniature society in Das Vorschutz, and he defended us all. I am certain that he would have sacrificed his life to save me or Mother if it had been needed. But at the same time—if a paradox may be permitted—he would have saved us for his own sake.

Does this make him a better or a worse stuffed animal? I would prefer to leave that unsaid.

My father, the daring Karl Beaver, if he had had the opportunity to consider and judge my life, would have brooded a great deal. Now it will soon be five years since the red pickup fetched him, and in many respects he remains a mystery to me, just as I would grow up to be a mystery to him.

Oh well, genuine love allows mysteries to remain unsolved. This I have learned from Maximilian, and this I have learned from love itself.

The first six years of my life I spent in Das Vorschutz. I never left our securely staked-out part of the massive forest; there was no reason to. Hans Beaver and his Olga Woodpecker and Anders Beaver and Bluebird Niklasson had each had a cub of their own delivered the same year I myself arrived with the green pickup. Together with my same-age companions Weasel Tukovsky and Buzzard Jones, I kept myself occupied from early in the morning until late in the evening.

This self-imposed isolation, encouraged and upheld by the grown-ups in Das Vorschutz, may seem strange to an outsider. Early in the morning or in the middle of the afternoon, it took less than an hour to get to the Star, the roundabout where the four avenues—rectilinear parade streets in each direction—meet in the middle of Mollisan Town, but we pretended not to notice. Without wanting to, we were part of a city that in every detail made claims to be more complete than our beloved forest. What was called civilization was, according to our way of seeing it, a single, gigantic life lie. How could stuffed animals close their eyes to the most fundamental of truths: that their ability to develop creation—I mean all the technical, medical, and psychological advances made during the last hundred years—could not be considered more than a youthful attempt in relation to Magnus's own creation?

The authorities left us alone.

The forest guards were managed by a division of the Environmental Ministry that was also responsible for roads and road maintenance. The ministry officials encouraged, even stirred up, our rebellious isolation. Perhaps this was simpler than the opposite? However it was, we were allowed to provide our own schooling as long as we adhered to the prevailing curriculum; a doctor came out to the forest glade once a month and attended to our physical health; and over and above grocery shopping and more infrequent clothes shopping, there was no real reason to set our claws and paws on the colorful asphalt of Mollisan Town.

When I was little, of course I didn't think about this. I lived the only life I knew, and I loved every second and minute of it. How could it be anything other than an idyll? Buzzard, Weasel, and I took care to develop our personalities in different directions: We were laying the groundwork for our adult lives. Buzzard, aggressive and demanding, a challenger and a leader. Weasel, an admirer who accepted Buzzard's challenges and survived them, thanks to his unpredictable imagination. And finally me, the silent wolf, the observer whom the other two needed to be able to perform and accomplish, show off and go further.

The year we turned seven, our days of play and voyages of discovery were almost imperceptibly transformed into school days. It was my mother, Carolyn Nightingale, who in her evasive, cautious manner shifted our youthful curiosity from Weasel's imaginary worlds to the subjects she chose. Our schoolhouse was at our home, in a room next to the first-floor dining room that I had hardly noticed until then. This room, we now discovered, had served through the decades as the Forest Cubs' classroom. A corresponding room in the home of Hans Beaver and Olga Woodpecker was used as the doctor's consultation room, while in the house where Jonas Beaver lived with his family, the same room was used for the weekly meetings of the forest guards.

My mother lured us to the classroom in the morning with apple tartlets she had made famous far up in north Lanceheim. The slightly salty dough in combination with the sweetness of the cinnamon and the acid fructose of the apples was a perfect taste experience, impossible to resist. In that way I always came to associate learning with the most obvious sort of physical satisfaction.

During the following three years, Mother began every school day by reading selected passages from the great classics to us. My memory is distinct. The odor of tar that came in through the open window—it always smelled of tar from the wooden houses—and the aromas from my classmates' cotton bodies where they sat on the inherited benches. The taste of the tartlet on my tongue, Mother up at the lectern, and the massive blackboard behind her, which made her look smaller than she was. And the words that came out of her mouth. Some were too difficult for us, the plots of the books might fly high over our heads, but even then I enjoyed the sounds and the rhythm of Mother's voice.

Mother was in charge of the lessons in language, social studies, and mathematics. We did not devote ourselves to any other subjects those first years.

In third grade we got two new teachers. Mother remained our main teacher and spent most of her time with us, but in addition Weasel's mother, Bluebird Niklasson, started teaching chemistry, physics, and biology. Eva Whippoorwill came to the classroom once a week to give us lessons in something that was called Physical Improvement. I was unexpectedly on the verge of a decisive awakening.

It happened during Eva Whippoorwill's first minutes in the classroom. She had told us to stand up, and with inquisitive looks she complained about our poor posture and substandard stuffing. In my whole body, along my back and down through my hind legs, along my upper arms in toward the armpits and above all in my chest, in my heart, a form of shaking began to take shape.

Of course I got scared. What was happening to me?

I looked down at my body and confirmed that, despite the fact that it felt as if all of me was a jackhammer in use, I stood steady and unmoving by my bench. How was this possible? The sweat broke out on my forehead at the same time as I felt dry in the mouth. I observed, without daring to turn my head, Eva Whippoorwill's slender, beautiful legs, heard her admonitions, and blushed when I admired her ample chest area.

For the first time in my young life I was on the way to falling in love.

That the object of this storm of emotions—whose symptoms were mostly reminiscent of a serious case of stomach flu—was my almost thirty-years-older teacher meant that I was following in the footsteps of many young students. But this I knew nothing about, because I had not made it that far in the luxuriant flora of epic literature.

When Miss Whippoorwill was through with her inspection, we sat down again, and she then spent the hour expounding at the blackboard on the various groups of muscles that she promised to develop in us during the coming year. I read scarcely a word of what she wrote. All I saw was her graceful neck and the shimmering red nuances of her beautiful, slender beak.

The lump in my stomach sank deeper down in my body in a way that made me both nervous and jubilantly happy. The feeling was inexplicable, but when the lesson was over and Miss Whippoorwill left, I knew that I wanted to experience it again. I glanced furtively at Buzzard and Weasel to see if they realized what had happened—had they too been afflicted by this strange influenza? But they were on their way out the door as if this day was only another little cog in the perpetual motion machine that we still imagined life to be.

I took my time. My friends were not unaccustomed to Mother keeping me behind in the classroom a few hours after the end of school. She had no natural aptitude for doing dishes or cleaning, and I gladly helped out.

But not this day. I waited until I no longer heard my classmates, and then headed directly to the second floor. I knew exactly where I should go. From the windows in Mother and Father's bedroom you could see right into the upper floor of Sven Beaver and Eva Whippoorwill's house; I had known that for a long time. Sven Beaver liked watching TV in the evening; Father despised the bluish glow from the neighbor's house. It disturbed him even when he closed the curtains.

I was breathing heavily and dry in the mouth when I came into the bedroom. I had a single thought in my head: Eva Whippoorwill. Despite the fact that I had seen Miss Whippoorwill almost every day since I was little, despite the fact that she and her husband ate dinner at our house once a month, she had been transformed during a few magic moments into someone else. I too was changed beyond recognition. It was only when Mother amiably asked what I wanted that I realized I was not alone in the room. Blushing with shame, I fled. The marvelous, painful fever of being in love had taken possession of me, and—it was wonderful.

Many years later I can imagine that my first, earthshaking passion must have taken nourishment from the mysterious shimmer that surrounded Eva Whippoorwill at that time. She was different from the other females in Das Vorschutz, and there were several reasons. She had a dialect that placed her in Mollisan Town's southwest sections, somewhere in south Amberville, and the manner in which she pronounced the soft vowels had always fascinated me. She dressed in a more modern—and youthful—style than anyone else, and it even happened that she wore lipstick. But above all, in contrast to Buzzard's, Weasel's, and my own mother, Eva Whippoorwill was not anyone's mom.

The maturity and knowledge that experience grants to us stuffed animals with the years unfortunately replaces the razor-sharp intuition with which we are equipped when little. Without really understanding how or why, I had—despite my mere ten years—noticed the tragic aura that surrounded Eva

Whippoorwill. I perceived the melancholy that was concealed in the corners of her eyes and heard the echoing desolation of her words, so unlike my own mother's satisfied voice.

Just as clear but unexpressed was how differently Eva Whippoorwill and her husband, Sven Beaver, lived compared to the other couples in Das Vorschutz. This had to do with the way in which they communicated, low and intensively, as if they held each other's secrets close by and protected them. Jealousy burned in my chest. The other grown-ups in the forest always spoke about Eva and Sven in a special tone of voice. There was no envy, but perhaps a kind of reserved consideration that I could not properly interpret, despite the fact that I heard it.

I was too little to understand that all this had to do with Eva Whippoorwill and Sven Beaver's cublessness. In solidarity, the other forest guard families had supported Eva and Sven's more and more resigned struggle against the authorities. Testimonials had been sent and references given, meetings had been arranged and Jonas Beaver had even been up at the Environmental Ministry—the authority that was responsible for the Cub List—to discuss the matter with the official in charge. But nothing sufficed.

In time the rumors were born. That the ministry denied Eva Whippoorwill a cub, certain parties in the forest glade reasoned, must be due to something. What did we really know about Eva? Spiteful slander, of course, but I could even hear my own mother hint at how dark secrets from the female neighbor's past had something to do with the matter.

For a young, newly in love whippersnapper the thought of Eva Whippoorwill's doubtful past was naturally a kind of icing on the cake. These fantasies occupied me while I waited for hours to catch a glimpse of her through the windows opposite. During the weeks that followed, I learned things about myself that would prove to be just as true twenty, thirty, and forty years later. I understand that the reader who is inclined in a more rational direction may think this confession a bit woeful. I am just as certain that the individual romantics who read me are nodding in concurrence. Besides, if I was not so fixated on Eva Whippoorwill, if I had not sought every occasion to see her and talk with her, I would never have stumbled across the preludes to the event that would come to change my life forever.

Heimat, the large lake in Das Vorschutz, was ten minutes northeast of the forest glade where we lived. Every morning my Eva Whippoorwill made her way there.

Eva was an animal of habit; after a few weeks of reconnaissance I could affirm that she had constructed an entire life of routines. This suited me fine. I learned when I should slip up to Mother and Father's bedroom to be able to see Eva sit down with a cup of tea and a book in her living room in the house opposite. I knew when she jogged in the evenings, and what route she took. And if I climbed up in one of the aspens behind the house where Buzzard Jones lived, I could see her fixing dinner in the kitchen.

In the mornings I got up earlier than I ever had, dressed quickly, and, by the time it was getting cloudy, sneaked down the stairs and ran the whole way to Heimat. I made myself comfortable behind a large stone and awaited my beloved. Alongside the stone was an overturned majestic tree; judging by the moss, it must have fallen many years ago. The roots of the tree were perfect for spying through without being seen. I was ten years old, and neither understood nor cared about what drove me to this.

Eva came walking on one of the larger paths. She walked almost the entire way up to the lake, but turned off right before the shoreline. For a few moments she disappeared out of my sight, then I saw how she was climbing up into the old willow tree. The branches extended longingly out over the glassy water of the lake, and when Eva had reached the forked branch where she would sit, she started to sing. Every morning for twenty-three days she followed the same routine, and at a distance of about fifty meters I lay listening to her. I could not hear what she sang, but it was the same song every morning. I have never in my adult life heard it again.

With a cub's intuition I realized, as I lay quivering with excitement and nervousness behind my root, that Eva's song had a religious significance. The falling tones sounded like a kind of lamentation. It was so beautiful, and at the same time infinitely mournful. She sat quite still and executed precise movements in fast-forward with her wings. The first time I thought she was in a trance, that the movements were unconscious, but soon I discovered that she was following a well-rehearsed pattern. It was a matter of turning her wings at angles against one another and against her body in a long series of positions that probably had significance beyond my comprehension. I have not seen these types of movements since either, although my life by now has been both long and eventful.

If I had already been enchanted by Eva Whippoorwill before, these mornings deepened my feelings, and they were etched in my memory for all time—the forest that stood densely around the bottomless lake, the dew that still lingered in the spiderwebs that had been spun over the tree roots during the night, and the whispering reeds only a few meters from my hiding place. And on the branch of the willow tree, this apparition, my love, who executed her mysterious and complicated ritual.

The twenty-fourth day was different.

I lay as usual peering between the roots. High above us the dark clouds were forming in the sky, but there was still more than half an hour remaining until the rain. About halfway through the song Eva Whippoorwill fell silent. It happened suddenly, without warning.

I realized immediately that something was wrong. She sat completely still on the branch, and I feared for a few seconds that she had discovered me. She turned her beak up in the air, drew her wings next to her body. It was as if she was holding her breath, or else it was just me who was doing so.

Then everything happened very quickly. Without my even seeing how it happened, she was out of the tree and down on the ground in seconds, and had started running up toward the forest glade.

Confused, I remained in my hiding place for a few short moments, but then curiosity got the upper hand. As fast as I could, I followed Eva Whippoorwill back up toward the forest glade.

I heard the commotion at a distance. The forest guards were usually soft-spoken; they were a taciturn breed. Now their voices were heard through the forest at a great distance.

When I came up, I saw all of our small population gathered on the circular lawn between the five houses of the forest guards. Mother discovered me as soon as I came out of the edge of the forest, and she ran up and took hold of me.

"Where have you been?" she asked.

But she did not wait for a reply; she was not interested. Instead she dragged me with her into a circle of stuffed animals on the lawn. I immediately joined up with Weasel and Buzzard, who stood next to their older siblings a little apart from the others.

"What's happening?" I asked.

"It's Sven," Buzzard began. "He—"

"He found something in the forest," Weasel filled in.

"Rolled up in a sheet. It was in a magpie's nest that had fallen down out of a tree."

"It was pure luck."

"It's something that's alive," said Buzzard.

Round about us I heard the grown-ups talk about Sven Beaver and what he had found, but here and there I perceived an agitated tone of voice, even an individual angry word; there seemed to be differences of opinion on the lawn.

"Something that's alive?" I asked Buzzard.

"They don't know what it is," said Weasel.

"Not a stuffed animal," said Buzzard.

"But not a forest animal either," said Weasel.

"Shut up now!" Buzzard's big brother roared at us, and we fell silent.

But not only us. The silence settled in a dignified manner over everyone on the lawn, just as darkness settles over the treetops in the evening, and our glances were turned toward Sven and Eva's house.

I too turned around, and saw Eva Whippoorwill come out on the stoop. She was carrying a peculiar bundle in her wings. I understood immediately that this was what everyone was talking about, what Sven Beaver had found in the forest. Eva looked down at the bundle in her arms, and then turned toward us.

"His name is Maximilian," she said loudly. "And he is Sven's and my cub. Be happy for us."

Her voice was tense, hollow, and the words were astounding. I think we all perceived her as stark raving mad at that moment. But at the same time she made us all embarrassed; her pride was unshakable, and her will so powerful that no one dared utter a word. We were staring at her. She stared back at us from up on the porch. Sven Beaver was not to be seen. When the silence had just about become unbearable, she turned around and went back into the house with the bundle in her arms.

Immediately the whispering started again.

"But what kind of thing is it?" Buzzard wondered in a low voice.

It was the question we were all asking ourselves, but no one could answer. When the first raindrops fell, everyone disappeared into their houses. Mother again took hold of my arm and pulled me away, but I heard Hans Beaver whisper to the forest guards to meet him for a deliberation as soon as the rain dispersed.

The forest guards' deliberation was held at the home of Jonas Beaver. A few years earlier, Buzzard and Weasel and I had discovered that in the closet in the guestroom on the upper floor at Jonas and Magpie Tagashawa's, one of the floor planks could be loosened. The closet was situated above the room where the deliberation was held, and without the floor plank it was almost like sitting at the table. It was always exciting to eavesdrop on the grown-ups, even if it was seldom that anything secret was said.

Raccoon Olsen—Jonas and Magpie's oldest son—had been our partner in crime from the start, but then grew away from us. He was a well-behaved sort who had begun his studies in economics in the city and would soon move from Das Vorschutz. The morning when the deliberation about Maximilian was held, however, Raccoon Olsen was standing with us inside the darkness of the closet, smelling the odor of mothballs and laundry soap and listening to the forest guards' harsh voices one floor below.

The prelude was cautious.

The beavers talked about the day ahead, about the week that had passed, about a spring they had discovered a few months earlier that could still not be traced to the Dondau, the river that ran inside the mountains and was only visible for a few kilometers inside Lanceheim.

Up in the closet we were getting impatient, and Weasel Tukovsky—who always had a hard time standing still—began drumming nervously against the floor with his paw. I silenced him with a sharp glance, and then we finally heard Jonas Beaver clear his throat down at the table and address the question of the day.

"Well, then," he said, "we all realize what this is really about, don't we?"

"She can't keep it," I heard my own father declare in his gruff way.

His voice always had a different ring when he was talking with his colleagues, at the same time gentler and more definite.

"Of course not," Anders, Weasel's dad, concurred. "On that point the regulations are crystal clear. Things that are found in the forest, which can be assumed to possess a certain value, must be turned in to the ministry, without exception."

"I'm sorry, Sven," said Jonas.

It became silent, and the silence went on for a time. As if to soften the significance of his regret, Jonas said at last, "But tell us, where did you find . . . Maximilian?"

Sven Beaver had been sitting silently until then, but now he began to speak.

"I was on my way home," he said.

His voice was flat. It was as though he was exerting himself not to betray any feelings.

"I'd been out since the day before yesterday. To the north. I'd been told that there was a fox, a forest animal, with an injured paw. I found the tracks, but never found the animal, and finally I was forced to give up. Yesterday evening, after the storm, I was on my way toward a Sleeping Place. I think it was you, Anders, who showed it to me. That was a long time ago. Where the mountain slopes in toward the bog, west of the spruce forest?"

"I know which one you mean," said Anders.

Several concurring hums were heard.

"Right before I got there, I heard the scream," Sven continued. "It was a call that I had never heard before, and I readily admit that it . . . made me worried. I can't say that I was scared, the call was . . . too little . . . for you to get scared. But I seldom hear a sound in the forest that I don't recognize. I waited awhile, and then I heard it again. This time more like a wailing. It was coming only a few meters from where I stood, and he wasn't hard to find. He was wrapped up in a blanket, which in turn was carefully placed on top of the ferns. When I picked him up . . . I knew that he was the one we had waited for. The one Eva and I had waited for."

No one said a word. Up in our closet we hardly dared breathe. Before me in the darkness I saw the image of Eva Whippoorwill in the willow tree, and how she abruptly stopped singing.

"But what kind of thing is it?" Hans Beaver finally asked. "I mean, it is naturally as you say, Anders, that things of value that are found have to be turned in."

"So it is," confirmed Anders.

"But it seems to me that in this case we don't know the value," Hans continued, "because we don't know what it is. And so we can't put it back either."

"It's something that's alive," my father declared.

"It's a kind of animal," said Anders.

After that, silence again fell around the table. Up in the closet we realized why, and we held our breath in excitement. The forest guard who looked after the forest animals, and had the deepest insights into the subject, was Sven himself. It was easy to imagine that all gazes now rested on him.

"It is a prayer that's been answered," he said at last. "That's exactly what it is. A prayer that has been accepted, and a cub has been granted to us."

"But, Sven—" Anders began.

"Sven, listen—" said my father in the same breath.

"We know how you feel, Sven, but—" interrupted Hans.

"We have rules to follow," Jonas almost whispered.

Silence again. Then we could all hear the scraping of a chair being pulled out from the table.

"Dear friends and colleagues," said Sven Beaver with a certain authority, and in the closet we understood that he had stood up, "I ask you, let me handle this in my own way. Just as you would let me treat an injured deer, or an eagle chick that fell from its nest. I promise you, I am not going to break any of the rules, I will follow every paragraph of the law that we forest guards have to follow."

The silence that ensued was solid.

"It's about trust," Sven added in a somewhat lower voice. "By granting your consent, you show that you rely on me. And we forest guards have to rely on each other."

"Sven," said my father at last, "don't do anything stupid."

I recognized the tone of voice; I knew that Father had just given his assent.

Without any further words we heard steps across the floor and then the door being shut. There was no doubt that it was Sven Beaver who had left the deliberation.

"If only we don't come to regret this," said Jonas Beaver quietly.

No one answered him.

During the months that followed, Eva Whippoorwill and Sven Beaver would adopt the little bundle that we all came to call Maximilian, just as Eva had said we should. The adoption occurred after a series of processes of both a moral and legal nature. Sven reported his find to the police, and was first forced to await the court's decision that no one else had a claim on Maximilian. Subsequently they went through the meticulous adoption process, where one of the more surprising problems had been to define Maximilian's type. That the bundle was not an ordinary stuffed animal was easy to ascertain; it was only necessary to take a look at him. Despite the fact that he had eyes, nose, and mouth, he was different in an—remember, I was only ten years old at the occasion in question—unpleasant way. Above all it had to do with the structure of his light beige fabric: like silk without the sheen, and the seams could scarcely be seen.

Eva and Sven had first sent in the papers without filling in the information about Maximilian's attributes, but they were rebuffed. Then they had to write "imaginary animal" instead, without specifying that further. Most of the imaginary animals in Mollisan Town could be categorized as "dragons," "prehistoric animals," or "fairy-tale animals." But some, a very few, were impossible to trace to a breed or a category, and it was among those that Maximilian was counted. The Ministry of Finance finally sent a dog out to Das Vorschutz, who with his own eyes could ascertain that the lack of a category was correct. The dog stared down into the crib and saw there a bundle, as small as a cricket bat, but with highly peculiar ears and without any similarity whatsoever to any of the known types of stuffed animals.

When the adoption went through, the commotion around Maximilian subsided somewhat. I will not go so far as to maintain that everything returned to normal, but it was well on its way. During the weeks that followed my love paled, and Eva Whippoorwill was transformed: in my eyes she became Maximilian's mother. The mystical shimmer around her remained, however. Again and again I saw in my inward eye how she interrupted her morning ritual by the lake that morning. As if she had known. She must have known.

How was that possible?

REUBEN WALRUS 2

Reuben Walrus sat down in row 15, seat 354, in the middle of the orchestra. He had little use for superstition. At the very most he might accept that faith was a balancing factor during a long life. Yet he always picked the same seat on the parquet when he rehearsed with the Lanceheim Philharmonic. He pretended that it had something to do with the acoustics. In an empty concert hall it was easy to mistake the tonal colors. The gilded, arched box seats along both edges of the stage gaped like greedy mouths above each other. True, the red velvet on the hundreds of chair seats and backs in the parquet did dampen the sound, but not in the same way as when the hall was filled with the cloth bodies of many hundreds of stuffed animals. This seat, in the middle of the parquet, was, for lack of a better, the most representative, Walrus reasoned. Here the tone remained intact.

The fact that he had sat in seat 354 when he directed his Piano Concerto in D Major, which got an exuberant reception ten years ago, had nothing to do with it. The fact that he had sat in seat 354 when he rehearsed the successful one-act opera *Sarcophagus*, which had been playing on one of the city's stages without interruption for at least fifteen years, had equally slight significance. And it was of no interest that out of sheer cussedness he had refrained from sitting on seat 354 when he suffered the fiasco with the Sonata for Violin and Harpsichord five years ago.

Despite the fact that the evidence was overwhelming, Reuben stubbornly refused to see himself as a victim of superstition. He had reached a mature age, he was en route to his sixty-fifth birthday at a furious pace, and yet he was still struggling with his self-image. Every morning he got up and wished that it were a different face that met him in the bathroom mirror. Someone whose forehead was not as high, whose eyebrows were not quite as grandly white and bushy, someone whose nose was less moist and who did not have mustaches that were quite so long and dense. He hated his large, heavy body, and he suffered from being nearsighted, even if he refused to wear eyeglasses in public. His egocentricity had made him a miserable spouse and a blind parent, and his friends had abandoned him long ago, because he always prioritized his work. He had unintentionally become something of a recluse, a type he despised, but he could not decide what he should sacrifice to become part of the community. The only thing he appreciated in his mirror image on certain mornings were the large, glossy eyes whose luster revealed talented melancholy. Reuben Walrus's vanity—for this was a matter of vanity and nothing else—was only one of many signs of his unfathomable need for acknowledgment. The maturity he had reached with the years meant that nowadays he knew that this need for acknowledgment would never be satisfied. But he also knew that it could never be ignored.

Walrus was latently dissatisfied, but also with dissatisfaction itself, which saved him from being impossible. Instead the surrounding world often seemed to appreciate his blunt cynicism and cutting irony, which in nine cases out of ten was aimed at himself.

The words that Dr. Margot Swan had spoken refused to become comprehensible during the afternoon. Reuben Walrus pretended as if nothing had happened. He positioned himself up in row 15, clapped his hands, and the musicians returned from their long break. Patiently he let them slowly take their seats, and then it was time. They started playing again, and Reuben concentrated on the music, closing out everything else . . . then he heard it again.

Seven minutes into the first movement of the symphony was a passage where the cellos along with the violins should build up to a successive, violent crescendo. It didn't work. It didn't work at all. Instead of creating interest in the variation on the theme that awaited in the following movement, it led the insistent cellos up to an anticlimax. It hesitated too long. The theme had to return sooner. Perhaps not completely, but in some form. The dissonances and chromatic changes that Reuben usually exploited were not enough in this passage.

Reuben stood up and waved deprecatingly. Frustration was pounding in his temples. When no one saw him, he began jumping up and down in the row of seats, waving his fins and shouting. The chastened philharmonic stopped playing.

"Damn!" shouted Walrus, but he knew that Malitte, the lord of evil, could not help him. "Damn, damn, damn."

He made his way out along the empty row of seats, hurried along the middle aisle of the concert hall, and ascended the stage via the short staircase on the right side. He ran past the violinists over to the cellists and grabbed hold of the score. He held it up in the air, staring at the notes and closing his eyes.

He listened.

This was the second day of rehearsals. Except for the timpanist, a blue elephant with a name no one could pronounce, everyone in the orchestra had worked with Walrus before. They knew what this meant. Therefore, when the timpanist with a superior smile on his lips—as if to say, "Is this pretentious or what?"—turned to the flutes, he got no response. Seeing Walrus standing on the edge of the stage with closed eyes, fanning the air, might perhaps be a sorrowful sight if you thought that the composer had fallen victim to his own myth. Later, however, someone—perhaps one of the sweet violas or one of the oboists, generally considered the most social section in the philharmonic—would let the blue elephant know what he had witnessed.

This is what Reuben Walrus's creative process looked like. He apparently heard melodies and harmonies within himself, silences and dissonances, orchestrations and parts. The philharmonic in Lanceheim had witnessed this several times—how Walrus stood among them, yet in his own world, and with closed eyes directed his inner orchestra, the one that never played a wrong note, neither hesitated nor questioned.

After a few long minutes the composer finally opened his eyes and turned over the music paper he was holding in his right fin. With his scratching ink pen he frenetically wrote down five, ten, and finally fifteen different parts that he had just "heard." Not once did he hesitate.

"I'll write out new ones for everyone," he mumbled, "just now it's only the cellos I want to hear. Only cellos."

And then he set back the score in front of the cellists.

"Play," he nodded and closed his eyes.

The cellos were heard again, the violins picked up where they felt comfortable, and Walrus nodded without opening his eyes.

Better.

. . . .

The Music Academy was celebrating its one hundred and twenty-fifth anniversary, and Reuben Walrus had been invited to write the piece that would inaugurate a week bulging with musical festivities. The invitation had arrived almost two years ago, and Reuben, after a year of hesitation, had accepted the commission. Even if he could not maintain that he had exclusively agonized over this Symphony in A Minor since then, he had devoted much effort to it. Whatever conflicts he may have had with the Music Academy over the years—and they were numerous, despite the fact that he could not recall any of them in detail—the invitation was a major official recognition. He had been asked due to past qualifications, but those past qualifications would not bring him through this in one piece if this symphony did not live up to what his reputation promised.

And it had been a while since he had tackled something of this scope. With the years and their successes, many other things made demands on Reuben's time. The actual composing he did was confined to simpler things. Last year he had squeezed out a couple of string quartets, but not more. The year before that, a few arias and ten sonnets was all he managed. To be quite honest, none of these compositions were more than deft elaborations on the sort of thing he had done previously, and for the sonnets in particular only neglect awaited. Since the Piano Concerto in D Major had been performed for the first time exactly nine years, eight months, and . . . a few days ago, there had been nothing other than trifles.

But the years passed. His time went to conducting or at least sanctioning recordings of previous works that musicians, orchestras, and smaller ensembles from the various corners of the city asked for. Reuben Walrus had been pro-

ductive when young, inconceivably and inexcusably pro-
ductive, he might think; a few things were best buried in
the compost heap of time. Devoting yourself to the past en-
tailed making revisions. He reorchestrated pieces for new
sets of instruments or transcribed symphonies to keys better
suited to tonal colors that had not been available when he
wrote them. The development of technique had opened unexpected paths for contemporary composers, and Reuben
was fascinated by the possibilities that he had never had.

His daily routines also included managing the financial
aspects of his own musical activity. As he found these tasks
inconceivably boring, they took him a disproportionately
long time. Many, not least his ex-wife, had again and again
suggested that he ought to let someone take care of book-
keeping, invoicing, and investing, but he would not. Some
called this stinginess; others emphasized his certified need
for integrity. Reuben himself answered, pressed and dis-
agreeable, that it was certainly a little of both.

Finally, Reuben's private life in recent years had been
equally hectic and turbulent. Not only due to his companion, Denise, although she clearly demanded the kind of attention that only a young, spoiled, and beautiful animal had
the right to demand.

The invitation from the Music Academy scared him to
death. But at the same time it was his salvation.

While the philharmonic continued into the grandiose madness of
the symphony, Reuben Walrus stepped down from the stage.

Three weeks was all he had before it was time to play the
symphony for an audience, and the last third was still left to
write. He had been noncommittal with the philharmonic.
They had asked of course for the last pages of the score.
He thought that when rehearsals got going, he would find
inspiration more easily. Well, that remained to be seen.

. . . .

When the Afternoon Sky had reached its most saturated blueness, Reuben Walrus again clapped his hands, but in a different way, a way they all recognized. Rehearsals were over for the day. The musicians set down their instruments. A couple of them, old friends, intended to exchange a few words with the great composer, but Reuben quickly fled the concert hall, with his coat over one fin and the score under the other. He was still holding Dr. Swan in check. Her words were encapsulated in the darkest corner of his brain, and they could only remain there if he avoided talking with anyone. Out on the sidewalk he turned right, and went north as fast as he could.

This was his block. The street where he lived, sea blue Knobeldorfstrasse, was no more than a stone's throw from the concert hall. Over the past few years the neighborhood from Dieterstrasse up to Rosdahl had gained a reputation as being pretentious and expensive, but the pendulum always swung back. When Reuben bought his four-room apartment ten years ago, the area had been exciting and slightly dangerous. The price of the large apartment was lower than that of some studios he had looked at farther south. And once they had carried the grand piano up the six flights of stairs, Reuben swore never to move away.

He loved Knobeldorfstrasse. He loved the old rooms—their musty odor that he had made his own, the yellowed wallpaper that reminded him of times past, and the creaking floorboards that responded to his steps like old acquaintances. The water in the sink remained cloudy until it ran for a minute or two. The bathroom was too cramped for a washing machine, and for that reason he could take his clothes to the dry cleaners with a good conscience. The obligatory drying cabinet—where stuffed animals sat if they happened to end up by mistake in one of the day's rain showers—was of an old, obsolete model, and it smelled burnt in a manner that caused him to feel hungry.

He loved the view from the bedroom toward the shady inner courtyard and the rusty bicycles that no one seemed to own and that could stand in peace year after year. And the contrast on the other side, facing Knobeldorfstrasse, where the pulse beat faster every day and the formerly abandoned apartments had been transformed in recent years to trendy cafés and boutiques that constantly changed ownership.

The sixth floor, the apartment under Walrus, stood empty. It had always been that way. The low rent level in the building allowed the tenant one floor down, a fairly successful milliner with stores in both Lancheim and Tourquai, to use the apartment as a storeroom. This meant that Reuben could play his piano as much as he wanted, any time of day whatsoever. This was perhaps Knobeldorfstrasse's best quality.

Reuben Walrus managed to make it the whole way home without Dr. Swan's words penetrating his defenses, but once he was inside the door his powers of resistance ran out, and he collapsed on the carpet. It could not be true, he thought. It could not be true.

Three weeks.

Kleine Wallanlagen was not the largest park in Mollisan Town, nor was it the smallest. Around a hill that was considered a mountain by Lanceheim loyalists, the city had laid out a gravel path. Lanterns were lit along it throughout the night, but still most avoided going into Kleine Wallanlagen when darkness fell. It was long ago that there was justification for the rumors of drug dealing and prostitution, but the gravel path was edged by dense bushes and ancient oaks, and the many hiding places contributed to fantasies.

Reuben Walrus stood hidden in the dark shadow of one of these mighty trees. Peering toward the building facades on the other side of pepper red Mooshütter Weg, he took a gulp of cognac that he had poured into a steel pocket flask. He had the flask in his inside pocket, while he carried the bottle of cognac in his coat pocket; drinking straight from the bottle was, despite everything, unthinkable. He was not used to drinking, and was already thoroughly intoxicated. The night had just passed its climax; the darkness was compact, and the chill penetrated right through the walrus's shiny fabric. This did not bother him. He was directing all of his concentration toward the windows on the third story of the building opposite, and he saw clearly how the two animals inside were preparing for departure. The female stood impatiently by the door while the male ran back and forth through the rooms, perhaps in pursuit of belongings, but just as likely on the lookout for excuses to stay behind.

Reuben bided his time. If he had waited this long, he could wait a little longer. He emptied the flask of alcohol and poured in more from the bottle. It became more and more difficult to hit the little opening, but it made less and less difference if he spilled. In the corner of his eye he saw how the entryway opposite opened and closed. He waited until the sound of the strange male's hooves were no longer heard on the sidewalk, sneaked out of the park, and slipped quickly and soundlessly across the street. He punched in the code expertly and opened the door to the stairwell without turning on the lights. In the darkness he fumbled his way up the two flights of stairs and fell three times before he was standing outside her door.

He had a key. She didn't know, Fox von Duisburg, that someone else had the key to her home. Reuben chuckled to himself and unlocked.

Inside in the dark hallway he remained standing, suddenly doubtful. Was this really a good idea? He tried to think about it, create a little distance between himself and the situation, but the cognac allowed no such thing. Instead he tittered at something he forgot at once, and then the ceiling light in the hall came on.

"You!" exclaimed Fox von Duisburg.

She was wearing a thin red dressing gown over her silk pajamas, holding a baseball bat in her paw, and staring at him.

The unexpected light made him jump. He was frightened when he saw the raised weapon, yet he could not control himself. Fox's face transformed his tittering into a bubbling, deeper and deeper laugh. Although he knew he shouldn't, he found he could not put a stop to it.

"You're drunk," he heard Fox von Duisburg declare with a certain surprise.

He neither could nor wanted to deny this. He held his stomach and fell forward in new spasms of laughter, so that he was transformed into a panting pile of fabric on the floor in her hallway.

This had at one time been his hallway.

"Old boy," said Fox, crouching down to raise one of his fins and place it around her neck. "Help out now."

And then she pulled him up from the floor and dragged him into the living room. When she dropped him off on the couch, his laughter had been transformed into shaking sobs. Fox von Duisburg had been married to Reuben Walrus for twelve years, but never before had she seen him cry. For a moment she felt paralyzed, completely empty. It was late at night, and her lover had finally left. Instead of falling asleep in her cozy bed, she found an intoxicated, crushed ex-husband in the hallway, and realized that the night had only begun. With an inaudible sigh she sat down beside him on the couch and placed her arm on his back.

"She gave me three weeks," snuffled Reuben.

Fox stroked him across the back and asked who he was talking about.

"In three weeks it's over," he explained.

"What happens in three weeks, darling?" she asked.

"In three weeks I am never going to hear again," Reuben forced out. "I am never going to compose again. My life is over."

Fox von Duisburg made coffee for them. Reuben sat at his place at the kitchen table and watched as she stood by the old wood-fired stove that she refused to replace for reasons of nostalgia and whipped the warm milk foam just stiff enough. The scene was familiar, except for the dense darkness outside the windows. They had been divorced for more than fifteen years, yet he felt secure and domesticated at her breakfast table. The table and stove were both remnants of Fox's childhood. She had lived in this apartment her entire life. From the apartment's perspective, Reuben Walrus was only a temporary resident who stayed longer than he was welcome.

"We never should have moved apart," said Reuben.

"Do you mean it's been a long time since you had coffee with foamed milk?" answered Fox with a broad smile.

The aromas made him nostalgic: the smell of the wood burning in the little opening, the milk that was warmed in the saucepan, the soft detergent she used when she washed her dressing gown.

"Sure, it's been a long time since I had coffee with foamed milk at three o'clock in the morning," he admitted.

"It's a good thing we don't live together anymore," smiled Fox. "I would never manage my days if the nights were like this. Not at our age."

"If we move in together again, I promise that I will never ask for foamed milk before the Morning Rain at the earliest," he offered grandly.

"Fantastic," she said, pouring the milk into the coffee cups. "No suitor could be more romantic than that. When can you move in?"

She set out the cups and sat down across from him at the kitchen table. He smiled, tasting the hot coffee carefully, whereupon the foam stuck to his long mustache. This caused her already tender heart to break, and spontaneously she placed her paw on his fin on the table and patted him.

"Say it like it is, you don't want me to move in at all," he said.

"You don't want to move in, you only want to hear me say no."

He shrugged.

"It suits me to pine, it suits you to reject."

"In your world, perhaps," said Fox.

"You used to like my world," Reuben replied.

"I loved your world, oldster. It was the best of worlds. I would recommend it to anyone."

"That's not what you said to Veronica," Reuben reminded her.

Fox remembered Veronica, and smiled broadly.

"If you drag your lovers here for the sake of comparisons," she said, "you can't count on me making it easy for you."

It had been a strange evening a few years ago. How he had come up with the idea of bringing together his new young female and his ex-wife he did not recall; they reminded him of each other, therefore they ought to meet. It was one of his stupidest ideas. All females paled in the glow of Fox von Duisburg.

He sighed heavily.

"I am never going to love anyone like I loved you," said Reuben Walrus.

"That's the least I can demand," replied Fox von Duisburg.

The moon was still half when he managed to convince her to take a walk. Her eyelids had become dangerously heavy the last quarter of an hour, and the idea that she could fall asleep and leave him alone was worse than he could endure. Fresh air and exercise was the medicine.

They walked arm in arm, a single shadow across sidewalks and on facades, wandering this way and that through north Lanceheim. After the divorce he had found a new apartment in this neighborhood, not least to be close to Fox and Josephine. He no longer remembered why they had separated, he hardly remembered it when he wrote the divorce documents, but he knew that it had been a wise decision. He loved her, perhaps she loved him, but they should each live on their own. Relationships had never been his strong suit; he had a tendency to forget about them even while they were going on, and when he remembered, they were over. He lived for his music, and when it took possession of him . . . when the harmonies were flowing through him . . . when the sounds revealed themselves to him and suggested how he should orchestrate them by means of string quartets, brass quintets, or entire orchestras . . . when the visions intoxicated him, and the joys of the work were in the keys under his sensitive fins . . . then there was no place for anything else.

Not even for Josephine.

He had not been the best of fathers, but he knew some who were worse. Reuben was forty and some-odd years old when they got Josephine Lamb, and it was too late to conquer the role of dad. He was who he was. Fox never became a mom either; she was her cub's girlfriend right from the start. Had he felt left out, set aside? Was that one of the reasons for the divorce? But he thought that contact with Josephine got better afterward, when he moved down to Knobeldorfstrasse and could devote himself to her when she came to visit. He taught her to play the piano, and he taught her to play the violin. The tuba was her own decision.

"I am never going to hear again," he said, as a cold breeze came around the block and searched its way into their eyes. "I am never going to know if what I experience inside me is what the orchestra is playing. Never again will I dare put my music in print, because I will never again discover where the mistakes are hiding."

She did not reply.

"I am never going to . . . ," he said, but there was nothing more to say.

The wind picked up. After ten meters or so they turned onto gray Friedrichstrasse, an alley so narrow that the wind could hardly find a place there. She stopped, and took hold of the lapel of his coat.

They looked at each other. She was older than he remembered. The fur on the side of her eyes was worn, and her gaze encompassed experience that had not known any detours.

"You can't give up," she said slowly. "What you are talking about has not yet happened. It hasn't happened. You can't give up."

He nodded. His wise fox. His strong fox. She released her hold, and they continued in silence back to Mooshütter Weg. The night would soon be over, dawn was on its way, he could see it in the sky, a premonition of daylight along the horizon. He was more or less sober when they were again standing outside her entryway, across from Kleine Wallanlagen. Inside his soul it was black, empty and desolate. The panic from yesterday evening had turned into a sort of apathy.

He would become deaf; he had three weeks' dispensation from Margot Swan, but then it was over. Whether Drexler's syndrome was fatal or not did not interest him; if he could not hear, he could not compose. And if he could not compose, the Chauffeurs might just as well fetch him.

He tried to cheer himself up.

"Thanks for a wonderful night," he said.

"Yes, I guess we've reached the age where we have to see this as one," she replied with a smile.

"If I can't take it, I'll come back this evening," he warned.

"You are welcome."

She hugged him. But when he turned around to go, she added, "Reuben, forgive me, but that door key you saved— don't you think I should get it back?"

He heard, but ignored her. He'd feel better if he kept it.

WOLF DIAZ 2

Of Maximilian's first seven years I have very little to relate, because I know little about them. My own life took me into puberty. When I turned fifteen, I was forced for the first time to become acquainted with Mollisan Town in general and Lanceheim in particular, because Weasel, Buzzard, and I started high school. The school in our extra room was transformed into a memory. The city did not allow higher education to be conducted at home.

Leaving the forest was thus not our own decision. On the contrary we were upset, and devoted most of summer vacation to cursing the authorities' lack of imagination. Without a doubt all three of us were terror-stricken. The contempt with which the grown-ups in Das Vorschutz talked about the city had rubbed off on us. Evil, sin, and destructiveness were the result of the artificial life that stuffed animals lived there, and now we too would be subjected to it. It was not strange that we took turns displaying inventiveness and a certain originality as we fantasized endless variations of blowing the Ministry of Education to smithereens.

All three of us were accepted into Lanceheim's Normal

School, which was customary for us Forest Cubs. The school was in Kerkeling Parish, a less attractive area in northeast Lanceheim, not far from Eastern Avenue, which led past the Garbage Dump and King's Cross out to Das Vorschutz. Lanceheim's Normal School was not one of the more sought-after educational institutions, but considering that our grades had been set by our mothers, we could not demand anything better.

On trembling legs we showed up for roll call. I cannot keep from thinking about it with a slight blush of shame. Weasel, Buzzard, and I roved about in the dark corridors of the massive school as if someone had sewn us together. We never left each other's side; we were constantly whispering, using language from the wretched novels for young animals we were forced to read when little: "All these stuffed animals!" "All these classrooms!" "All these sounds, streets, and houses!" For several weeks we continued to talk like that, with exclamation points: "All this stress!" "All these lessons!" "This whole city!" "All this evil, anger, joy, and desire!"

And personally, for me more than for Weasel and Buzzard, "All these beautiful, seductive females!"

The presence of so many new stuffed animals of the opposite gender set my emotional life swinging so that for several years I would walk around in a constant fog, slightly seasick. The opportunities were too many, the longing too great. On an ordinary day I would fall headlong in love with at least one, but more often two, of my classmates, one of my fellow travelers on the bus, or one of all the beauties that I met on Lanceheim's streets and squares. In the evenings I was as exhausted as an empty banana peel, and I had a hard time keeping up with my studies.

I did not devote many thoughts to the strange Maximilian during this period, despite the fact that in secret he executed a magic trick of the greatest distinction.

He got bigger.

Eva Whippoorwill did her best to conceal this disturbing fact, but nonetheless we could all see it. The little bundle that Sven Beaver had found in the forest was not so little anymore. If Maximilian had been tall as a table leg to start with, after seven years he was twice as tall. And as he grew, he changed appearance. This did not happen overnight; it was a subtle, drawn-out process, and among the stuffed animals of the forest, amazement at the phenomenon decreased and increased like ebb and flow. At times there was much talk about the matter, on other occasions less, but one thing stayed the same: we talked only with each other. No one outside Das Vorschutz knew anything about Maximilian; we had the feeling that no good would come of that.

Eva Whippoorwill did her best to protect her son from curious gazes. It was not the case that she hid him—she was far too intelligent for that. On the contrary, this would have led to even more gossip. But she participated sparingly in social gatherings, and she let Maximilian go his own way.

As I have already admitted, I was absorbed in my own emotional life and was far from being as attentive as I should have been. My attitude was like everyone else's: when Maximilian came up in conversation, I experienced a certain discomfort. I did not think the peculiarities that surrounded him were either exciting or interesting. We were already sufficiently vulnerable as it was in Das Vorschutz.

This meant that if Eva Whippoorwill took care to keep her adopted son to herself, we would do our best to avoid him.

I do not recall the reason that I took Maximilian along on a walk. It was not uncommon that I walked by myself in the forest. I had just turned seventeen and was filled with existential torments due to the endless series of more or less unhappy love affairs that fate—as I called Magnus at that time—had thrown in my path. The forest had always been my refuge; its heavy gloom and tender melancholy suited me fine. On this day someone asked me to take Maximilian along.

True, I was irritated—I specifically remember that—but the irritation quickly went away. The cub was still only seven years old; he had a serious, taciturn disposition, and thus did not disturb my equally lovesick and profound trains of thought.

We took the road toward Heimat, but turned off to the east before we came up to the lake. The air was clear after the Afternoon Rain, and Mother had forced both me and Maximilian to put on clothes that withstood the cool breeze. I recall that we were told that we should be gone for a full hour, but what sort of preparations set this time frame I do not remember. However it was, I went ahead, deeply submerged in brooding. My love on that occasion was named Sarah, and she let me taste her beautiful ears but then pushed aside my paw when it glided down across her cheek.

Maximilian followed a few meters behind. Like me, he was the son of a forest guard and therefore naturally knowledgeable about the forest. He moved lithely; he walked silently and expertly. Deeper and deeper into the pine forest we penetrated, on paths that our fathers' predecessors had trod. And because this Sarah was at that point the most beautiful but also the most standoffish stuffed animal I had ever met, I do not know how long Maximilian and I trod on eastward.

A sound, so terrible that I myself let out a cry, caused me to waken abruptly out of my musings.

Ten or so meters ahead, to the right of the path, was a wounded stuffed animal, a badger, and he was whimpering as though he had already landed in hell. His entire body was torn, and in some places the tears were so large that I could see the cotton inside, despite the fact that I was standing some distance away. He had heard us coming, and his whimpering was in reality a cry for help.

I stopped where I was and simply stared. I was young and inexperienced, and what I felt was fear. My impulse was to turn around and run away. I am being brutally frank, but that is the least you have the right to expect of me. I was simply scared to death.

As I stood there, considering this cowardly retreat, Maximilian forced his way past me on the narrow path and hurried over to the badger. I was astounded to say the least, because I had managed to forget that Maximilian was even there.

Before I could say or do anything, he turned around and said, "Water. The badger must have water."

Then I heard. The moanings that the dirty, torn stuffed animal was forcing out were unhesitating variations on this very word: "Water."

In Maximilian's eyes was a force I had never seen before, and that made me even more confused.

I looked around. How far had we really gone? The forest around us consisted mostly of fir trees, and it was difficult to glimpse the sky between the dense treetops. To my surprise I realized that the sun had already started to go down, which meant that we must have wandered for more than two hours due east. There was no water here.

I shook my head.

"There's no water here," I replied stupidly. "What's happened to him?"

I asked as if Maximilian were an interpreter between me and the badger. Maximilian did not seem to have heard what I said.

"He needs water," he repeated. "Help out."

Maximilian went over to the badger, taking one of his arms and putting it around his own neck. I hurried over and did the same thing, on the other side. The badger was hanging between us as if we intended to dry him in the wind.

"That way," said Maximilian.

Afterward I wondered why I didn't react, why I didn't refuse. It would have been natural, I knew the forests better than Maximilian—there was no water in the direction in which he wanted to go. But I kept silent and, without asking, did as I had been told.

We walked quickly, with the badger between us. He was no longer mumbling; he had used the little strength he had, and I doubted that he was even conscious. The fear had not released its hold on me, and perhaps that was why I simply continued to walk. I had no idea where we were going.

No one knows how far east the mountain range that we call Pal extends. No one has gone to its end and come back again. What is no more than a hill within Lanceheim becomes a ridge at the city limits and first forms what might be called a small mountain a few hundred meters south of Das Vorschutz. Twenty or thirty kilometers into the forest, the mountain rises so high that it takes a whole day of climbing to make it over to the other side.

Together Maximilian and I hauled the badger straight toward the mountain. My mental recollection was that the cliffs at the pine forest rose both abruptly and steeply, but because Maximilian seemed so single-minded, I thought perhaps there was a crevice, a ravine that I did not know about. And what if there was also a mountain spring, a natural well that I had not heard about? We were walking at a rapid pace. The badger hanging between us rattled unpleasantly when he breathed, and even worse, this rattling was coming at longer and longer intervals.

Soon I saw the cliffs. And just as I thought, the mountain rose like a wall before us. It was impossible to climb. Despite the fact that Maximilian must have seen this too, he did not slow his pace. On the contrary, he seemed to walk a little faster, as if now he was in the vicinity of where he wanted to go.

"Shut your eyes," he said.

We were walking quickly alongside each other. I was starting to get a little tired; I have never been an athlete. I tried to protest.

"Shut your eyes," he repeated, still without reducing speed.

Once again I did as he asked me. He was seven years old, I was seventeen, and I obeyed him. Soon this would prove to be the least remarkable thing about this late afternoon.

I closed my eyes. When I could no longer see, my other senses were sharpened. I felt the weight of the badger's arm around my neck much more clearly, heard the pine needles that crunched under my shoes, the wind that whispered in the branches of the trees, and felt the gentle breeze against my whiskers.

Then it suddenly got cold. First around my face, then around my whole body. It was a very tangible, physical experience, and involuntarily I opened my eyes. This happened at approximately the same time as the sounds of the forest abruptly disappeared, as if someone had hastily turned nature's volume control down to zero.

The shock was . . . I cannot describe it.

I stopped, blinked, my jaw dropped, and I was not capable of intellectually comprehending what was obviously a fact.

We were inside the mountain.

Before me was a type of deep, high grotto where a brook

was purling by our shoes. From above, daylight forced its way in as finely sliced sunbeams through what must be cracks in the stone. Maximilian hauled the badger down to the water vein while I remained standing.

I closed my eyes, opened them again—nothing was changed. I turned around. There was no opening, no entrance, only thousands-year-old rock. And deep inside I knew what had happened without daring to admit it.

The badger, Maximilian, and I had passed through the ancient, solid rock as if it had been air. Our molecules had been dissolved and put together again during the course of a few seconds. Or else it was the mountain that dissolved before us. That didn't matter. What had happened was impossible, yet I was standing there.

The badger lay on the floor of the grotto and drank directly from the clear mountain brook. Maximilian sat alongside, holding him by the shoulders. I observed them a while without seeing them, and then turned around again and searched for the opening in the rock.

I knew there wasn't one, but I was still compelled to look.

And the impossible would happen again, when we left the grotto after an hour. By then, the badger had recovered to the point that he could walk by himself. Maximilian asked us to hold his paws, and after that he told us to close our eyes. We did so.

This time the chill that embraced me for a few, to be truthful, unpleasant moments was even more ghastly, and the relief when I again felt the breeze against my ears was enormous. I did not dare look at either the badger or Maximilian when I withdrew my paw and continued walking.

We returned to Das Vorschutz; it took a little more than an hour, and I went directly home and up to my room. I did not want to see or talk with anyone. Obviously I did not say what I had been involved in, for the reason that my reader will very well understand. Who would believe me?

I never did find out who the badger was and what he was doing out in the forest, but the wound on his body was due to an encounter with a forest animal, a fox.

I myself had witnessed a miracle.

REUBEN WALRUS 3

It was a matter of taking a deep breath, making yourself invulnerable, throwing open the doors to the large hall, and exceeding expectations. Be brilliant, humble, and empathic. Be eccentric, stately, and tragic.

At the same moment that Reuben Walrus heard the murmur, perceived the aromas, and saw the glow from the massive chandeliers, he regretted that he had let Denise Ant convince him. He took a firmer hold of one of her arms, as though he were clinging tight with his small fins, and she smiled encouragingly.

Denise Ant loved Reuben Walrus when he was miserable.

Every year Reuben led a course in free composition for the graduating class at the Music Academy. He maintained that it kept him young to meet, and be challenged by, the coming generations. In the office, the refined hens gossiped that he used his position to pursue young females at the school.

Denise Ant had been one of his pupils, the most critical of him in her class, and also the most yearning. So as not to feed the gossip, Reuben had been careful to avoid Denise the whole semester, and he only phoned her six months after she had finished at the school. They met at a gloomy pizzeria that smelled of old oregano, located a stone's throw from Denise's apartment in Amberville. At the restaurant she gave him a good dressing-down. First she scolded him for not calling her. Then she scolded him because he had called her, thereby exploiting his position as her former teacher and model.

He had ordered a pizza with mushrooms and onions; she had chosen a vegetarian combo. When the food arrived, Reuben ate in silence while Denise dissected one of his symphonies and, stanza by stanza, showed where he had stolen the various sections. Over coffee it was his lack of talent as a lecturer that she tackled. He longed for the check and to be able to leave this angry ant to herself, but when he finally got up, she asked if he wouldn't like to accompany her home. In pure astonishment he answered yes, and then they cuddled the whole night.

Denise Ant did not move in with Reuben. She refused to give up her life, refused to give up her apartment, her pride, and identity. Reuben was careful not to agree too quickly; a single thoughtless nod might very well cause her to move in on Knobeldorfstrasse the same day.

She appeared indifferent to the outside world's contemptuous looks, which suggested that she was only one in a series of Reuben Walrus's young lovers. She was unruly but reasonably predictable in her fierce defiance, and she had an energy that he found irresistible. He missed her on those days that they didn't see each other, but got enough of her after only a few hours when they finally met. Hundreds of times he rehearsed in his imagination the quarrel that would finally put an end to the relationship, and just as many times he refrained from saying the words out loud.

He assumed that she was just as divided as he was.

And with that, the first year was added to the second, and Reuben and Denise remained a couple.

. . . .

They were standing at the top of the stairs in the entranceway
of the music hall, and heads were turned in their direction
from everywhere in the murmuring room. Reuben could
see some he knew well, others he knew vaguely, and some
he had never seen before; thirty-some stuffed animals who
were sipping colorful drinks and who all felt they had a
special, close relationship with him.

Slowly Reuben and Denise began to go down the stairs.
A whisper passed through the assembly, an empathic silence
spread. It was unbearable. How had it happened? Who had
leaked it? Someone at the hospital laboratory, perhaps? The
secretary outside Dr. Swan's office? It was of no importance.
Yesterday he had received his sentence, today he was hung
over, and everyone seemed to know what had happened. Flowers had been delivered to Knobeldorfstrasse all morning. As of
now, he was the tragic genius, whose career and life were over.

When he and the ant reached the bottom step, the guests
had grouped themselves along the sides and in this way left
the field open for the host of the evening. Jack Elephant
could greet the late-arriving guests in solitary majesty.

"Reuben," the elephant rumbled, "that you manage, that
you show up, it's incomparable!"

"Incomparable," agreed Reuben.

"And Denise Ant," continued Jack, "more beautiful than
ever!"

Denise clicked her tongue lightly, as she always did when
something irritated her, but the smile she had put on remained unmoved.

They exchanged a few more words with Jack, but moved
in toward the hall and ended up beside Vincent Tortoise,
the head of the Ministry of Culture.

"Reuben," said Vincent in a voice vibrating with compassion, "I heard about what happened."

"Anything else would have shocked me," mumbled Walrus.

"This is not a topic of conversation for an evening like this," said Vincent, and Reuben felt deep gratitude toward the politician, who continued, "I'll be in touch during the week, so we can talk a little, the two of us?"

Reuben nodded, and Vincent Tortoise was swallowed up by the crowd of animals, who closed ranks and turned up the volume. Walrus snatched a glass of champagne that was being carried past on a large tray, forcing himself to smile politely and listen to the complaints from Countess Dahl. She let all her chins quiver with annoyance as she recounted the ignominy she was subjected to when her chauffeur for the evening proved to be a snake.

Reuben nodded to the right and nodded to the left, feeling like all eyes were on him as he elbowed his way up toward the high windows where his ant had taken her station.

"We never should have come here," he whispered. "Everyone knows! Everyone. How is it possible?"

But before Denise had time to reply, they were attacked by another wave of admirers or backbiters, it was impossible to decide which; everyone smiled equally ingratiatingly and tenderly, anxious to express their dismay and concern.

Jack Elephant had become a widower two years earlier, and these musical soirées were expensive pretexts to avoid spending evenings alone. Jack had been president of the Music Academy for many years, and Reuben Walrus did not dare say no to his invitations; he was not an enemy that Walrus could allow himself.

On his way through the elephant's sparsely furnished drawing room toward the grandiose dining room, Reuben walked close beside Denise. He had told her about Drexler's syndrome that morning over a cup of coffee—which did not relieve his headache—at Gino's. She was livid. How did he dare? To subject her to this? And when it was clear to her how little he knew about the disease, how he had only accepted the doctor's diagnosis, she promptly got up from the table and left. After the rehearsals in the afternoon, they had met at his place, and then she refused to talk about the matter.

In some absurd manner this denial was pleasant; an angry look was preferable to a pitying one. Walrus refused to let himself be reduced to a victim, a poor thing. The sentence he had received was unmerciful, anxiety tore at his heart, but he still lived—and heard.

He walked a half step behind Denise, breathing in the aroma of her perfume, the smell of cloth surrounding her hard-packed body, and for a few seconds he closed his eyes and tried to feel happy about getting to be so close.

In honor of the evening, Jack Elephant had placed Reuben Walrus at the short end of the table. He sat between a pianist he knew but whose name he could never remember, and a vivid green dog with red eyes from Amberville who lisped when she talked and introduced herself as Annette Afghan. The pianist was dressed in a tight-fitting black dress, which helped Reuben to recall her as a boring, honest, and ambitious stuffed animal. The dog was wearing something low-necked with ruffles.

Denise Ant was sitting far away, between a duck that Reuben did not know and Tom Whitefish, music director at Radio Mollisan Town, who many considered to be the real power in the city's musical life.

"Oh, so unexpected," said Afghan as Reuben pulled out her chair and they sat down for dinner, "getting to sit next to a real TV star."

"TV star?" said Reuben with a self-conscious smile. "I don't know if I—"

"Do tell," continued the Afghan, "how you can read the

news and look right into the camera at the same time? I stumble even when I read silently from a book."

"But I don't read the news on TV," Reuben answered with surprise.

"You don't?"

"No."

"But . . . I was sure that . . . ," stammered the clearly disappointed and shamefaced dog. "Excuse me, but I know that I recognize you from TV. Or somewhere."

Reuben told who he was, the Afghan laughed with embarrassment and maintained that of course she knew about him and his work just like everyone else, that she had heard several of his . . . songs . . . and that she had only made a mistake because she felt a little tipsy from the champagne. Reuben smiled amiably and asked what kind of work she did.

"I work with stuffed animals," she said, suddenly serious, and nodded her sweet head. "There are so many that are doing poorly these days, you know? So many who need someone to talk to. You have to believe in something, you know? There are so many who don't believe in anything."

"And you yourself believe?" asked Reuben amiably.

The appetizers were served. Walrus saw from the corner of his eye how Denise was laughing at something Whitefish said, and he turned again toward Annette Afghan. The atmosphere was already lively around the table. The cook had blended mild mold-ripened cheese into the ground steak tartare, and white wine was being poured into the glasses.

"You have to believe," answered Annette Afghan. "I believe in my inner power, and how I can develop it. Magnus is in all of us, you know? In you too."

She riveted her eyes on him, as if what she said was a reprimand.

"Shall we see if Jack's white wine is just as good as the red usually is?" Reuben asked, raising his glass to his nose.

Afghan ignored his attempt to change the subject.

"Do you know," she asked, letting him sip the wine alone, "how many there are who come into the store and ask for rainbow stones? Every day?"

This Reuben did not know. He had not even heard of rainbow stones.

"It's not one or two," Afghan answered her own question. "It's considerably more. And shall I tell you what they really want? They want to believe. You know? But Magnus is already in them, it's a matter of discovering him. Or her," added the Afghan, blushing.

Reuben took a piece of steak tartare on his fork. It was going to be a very long dinner, he thought unhappily. The Afghan was making sure to completely monopolize him, and he almost longed for the boring pianist on the other side.

"If Magnus lives in you," Reuben interrupted at last, "then we can be sure in any event that he's a good listener."

Despite Annette Afghan, it was still the pianist who, right before dessert, disrupted the evening. At that point Reuben had still not given her more than friendly smiles. It was only when Annette Afghan got up to look for the restroom that he got a chance for courtesy. The pianist did not lose the opportunity.

"It's so terrible," she said. "You must excuse me, but I don't know what I should say."

Reuben had consumed a number of glasses of Jack Elephant's excellent white wine and then a few glasses of the red, but was still relatively sober.

"Say about what?" he asked.

"About . . . about . . . ," stammered the pianist, "about . . . the tragedy that has struck you. That has struck us all, indirectly. It's . . . terrible."

With the babbling Afghan Reuben had temporarily forgotten his anxiety, Drexler's syndrome, and the fate that awaited him. He had partaken of the garlic gratin and the breaded flounder. Like an executioner's ax, melancholy now fell over him.

"Hmm," he replied.

"We have worked together many times," the pianist continued, "and I know what hearing means to you. I mean . . . for you in particular. Oh, I don't know . . . however I put it . . . it sounds so stupid . . . I . . . I don't know what I should say."

In all honesty, Reuben Walrus didn't know either, and therefore it felt like a gift from above that Annette Afghan returned at the same moment. Reuben had an excuse to get up, pull out the Afghan's chair, and thereby puncture the unpleasant moment. But the pianist was not prepared to let go. She leaned past Reuben, drawing Annette into the conversation.

"We were just talking about the Tragedy," she explained, nodding at Reuben as if the walrus were not present.

"The tragedy?"

"About Reuben's illness," she explained. "Mollisan Town is grieving one of its greatest composers of all time."

Annette Afghan turned with an uncomprehending look toward Reuben, who was absentmindedly pulling on his mustache. The pianist was more than willing to tell.

"But that's just terrible," exclaimed Annette Afghan when the pianist was done.

"The worst is that he won't be able to compose anymore," the pianist maintained.

"But isn't there anything you can do?" asked Annette. "Aren't there any medications, any . . . treatments?"

"Nothing," said the pianist, shaking her head ominously.

"But . . . this is just terrible!"

"He got the diagnosis just a few days ago," the pianist

explained, and added in a lower voice, "I don't know if he's understood it yet."

"He has to go see Maximilian," said Annette Afghan.

And she turned directly to Reuben, who had followed the conversation with distress without getting into it. Annette looked him sternly in the eyes.

"You have to go see Maximilian."

Denise Ant wanted to dance before they went home, and Reuben Walrus sat in Jack's library with a large glass of cognac and waited. He despised dancing and had never—besides the waltz at his own wedding—done it. He sat down on one of the elegantly worn leather armchairs and was immediately joined by first one animal and then another who wanted to complain and dramatize. It was as if they were talking about someone else, and soon Walrus also felt anguish: what this city was about to lose! Cigars were smoked and there was the smell of leather, and on the whole Reuben thought that the role of poor wretch could also have its special pleasure.

It was not until his third glass of cognac that the pianist from dinner sat down in the armchair beside him, and conspiratorially leaned forward to address him in a low voice.

"Do you know about Maximilian?" she asked, getting right to the point. "Maximilian that Afghan mentioned?"

Reuben smiled in collusion. The alcohol had lightened his heart a little.

"Afghan won on fatigue," he replied. "And dinner was a pleasure. But you cannot forgive her ecumenicism. And this . . . Maximilian . . . is no one that I—"

"She was right," interrupted the pianist.

Reuben looked at her with surprise. Even if he did not remember her name, he knew that she was a talent, a serious musician with a solid reputation.

"What do you know about Maximilian?" she asked.

He shrugged his shoulders. "Nothing, really," he answered truthfully. "It's clear that I know about the phenomenon, but I've never believed that—"

"I've heard a story," the pianist began, but corrected herself. "I have heard many stories, but I'm thinking about the story about the giraffe in particular. He is still living. I think his name is Heine and he lives down in Yok. The giraffe was sick. Fatally sick. If I've understood the matter right, it was cancer of the throat, and metastases down in the stomach. It was a matter of weeks, perhaps days, before the Chauffeurs would come and fetch him. When he was walking around in the neighborhood where he lived, he seemed to often see a red pickup driving by. Because he was in so much pain, it would in a way also be a release.

"One day, wandering aimlessly on the street—he wasn't eating anymore, could only drink because the cancer had almost entirely corked up his throat—the Miracle happened. Down from the sky came an animal who did not look like any stuffed animal. I know that you think it sounds ridiculous, Mr. Walrus—I thought so too when I heard it the first time. But since I have heard the same type of story from so many places, with such similar variations, at last I was forced to believe in it. If it was down from the sky or up out of the ground I don't know; the important thing is that this animal, Maximilian, came out of nowhere."

"What do you mean, he doesn't look like a stuffed animal?" asked Reuben.

"Exactly that. I don't know how to explain it, because I haven't really understood it myself. He lacks a category, he is simply . . . Maximilian," the pianist answered, shaking her head lightly.

"Back to the giraffe," prodded Reuben, who was curious to know how the story would continue.

"The giraffe was out on the street, and suddenly Maximilian was standing in front of him," said the pianist. "He knew it was Maximilian, because Maximilian introduced himself. What the exact words were, I don't know. Some say one thing, some say another. It seems as though the giraffe began some kind of conversation, where he complained about no longer being able to eat corn on the cob. Or corn. Before the giraffe had clarified that it was due to cancer of the throat, Maximilian said: 'Go and buy corn. As of now you can eat as usual again.' "

The pianist fell silent with an urgent look.

"And so?" said Reuben.

"And so it was," said the pianist. "There and then, at the same moment as Maximilian said the words, the cancer disappeared from the giraffe's throat. It was a miracle."

The walrus sipped his cognac. The pianist's story made him ill at ease.

"There are hundreds of stories about Maximilian," she said. "But I happened to think of this one."

"Yes?"

"Mr. Walrus," said the pianist, looking him straight in the eyes, "Maximilian can perform marvels. I have heard stories . . . he can fly . . . he has performed miracles . . . he can heal the sick, Mr. Walrus. *He can heal the sick*."

Reuben nodded but looked as if he were thinking about something else.

"The Afghan is right," said the pianist, getting up. "You have to go see Maximilian. It is your only hope."

She stood a moment, staring at him, with melancholy in her gaze. Then she left, and Walrus remained sitting with his cognac glass in his fin, and his thoughts in disarray.

WOLF DIAZ 3

The outing to Sagrada Bastante was mandatory, and not just for us Forest Cubs but for all sixth-graders in the city. The magnificent cathedral with its thirteen towers was located at the Star. The archdeacon of the city, Penguin Odenrick, was responsible for Sagrada Bastante. He was also the superior of the four prodeacons, from Amberville, Lanceheim, Tourquai, and Yok. In each part of the city there was a series of parishes led by humble, industrious deacons who did their best, most often with limited resources. The church was prosperous, and it intended to remain so. That explained the extreme thriftiness.

In Das Vorschutz we had all been brought up religiously. It was part of who we were; the forest was the creation of Magnus, and we were his humble servants. For that reason it was a solemn experience to enter the massive cathedral for the first time together with your schoolmates, and see with your own eyes the fateful ceiling and wall paintings, which depicted portions of the Proclamations in a manner that must be called dramatic. I recall it as if it were yesterday. I walked slowly so as not to stumble. Despite the massiveness of the church and its windows tall as flagpoles, an ominous darkness rested over the floor of the cathedral. Shadows of carved ornaments and decorations stuck out from walls and pillars, and the intention was surely to instill proper respect in the poor Magnus-fearing visitor. I thought it impossible that the church had been built by the paws, claws, hands, and tails of stuffed animals; this was a work by Magnus himself.

The church in Mollisan Town saw its mission as being to remind the stuffed animals in all situations about their pitifulness, smallness, and mortality. The thirteen towers of Sagrada Bastante rose high above the surrounding neighborhoods and functioned as a part of this constant reminder.

I was sitting at the kitchen table having breakfast the morning my mother, Carolyn Nightingale, led her sixth-grade class to Sagrada Bastante. She had only two pupils who were twelve years old, Maximilian and Weasel Tukovsky's little brother, Musk Ox Pivot, and therefore she had arranged the showing with one of the schools in Lanceheim. Her good friend Theophile Falcon worked there, and in his school there were five parallel sixth-grade classes.

"Good morning," I greeted.

Maximilian and Musk Ox looked suspiciously at me. Even if I often visited Mother and Father at home, I was no longer one of the residents of Das Vorschutz, and so the Forest Cubs viewed me with skepticism. I recognized the behavior; I had acted the same.

That morning it was almost exactly five years since Maximilian and I had met the wounded badger in the forest. For me the experience had led to existential brooding of the most painful sort, and many times I wished nothing better than to be able to tell someone what I had been involved in. Still, I said nothing. Something held me back.

Sometimes there was talk about Maximilian. He was an odd character; his gifts were beyond the ordinary, and he radiated a sort of integrity that could feel annoying, especially considering his age. No one yet identified this radiation as "goodness"; that came later. I refrained from taking part in these discussions, but no one asked why. I had a reputation for being a taciturn wolf.

"Are you spending the night?" Mother asked.

"Probably," I replied.

Weasel and I had each moved into our own studio apartment in south Lanceheim, while Buzzard was living at home with his parents again for the time being. Naturally we teased him about this, but often we too—with bags of dirty laundry and growling stomachs—sought out our compassionate mothers.

"We're having lasagna," said Mother to further convince me, and after that she shooed her two schoolchildren out to the taxi that would drive all three of them to the cathedral.

I watched Maximilian as he was leaving. He had continued to grow, and was on his way to being the tallest stuffed animal ever. His appearance seemed to be in constant change, but it was still impossible to see what he resembled. Mother had been nervous about the reactions he would arouse in the other children, but with baggy clothes on his thin body and a cap pulled down over the strange ears, he looked less striking.

" 'Bye now," I called after them.

I spent the day in the living room with my abstracts and legal cases. After high school, I had applied to and been accepted in the law program at the university in Tourquai, and I can't say that I felt at home there, but neither could I complain of discomfort. I had been doing schoolwork for so many years that it seemed obvious to keep going, and I liked the idea of constantly trying to separate right from wrong, evil from good.

Mother came home right before the Afternoon Rain, but she slipped right into the kitchen. Soon the aroma of garlic-sprinkled broccoli and full-bodied cheese sauce spread through the house. I found it more and more difficult to concentrate, and was relieved when there was a knock at the front door.

Outside stood Eva Whippoorwill.

"Is your mother at home?" she asked.

I nodded and asked her to step in. She looked angry and afraid. She was wearing a dark blue dress with pleated skirt and polo collar, and even if the memory of youthful infatuation had faded, I still thought she was beautiful.

I followed her into the kitchen.

"Where's Maximilian?" Eva asked as soon as she caught sight of Mother.

"Maximilian?"

"Where is he? You should have come back before the Breeze. Musk Ox is already home; I just spoke with Bluebird. Where is Maximilian?"

With rapid, definite movements Mother set aside the grater and cheese on the counter, untied her apron, and quickly stepped past Eva Whippoorwill out into the hall where the telephone was. Eva followed nervously.

"Carolyn, what has happened?" she asked.

Mother did not reply. She dialed a telephone number and waited with the receiver pressed against her ear. She looked resolute. When Theophile Falcon answered, she got right to the point.

"Theophile, this is Carolyn. I'm calling about Maximilian. Was there anything that . . . ?"

Mother fell silent, listened, nodded to herself, and replied with a brief yes or no at regular intervals, all while Eva Whippoorwill and I anxiously watched her.

"Good," she said at last on the phone. "We'll come there."

She hung up, turned around, and said to me, "Eva and I will borrow Sven's car. Tell Father that we'll be back later. Maximilian is apparently still in Sagrada Bastante, and we have to bring him home."

And with no further delay or explanation, Mother and Eva Whippoorwill left.

They did not return until long after the Evening Storm, and Father and I were extremely curious by that time. We had prepared tea and sandwiches—Mother had not eaten anything since lunch—and while she stilled her hunger at the kitchen table, she told us about what had happened.

A quarter of an hour after the guided tour had begun that morning, Musk Ox Pivot got sick to his stomach. Mother was compelled, not without a certain irritation, to sit with the patient on one of the benches in the inner courtyard, while Maximilian followed along with the other sixth-grade classes under Theophile Falcon's supervision.

Carolyn thought the nausea would pass, but on the contrary it got worse. After sitting on the bench a while, Musk Ox became seriously ill, and threw up in one of the cathedral's many exquisite rose beds. The fact that some of it got on his clothes did not make things any better. Carolyn asked poor Pivot to wait where he was sitting, and then ran to catch up with Falcon and the other cubs. She had to return to Das Vorschutz with the sick musk ox; could Falcon take charge of Maximilian and see to it that he got home later?

Falcon nodded; it was no big deal.

It was only during the afternoon sabbath that Schoolmaster Falcon discovered that Maximilian had disappeared. Few stuffed animals observe the sabbath nowadays, but it is only necessary to go back a hundred years to find that all activity in Mollisan Town more or less halted during the hour in the morning and the half hour in the afternoon that the rain fell. In the church the sabbath was still holy, and so only then did Falcon get a chance to count all the cubs.

Maximilian was gone.

Falcon went off on a hunt through Sagrada Bastante, following his own tracks through the church, and it was not long before they found him. In a room inside one of the lecture halls in the oldest part of the building sat two all-deacons and a deacon at a round table, listening seriously to the twelve-year-old Maximilian. The room was dark except for a kerosene lamp, and Theophile Falcon got the feeling that he was interrupting something important.

Maximilian fell silent when the door opened, and the all-deacons turned around.

"Excuse me," said Falcon, "but Maximilian . . . is part of my school class?"

The all-deacons and deacon looked startled and doubtful. They exchanged quick glances of mutual understanding, and then asked amiably for leave to keep Maximilian a while longer.

"I don't know . . . ," Falcon replied. "I promised to take Maximilian home to Das Vorschutz this afternoon, and . . . pardon me for asking, but . . . what are you talking about?"

"About evil and good," said one of the young all-deacons.

"About right and wrong," replied the other.

"We promise that young Maximilian will come home in a safe manner," said the deacon. "No later than dinnertime."

Falcon nodded, perplexed. He did not understand what young Maximilian could tell the stuffed animals of the church about good and evil.

"Are you sure?" he said. "Because I promised that—"

Adam Chaffinch, the deacon who was the leader of the small circle, interrupted him and promised once again that Maximilian would be delivered home to Das Vorschutz, and Falcon was content with that.

When Carolyn Nightingale and Eva Whippoorwill parked Sven Beaver's old Volga Kombi in front of Sagrada Bastante, the sky was already dark. They ran into the church, asked for Adam Chaffinch, and soon found the room where Theophile Falcon had received his assurance many hours earlier.

"Mother?" Maximilian exclaimed in surprise when he saw Eva in the doorway.

Deacon Adam Chaffinch asked what the weather was, and then begged pardon of both females over and over again. They had completely forgotten the time. Would it be possible to keep Maximilian another hour? They were in the midst of an especially important train of thought.

Eva Whippoorwill became furious.

Deacon or not, you didn't behave like that.

Four minutes later Eva and Carolyn were again sitting in Sven's car, this time with Maximilian in the backseat, en route home.

"He's a strange one, that Maximilian," my mother asserted, eating up the last bite of her sandwich.

Through the windows of the barn, to the north, south, and east, the cubs saw kilometer upon kilometer of fields, nothing else, just tall wheat that swayed invitingly in the gentle breeze. To the west a blue streak could be made out on the horizon, the sea, and Hillevie, the stuffed animals' vacation spot near Mollisan Town. Between the city and the sea was agriculture, the fruit farms, where an old-fashioned rural life lived on. The small number of farmers who worked the soil lived in isolation, here and there a sporadic settlement, but nothing that with the best intentions in the world could be called a village.

Together with seventeen confirmation students of the same age, Maximilian was sitting in the renovated barn, looking now and then out the window. A few hours ago All-deacon Chiradello, a light yellow seal pup with bushy eyebrows and a hint of acne, had told the story of Magnus and Noah Whale. Chiradello was young and could therefore be traditional without being accused of conservatism. He stood up at the lectern, which in turn stood on a little rise at the farther short wall. Through the window behind him the confirmands could rest their gazes on the swaying wheat, a kind of meditative view that, according to the all-deacon himself, deepened concentration and understanding.

The barn was exactly 143 square meters in size, and it was seven meters up to the exposed ends of the roof. Besides the large window behind the lectern, there were four windows on the side walls, but they were small and narrow.

Chiradello had set out eighteen chairs in a half-moon on the floor, and there sat the confirmands. They felt exposed, unprotected, and that was the point. Magnus had created an immense universe for us; we stuffed animals were only pitiful trifles in that context. There was a faint odor of dampness in the room, despite the fact that a pair of electrical space heaters stood humming in the corners. Out here on the plain the ground never really got dry.

"Does anyone know the name of the first stuffed animal whom Magnus appeared to?" asked the all-deacon.

He looked around. His lidless gaze wandered curiously from one to the other. The few but rigid whiskers pointed straight out in the air. He had a light voice and a tone that was equally chiseled and precise; he spoke with a studied precision.

An albatross raised his wing. The all-deacon nodded.

"Noah," he answered.

"That's right," Chiradello called out with exaggerated enthusiasm. "And does anyone know when that was?"

The seal pup was not standing behind the lectern; he knew that created a barrier between him and the cubs. He stood up on the podium, and instead of the long, black robe that the animals of the church usually wore, he had put on a tweed jacket and a pair of jeans for the day. It was about creating trust.

A farm cat cleared her throat.

"Yes?" said Chiradello, smiling amiably.

"A thousand years ago?" said the cat.

"A thousand years ago." Chiradello nodded encouragingly. "That's what we always say. A thousand years ago. But that doesn't mean that it was exactly one thousand years ago, does it? When I was confirmed, the answer to that question was also a thousand years. And in ten years we will probably continue to say the same thing. It's part of the tradition. 'A thousand years ago' means a long, long time ago."

There was nodding around the room.

"And why?" asked Chiradello. "Why did Magnus show himself to Noah Whale?"

It became silent in the barn. The all-deacon made a little victory lap up on the podium. He liked this: going from religious generalities straight into the darkest holes of metaphysics with simple questions.

"No," he said when he thought the stage pause was long enough, "it's not equally obvious. And at the same time, that is what we will focus on during the coming—"

"Excuse me, Schoolmaster?"

The all-deacon fell silent. He saw that it was the cat who had interrupted him, and with concealed irritation he said amiably, "Yes?"

"Him over there, with the scarf on his head, wants to say something," said the cat and pointed.

And that was correct. When All-deacon Chiradello looked, the strange animal who had a kind of scarf wrapped around his head, the one who was sitting at the far end of the row, was holding up his arm.

"Was there something in particular you were thinking about?" he asked.

He hoped that he still sounded nice.

At every camp there's an oddball, Chiradello had learned; someone the others would laugh at if you didn't ward off the situation. In this group the oddball was the animal with the scarf on his head. Chiradello had decided to do his best not to let him be picked on by the others.

"What was it you wanted?" he asked again.

"It's not what the puzzle depicts that is important," said Maximilian, touching his headgear lightly, "it's how you solve it."

Before I continue telling about Maximilian's confirmation camp, I would like to address a few words directly to the skeptical reader. I intend to cite Dolores Deer. Straight out I admit that the reason I am going to cite Dolores is that I feel the need to justify myself. I am going to betray a confidence, and thereby make her my character witness. It is probably an unattractive thing to do, but it is important that you, readers of my assuredly flat but significant narrative, do not remain ignorant of what I have to put forward in my defense. Yet it is impossible to mention Dolores without devoting a few lines to her eyes.

Dolores's eyes were the most beautiful I have ever seen.

It was many years ago that by chance I ended up at an espresso bar I had not noticed before. It was hardly more than a hole in the wall, not far from Maria's House. Its furnishings consisted of a long bar counter and a couple of stools.

I ordered a double macchiato from the waitress at the espresso machine, and dug in my coat pocket for change while she ground the beans. I set the money on the counter at the same moment that she set out the cup, and it was then that I saw them: Dolores's eyes.

It was an explosive moment of absolute stillness. Her speckled blue irises shone like the sky above a sea, and the distinct black pupils widened like a personal invitation. I got weak in the knees, my mouth got dry, I could not get out a word. If I had fallen for females before, the fall had never been as dizzyingly long as when I looked into Dolores's eyes for the first time. They awakened a desire that made me blush when I, mumbling, raised the cup of macchiato and attempted a smile. She had to be mine. If I did not get to look into Dolores's eyes again, life as I knew it would lose a dimension.

I don't intend to go into details. It worked out. A few weeks later, over a small restaurant table in north Tourquai, Dolores leaned over and said, "Wolf Diaz, you are the most intuitive stuffed animal I have ever encountered. I am sure you would be able to recount my entire childhood without even knowing about it. Your imagination and your empathy are like a crystal ball where you can see both the past and what is to come."

In principle that is what Dolores Deer said.

By this I do not mean to say that this depiction of Maximilian's confirmation camp is correct or complete. I do not want to boast or make commitments that I cannot live up to. But when the critical reader questions how I have the gall to put words in Maximilian's mouth or dress Alldeacon Chiradello in a certain facial expression, I will only remind you of Dolores's words, and assure you that I also remain humble and choose an open interpretation to the extent I feel the least bit uncertain about how things actually happened.

It was during the weeks at confirmation camp that the stuffed animals realized that Maximilian was good.

"Good" is not a grand character trait. On the contrary, if anything it seems a bit lame, and the semantic problem of the word is, as I see it, one of the concept's fundamental concerns. From a subjective perspective we are all good, aren't we? That is to say, we regard ourselves as basically good. With any amount of objectivity, however, we can observe and evaluate our actions, and understand that they do not all spring from goodness. But we are quick to excuse ourselves; you do what you do, deep down we can always distinguish right from wrong.

May I suggest a brief exercise for the soul-searching reader?

Shut your eyes.

Peel off coquetry and ironic winking.

Penetrate within your intellectual defenses and place yourself all the way inside your innermost core.

Answer this question: Are you good?

The answer is: "Yes."

And open your eyes again, and confess: It's not true. No more than in parts, sometimes, if the conditions are right, not to say perfect.

With Maximilian it was, and is, different. Maximilian is good. Without reservation, without weakness. Perhaps he is even Goodness itself?

It was All-deacon Chiradello who formulated it. It was he who spoke about "good" in connection with Maximilian for the first time, instead of calling his radiance "integrity" or "talent."

Once upon a time many thousands of years ago Magnus created the universe. One aspect of the creation was the creation's own possibility to develop. Therefore Magnus appeared on the earth three times, and let himself be escorted through the world that he himself had initiated and watched over ever since. A thousand years ago, for three months, three weeks, and three days, Noah Whale had shown Magnus how the sea, the coast, and the land connected to the coast had developed. Many hundreds of years later, it was Jean-Jacques Fox who for two months, two weeks, and two days became Magnus's cicerone in the forests.

For the Forest Cubs from Das Vorschutz, the second part of the Proclamations, the one written by Fox, was the easiest to absorb. In Fox's Proclamation there was everything that we Forest Cubs recognized: the trees and lakes, mountains and vegetation, forest animals and paths.

All-deacon Chiradello devoted himself to the gospels of Jean-Jacques Fox during the second week of confirmation studies. Perhaps he believed—and surely hoped—that Maximilian could strengthen his position with the others when the forest came up for discussion. He gave great scope to Maximilian to answer questions and show himself to be knowledgeable, but to no effect. Maximilian was just as taciturn as before. Either he answered when addressed, directly and clearly but never with a word too many, or else he answered with the similes that fascinated Chiradello to an increasing degree.

The seal pup was soon brooding just as much about these similes as about the texts he had selected from the Proclamations for the sake of instruction. He could stand before his eighteen confirmands in the barn and talk about Jean-Jacques Fox's famous depiction of Magnus and the stumps, and at the same time wonder what Maximilian meant with his simile about the puzzle and how you solve it.

Slowly Seal Pup Chiradello realized that there was a connection between Maximilian's similes and the texts of the Proclamations. Chiradello could not account for how he arrived at this connection or exactly how it appeared, but he was nonetheless convinced of it.

The third week of confirmation studies was devoted to the last part of the Proclamations and the stories of Rachel Siamese. For a month, a week, and a day Magnus walked around the streets and squares in the four cities that, much later, would merge together into Mollisan Town.

"It requires consideration," said Chiradello, while as usual he let his large, dark eyes sweep across the row of confirmands. "What must Magnus have experienced? How we consistently show that we reject His creation by re-creating what he has given us in every detail and changing it into something else. Water and sand become cement. Stone and ore, we make into metal and steel. Coal and copper become light, and light becomes energy. He gives, we receive and transform."

The all-deacon fell silent and lowered his gaze, as if he personally had displeased Magnus the Almighty. Outside the barn the Afternoon Weather was reaching its end, the wheat fields stood untouched by the wind, and the heat was about to diminish. The sun had reached so far across the sky that its rays could make their way into the barn; the ripening yellow light settled like square panes in the laps of the confirmands. They all felt ill at ease, and at last someone said, "But the wrath of Magnus, is it . . . I mean, that was a long time ago, wasn't it?"

"Yes," replied the all-deacon slowly. "That was a long time ago. But in the Proclamations it is not always what is written that is being referred to. And what is written is not always all that ought to be understood. You have to think for yourselves. This is, and remains, the challenge to you confirmands, even if it is the only thing you learn during these weeks. Think for yourselves. What makes Magnus angry? Is it that we devote our brief lives to re-creating what has already been given to us? Can Magnus have perceived it in such a way, that we transform His natural assets so they are in better accord with our own laziness and vanity, our insecure searching for acknowledgment, and our endless striving for simplification?"

"But," an anxious voice was heard, "I haven't re-created anything."

The all-deacon knew that the third part of the Proclamations was always experienced as unpleasant by the confirmands. He had never felt comfortable with frightening anyone into belief, and he was about to answer when Maximilian unexpectedly got there first.

"I want to say this to you," said Maximilian. "He who owns a dollhouse, seldom lacks a doll."

The silence in the barn intensified. The cubs looked nervously at one another; no one knew anymore how they should handle Maximilian's comments. They had laughed and ridiculed them, they had sometimes tried to take them seriously. But nothing made them comprehensible, it seemed.

"Maximilian," said the all-deacon from the lectern, "I do not think that—"

"But that's so sick," interrupted Agnes Python.

No one could mistake the irritation in her voice, and for once she was not only speaking for herself.

"I'm getting tired of hearing these idiotic similes," she continued. "What does he mean by talking like that? Does he even know what he means?"

A buzz immediately went through the barn, the confirmands turned to each other to exchange quick comments. It was a relief that someone had finally dared say it. Maximilian remained unperturbed.

"Can you perhaps explain what you mean?" asked All-deacon Chiradello as the buzz subsided.

"The one who owns a train seldom lacks cars," Maximilian clarified, and continued. "A stuffed animal came wandering along the road. On the field beside him was a scythe, and on the scythe spiders had spun their webs. In the grass a stuffed animal was sleeping. The scythe was the sleeping animal's tool. 'Shall you not get up and use your scythe?' asked the wanderer. 'No, I don't have the energy for that,' answered the animal in the grass. 'The desire exists, and the understanding of what must be done, but no longer the energy.' Then the wanderer took the scythe and threw it into the field so that it disappeared from sight. 'Now your desire and your understanding will soon be as little as your energy,' said the wanderer. And with that he continued along the road."

It was silent in the barn, so silent that Chiradello could hear his own heart beating. Never before had they heard Maximilian say so many words at one time. No one understood what he meant by his story, but the confirmands could see from Chiradello that something significant had occurred, and they felt a kind of veneration before the moment. Even Agnes Python kept quiet.

I have to contact Chaffinch, thought Chiradello. I can no longer keep this to myself.

During the weeks of confirmation camp the sabbath was observed. As long as the Morning Rain and the Afternoon Rain fell, the pupils were forced to pray one or more of the fifteen prayers that could be read in Noah Whale's part of the Proclamations. The only exception was made on the day before the confirmation itself, a day filled with preparations and nervousness. Then suddenly a "dignified" cleaning of the cupboards in the dormitory was allowed. The modern-day church's concept of what was and was not allowed during the two periods of rain during the day was somewhat diffuse. There was talk of "dignity" or "contemplation," but exactly what this meant remained unclear to the confirmands. There was of course a long list of prohibitions, but the list was taken from the Proclamations and in need of contemporary adaptation.

After breakfast, everyone gathered out in the barn. Alldeacon Chiradello went through the program. By afternoon they would all leave for the city, and the confirmands would sleep in their own homes the night before the solemn ritual. Early the next morning there would be a gathering in the church in Kerkeling. Then Chiradello proceeded to describe the ceremony as expected, practically speaking, minute by minute. The questioning itself would take place right before lunch, and then it was time for the confirmation.

The last day at the farm was devoted to cleaning, and Chiradello took the opportunity to quiz the cubs one last time on the questions that awaited the next day. The answers came like running water; it was not the idea that anyone should fail.

The bus that was to drive the cubs back to their homes showed up right before the Afternoon Rain. The confirmands fell into line, and one by one they climbed aboard. At the door of the bus Chiradello stood and said good-bye. Maximilian was the last in line, and when it was his turn, Chiradello said, "I can drive you in a little later—there is someone I want you to meet first." He then made a gesture to the bus driver, who closed the door and drove off with seventeen soon-to-be confirmands.

"So we meet again," said Adam Chaffinch.

The chaffinch was sitting on one of the eighteen chairs that were still in a half-moon formation in the middle of the barn, and he got up when Maximilian and Chiradello came in. He had on a long black suit, under which his gray plumage stuck out. His eyes were dark, and his beak was stern.

"We've met before," he continued. "A few years ago, in Sagrada Bastante, where we carried on an exciting discussion. Didn't we?"

Maximilian nodded and smiled vaguely. All three of them sat down.

"I am Adam Chaffinch. I work in Kerkeling Parish, and tomorrow I am the one who will confirm you and your friends."

Maximilian nodded again. There was not a trace of friendliness in the chaffinch's voice; he spoke as if he were preaching.

"But I have a proposal that I think you should consider. I know that you have applied to Lanceheim's Normal School, and there is nothing wrong with that. But if you would prefer, I can offer you a place at Kerkeling High School. It is the only educational institution run by the church in Mollisan Town, and we do it because we sometimes feel that special talent is at risk of being lost if a little extra care isn't taken with it. The high school is a kind of boarding school, which means that you get to stay in an apartment right next to the school."

"Take it," urged Chiradello, turning directly to Maximilian. "Kerkeling High School will suit you much better than Lanceheim Normal."

"I thought this when we first met in Sagrada Bastante," said Adam, "and Seal Pup has had the same impression during the weeks you have spent together. We believe that with the extra attention we can give you in Kerkeling, you will be able to develop even quicker."

"Take it," repeated Chiradello.

Adam got up.

"I'm on my way," he said. "This is not something you need to decide right now. Speak with your parents, and then you can get back to me when you have thought about the matter."

Maximilian also got up, and nodded again. Thoughtfully he said, "A jump rope is only a rope if no one jumps."

Chaffinch nodded, smiled an ambiguous smile, and left the barn.

REUBEN WALRUS 4

Reuben Walrus was under considerable pressure.

That was his excuse.

The illness was gnawing deeper and deeper into his awareness. At times he imagined tiny microbes literally eating up the cells in his ear passages. The rehearsals progressed, but more by randomly skidding in the right direction than by the orchestra taking clear, determined steps with steady improvement. It was Sunday, the sixth day of rehearsals. Dag Chihuahua, the philharmonic's first violinist, snorted audibly.

"I can't work if I think about it," he said shaken up, setting aside his bow on the edge of the stage. "It doesn't work. I'm sorry. In my eyes nothing has changed. I don't intend to be nice."

"Nothing would be more foreign to you," Reuben corroborated.

They were standing a short distance away from the orchestra and talking so that no one could hear them. Chihuahua was wearing a sky blue velvet jacket with a dark red silk scarf around his neck instead of a tie. His large eyes swayed uneasily in his head, and the narrow nose bobbed downward as he spoke.

"Not being able to present a finished piece is unforgivable, Mr. Walrus," he continued. "How do you think a professional musician can interpret the symphony without knowing the ending? You have only yourself to blame for the uncertainty you are hearing in the orchestra, Mr. Walrus. Give us the final movement—then we will give you the strength and sensitivity of which we are capable."

"Dag, I—"

"And I don't want to hear anything about your . . . condition," objected Chihuahua.

"Dag, I—"

"Not a word!"

"How long have we known each other, Dag?" asked Walrus, forced to raise his voice in order not to be interrupted a third time. "Twenty years? Is it thirty? It's one thing that you refuse to call me by my first name, but I demand a different kind of respect. I am doing my utmost. You will get new scores tomorrow, perhaps the day after tomorrow. Until then . . . I do not expect . . . great achievements . . . but simply that you lead your musicians in a manner that makes us both feel . . . proud. That is not too much to ask."

Chihuahua snorted.

"I'll go out and get Denise," said Reuben, "and then we'll try again."

And without awaiting the violinist's blessing, Reuben went out to the lobby where Denise Ant was sitting curled up in the window recess, reading. Reuben had finally given in and let her come along to the rehearsals, but he had regretted it as soon as they started this morning. Now it was too late.

"Are you coming, darling?" he said. "We're starting now."

They went into the concert hall together. He felt heavy and stiff beside her; she moved like a romping cub. The idea struck him the very next moment: she *was* a romping cub.

The musicians on the stage resumed their places, and the customary racket broke out as the instruments were tuned and checked. After a few minutes, order was slowly restored.

Reuben and Denise went into row 15. Reuben had placed his briefcase with calculated nonchalance on seat 354 so that Denise would not sit there by accident.

"I was thinking," said Reuben with a loud, authoritative voice to the musicians as Denise sat down, "that we should devote the afternoon to the andante of the second movement, and focus in particular on the intention behind the chromatic changes. Up till now we have played them . . . deliberately. As if we were full of how gifted we are. As if we were playing and at the same time admiring what we had produced. This afternoon I want to let the emotions loose. You're starting to know this. You don't need to read the notes. Forget yourselves, forget your instruments. Play because you love it. From . . . page fifteen in the score, second measure, the violins start on G sharp."

Reuben raised his conductor's baton; the room was filled with tension, the discipline that a few moments ago seemed distant was again razor-sharp. And through a quiver from his fin the music exploded from the stage.

Reuben stole a glance at Denise. She was sitting on the edge of the seat, and her eyes were shining. She loved this. Being part of a world of vanity and musicality, consummate professional skill and heavenly talent. But she would never completely understand, Walrus thought with melancholy, and his thoughts wandered hastily on to his daughter, Josephine. Like Denise she was self-sacrificing and pragmatic, but she did not have the talent. So cruel, he thought.

. . . .

Reuben Walrus stopped the music as the orchestra musicians were on their way out of the second movement of the symphony. There was much to talk about, to think about. He knew that he was disappointing Denise—she would rather have continued listening—but the rehearsals were not for her sake. Besides, she had heard enough to be able to brag about it.

"Dag, are you coming down for a little while?" called Reuben, and Chihuahua carefully put down his violin and climbed down onto the parquet.

It was the customary procedure. The composer and the first violinist conferred, came to an agreement about what had been good and bad, and decided how criticism could best be conveyed to the orchestra to lead to positive changes.

"Will you excuse me?" Reuben asked Ant.

She nodded, with a knowing expression. It irritated Walrus that Denise presumably knew along what lines he was thinking. She had an unpleasant way of understanding him. Together with Fox von Duisburg, over the years Reuben had cultivated the role as mystical and eccentric. Through her understanding, Denise reduced him to something hopelessly predictable.

Reuben took Dag aside and discussed the weaknesses that he still thought were apparent. The soft, dreamy atmosphere that was in the composition was missing in the concert hall, the melody was forced along; it was as if the musicians were taking the notes a fraction of a second too fast. Perhaps it was primarily the brass players who were causing the problem, the tubas who were standing out?

Dag Chihuahua was not only a musician, he was a composer as well. Not on a level with Walrus, at least not in the eyes of the general public, but Reuben had the deepest respect for the violinist's creative vein. The dog had, however, developed a combination of shyness and perfectionism that meant he very seldom managed to complete his compositions. Reuben had tried to encourage and support him as much as possible over the years, but to no end. Dag Chihuahua was a musical snob of the worst sort, which primarily affected himself.

"Can't you just ask them to shut up for once?" asked Walrus.

Chihuahua nodded. His job was to communicate the director's ideas in such a way that the orchestra did not immediately resign and leave the concert hall. Reuben was a full-blooded egotist and saw his own interests first and last; he had never devoted time to consoling or feeling. He believed this was class-related. It was about how hard you were forced to fight for your successes. It was different with animals like Dag Chihuahua, or for that matter, Fox von Duisburg. Fox had never had to fight to be seen or appreciated. From her early years she carried with her the knowledge that there would always be a place for her in Mollisan Town's upper crust. Due to that fact she could easily decline an invitation, refrain from an acquaintanceship, and quietly observe a course of events that would affect her. He had always despised this calm. When he accused her of snobbery, of elitism, she smiled amiably and asked whether the word he was actually looking for was *self-esteem*.

She was right.

This made him furious.

Dag Chihuahua concluded his conversation with the wind players, turned toward Reuben, and gave the conductor a brief nod. It was taken care of. During Chihuahua's deliberations with the tubas, the rest of the orchestra had carried on quiet conversations and, with paws over keys and valves, practiced difficult passages silently to themselves. Now Reuben resumed command.

"We'll try again," he called. "From the same place, and . . ."

He raised the baton, closed his eyes, and searched in his memory for meter and mood. Then he let loose the philharmonic.

After only a few minutes he heard the improvement. He could not keep from sneaking a glance at Denise. She was looking at him with admiration and veneration. She heard what he heard. She affirmed him. There was a connection between them that was strong.

Yet he was aware of the unexplainable.

Tonight he would lie to Denise to go over to Fox and let himself be taken care of and rebuked. If she had time. He needed Fox more than ever.

Perhaps, he thought, he could use his planned lunch meeting with Tortoise to be rid of Denise as early as this afternoon?

'm going to be completely frank," said Vincent Tortoise. "I don't really know how we should handle this, I've never been involved in anything like it."

The head of the Ministry of Culture was sitting with Reuben Walrus in one of the many restaurants along Grindelhof. They were sitting at a table where they could talk undisturbed. Tortoise knew the young chef at the place and, when he could, frequented the restaurant, which served a type of fusion that in the eyes of the minister seemed modern. Now it was lunch and the restaurant was full; from all directions there were surreptitious stares at the two distinguished guests. Both Tortoise and Walrus had become accustomed to these looks many years ago. Tortoise had also, contrary to his personality and character, developed a frightful taste in clothing. He was wearing a glistening bright red velvet jacket with a loud multicolored tie, and the stuffed animals who by chance did not know who he was looked anyway.

"What did you say?" asked Reuben, who as always was dressed in black and gray.

He was not sure that he had actually heard wrong, but because Margot Swan had told him that his hearing would get worse and worse, it was nearly impossible to distinguish imagination from reality.

"I said that we haven't decided yet, we have no plan," Tortoise repeated in a somewhat louder voice and clearer articulation. "We've been deluged with letters and calls, from ordinary stuffed animals everywhere in the city, and everyone will in some way . . . I don't know . . . share your suffering . . . or at least declare and share their sorrow?"

Reuben Walrus did not know how he should answer. During the week that had passed he had made a follow-up visit, and Margot Swan had explained that now it was determined beyond all doubt that Drexler's syndrome was ravaging the composer's ear passages.

"What do you think, my friend?" wondered Tortoise. "Normally we would not get involved, but opinion is over-whelming. Would you be embarrassed if . . . we did some kind of recognition?"

"I don't know," said Reuben. "In a way you hate being a poor wretch, but at the same time . . ." He laughed. A deep laugh, contagious, coming from his belly.

"It's wisdom that causes you to give in." Vincent Tortoise smiled.

"It's age," answered Reuben.

"It's the same thing."

"What did you say?"

"It's the same thing," repeated Tortoise. "Age and wisdom."

"If it were only that easy," sighed Walrus.

Vincent did not reply. His old friend was in the process of losing his hearing, losing the ability to compose, and if he did not want to maintain a light tone, it was understandable. Vincent had no need to gloss things over either. They had known each other a long time. Their parents had been superficially acquainted, and they had gone to the same schools in Lanceheim long ago. Reuben was a few years older, and he had been one of the enviable ones, not only successful with the opposite sex but a model student besides. When Vincent got to know Reuben better, he saw that this perception did not hold up. Walrus's charisma was actually more convincing than his academic achievements, while with Tortoise it had been the opposite.

"A statue has been proposed," said Vincent.

"What the hell?!" exclaimed Walrus, his mustache bristling. "You must be joking! A statue? Why that?"

"Someone talked about naming a street after you. Perhaps a square, even if the squares are more sought after because there are fewer of them."

"Now you must be—"

"Easy," said Vincent. "I know it seems like a bit much. But we have to do something. The pressure is . . . inconceivable. I mean, you know that I've always been one of your greatest admirers—"

"Bullshit," said Reuben amiably. "You've never understood a note of what I've done."

"Possibly. But I have always understood that it is wise to appear to be one of your greatest admirers."

"It's not your political talents I'm talking about, it's the musical," mumbled Reuben with a wry smile.

"However that may be, you're not exactly a national poet. And yet . . . I mean . . . no one has officially said that you are ill. Yet Mollisan Town appears terrified at the thought of never hearing a new Reuben Walrus composition again."

Reuben did not reply. They had each ordered an endive salad with marinated quail egg, but neither of them had touched it. Perhaps because it reeked of vinegar, perhaps because they had no appetite.

"Personally I thought that perhaps we could get Radio Mollisan Town to devote Sunday afternoons to your works for some time to come? Until the worst has passed."

"That will bring in a little cash anyway," answered Reuben. "Sunday afternoons?"

"It was only an idea. But it would show the stuffed animals in the city that we're doing something."

"Mm," said Reuben. "Worth thinking about."

"Just so you know, you're not the one who makes the decision in this matter," Tortoise clarified sternly.

"Not you either, not without my approval," grunted Walrus. "I'm not dead yet, you know?"

"I know." Tortoise smiled.

But in a way Reuben Walrus felt dead, grieved for, and missed. As long as his concentration was focused on rehearsals and the problems with the unfinished symphony, things were going okay, but when discipline wavered . . . Despite the fact that part of his awareness knew how important it was to keep associations under tight rein, another part of him allowed his thoughts to roam freely. And this caused him pain and anxiety again and again.

"Listen, I have a question," said Reuben when lunch had advanced so far that the check was on the table, something the great composer showed no sign of caring about. "You must have heard about someone called . . . Maximilian?"

The reaction was immediate. Vincent, who had raised his glass to drink the last drops of water, remained sitting with his arm raised and mouth open. He stared distrustfully at his old friend, and in his gaze was a severity that he seldom showed.

"What about him?" he asked.

"No, I was just wondering," said Reuben. "I got the suggestion of looking up this Maximilian, and it appears . . . a little ridiculous?"

"Who gave you this suggestion?" asked Tortoise.

"No, it comes from . . . various sources," said Reuben truthfully.

"I would appreciate it if you could be more precise than that."

"What did you say? More precise?"

Tortoise hesitated. He knew what he had to say, but he was not sure how Reuben would take it.

"Do you remember . . . the Night of the Flood?" he asked.

Reuben thought about it. He had a vague memory of something like that, a Night of the Flood, it must have been fifteen, twenty years ago.

"It was a riot, wasn't it?"

"It was a catastrophe," asserted Tortoise. "And it was completely due to Maximilian. He arouses . . . emotions."

"Now I remember," said Reuben, whose memory worked slowly. "It was somewhere in east Lanceheim, wasn't it?"

"It was over the whole city, but it culminated there. It's a long time ago, but we still try to keep track of stuffed animals who . . . have anything to do with Maximilian. If you have any names . . ."

"Track?" asked Reuben, and he couldn't refrain from adding, "Yes, you're good at 'keeping track.' And it sounds so exciting."

"It's not particularly 'exciting' at all," snapped Tortoise. "There are stuffed animals who make use of this poor Maximilian to challenge . . . the structure of society . . . for their own purposes."

On a different occasion Reuben would have made fun of this "challenge the structure of society," but now he was more interested in the main subject.

"What is 'poor' about Maximilian?"

"They are exploiting him!" exclaimed Tortoise. "He's a harmless lunatic. He's been in King's Cross, and from what I understand from the prison records, then—"

"Do you have access to the prisoners' records at King's Cross?"

"Don't be naive," said Tortoise. "I am head of the ministry. I have access to whatever I want."

"Now then, a quote to use in the next election campaign," Reuben sneered.

"Maximilian could be anyone at all," continued Tortoise, ignoring Walrus. "They spread their stories about him and get poor and sick stuffed animals to hope when no hope remains."

"And you want to stop that?"

"There are underlying objectives."

"Such as?"

"That I cannot go into, Reuben. Not even with you."

"Because you don't know what they are?"

"I know about more than you want to know."

"Hmm."

"What is that supposed to mean?"

"Hmm."

"You're doing that to annoy me," said Tortoise.

"Hmm," repeated Reuben for the third time, just to annoy him, and he knew that he was doing it with success.

Vincent Tortoise seized the check and angrily counted bills from his wallet.

"Keep away from that," he said. "That is my firm advice, Reuben. Keep away from Maximilian and the mob around him. You're going to regret it if you get involved in that game."

"So you say," answered Reuben, adding for the sake of peacekeeping, "And just so you know, I didn't think that thing about Sunday afternoons was a bad idea at all."

Tortoise belched out a kind of coughing groan, and they both got up at the same time.

"It wasn't a promise," said Vincent. "It was just an idea."

"I realize that," said Reuben. "But it was a nice idea."

Under the hot sun they accompanied each other out onto Grindelhof before it was time to separate. They talked about meeting again in the coming week, but nothing was decided.

Reuben continued down toward Pfaffendorfer Tor, and he felt a certain relief. The idea of Maximilian had irritated him because he had not been able to decide, but now he had made his decision. This evening he would make a few calls.

It was time to act.

WOLF DIAZ 4

I have no difficulty imagining that Sven Beaver and Eva Whippoorwill were, to put it mildly, surprised when Seal Pup Chiradello showed up together with Maximilian in Das Vorschutz the evening before confirmation. They were even more astonished when they heard what Chaffinch had offered.

I stayed at home that evening, and the rumor spread with the velocity of the wind between the houses. The church had offered Maximilian a place to live and a place at the high school. What had actually happened at the confirmation camp?

At the same time, I believe, there were many in the forest who nodded in affirmation to themselves and thought that this was right and proper. There was something about the cub that separated him from the rest of us. He was obviously academically gifted, he always had been, but still it was difficult to imagine an academic career for him; it was difficult to imagine any career at all, actually. The church? Yes, it might very well be there that he belonged.

This is speculation, of course, but I think that Maximilian's father immediately accepted the idea of sending his son off to Kerkeling High School. It was different of course with Eva, my once so beloved whippoorwill. Not even when summer was over and Maximilian went off with his father to his new school and a life at the boarding school would Eva accept that Maximilian had left home.

The church's gloomy little apartment building on bark brown Leyergasse was squeezed between a pharmacy and a dance academy. The latter sounded glamorous, but the academy's heyday had been more than forty years earlier, and the dancers were the same then as now.

The entryway was dark and worn. The stairwell ceiling was low. The church had installed a beautiful stained-glass mosaic in the windows the whole way up to the fifth floor, but many pieces were cracked and broken, and no one had repaired them. Maximilian lived on the third floor, and considering it was a student residence and likewise the first apartment of his own, the two rooms were both comfortable and well utilized. It was not in Maximilian's nature, however, to take note of comforts, or to care about how he lived. When I moved in—that is a later story, which I will soon return to—he had been living at Leyergasse for almost three years, and the kitchen table and two chairs, a bed in the bedroom, and a shelf in the living room were still his only pieces of furniture.

In Kerkeling High School it was soon evident that the ease with which Maximilian made his way through elementary school had not been due to home instruction. While others agonized and were forced to devote afternoons, evenings, and weekends to their studies, Maximilian absorbed most of his knowledge during the lectures. On some isolated occasions he seemed to completely misinterpret the essay questions and give answers that were incomprehensible, but as a rule he got all or almost all correct on all tests in all subjects, and without visible exertion at that.

His grades were not unimportant, but it was not due to them that Maximilian was soon perceived as an eccentric. He was really very quiet, and when he did speak, few or none understood the similes he used. In addition to that, he radiated what Chiradello identified as "goodness." He never seemed to be irritated or angry; he seemed to understand and forgive everyone, and it is not strange that this appeared provocative. You do understand what I mean, don't you? Personally I cannot say that I am particularly aggressive, but when, in the midst of a traffic jam whose origin you do not understand and whose extent you only sense, and moreover on your way to something you have looked forward to for a long time and are planning to enjoy a great deal, swearing to yourself and at times with one paw on the horn, you see a strange driver in the car next to you who is smiling and waving amiably, this is provocative behavior.

It was the same thing with Maximilian.

Semester after semester he forgave cheaters and bullies, slackers and lazybones. He refused to judge the sadistic teachers who surprised their classes with unannounced tests or gave apparently unjust grades. After a few weeks in the new school, a puma in the second year designated Maximilian as his particular victim. As soon as the puma could, he started in on the younger pupil with taunts and calls, but also with shoves and sometimes a kick. Again and again he received Maximilian's forgiveness, which naturally annoyed the puma even more, and the bullying continued.

The last month during Maximilian's second year in Kerkeling High School, the puma snatched Maximilian's headcloth for what must have been the hundredth time. But instead of hiding or soiling it as before, he tied it around the history teacher's leg without the teacher noticing anything, whereupon Maximilian was forced to look for said teacher in the teachers' lounge and with a blush of shame on his cheeks ask to get the headcloth back in front of the whole faculty. Then the stuffed animals in Maximilian's class thought that the puma had gone too far. They gathered around Maximilian in the corridor where the class had their lockers, and explained that they were on his side. The puma had been harassing their classmate far too long; now the time for retribution had come. But Maximilian looked at them, smiled, and said, "The higher the height from which a ball falls, the higher it will bounce upward."

As usual no one understood what he meant, and at last someone dared ask.

"At a table in a prosperous home a duck sat and ate," Maximilian explained with customary patience. "It was in the evening, and there was an unexpected knock at the door. The duck was not expecting a visitor, but still he got up and let in the stranger. 'I am hungry and poor,' said the stranger. 'Can you help me?' The duck gave the stranger food and lodging. When he awoke the next morning, he was tied up in his bed. The stranger was standing before him. 'I'm going to take everything I can find in your house,' said the stranger. 'And I'm going to tape your mouth shut before I leave, so that no one can hear you cry for help. Only if fate wills it, will anyone find you here.'

" 'Why are you doing this?' asked the duck. 'I invited you into my home, I gave you something to eat, I offered you a roof over your head.'

" 'Because I can never be you,' said the stranger.

"After that he taped the duck's mouth shut, and left the house forever."

Maximilian fell silent.

His classmates stared at him in confusion. If the first simile was difficult to interpret, the longer parable struck them as completely incomprehensible.

. . . .

It was during Maximilian's second year at Kerkeling High School that I reestablished contact with him; after that I would never leave his side.

The visits to Das Vorschutz had become more and more sporadic on my part the last few years. I was living on banana yellow Hüxterdamm in an apartment building with an unpleasant stairwell that stank of urine and where the lighting never worked because the tenants stole the light-bulbs that the landlord replaced on rare occasions. I still had not concluded my legal studies. Uncertainty about my direction and future kept me at the department. I got by through tutoring first-year students and helping a couple of professors with research while I agonized over my remaining requirements. Life was waiting for me, but I was not ready to make myself known.

One of "my" students was a talented millipede who lived in a neighborhood of townhouses in northeast Lanceheim. We had a standing appointment on Sunday afternoons, but it took five weeks before I caught sight of Ulla Guinea Pig for the first time. I was completely distracted, probably gaping like a fool, and the poor millipede was forced to introduce us.

"This is my little sister, Ulla," he said. "This is my tutor, Wolf Diaz."

I extended my paw, she took it, and between our bodies an electrical charge arose that caused me to vibrate from my belly down to my knees. I saw that she felt the same. I had never experienced this before; this was love of a super-animalistic type. The following night I brooded for the first time about soul travel and reincarnation. If we had never met before, I asked myself, how was such an immediate contact possible?

She was younger than me. Considerably younger. And

in normal cases I would never have taken up with such a young stuffed animal. But I was helplessly in love and had no other choice than to adore her. When a few weeks later in the kitchen at home with Ulla Guinea Pig I heard Ulla talking about a terrifying recluse of a classmate who always wore a headcloth, I realized that she was in Maximilian's class at Kerkeling High School. I remembered that I had babysat for Maximilian, and I realized that I could have been a babysitter for Ulla.

This was a sobering occasion.

The story she told was astounding.

The day before, the class had a lecture with Schoolmaster Slovac. He was one of the oldest teachers at the school, but also one of the best. He taught mathematics and physics, and gave his subjects such a philosophical tinge that the mathematical topics appeared to be secondary matters in a larger context. He stood up at the blackboard and discussed the dilemma of infinity with a piece of chalk in his claw. In the middle of a sentence he fell silent, and sank down to the floor.

It took a few moments before the class reacted. Some kind of stroke, perhaps a heart attack, it was obvious. Half of the pupils ran up to see what was going on with the teacher; the other half rushed toward the door to escape. If Slovac really was about to die, the Chauffeurs could bang on the door to the class at any moment. The fear of encountering these henchmen of death could cause anyone to run for their life.

Maximilian, however, was not in a hurry.

He forced his way slowly through the circle of pupils and squatted down next to Slovac's unconscious body. Ulla had been among those who first approached the fallen teacher, but she explained that somehow everyone understood that they should make room for Maximilian.

"It was as though we knew," she said, looking at me as if I would be able to answer her unspoken question.

Ulla had held Slovac's claw and thus been the only one in the room who knew that it had already happened. There was no pulse; it was too late.

"But I didn't dare say it," she admitted to me and her brother. "I didn't dare say it, I hoped I was wrong."

Maximilian sat next to the lifeless stuffed animal and placed his hand on Slovac's head. Then something happened that Ulla Guinea Pig could not describe. It was, she said, as if the expressions and gestures of her classmates were transformed into rigid looks and grimaces. As if time slowed down, everything stopped, life and reality. She noticed that she was breathing again at the same time she felt that the blood was flowing in Slovac's veins.

She let go of the claw in terror; it fell to the ground.

"He brought him back to life," Ulla said quietly. "You won't believe me, but that was what happened."

"Wolf Diaz!" exclaimed Maximilian.

I had waited for him on the sidewalk outside the school. When he came out, alone and long after the other pupils, I let myself be known.

"I will gladly help out," I said.

"With what?" asked Maximilian amiably, at the same time starting to walk.

"With whatever your purpose is," I replied, at once pretentious and self-occupied, and joined him.

Ever since Ulla Guinea Pig told me how Maximilian had saved his teacher from the Chauffeurs, I hadn't had a peaceful moment. I had suffered all the torment of doubt. I was probably late in my existential puberty—the testosterone had protected me from the tribulations of melancholy; females had occupied all my waking time. I was, as I already mentioned, twenty-six years old when I stood on the sidewalk and addressed Maximilian that day. I ought to have made my peace with the meaninglessness of existence and accepted that a legal career was neither more nor less hopeless than anything else. But I matured late—I am still maturing—and for nights and solitary morning hours that week I came to see that there was meaning to the electrical jolt that Ulla Guinea Pig had given me. It had nothing to do with her; it was about Maximilian.

"I have some notes," said Maximilian without looking at me or slowing his pace, "that perhaps you could make a clean copy of?"

I followed him home that afternoon, and found drifts of paper in his apartment. It would take me more than two months simply to organize the notes before I even started to write them out. During that time, I also understood how alone Maximilian was, and after the incident with School-master Slovac, it only got worse. If his classmates had already kept him at arm's length before, now the faculty was also suspicious. But Maximilian did not seem to suffer from this. He was a singular animal, and when one morning I found the following parable in a thick folder on his book-shelf, I knew that I had found my place in life.

In his childish handwriting he had written the following:

Once upon a time there was a miller who had three daughters. The first one was beautiful, the second was prudent, and the third daughter was sly. The miller tried to treat all three of them the same. Being just was a virtue. But the years passed, and this became more and more difficult. He gladly smiled at the beau-tiful daughter, he gladly conversed with the prudent daughter, but he preferred to keep away from the sly daughter. This tormented him. The miller therefore tried to smile at the sly daughter, converse with the beautiful daughter, and keep away from the prudent daughter. He kept a notebook, and there he made note of how many smiles, conversations, and evasive maneuvers he executed during the day in order to be certain of his irreproachability.

When the prudent daughter fell one day and hurt herself, the miller wept tears of sympathy for her. At once he became afraid that he had treated his other daughters unfairly, and therefore he sought them out as soon as he could and sat down with them and wept corresponding tears. When he laughed at something the beautiful daughter did, he ran off, dismayed, and laughed at the other daughters in the same way.

One day a wise lion came to visit the miller. The lion observed in silence how the miller exercised his fairness, and in the evening he asked the miller to sit down for a talk.

"You are a just father, aren't you?" asked the lion.

"I do my best," answered the miller, who was more than a little proud about how just he actually was.

"But when you laugh with the daughters who haven't done anything funny, how do you think they feel?"

"They feel content that they haven't been wronged," replied the miller.

"And you yourself?" asked the lion craftily.

"I feel content at being fair," replied the miller.

"Fool!" said the lion, getting up and pointing at the miller with one of his powerful claws. "What you call fairness is dishonesty. What you think are feelings, are calculation and envy. You are afraid that you cannot love your sly daughter the way you love the other two. But I will tell you one thing, Miller: Love is just as strong as bamboo, and just as pliant. If you learn to lavish it, it will find ways to reach all of your daughters. You have squandered your time up until now."

. . . .

Every afternoon I went home to Maximilian at Leyergasse
and helped with household tasks: he did not seem to care
about either dishwashing or laundry. We conversed, on his
special terms, of course, and I wrote down the things he
said as well as things deciphered from his own fastidious
notes.

The thought of leaving my legal studies had been on
my mind for several semesters. At the time of these events,
Maximilian was fifteen years old going on sixteen, and I
was ten years older. If I had had a genuine interest, I would
already have finished my law degree, and the reason for my
continued uphill struggle—with deferred exams, requirements postponed, and more and more pressure—was that
I did not dare tell Mother and Father about my decision. I
had my own small apartment on Hüxterdamm; I was living
on student loans and the money I earned as a tutor. The
law program felt less and less urgent as my fascination with
Maximilian grew.

At last I gathered my courage and drove out to Das
Vorschutz and Mother and Father. My life was about to
take a different direction, and I felt content. That ought to
be enough for them too. But there I deceived myself; it was
a terrible evening that did not flatter any of us, and I would
rather let it remain sealed up in my memory.

I do not have a confessional nature, but this I admit:
without Maximilian, my own life would hardly be worth
anything. I became his biographer, his permanent secretary
and clerk, long before Adam Chaffinch appointed me as the
Recorder. I found meaning in an existence that otherwise
would have remained a mystery to me.

The church in Mollisan Town talked about love. Each
and every one of the three preachers wrote, in different
ways, about the all-encompassing love of Magnus for us

stuffed animals, and how we were unworthy but nonetheless compelled, according to our pitiable capability, to repay it. Like all other messages that the church had interpreted from the Proclamations, there was an underlying threat in this talk about love. No promises were given to the one who could love, but clear threats were whispered to the one who loved wrongly. There were elements of obligation and compulsion in Magnus's love for his creation, and thereby our love for Magnus should have a similar makeup.

Maximilian's message was a different one. Personally, I believe that it was one of the contributing factors to the fact that, over time, he came to have such a large following. The faith he preached was free from threats. All-deacon Chiradello saw "goodness" in him, but that should not be mixed up with "niceness." Maximilian's morality was absolute and his ideas a clear guide.

The story of the miller and his daughters had a clear moral for me. It was about being able to lavish love so that it extended to everyone. And this was exactly my nature; something I had been ashamed of until then. Growing up in an environment where you stayed together, where love between a he and a she was something absolute and irrevocable, I had always felt deviant. When passion struck me—and that happened several times a month—I was so ashamed that I didn't dare talk about it with anyone. In every beautiful, mysterious, and fascinating female I met, I seemed to see an opportunity. But until then my happy, aching, and double-beating heart had been my dark secret. I too lavished my love—my love for females, anyway—and through his story, Maximilian freed me from guilt.

From that moment my place was with Maximilian, and nowhere else.

Maria Mink pressed herself closer against the brick wall.

Her long coat dragged on the sidewalk, and just moments ago the first drops of the Afternoon Rain had fallen on her coat sleeves. The thick tweed fabric immediately soaked up the liquid, and Maria regretted that she hadn't put on a raincoat. At the same time she assumed that they never would have let her stand here in a coat that shone bright red or festive blue. There were no written instructions, no rules that she had heard mentioned; and yet she knew. Those who were getting in line on the cramped, dark turquoise Herzoger Strasse right before the Afternoon Rain were all wearing dark, anonymous clothing. And the tweed-patterned gray coat she had inherited from her mother was the gloomiest piece of clothing Maria Mink owned. In addition it smelled of mothballs, and every time she put it on she started to sweat.

Of the four streets that surrounded the church in Kerkeling, Herzoger Strasse to the east was decidedly the narrowest and least traveled. In that direction the facade of the church was windowless, and apart from a small door used by the church caretaker to take out garbage, the dark stone wall rose lifeless and without openings straight up to the sky. The building opposite housed the long-defunct Halz-bank Verlag book printers, and even if the well-formed windows were large and lovely, no one was ever seen at the large machines and conveyor belts.

Down on Herzoger Strasse, squeezed between its hefty office buildings, the alley was so narrow that a car could not drive through it. There was no room for either lampposts or hanging streetlamps, which meant that when the sky darkened, as it did now, a merciful dimness fell over the stuffed animals assiduously lining up along the street. This was not the first time for Maria Mink. She had made an attempt the week before, and a few times last month. But if you arrived too late, the line was much too long. And if you arrived too early, you were shooed away by one of the church caretakers.

Today she was in luck. There were only two animals ahead of her.

"What's a beautiful mink like you doing in a place like this?"

The ox in front of Maria turned around and addressed her. She gave an involuntary start. She did not talk to strange males; she was scared to death of this sort of confrontation. For that reason she lowered her gaze toward the street and acted as if nothing had happened.

"Yeah, yeah," said the ox, obviously annoyed. "I don't look that freaking dangerous, do I?"

"No, no," the worried Maria hurried to reassure him, "not at all. It was just that I—"

"You uptight females are the freaking biggest downers I know," the ox spat out, as if he belonged to a different decade.

To this Maria had no reply, and she looked down at the street again.

"What are you standing here for?" asked the ox in a somewhat friendlier tone, and added with a nod at the grasshopper at the head of the line, "You hardly need to ask him."

The grasshopper was standing upright with the help of a pair of crutches, and pretended not to hear. His right leg was bent at an incomprehensible angle and stood straight out from his green body. Maria could not even guess what had happened.

"I . . . ," she began carefully, "have a little pain . . ."

"A little pain?" repeated the ox.

"Pain," she nodded. "I have pain. Lots of pain."

"Where does it hurt?"

"Here and there," she said, but corrected herself when she saw his stern look. "I have pain in my shoulders. Most often in my shoulders."

"I can massage you a little, sweetie pie," the ox suggested, licking his mouth with a long, dark red tongue. "Pending a miracle, may I massage you a little? At my place?"

"No, thanks," Maria replied politely and turned away from the ox.

She was scared to death.

"Are you turning your back on me, you stuck-up little—"

"No, no," said Maria, turning back again. "It wasn't my intention to—"

"Oh, what the hell," sighed the ox, turning so that Maria Mink was staring at his broad back.

They were called in at the same time: the grasshopper with the broken leg, the unpleasant ox, and Maria Mink, all rescued from the rain when the modest door at the back side of the church was opened from within.

I can imagine how they experienced it, because I was the one who opened the door. I had opened it every day for several months at that time, always equally uneasy that someone might see me. With a pounding heart and alarming buzzing in my ears, I whispered, "Come in, come in," to the one who stood first in line.

On this day it was a grasshopper.

There was always the risk that one of the all-deacons in Kerkeling's church would pass by, even if I had never seen them walking on gloomy Herzoger Strasse. Perhaps I sensed the danger because deep inside I wanted to be revealed? The subconscious can play those kinds of tricks on us; if we knew our own soul as well as we know our desires, we would all be happier stuffed animals. I had a continual bad conscience over the fact that we were doing this to Adam Chaffinch. He was our friend and protector.

"Come in, come in," I whispered.

I took in three animals on this day; we had only half an hour at our disposal during the afternoon sabbath.

"Wait here," I told the visitors, and ran off into the church to see if Maximilian was ready.

Maria Mink looked around. I had asked them to wait in a storage room, small as a cubbyhole and dark as a cellar.

"What the hell is this?" roared the ox, but he no longer sounded as impudent.

Maria made no reply, nor did the grasshopper. There was a faint odor of cumin in the room, and Maria noticed that the ox smelled of alcohol. She had never had any dealings with drunken stuffed animals. She stared straight at the light that seeped in through the cracks in the doorway. She did not like darkness. Her shoulders ached even more, but she did not make her torment audible; the ox would only make fun of her. Then the cramped room became completely dark, and in the following second the door opened.

"Grasshopper," I said, "we'll start with you."

The grasshopper made his way out bravely on his crutches, and while he was hopping away into the church I quickly explained to the ox and mink, "You have to keep quiet. Stay here and remain quiet. I will get you when it is time. If anyone hears you, that will be the end of it. They would . . . I do not even want to think about what they would do."

"Aw, what kind of melodramatic crap is that?" the ox protested without using the low, almost whispering tone I myself had used, and which was usually contagious. "No one's going to do a damn thing."

I admit that his attitude made me feel embarrassed. I could not recall anyone questioning my rules up to that time.

"I have a buddy," continued the ox, "who has done this. He didn't say a thing about you, Wolf. You're not the one we came to see."

"I am merely a humble—"

"Where's the magic animal?" asked the ox.

"There is no magic animal here," I replied.

"Aw, but lay off," said the ox.

He was a normal-sized animal, but his broad shoulders gave his form a certain physical advantage and inspired respect.

Maria Mink had squeezed herself as far into the cubbyhole as she could get. She was whimpering in a way that made me realize how scared she was, or else it was the rheumatism that attacked her with its cutting pain.

"No wizardry goes on here," I said in a valiant attempt to cheer myself up and regain control. "And if you remain calm, you will see it with your own eyes. This is a matter of believing."

"I don't believe shit," announced the ox. "And least of all you."

"It's not what you think that you believe," I explained. "This is for real."

A sound was heard from within the church, a kind of thump, and it made me nervous. Outside the Afternoon Rain was pouring down. The church was empty, all activity in abeyance. I was in constant fear that someone would come upon us. We were borrowing the church without permission, and during the sacred sabbath besides.

"Wait here for your turn," I said once again, and carefully closed the door on them.

Then I ran off to see what had happened, and to help the grasshopper up on the podium where the altar was.

The ox opened the door the same moment I had left.

"We can't stay here," he mumbled, as much to himself as to Maria Mink. "There's no damn danger. Come on, let's go check it out."

But the ox did not dare step out of the waiting room alone. Instead he reached for the poor mink, and with a forceful tug he shoved her across the threshold.

"Good," he said sarcastically as he continued to push the resistant mink ahead of him, "now we'll see what this is about."

In this manner the ox and mink made their way into the church. In the darkness the already terrifying sculptures and decorations were even more threatening; the stillness that prevailed was unnerving, not peaceful. From where the stuffed animals were standing they could, if they bent forward, see up toward the altar. I had, as usual, lit the fifteen tall candles that I carried with me in a bag every morning and evening, and which I placed in a half circle around the altar ring. The glow of the wax candles was the only light; outside the windows, as I already mentioned, the dark rain clouds prevailed in the sky.

Maximilian and the lame grasshopper were standing in front of the altar, outside the altar ring, quietly conversing.

In comparison with the stately shadows along the church's massive vault, the animals there looked ridiculously small. In the ominous silence that prevailed, Maximilian's voice was clearly audible. The mink and the ox sat down quietly at the far end of the nearest row of pews.

Up at the altar the grasshopper was executing a kind of strange bow. The broken leg made this difficult. He crouched as well as he could, making his right leg look even more grotesque where it stuck out.

Maximilian placed a hand on the grasshopper's head, and asked him to tell what was the matter. It was difficult for the ox and Maria to catch what the grasshopper replied. Like many stuffed animals before him during the past months, the grasshopper was filled with a nervous humility caused by the church's splendor and gravity, the long wait that had at last allowed him to stand before Maximilian, and finally the friendly address; the grasshopper did not venture more than a quiet and partly snuffling mumble.

The ox soon tired of trying to listen to the conversation. At first the glow from the candles at the altar did not seem to suffice, but as his eyes adjusted, it allowed more light than the ox had thought, and he looked around. He had never set his hoof in the church before and was astonished by its size and splendor. This was not apparent on the outside. The parish had not always been poor. The entire inside ceiling— thousands of square meters—was decorated with a massive painting. The image had been taken from the Proclamation of Fox: It depicted the occasion when Magnus returned up to heaven from the forests. Several hundred angels hid themselves in the painstakingly painted crowns of trees, and they all seemed to look down at the ox where he sat. In the three large church windows on the short side behind the altar, the mosaic was subdued and beautiful. Here too, in colorful patterns, images from the Proclamations were incorporated, but they were harder to identify; the ox had not read the sacred texts since confirmation. To the left was the church organ with its hundreds of pipes, an instrument so monumental that the ox did not even realize what he was looking at when he turned his gaze toward it.

"Stand up!" exclaimed Maximilian.

The ox winced. He had been mesmerized by the church building itself, and for a few moments forgot the two at the altar. When he now directed his gaze there, he saw something that caused him to blanch. Before his eyes, in the mild light from the wax candles, the grasshopper's broken leg slowly resumed a normal appearance.

The ox gaped.

The grasshopper up at the altar was also staring at the miracle that had occurred. He seemed just as surprised as the ox. He got up, gingerly put his weight on the suddenly healthy leg, and found that it held. He set aside his crutches and bowed again before his savior; this time he did it with no trouble.

This was more than Ox could handle. Pale as a ghost and without a word, he got up from the pew, turned, and ran out of the church. He did not know what he had expected, but not this. He ran because what he had witnessed scared him, in the same way that we had frightened many others during the past months. Ox would tell about the demon that reigned in the church in Kerkeling for several years to come, and in my naïveté I did not understand that such stories had already spread all over Lanceheim.

One morning, months before, Maximilian had woken up, sat up in bed, and exclaimed, "All this suffering. All this pain."

That was how it started.

Everywhere, Maximilian encountered stuffed animals who were weighed down by the deepest anxiety and who time and again had been struck by the unpredictability of life: the handicapped and the accident-prone, the mortally ill and the abandoned. By talking with them, touching them, and understanding them, he could ease their afflictions, fix them, and heal them. For me this was no surprise; I already knew what he was capable of.

The reason that we ended up in the church during the sabbath was practical. We needed a place to be, somewhere where the sick could find us, and we did not want to attract attention. In the beginning Maximilian received visitors at night at home on Leyergasse, but the neighbors soon complained about all the running on the stairway and slamming doors, and therefore we were forced to find someplace else.

We found an unlocked trash room a few blocks away, approximately halfway between Maximilian's apartment and Kerkeling High School, and continued our activity there. Throughout the night Maximilian received stuffed animals, while I tried to help to the best of my ability. I maintained order in the line and took care of the practical aspects. Sometimes the police came past; here too there were complaining neighbors, and the animals who stood and waited did not always know how to behave. We thought we could make the police listen to reason, but after a few weeks they brought us in for interrogation and gave us a proper warning.

At the same time Maximilian failed an examination for the first time. He fell behind in school. The work at night had taken its toll; Maximilian hardly found time to rest, and one day Adam Chaffinch came by and asked what we were up to.

Maximilian explained it in his own way, but I am not sure that Adam really understood. I realized that if Maximilian did not live up to academic expectations, they would throw him out of the school.

Therefore I was the one behind the idea of moving our activities to the church in Kerkeling. This solved several problems at the same time, and Maximilian had nothing against working during the sabbath.

"They are so many," he confided in me, "and I can help them."

At the same time I forced him to prioritize the lectures in school and not be truant. Therefore our sessions in the church became capricious in a way that I imagined was only good. Regularity would make it easier to uncover us.

When both the ox and the grasshopper had left, I went and fetched Maria Mink. I did not scold her for leaving the dark waiting room, nor did I say anything about the fear I saw in her eyes. I had seen it before.

Maximilian was waiting up at the altar. He was wearing a thin white tunic, and around his head and ears he had wrapped the veil he used when he worked: white with embroidered red briars. Something otherworldly rested over his form; Maria Mink reacted just like all the others.

She was faced with something she had never experienced before.

With a gesture I showed her the way up to the altar. She met my gaze doubtfully; would she dare? But just as courage was deserting her—it was, after all, just a matter of walking up there—her right shoulder twinged in pain, and she stepped up onto the podium. Without a sound I went to one of the rows of pews and sat down on the hard wooden seat. The church pew sloped forward a little, which made it even more uncomfortable.

Together with the hundreds of angels on the ceiling painting, I observed the terrified mink on her way up to the altar. Her life would be different in a few minutes. Her pains would disappear forever. I had seen it happen many times; I could see it as many times as I'd like.

"Come now, don't be afraid," said Maximilian amiably.

Maria got down on her knees, just as she had seen the grasshopper do before her. I had never needed to instruct anyone; it happened by itself. Maximilian placed his hand on Maria Mink's head.

"Tell me," he asked with his light voice.

She told about her pains. She stared shyly down at the floor, but told everything. How the pain came one day, and never left her after that. She told about visits to doctors and diagnoses, about the advice of good friends and how her mother had similar experiences when she was young. Maximilian listened patiently, and after a few minutes, when Maria paused for breath, he said, "And love?"

The mink fell silent and looked up in terror.

"What did you say?"

"A long time ago," said Maximilian, "so long ago that you have almost forgotten it, you loved. Do you remember how it felt?"

"But . . . ," Maria Mink stammered, "I . . . this is about my pain? I'm in pain. I came to—"

"I know why you came," replied Maximilian. "Tell about love. Have you experienced it?"

Maria stared at him. She was even more afraid now. She knew exactly what Maximilian was getting at. It was a secret that she had carried for many years without revealing it to a single stuffed animal. How could he know?

"One time," she forced out, "one time I have known love. I don't want to think about it."

"But that is exactly what you are doing," asserted Maximilian. "You are thinking about it, because it frightens you. More than anything else, it frightens you."

Maria Mink protested. "I want to talk about my aches!"

Maximilian nodded, closing his eyes but keeping his hand on the mink's head. Maria babbled on about rheumatism a while, and when she lost the thread, Maximilian asked again, "What do you remember about love?"

She shook her head.

Maria's confusion intensified, and I smiled to myself. This drama was always equally fascinating to see. Soon she would tell him what he wanted to hear; she had sought his help, and he intended to give it to her.

The Ministry of Culture's extravagant headquarters of glass, bamboo, and granite had been erected during the next to the last of the boom periods at the end of the previous century. The building was situated at Schwartauer Allee in east Lanceheim, four blocks north of Eastern Avenue. It was a modern temple, overwhelming in its ambition to impress. On the doors in the lobby was a picture of the medieval war when King Carl united the four parts of the city and created modern-day Mollisan Town. The animals of the ministry left it up to the visitors to interpret the symbolism.

The Ministry of Culture was closer to the Garbage Dump than to the Star, Vincent Tortoise had joked when, as a young clerk, he had taken a position at the agency.

No one had laughed. Then as now an atmosphere of seriousness prevailed at the Ministry of Culture. It was the same at the Ministry of Finance and the Environmental Ministry. It was as if these workplaces demanded affirmation by an excess of seriousness. Unending care was devoted to things that were demonstrably unimportant, or at least decidedly less important. Nothing was allowed to stand

out as more or less significant at the ministry. This was a
principle of solidarity: here everyone and everything were
equally important.

Was this simply stupidity? Over the years Vincent Tortoise had asked himself that question many times. Was it
all the same? All the resources and energy that were applied
to cultural manifestations, to the media, to education, was
it unnecessary? Would those animals who were inclined
toward the humanities—the seekers and thinkers—produce
the same things for the most part even without the solici-
tude of the ministry? And the others, the uneducable and
the uninterested: Could they be disregarded?

Vincent Tortoise was doubtful. Doubt he had never been
able to get rid of. He counted this doubt as his greatest asset.

The morning that I have chosen to introduce my careful
reader to Vincent Tortoise, the newly appointed head of the
ministry parked his car in the garage without granting the
injustices within the agency a thought. The tortoise drove
a mint green Volga Mini. Each promotion had slowly but
surely brought him closer to the most desirable parking
place in the garage, the one right next to the elevators. As
democratic as the agency wanted to appear aboveground,
the structure was mercilessly hierarchical under the surface.

He was brooding, and encountered his mirror image in
the elevator on the way up without recognizing it. In recent
years he had aged more rapidly than could be attributed to
time alone. On the surface he looked as he had when he was
delivered from the factory, a green and wrinkled tortoise
with a small, grudging nose and a velvet shell that was as
soft as whipped cream. But in his eyes was a fatigue that was
not there before, and any day now it would overpower him.

Outside the elevators on the fifth floor in the ministry
building was a reception counter, and alongside it a narrow

couch where visitors could sit and wait. There were not many, however, who came to visit the fifth floor; it was mainly employees at the ministry who moved about up there.

This morning Armand Owl was sitting on the couch, waiting for Tortoise. Vincent nodded as he went past, but continued without stopping. He assumed that Owl would follow.

Tortoise had been assigned a cubicle, which, in the spirit of democracy, was just the same size and equipped in the same way as those for all the other official animals at the ministry, but he was seldom there. Instead he had more or less annexed the adjacent conference room. There was a door between the rooms, and it was always open. Eighteen stuffed animals could sit at the conference table, and to start with it had felt a trifle large to use as a desk.

In time, however, Tortoise got used to it.

Constance worked in the cubicle next to his own. She was not his secretary; she was his assistant.

"Good morning," she said when Vincent tried to sneak past. "You already have a visitor."

Tortoise stopped unwillingly. With a glance over his shell, he verified that Armand Owl really had followed him.

"I assume that it is too late to ask him to wait in the reception area?"

"I think so," Constance confirmed with a smile. "Good morning, Armand."

"Constance." Armand Owl nodded.

She thought the owl was stylish. Always dressed in well-tailored clothes of the latest cut, he accentuated his beautiful figure and his white-flecked head, from which a sharp little black plastic beak looked out. There was something gruff about him, but at the same time exciting. Constance lowered her gaze to her desk.

Vincent felt irritated. His mood this morning was miserable, because he had trouble with the garbage pickup, and on top of it all he would now be forced to put up with Armand Owl. They passed the tortoise's cramped office, hung their coats up on the hangers in the conference room, and sat in leather-clad rocking chairs at the beautiful conference table.

"There's something special, I presume?" said Tortoise.

"Yes, the hell if I'd have my morning java with you voluntarily," replied Owl.

Vincent sighed audibly. The hard-boiled jargon that Owl used agreed neither with his appearance nor his background. One time long ago Vincent Tortoise had hired Armand Owl, who until then was the best researcher Vincent had come upon. After a few years in the archives, Armand showed an interest in work in the field, and Vincent accommodated him. A few weeks on the streets was enough, and then he took on the role of the experienced, superior agent. But he played it in an inferior manner, Vincent felt.

The head of the ministry stole a glance at his in-box and the piles of paper that waited, and nodded.

"Let's hear it," he said.

"I think we have a problem," said Armand. "I don't know for sure, but I think that we may have a hell of a problem. Not now, but in a couple of years. But that's just what I believe."

"In a couple of years?" repeated Tortoise.

"If we don't do anything about it," Armand confirmed.

"You come here unannounced before breakfast because we may have a problem in a couple of years?" Tortoise asked. "But how would it be if we took care of the problem when it arose, in a couple of years?"

"Did I mention that imaginary animal in east Lanceheim?" Armand replied, without taking notice of Tortoise's sarcasm. "I think that it could potentially be a hell of a problem. There is something about that . . . I heard talk about it even a few months ago. They say that he is a demon, that he has been sent by the lord of the underworld, Malitte, that he is gathering souls, that he takes them in payment for healing the sick and deformed."

"Souls?"

"That's what they say. The stuffed animals in east Lanceheim are superstitious fools. But last Monday they were arrested by the police—Maximilian and his companion, a wolf. I got hold of the record of the hearing. It made me uneasy."

Armand took a plastic folder out of his briefcase and gave it to Tortoise. While the head of the ministry read, Armand offered his own analysis.

"You see what the problem is?" asked the owl, and continued as Tortoise read on. "He's not a swindler. He is possibly crazy; in principle I don't get a bit of what he says, those ridiculous parables about rocking horses are damned pathetic. But that's not the point. The point is that if he were a cheat, he would have made himself comprehensible. He would have answers to the questions. Now he appears . . . as if he is actually not guilty."

"Hmm," said Vincent Tortoise, setting aside the police protocol.

Excuse me if I interject a brief reflection that I nonetheless consider to be in its place right here and now. I have been on this subject previously, and take the opportunity to remind the interested reader that I am simply a dutiful clerk.

Did Armand Owl already understand at this meeting what this was about? The question is open, and—I believe—relevant.

What Maximilian was occupied with, was to reveal the fears of stuffed animals and thereby free them from the clutches of terror. This was of course not all that he was doing—there were dimensions of his healing that I will never understand—but expelling terror was one of the main issues. He himself revealed this to me. And if you were to compare Maximilian's faith with the church's, and his undertakings with the gospel of the Proclamations, it was the same way. What Maximilian offered us stuffed animals was a faith without fears. I may happily expand on this point later on in the text, but to get right to the point: From the perspective of the government, this was extremely dangerous.

Did Armand Owl understand this even then?

Did Vincent Tortoise understand it?

"Are they operating in the church? During the sabbath?" asked Tortoise that morning, as Armand Owl continued to tell what Maximilian and I were up to.

"But, what the hell, aren't you listening to what I'm saying?" said Armand.

"Sure, sure . . . ," Tortoise replied absentmindedly. "I wonder if I shouldn't make a call to Eagle Rothman anyway. . . ."

Do you, dear reader, recall where we were? Maximilian was standing up at the altar, and on her knees before him was Maria Mink. His hand was still on her head, and they had just stopped talking. Maria took a deep breath. The air in the church was still. The subsiding Afternoon Rain fell against the roof and was heard as a distant murmur. I experienced a light dizziness, as I sometimes do when I haven't had enough to eat for lunch. Once again Maximilian had coaxed the truth out of a stuffed animal, once again he had—by understanding and expelling her innermost terror—transformed pain into a memory. I was the only living being who had seen it happen, and at the same time I had company. Mute, the angels on the ceiling witnessed what was going on. Farmers, fishermen, and city dwellers who appeared out of the glass mosaic in the high church windows behind Maximilian's back had been there the whole time.

"Maria Mink," said Maximilian in his gentle voice, "you have—"

Then it happened.

The doors of the church were opened.

A bang was heard, and I winced, turned around, and felt my heart stop and my pulse rush at one and the same time. Up at the altar Maria Mink reacted the same way. She had been sitting on her haunches, but the surprise caused her to wobble and fall sideways.

Maximilian on the other hand turned calmly toward the gray daylight that suddenly ran along the middle aisle like an uninvited guest. The odor of rain and dampness filled the building. The noise from the stuffed animals that suddenly made their entry was earsplitting in contrast to the dense silence that the church had contained seconds before.

First came Eagle Rothman, the prodeacon in Lanceheim. I had never seen him before and therefore did not recognize him. His high-handed posture and the rapid, long steps he took up to the altar demanded respect. There was no doubt of the fact that this was power approaching on foot.

After Rothman, a small flock of stuffed animals came running. I recognized several of the all-deacons in Kerkeling, and there of course was Adam Chaffinch too. Following after them were mammals that I had never seen before, dressed in more official-looking clothing. All of them tried to keep pace with the prodeacon, which meant that a few were forced to jog. Adam kept to the side of the lot, but like all the others he was staring intently up toward Maximilian. There was no surprise in the deacon's gaze, but there was deep disappointment.

Shame besieged my heart and overpowered the terror. I still didn't have a close relationship with Adam Chaffinch, but Maximilian and Adam met regularly, and it was thanks to Chaffinch that all of this had been possible. He was without a doubt Maximilian's patron.

"So it's true!" shouted Eagle Rothman.

He raised his massive wing dramatically and pointed with the tip toward Maximilian up at the altar.

"Heretic!" Prodeacon Rothman spit out; the word was tensed like a bow in the eagle's throat and shot away like an arrow.

No one paid any attention to me, despite the fact that they all saw me. Maximilian was their prey; he was the one who was the danger. The procession stopped a few meters in front of the foremost row of pews, on the threshold to the podium where the altar stood.

"What was it I said?" asked Rothman triumphantly.

The words were aimed at Adam Chaffinch. It was Chaffinch who would bear the responsibility for this: It was in his parish, in his church, that witches' arts were being carried out during the sabbath. The all-deacons and animal officials lined up at the prodeacon's side and formed a kind of semicircle, a wall through which Maximilian would not be able to flee. Adam Chaffinch stepped up on the podium a few meters from Maximilian.

Poor Maria Mink did not know where she should go. She stood on all fours, staring terror-stricken at the stuffed animals, all of whom looked past her. Carefully, she began to creep across the podium, and when she realized that no one was paying any attention to her, she increased her pace. She disappeared out of sight, and it would be many years before I saw her again.

"We know what's going on," Rothman cried out in his powerful preaching voice. "You play the part of a healer, but you are a charlatan! Do you dare deny it?"

The whole time he had the tip of his wing aimed at Maximilian's chest.

"Animals are in pain," Maximilian replied simply. "I help them."

I observed Adam Chaffinch, and his facial expression caused the hair on my neck to rise. Chaffinch was a strong, unyielding leader, uninfluenced by his surroundings, it seemed to me. But all of his being signaled danger when Rothman was speaking, and it would take a lot to make Chaffinch nervous.

"You don't deny it?" Rothman asked again.

Maximilian did not reply, but his gaze was steady.

"You confess?" said Rothman.

I saw how Adam Chaffinch indicated a negative twisting of his neck; it was probably unconscious, but it was a signal that Maximilian should have paid attention to. He did not. He met the eagle's gaze, unafraid, perhaps even surprised.

"This is a confession!" Rothman called out contemptuously, and one of the suit-clad stuffed animals took notes.

"Perhaps I can explain . . . ," I began, but no one heard me.

Both Chaffinch and Maximilian have forgiven me many times since then, but I still carry something of the stigma of a traitor after that afternoon; my attempts to stand behind my master were lame.

"During the sabbath," continued Rothman, "this animal has violated the peace of the church, and—"

"I don't believe that Magnus is offended," said Maximilian calmly.

Rothman lost his train of thought. This was the first time in many years that anyone had interrupted him. He tried to hold back his anger, but with little success. Without actually thinking about it, the all-deacons who had been standing next to Rothman up until then took a few steps to the side, as if they feared that the prodeacon might explode at any moment.

"You believe?" said Prodeacon Rothman at last. "You believe?"

Maximilian nodded. The calm, or more correctly stated, the assuredness that he radiated influenced all of us, and Rothman lost his composure.

"Your pitiful belief," hissed the prodeacon contemptuously, "is like a seed that has not come out of the ground."

"Excuse me, but I . . . ," said Adam Chaffinch unexpectedly, and everyone turned toward him, "I am certain that Maximilian's intention never could have been to . . . I have never met anyone whose goodness is so genuine, someone whose faith is . . ."

Adam lost the thread. Rothman's fiery gaze was now directed at him, and I could see that the stern, straight-backed Adam Chaffinch who stood beside Maximilian was only a splinter of the deacon I had come to know. Rothman was not only Chaffinch's superior, I found out later; he had also been Chaffinch's adviser through his entire theological education. What Rothman didn't know about Chaffinch's weaknesses wasn't worth knowing.

"Shall you talk about faith?" exclaimed Rothman contemptuously; he almost spit out the words. "*You?*"

I do not know what was worse, his tone of voice or Adam's facial expression.

"So your own faith is strong?" asked Maximilian.

Rothman twirled around and stared with a blazing look up toward the strange animal at the altar.

"My faith, young stuffed animal, can set a stone on fire."

"And Adam's faith . . . wobbles?" asked Maximilian.

"I do as well as I can," mumbled Chaffinch from his direction.

"Let me say this: Only when the bark boat sails do the cubs laugh happily," said Maximilian and turned toward Adam Chaffinch.

No one, not even Rothman, dared to disturb the mute concentration that had formed between them. In a gentle voice Maximilian asked Adam, "The almighty Magnus, do you see him in me?"

The words were no more than a whisper, and Adam was staring at him.

"Do you see Magnus in my soul?" he repeated.

"I . . . I believe so," said Adam.

"And you?" said Maximilian, turning toward Prodeacon Rothman. "Do you also see Magnus in me?"

"Magnus dwells in all of us. I see him even in you, my son," replied Rothman with all the superior condescension of which he was capable.

"Adam," continued Maximilian, turning back again, "do you see the image there, of Malitte? Do you see Magnus in Malitte?"

On the last pillar next to the altar the lord of evil Malitte was depicted. It was typical for the church that the pious stuffed animals' worst nightmare observed them sideways during the entire service. Malitte was painted right on the stone pillar, with his narrow black body full of knots and tassels, the long tail coiled around a stone, and one of his fangs bared in a malicious smile.

Adam did not reply. He was pale, and he shook his head slightly.

"And you?" asked Maximilian, turning again toward Prodeacon Rothman. "Can you see anything of Magnus in Malitte?"

"Obviously," said Rothman. "Malitte is a part of Magnus, just as we all are a part of him."

Then something happened that even today I hardly dare think about. The whole thing lasted no more than a few seconds, yet I know that we all saw it. The painted image of Malitte came to life. The bestial stuffed animal curled his upper lip and showed more of his razor-sharp teeth, and in the distance laughter was heard.

Prodeacon Rothman winced. His beak was open, but he could not get out a word.

"Without doubt, faith is worth nothing," said Maximilian.

The silence around the prodeacon was dense. He stared at Maximilian, and then looked again at the painting of Malitte. Suddenly what had happened was unbelievable.

"Get out!" hissed Rothman.

The silence remained undisturbed.

"Get out!" screamed the prodeacon, turning to the official animals and the all-deacons. "Throw out the sorcerer, throw out the heretic! Never again may this animal set his paw in any of the churches in Mollisan Town!"

It continued as if time stood still; no one moved.

"Now!" screamed Rothman. "Now! Now!"

And finally they came to life, all of Rothman's entourage. But Maximilian had already started walking toward the exit, and it was then that the first drops fell. Reality, as we knew it, was already out of commission; we had not managed to recover from the previous shock. At the same moment as the church door shut behind Maximilian, the rain began to quietly fall over us.

We felt it all together, and we reacted similarly. We twisted our necks and looked upward.

It was the angels in the ceiling who were weeping.

REUBEN WALRUS 5

He listened from outside the control room, trying to concentrate on the cello, because the cello was the key to the piece. To start with it was concealed behind the violins, then changing into an open struggle with the viola for attention. Its dominance in the last half of the work was thus heralded from the very first measure, and here the interpreters of Walrus's String Quartet in E Minor often made a mistake. More often than not they emphasized the struggle between the introductory viola and the concluding cello.

The idea with this series of recordings had been to let Reuben himself interpret and produce some of his most classic works. Not, perhaps, to correct so much as to comment on the sort of thing he, startled and paralyzed, had seen happen to his intentions over the years.

He knew the musicians well; he had chosen them from among many applicants, and the feeling of being chosen elevated their abilities this morning. Reuben listened and tried to be constructive. But just as during the rehearsals with the philharmonic string section yesterday afternoon, he realized that the illness was reducing his capability.

"It sounds fantastic, Daddy," said Josephine.

"Do you think so?" said Reuben without feeling, concentrating on the cello.

Like that, he thought. Not too carefully. He mustn't be too careful, not even in the beginning.

"Fantastic," repeated Josephine.

"Honey, be quiet now, please?" asked Walrus.

Walrus had not been able to sleep that morning. He had woken up long before dawn, felt the anxiety sitting like a damp blanket between his body and the sheets, and been forced to get up. He splashed water on his face and then sat in the drying cabinet a while. The sound of the fan drowned out the buzzing in his ears, which meant that he could fantasize that everything was as usual. But self-deception could not be maintained for any length of time. He got out, dressed, and left the house. The sun was on its way up over the horizon, and slowly he walked through a Lanceheim that was still resting in the approaching morning. The families that occupied the heavy, well-renovated buildings in his neighborhood would soon awaken; the apartments would be filled with stress and shouting, bathrooms occupied by teenagers and kitchen tables stained by the younger ones. Fathers and mothers would dress for the day's work and at the same time fill schoolbags with books and schoolchildren with admonitions.

He himself had been a lousy father. He regretted this, without doing anything about it. Josephine's birthday had been a few months ago, and he had not even made it by with a present. That was unusually lousy. And as always, when he thought about his daughter, he was seized by feelings of guilt that cut into his heart. The helpless cub who twenty-one years ago was delivered to pepper red Mooshütter Weg had not chosen her family. On the contrary, it was Reuben who had applied for a cub, only to initiate a long series of betrayals and shortcomings.

But it's not too late, thought Reuben Walrus, hurrying home through the deserted streets to call and wake his daughter and ask if she would like to go along to the recording studio that same morning. As soon as she, drowsy but happy, asked on the phone if she could bring her tuba and play for him, he regretted it. Her audition to get into the Music Academy was on Monday, and she needed all the advice she could get. He said yes, of course, and now they were here.

She was a sweet lamb with woolly ears and a pink cloth nose, but to be completely honest, he did not know her.

"She wants your acknowledgment," Fox had explained to the languid Walrus. "She wants to be seen and loved by you, and she thinks that the best way is by playing."

"But have I ever—"

"It is rather logical, isn't it?"

"Well, yes, but I—"

"You were perhaps going to say that you don't see anyone other than yourself, and that it's yourself you love the most?" asked Fox sarcastically. "Oldster, that is something I and all your friends have understood and accepted. But for Josephine's sake, you must exert yourself a little more."

He did that. It did not work.

"Your string quartets are what I like the very best," said Josephine from her corner in the studio control room, and Reuben sighed again.

The cello, he reminded himself. The touch of the bow. Quiet, not hesitant. The tone bides its time, it doesn't hesitate, it waits.

But Reuben Walrus was not feeling well, and to reveal this type of subtlety demanded acuity of which he was not capable. The recording studio was a claustrophobic place, cramped with a low ceiling and no windows. All the technology, the mixing board and cables and speakers and computers, smelled of plastic and oil. As usual the oxygen was about to run out after a few hours of work, and in the control room the thoughtful Sripen Dragon, the recording technician, turned down the lights. Still the headache crept in. Anxiety did not leave his body. Reuben was sweating, and restlessness made the slow middle section of the piece unendurably boring. Judging by how it sounded, the composer of this piece must have felt immortal when he wrote it, with oceans of time to swim around in. How naive could an artist be? Reuben asked himself, sitting heavily in the chair beside Sripen Dragon. He had worked with Sripen off and on for over thirty years, and he was ashamed. Never had he shown her this decrepit side before; never before had he felt so dejected. He leaned back in the rocking chair. Josephine sat on the leather couch that was on the short wall.

"Daddy, can we take a little break soon?" she asked. "I've been practicing what you asked me to, and I'd like to show you."

He did not remember what he had asked her to practice, and he realized that the risk of repeating himself was thereby imminent.

"Honey, can't we . . . ," he began, but reconsidered.

Why not exploit the opportunity for a break? He whispered to Sripen to take fifteen minutes, and then disappeared out into the corridor with Josephine. There were several empty studios on the same level, and they went into the nearest one.

While Josephine took out her instrument and got ready, Reuben thought about his unfinished symphony and the final stanzas that remained, just as unapproachable as they had ever been. On one level it was easy to emotionally imagine what ought to follow the introduction, but he could not possibly transform that feeling into notes and arrangements. He sat at home at his grand piano and plunked—that was the word, plunked—all through the night. But . . . nothing.

"Now, Daddy," said Josephine.

When she started playing, he strived to connect with her. He listened carefully to her youthful eagerness, her unfeeling clomping in the corridors of musicality, her practiced phrasing, and he tried for the life of him to think of something to say. He could not be too hard, but he wanted to be fair, he had to remain loving but still professional. And exactly like everything else that had to do with fatherhood, the moment became a task, and he himself was transformed from a stuffed animal of cloth and blood to a cliché.

Josephine stopped playing, lowered the instrument, and looked at him with ingenuous eyes. It was a look he defended himself against, because it hurt to encounter it. There was only hope and love, no dissimulation and no reservation.

"Yes, dear," he began, "that was not bad at all."

"You didn't think it was bad?" she repeated.

"What do you mean?"

"Did you like it? I've been practicing especially on the change to minor. Was it better now? I was thinking that I could play it on Monday. What do you think?"

"It's going to go fine," he said. "It's clear that it will go fine. And the change to minor . . . just take that as carefully as you possibly can."

"I'll do that, Daddy," she said, and she was radiant. "So you think I can manage it?"

What could he answer? He was her father; there was only one answer to give.

"I'm sure it will all work out."

"Oh, Daddy," she said, spontaneously giving him a big hug.

He felt lousy.

Back in the studio with the string quartet, Reuben Walrus was drained of energy. Josephine had left, but she left behind the love he could never accept, and he needed energy to repress this miserable performance. The frustration over the unfinished symphony was festering as he listened, yet another time, to the cello.

Then he realized that the moment had passed, that the string quartet inside the studio on the other side of the glass window was in the midst of one of the final passages. He rose, surprised, from the chair, saw that Sripen gave a start and the violist on the other side stopped playing.

"Was there . . . something wrong?" asked Sripen.

The three other musicians had also set down their instruments, and looked at him uneasily.

"I . . . was thinking about something . . . ," he stammered, "there . . . was nothing wrong. Not wrong at all."

He continued to shake his head; he had a hard time collecting his thoughts, and realized with astonishment that all the expectations being directed at him at this moment did not concern him in the least.

"I . . . have to leave to go to a . . . ," he said. "I have a meeting that . . . but I suggest that you play through the piece from beginning to end one more time, and if Sripen could record . . . then I'll listen to it this evening."

He held out his fins, realizing how he had disappointed them. Without waiting to reconsider, he was already on his way to the door.

"Sripen . . . I'll call," he mumbled over his shoulder.

He was out in the corridor before the dragon had time to answer, and he walked as quickly as he could without running.

There is always a female, thought Philip Mouse laconically. Life functions approximately as it was once intended, after a long day comes a long night, the bad animals are more numerous than the good, and whiskey tastes better without ice. Then comes the female—in Mouse's case a luscious puma who knew how to moisten her whiskers and put force behind her uppercut—and everything turns to chaos.

Philip pushed his hat up on his head and stroked his chin thoughtfully. It was still tender after the puma's stern reprimand the night before.

Why couldn't he stop thinking about her? Wasn't she simply yet another in a long series of females?

He got the ace of spades, but didn't know where he should place it.

Through the door's frosted glass pane Philip Mouse could see the contour of Daisy's backside as she bent over looking for something in the cabinet next to the desk. Her behind was as big as a beach ball, today draped in a tight red skirt. It would burst if she bent over a few more centimeters.

Philip Mouse sighed involuntarily.

He was sitting in the office beyond Daisy's. He had his shoes on the table and was leaning back in the worn black swivel armchair. The wooden shades in the windows out toward the street were half pulled down, and the room was in a striking semi-darkness. On the ceiling above the desk an old fan revolved slowly, acquired in an antique store not far from North Avenue. Over the back of his chair Philip had hung his wrinkled jacket, and over the jacket hung his empty holster. The pistol was in the middle of the mess on the desk, a .22-caliber automatic weapon he had bought from a rabbit at the Garbage Dump. It was impossible to trace.

The conspicuous disorder of the office was false evidence of work. During the morning, Philip had tried to play a new game of solitaire, but still after a few hours he did not understand how it was supposed to work out. As usual he wondered fleetingly how Daisy could keep herself occupied. He had not paid her in over six months, and therefore he assumed that she had found a side job to devote herself to. He did not intend to ask. It was beneath his dignity. Philip Mouse was one of Mollisan Town's few private detectives, and he intended to act like one. There was a code of honor.

Daisy found what she was looking for and sat down again behind her desk. She sat so that Philip could not see her through the glass in the door. In the inside pocket of the jacket he found a lumpy pack of cigarettes. He took one out, tore off the filter, and lit it with an old gasoline lighter he had inherited from his father.

Jack of clubs. He put it in the pile to the left.

She would probably call this evening, the puma. They usually called. Reflexively he grazed his chin again. A hot temperament, he thought, smiling to himself. It boded well.

. . . .

When there was a knock on the door to private detective
Philip Mouse's office, the weather was just before lunchtime. Daisy had already taken hers out. She set it on the
desk, opened the lid, and with a fork in her hoof started
eating directly from the box. Same food every day, saffron-
scented couscous with broccoli and ham.

Philip had ten cards left in his hand, and had just decided
that this was the last round; then he too would have lunch.
He usually had a cup of black coffee and smoked a few cigarettes in the shadow of Zeke's sidewalk café while he read
the sports page. The Yok Giants were Philip's team; most
likely they would have another miserable season.

There was a second knock. With the fork in her hand,
Daisy went and opened the door. Philip hardly looked up
from the piles of cards. Nine times out of ten the knocking
meant that the landlord wanted to let them know about
a power outage or elevator repairs. Sometimes he spoke
threateningly about the rent.

"We don't want any," Daisy's determined voice was heard.

"I . . . I'm looking for Philip Mouse," replied a dark voice
from out in the corridor.

Philip's office was the only one on the third floor; the
remaining doors led to ordinary apartments.

"Is it about the car?" asked Daisy. "I called last week to
say that there must have been a mistake at the bank. The
money went from here the—"

By the fact that Daisy fell silent Philip understood that it
was not someone who was sent to repossess the car.

"I . . . I have a little problem that I would like help with,"
said the dark voice.

A few moments of silence followed, until Daisy realized
that this actually was a client standing out in the hall.

"Absolutely," she said with a spark of recognition. "Problems exist to be solved."

And with a generous gesture she invited in Reuben Walrus.

Walrus nodded, preoccupied, and stepped into the office. He looked around. The room was empty. There was an odor of saffron. Without performing the scene that Mouse preferred that Daisy would play—she should ask the client to sit down a few minutes on the hard Windsor chair at the side of the door—she went right into his office.

"Here you go," she said to Reuben with a hint of sarcasm. "Philip Mouse, private detective."

Philip adjusted his hat and got up. Across the threshold came a walrus that he knew he recognized, but whom he could not immediately place. Due to the mustaches, walruses looked old even when they were young, and it was easy to be mistaken.

"It's a female," said Philip Mouse.

With a gesture he invited the walrus to take a seat in the chair in front of the desk, at the same time as he himself sat down again.

"It's always a female," he added.

Reuben concealed his smile, but sat obediently.

"No, not today," he replied, so as not to embarrass the mouse.

"If she isn't the question, she's the answer," said Philip.

"Mm?"

"Tell me why you've come to see me, Mr. Walrus," said Philip Mouse, taking a chance that Walrus was his surname and not his first name.

"Yes, well," replied Reuben uncertainly, thinking that this was going too fast; it lacked any sort of introduction. "Well, I don't know . . . do you know about Maximilian?"

Philip thought. This rang no bells. On the other hand, he remembered who the walrus was. Even if Philip Mouse did not listen to classical music, it was interesting that someone like Walrus sought out a private detective. Famous stuffed animals were usually afraid of such things. But when they did . . . they had very good reasons.

"Maximilian? Is this a composer colleague?"

"Ahem, no. Maximilian is . . . yes, to tell the truth, I don't really know what he is. That is, what kind of animal he is . . . yes, perhaps I should say that I don't even know if he exists. At all. Perhaps this sounds strange, but—"

"Only the normal appears strange," said Philip Mouse, letting his hat sink toward his eyebrows. "And why are you looking for . . . Maximilian?"

"Yes . . . ," said Reuben hesitantly, "I don't know if that really affects the matter. Or . . . I am certain that it has no significance—"

"Before we get to the more specific details," interrupted Philip Mouse, "perhaps we should talk about the essentials? You've sought me out because you want me to find Maximilian?"

"Yes, that's right," said Reuben.

"Good. I get five thousand a week, plus expenses. And as expenses I count all costs I consider necessary to solve . . . to find the animal in question."

"Per week?"

"Five thousand a week," answered Philip Mouse, who had a policy of never negotiating on the price. "Obviously I deduct for weeks with official holidays, and it can happen that in stubborn investigations, where the only talent required is patience, I'm prepared to discuss various types of discounts, but taken as a whole then—"

"No," interrupted Reuben, "it's not the price. I . . . I don't have weeks. Either I get hold of Maximilian now, or else it doesn't matter."

"Now?"

"Now."

Philip nodded in corroboration and poked a cigarette out of the crumpled pack. He lit it and blew the smoke at the ceiling.

"And how soon is 'now'?" he asked.

Reuben shrugged his shoulders. "A few days."

Philip Mouse considered this. He seldom had anything against assignments that dragged out in time. During longer periods of inactivity, which could affect even the best, he unwillingly even took on cases of adultery. This was a matter of pursuing married men and wives to uncover their extramarital relationships. The advantage of this type of work was that deep down the employer did not want to unmask his beloved other. Therefore weeks were added to weeks, sometimes months, before sufficiently incontrovertible evidence could be presented, all while the meter was running.

An assignment of a few days was something quite different.

"I'll pay . . . ," said Reuben, considering what he thought was reasonable, "five thousand for three days. If you think you can find him."

"There are no leads?"

"I can give you the names of stuffed animals who have told me about him," said Reuben. "As long as you don't say that it was me who gave you their names."

"And more than that?"

Reuben thought. "Nothing else."

"That's good," said Mouse. "It's a challenge, like life itself. I'll take the assignment."

He got up and held out his paw across the table. Reuben also got up, astonished at the conversation's unexpected development, and tried to reach Mouse with his short fin. He didn't succeed completely, and they both smiled apologetically at the mishap.

"It's a deal then," said Reuben.

"Three days. You can give the names to my secretary,

then I'll get started this afternoon. And, Mr. Walrus, I always work against an advance. In this case I think that half the total amount is reasonable. Daisy will take care of that detail too."

"Unfortunately I don't have that much cash on me," said the surprised Reuben Walrus.

"We take credit cards."

"I don't have a credit card on me either."

"How much do you have on you?"

Reuben took out his wallet from his inside pocket and looked. He had six hundreds and two fifties.

"Good," said Mouse. "The advance is set at seven hundred. You'll get a receipt from Daisy."

And with that Reuben left Philip Mouse's office.

The gentle breeze had just picked up when Reuben Walrus came out onto baby blue Knaackstrasse again. He began slowly walking toward mint green Eastern Avenue, and could ascertain that the buzz in his ear was a reality. The sun beat down from the blue sky, and the streets were again empty after the lunch hour. He saw a pedestrian or two, but in these anonymous blocks in south Lanceheim there were seldom animals on the street.

After lunch with Tortoise yesterday and the subsequent afternoon rehearsals, Reuben had devoted the evening to looking for Maximilian. He had called a usually well-informed journalist that he knew, and he had called the deacon in his own parish in Lanceheim. Neither of them had anything to relate, and both dismissed the Maximilian phenomenon as superstition.

During the night the buzz in his ears had returned. Reuben seemed to notice signs of worsening all the time, but in the darkness it was difficult to be strong. When the buzzing returned this morning, he called Margot Swan, who confirmed that the course of Drexler's syndrome might very well include buzzing.

It was then that he decided to hire a private detective.

He came down on Eastern Avenue and walked under the great oaks in the avenue that separated the western and eastern traffic.

It was pathetic, he thought.

Hiring a private detective who was obviously not reliable. Asking him to hunt out a ghost character who probably did not exist, with the intention of then convincing this ghost to perform a miracle that defied all medical expertise.

I don't even believe in Magnus, thought Reuben Walrus.

At least I didn't.

A taxi came by going in the right direction, and Reuben took a few steps out into the street and waved the car to the curb.

Fox would laugh some sense into me, he thought gloomily as he sat in the backseat and gave the address. I should tell her, hear how it sounded out loud, and then she would laugh and bring me back to reality.

When the car drove away, Reuben's gaze settled unintentionally on a character standing under one of the oaks in the middle of the avenue. He did not see him long enough to recognize him, but long enough to know that this particular animal, with his stiff posture and purple beak, had just been in the Radio Building.

Was he being followed?

But in the following moment the thought went away, as so many thoughts do.

WOLF DIAZ 5

Let me tell you about Adam Chaffinch.

Adam Chaffinch grew up in Kerkeling Parish in east Lanceheim. From an early age his individuality was apparent, and this was not simply part of his desire to be different. In school he hardly distinguished himself—he was blandly average, one of those no one remembered later. Nor was there a clear-cut role for him at home. Adam was the second to youngest cub in a group of four siblings. His father was absent for the most part, and when he did join them for meals he was absorbed in himself and seldom said a word. While he was growing up, Adam knew neither what kind of work his father did nor where he spent his time, and when he no longer showed up for dinner one day, they realized that the Chauffeurs had taken him. Adam was then fourteen years old.

Adam Chaffinch's mother was an industrious gnu who worked for a cleaning service that specialized in the offices in the skyscrapers of Tourquai. She left early each morning, before anyone else in the family had awakened, and returned home with food for dinner, which she prepared as soon as she came inside the door. After doing the dishes—she refused to let the cubs do dishes because the china was her only inheritance—she remained dutifully awake and listened to the cubs, who drowned each other out telling her what they had done or not done during the day, but Adam seldom got a word out before his mother raised her hand, silenced her group of cubs, and went to bed.

Adam Chaffinch therefore created his identity outside the home. From an early age he had the power of attraction; he was an animal that other animals wanted to be with. This did not mean that he was inventive or charming; he had neither money nor looks. Yet his classmates were drawn to him. With his intuitive, serious manner, he made them feel chosen and important.

Adam Chaffinch never showed off. On the contrary, part of his attractiveness was his unflinching integrity. If anything, he might seem blunt. When he expressed an opinion, he always did it definitely, even aggressively. He did not suck up to anyone. He was most often dressed in a wrinkled brown jacket and a white shirt that would never stay in place inside his belt. His short beak was seldom polished, he held his gray-speckled head bowed forward, and his intense way of speaking was in such sharp contrast to his physical image that it was almost comical. And whether he was sitting in discussion groups talking modern philosophy or jogging on the outdoor track, he remained himself.

The reason for his many, sometimes opposing, interests was not that he longed for participation; Adam Chaffinch was and remained a seeker in the literal sense of the word.

It was only in the third year of high school that Adam let himself be lured by the church's youth group. This transformed his life. By this stage he had acquired a broad experience of societies; he had sat in many worn-out armchairs, drinking coffee and eating soft ginger snaps and listening to jargon that was always similar and with the same intent: to create a "we" that could be placed in relationship to a "them."

The church's youth group was different.

There had been a caring atmosphere that Adam had never experienced before. Even the conversation was different. Instead of focusing on obscure details, as in other discussion groups, the youth of the church were willing to see the larger perspective. This appealed to Adam Chaffinch more than he could explain, because he was neither saved nor a believer. His former lack of faith increased the attention given to him. The others were eager to convince him, and perhaps he too wanted to be convinced. Before Christmas, Adam had already decided to apply to the theology department at the university after high school.

The department was in one of the medieval buildings on emerald green Via Westphal, and in connection with the roll call for the new theologians, the prodeacon of that part of the city held an introductory lecture in accordance with tradition. Then as now it was Eagle Rothman who ruled over Lanceheim's parishes and churches, and Rothman took immediate notice of Adam Chaffinch. When it was time to assign mentors, all-deacons or deacons who would guide and support the students during the five years of theology studies, Rothman made sure to assign himself to Chaffinch. The fact that one of the four prodeacons in Mollisan Town made himself available was unusual, if not unique. Adam and Rothman met once a month in Rothman's office in the church in Obersdorf Parish in central Lanceheim, not far from the Star.

Despite previous doubtful achievements as a student, Chaffinch easily navigated past the rocks of exams and the shoals of orals during the years that followed. Theology fascinated him, and that was all the help he needed.

From the beginning it was just as clear that faith remained Adam Chaffinch's stumbling block. This reluctance was not so much about Magnus and the creation story—the department proved to be open to interpretations and adopted a tolerant attitude within given frameworks—as about the reasoning around Malitte and the occurrence of evil in Mollisan Town. In his striving for justice and balance, Magnus had created Malitte, the lord of evil. At the same time the modern church judged every stuffed animal that was enticed by the servants of evil, judged them harshly and mercilessly, forgetful of the balance that even Magnus accepted. The conversations between Adam Chaffinch and Rothman most often revolved around this: that the Proclamations, and the church that spread the interpretations, would sooner emphasize a bad example than a good one.

Adam Chaffinch was initiated three days before his twenty-third birthday. One month later he was appointed a deacon in Kerkeling Parish. This was a sensation. The usual arrangement was that the initiated theological students took jobs as all-deacons in one of the city's twenty-three parishes. It might then be anywhere from five to fifteen years before a deacon position became open; these were the rules of the game, and no one protested. Adam Chaffinch was not only the youngest deacon in Mollisan Town when he took over Kerkeling Parish, but one of the youngest deacons in history.

It went so fast that Adam himself had difficulty understanding it. The first time he opened the door to his own church was an experience he never forgot—seeing clouds of dust floating through the air of the massive space inside in streams of light that fell in through the high windows, and on the other side, so far away, the gilded magnificence of the altar. All this was his to administer, to use. It felt absurd.

During the first service that Adam Chaffinch held in Kerkeling, however, not many recognized the searching, doubting theologian from his student days. There was only one way for a young stuffed animal to atone for the responsibility, the attention, and the good fortune that had fallen, apparently undeserved, to Chaffinch: through anxiety and guilt. In an insane attempt to put doubt behind him, the young deacon made himself hard and unmerciful. It was a doomsday voice that was heard in the church, a cold and unforgiving deacon who was not prepared to forgive sinners who did not feel guilt themselves; who was not prepared to turn a blind eye.

The entire first year continued in the same manner. The congregation came dutifully and listened on Sundays, terrified yet uplifted. There was still a force of attraction in this furious deacon who was appointed to tend their souls. Only when he went on the attack one Sunday against Rothman, who was perceived as the most liberal of the four prodeacons at that time, did Chaffinch go too far. He received a reprimand, and it was almost as if he had expected it. After that he became more careful, but the reputation of the "angry deacon in Kerkeling" continued to grow.

When Adam Chaffinch met Maximilian in Sagrada Bastante, there was an energy about the cub that Chaffinch had never run across before. The similes that Maximilian used fascinated the deacon. It was easier for Adam than for most to interpret them—or rather, no one else devoted so much time to them.

Adam offered Maximilian—as you already know—a place at Kerkeling High School, and when Adam realized that I was part of the package, as it were, he appointed me as Recorder. This made a virtue of necessity, or perhaps better, granted a title to something I had nonetheless already decided to do. In addition, becoming the Recorder gave me more than an alibi: I was paid for my efforts. Don't ask me how he had the means; a deacon's salary is not a kebab from which to slice juicy pieces of meat.

Then came the day when Rothman challenged Maximilian and Chaffinch in the church. After that, everything changed. The prodeacon knew that Maximilian was enrolled in the church's high school, and demanded that he be expelled immediately. There was nothing Chaffinch could do to prevent this, and Maximilian was forced to quit a few weeks before final examinations in the second tier. I had moved, but Maximilian was still living in the church's building on bark brown Leyergasse—I suspect that Adam arranged the matter simply by not raising the issue—and fortunately we were able to get Maximilian to understand that he would have to at least temporarily abstain from his sessions with the sick and handicapped stuffed animals. He suffered. He could help all the tragic stuffed animals he saw on the streets and squares, but he was forced to refrain.

Adam's frustration grew as well. With Maximilian in the school, the deacon had him close at hand, and now there was no longer a natural meeting place. Therefore Adam started something that would now come to have great significance for all of our lives: the Seminars on Faith, Hope, and Love. I realize that I do not need to say it, but I will say it nonetheless: This was my idea completely, even if I have heard differently over the years.

Two times a week, usually Tuesdays and Thursdays, we invited five or six stuffed animals to the apartment at Leyergasse. We were meticulous about who was allowed to come, and new participants were allowed only if they were recommended by two existing attendees. After half a year the interest in the seminars was so great that we could set up a little waiting list, and then it was easier to more systematically see to it that a mixture of new and old guests created an exciting dynamic.

It went like this. About half an hour after the Afternoon Rain, we gathered in the living room on Leyergasse. In most cases Maximilian himself was present, but we managed even when he decided not to take part. I do not know if it has been clear before, but to an outsider, Maximilian could appear to be very capricious. I, who saw him practically speaking twenty-four hours a day, knew that these "whims" occurred regularly and that the "caprices" were habits. But I readily admit that his respect for normal forms of social interaction was slight.

Adam Chaffinch led the meetings, with a starting point in one of the similes or parables that Maximilian had given us. We sat in the living room. I read out loud from the Book of Similes, and then the discussion started. It depended of course on the mix of stuffed animals, but it was seldom that everyone felt they had had their say when we dispersed at the time of the Evening Weather.

For my part, it was only in retrospect that I took a position on the viewpoints that were knocked around in the room; during the seminar itself, all my concentration was on keeping the minutes, a record that I appended on an ongoing basis to the steadily increasing Book of Similes. Only when reading and reflecting on my notes could I fully see Adam Chaffinch's significance and greatness. Without taking up too much room, without inhibiting the associations or lowering the level of thought, he guided the conversation in the direction he wanted. It sounds manipulative as I am writing this, and perhaps it was, but it was also necessary. Without Adam, the seminars would never have felt equally important or exhaustive. Direction was required with the openness that Maximilian created with his similes in order to bring home the point; this was Adam's role.

. . . .

On the private front, I made several attempts during this period to repair my relationship with my parents. After I had abandoned my legal studies, I seemed to detect disappointment, not to say sorrow, in their eyes when they looked at me. I only went out to Das Vorschutz occasionally, and therefore I was very happy when Father unexpectedly got in touch and asked me to come out and have dinner over the weekend. I could not recall when something like that had last happened.

Expectant and light of heart, I knocked on the door the following Saturday, but as soon as I stepped across the threshold I sensed unease.

"Where is Mother?" I asked.

Father did not answer, but instead led me into the kitchen. There the table was set for two, and judging by the folding of the napkins, it was Mother who had arranged this for us. Now I am sure that she was on the upper floor, but just then I did not think to ask.

"Isn't Mother going to be here?" I said.

"We have something to talk about, my son," said Father in his gloomiest and darkest voice, the one he only used on special occasions.

I sat down at the table. Although I feverishly attempted to think of what I had done that might be the cause of this seriousness, my lost career as an attorney was the only thing I could think of.

"Mother has heard talk about your . . . love life," said Father.

It was as though the air in the room ran out in a single breath. I was completely unprepared.

"We have not brought you up to be a . . . a . . . Mother has heard that you have various . . . friends?"

"Various friends?"

Of course I knew what he was saying.

"Mother has heard that . . . well . . . that you've lived with three different females the last few months. That can't be right? No one in our family has ever moved in together before they were engaged. You know that. This is not how we brought you up," said Father, who found it difficult to accuse me of something he thought was absurd.

"I'm not living with anyone right now," I replied honorably. "But Father, I would like to tell you what Maximilian has to say about love. And about living together."

"Answer the question," Father said quietly.

"Maximilian told me the story about the miller—"

"Answer me!"

But I couldn't. My father was very conservative about some things, and marriage was one of them. In his mind, adultery was a crime equivalent to poaching, and Father was a forest guard. Living with a female that you hadn't married, you were being unfaithful to Magnus and to the church. To live with three different females that you hadn't married was, well, worse.

"Father, let me tell the story. The miller—"

"Enough!" exclaimed Father.

He had still not sat down at the table, and I sensed that he would prefer not to sit down this evening.

"Have we not brought you up to respect Magnus?" asked Father, and his voice was so loud that it would certainly reach up to the second floor. "Don't we deserve some decent behavior from our only child?"

"Maximilian says that—"

"Enough! The Maximilian you worship is Eva's son, and Eva never has . . . been thinking straight. Don't come here and throw that cub's words in my face! Why don't you get yourself a wife?"

"Father," I pleaded, "will you let me tell you the story of the miller? Once upon a time there was a miller who had three daughters. The first was—"

"Are you defying me?" asked Father, and his face was dark, ominous.

"No, Father," I answered quietly. "But I—"

"Do you enjoy hurting your mother?"

"No, Father, I . . ."

Yes, every reader with even slight experience of life understands how the rest of that conversation continued. I will spare you, and only declare that I left there without having told the story of the miller, without having conveyed the idea of the goodness inherent in lavishing love upon the females in my life, and without having improved my relationship with my parents to any noticeable degree.

It was after one of our Seminars on Faith, Hope, and Love that I finally dared asked the question. Adam Chaffinch had lingered behind to look over our financial situation together with me. It was something we did on a monthly basis, nothing remarkable and seldom surprising. Maximilian and I lived a withdrawn, planned existence. We were sitting in the living room on Leyergasse, the young deacon and I, exhausted after hours of conversation, but also fired up by the discussion that had just concluded. We lit no candles; outside the windows the sky was colored red by the sun returning home. Maximilian sometimes suffered from migraines, and that was the case on this particular afternoon. He was lying down in his room, sleeping. A year and a half had passed since the angels had wept from the ceiling in Kerkeling's church.

"Do you ever think about that?" I asked. "About that day, with Rothman in the church?"

"Ever?" asked Adam. "I think about it every day."

"You do?"

I was astonished. To me, Adam Chaffinch was an immovable rock. I did not know about his youthful doubt and hesitation. He did not know that his stern seriousness concealed his doubt.

"It was then," Adam continued in the same tone of voice, "that I finally gained my faith."

"Then?" I exclaimed, perhaps a trifle insensitively.

"It was then," he nodded, seemingly to himself. "Up until that day, that hour, I had hesitated. But then I knew. It was so simple, just as simple as those tears that fell upon us. My doubt was my faith, not the opposite of it."

This paradoxical assertion reminded me of something that Maximilian himself might have said, and I decided not to go into the matter further; this seldom served any purpose. Instead I took the opportunity—as Adam Chaffinch was obviously in a confiding mood—to ask the question that I had harbored for several years, but never dared to utter.

"But is he the Messiah?" I said. "Maximilian? Is he the Savior that is talked about in the Proclamations? Is he? Because I . . . I believe that he is. . . ."

Adam Chaffinch looked at me for a long time before he answered. There was something searching, but also something appreciative in his gaze.

"That is what only you can decide," he replied.

"He does not want you to be here right now," said Duck Johnson.

I was standing out in the stairwell, aimless, looking down at the worn brown leather shoes that I had once bought because of their amusing spike pattern.

"He asked me to ask you to come back the day after tomorrow," said Duck.

I shook my head. I should have protested, argued, perhaps even yelled something. But I did nothing. How I despised my weak muteness at the moment.

"But," I finally forced out, "but . . . Maximilian and I have always—"

"Besides," Duck pointed out, "it will be too cramped. We were just talking about it. The apartment is simply not built for more than two animals."

And with that he shut the door in my nose. Self-contempt kept me from exposing myself to further ridicule, and I left, crushed. Possibly I could have viewed this as a test; that Duck Johnson was something the inscrutable Magnus had put in my way to tear me out of the secure—and happy— existence I had finally created.

But dismissed from Maximilian's apartment on bark brown Leyergasse, I was not capable of that kind of contemplative distance; Duck Johnson was my rival, and inside I was furious.

I myself had moved to banana yellow Hüxterdamm. At the time of Duck Johnson's appearance in Maximilian's life, the break in my studies at the university had lasted more than six years, and I no longer had any ambition to return. At first I had been enticed by the fundamental idea of the law: to attempt to distinguish good from evil in matters great and small. But with every semester that passed, I realized that this was not about good and evil at all; it was about argumentation techniques and power, patience, and hard work. If I had not had any alternative, I would surely have been interested in such things too, but weighed against the sort of seriousness represented by Maximilian, the decision was simple.

I was not living alone.

During the years that the Seminars on Faith, Hope, and Love were going on, Adam Chaffinch insisted that Maximilian's schooling should nonetheless be finished. Therefore it was my task to see to it that teachers of academic rank came to the apartment on Leyergasse to help with his studies. One of these teachers, who taught theoretical philosophy and geography, was named Maria C. Terrier, and she seduced me the first time she came to visit. On the way from Maximilian's room and out into the hall—this was a matter of a stretch of less than four meters, bordered by coats to the right and doors to the cleaning closet and bathroom to the left—she succeeded in turning my head and causing my body to quiver with arousal and terror. Her heavy, sweet perfume, mixed with the stench from the bathroom's cracked pipe and the old coats in the hallway, is an olfactory memory that even today causes me to shiver with enjoyment mixed with fear.

Maria C. Terrier moved in with me on Hüxterdamm later that same week. This was the start of a stormy three-year-long marriage. Maria C. was hotter than a gas stove. I do not wish to assert my qualities as a lover and male—practice gives proficiency even to the meek, and I had practiced quite a bit—but this did not go far.

At home Maria C. insisted on walking around in her underwear, extravagant little garments of red, black, and white she purchased in an elegant boutique two flights up on light blue Up Street in Amberville: garters and corsets, push-up brassieres and thongs. She liked to sit on the kitchen table as I had breakfast, leaning back theatrically and asking if there was anything else I was hungry for.

Why did we separate? Maria C. Terrier was notoriously unfaithful to me. I sensed it for a long time, but finally confirmed it. I do not intend to go into any sordid details. Let me simply say that her profound abilities in theoretical philosophy did not help that day. I was not the one who threw her out, I was not the one who petitioned for divorce; she carefully packed her bags and left me on her own accord for one of the many lovers who, befogged by the special sweetness of love, happily took her in.

This was a defeat, and I grieved for Maria C. for several weeks. Without Haddock Krausse and her warmth and empathy, it would have taken time to get over the terrier, but that is another story; perhaps I can come back to it. What I was about to tell was about the day when Duck Johnson showed up.

That week, a month or two after Maria C. had moved out, the Seminars on Faith, Hope, and Love were devoted to the incident of the colors.

Maximilian and I had been out walking when we found ourselves due north of Krönkenhagen, in the middle of Lanceheim's commercial center. On a gray asphalt wall, the backside of one of the many stores—a black ventilation grate was the only decoration on the facade—someone had painted graffiti. A kind of pattern, it might perhaps be called, broad round rings of yellow, green, and orange that together created a feeling of motion, confusion. To be honest, I would not even have noticed it if Maximilian had not stopped, apparently fascinated, and asked me to copy the graffiti in the notebook. I did as he asked, and on the same page wrote down his commentary: "Without lines to stay inside," he murmured, "color is nothing other than variations of mood."

The incident became a part of that day's notations. I did as I usually did, and read the incident aloud to Adam the following morning. It was a few weeks, however, before the deacon returned to the matter, and at the first seminar where the incident was discussed—another week or two later—Duck Johnson was present. He must have come recommended by two previous seminar participants, but which two I was never able to find out.

Duck distinguished himself from the first moment. He came dressed in an old-fashioned black suit, white shirt and dark spotted tie, shiny shoes, and a small hat. No one else was dressed like that. When he sat down on the couch by the window, an odor of mothballs and aftershave spread around him. He made a stiff, somewhat antiquated impression, and smiled courteously at everyone who happened to look at him.

Furtively I noted, however, that the suit was a few sizes too small, the shirt collar was almost laundered to bits, in the middle of the tie someone had failed to remove a grease spot, and when Duck put one leg over the other, I saw that there were holes in the soles of both shoes.

The seminar followed its usual pattern. After the first hour we took a break for coffee, and then Duck Johnson caught sight of me. I was standing in the kitchen, setting out a modest buffet.

"You really have a pleasant voice," he said.

Surprised and blushing slightly, I raised my eyebrows at the same time as I poured coffee for the guests.

"There aren't many," Duck continued, "who can read with such feeling, and at the same time preserve completely clear diction."

He was clever, that I will grant him. Reading aloud from the Book of Similes was a standing feature of the seminars. I had practiced, I had exerted myself, and I was secretly proud of my reading. For that reason Duck's flattery worked.

"Did you think it was interesting?" I asked.

"Very interesting," Duck replied with genuine warmth. "Maximilian is a fascinating being. And Chaffinch handles the situation masterfully."

"We are all impressed by Maximilian," I confirmed proudly, and added, "even if we don't always understand what he says."

This was an inside joke, a jargon that we maintained in the innermost circle; Maximilian's similes could be interpreted in so many ways that we sometimes jokingly called the exercises "Seminars on Faith, Hope, and Confusion."

Duck Johnson was about to comment on this when Adam showed up. The deacon took a cup of coffee and greeted the new guest.

"It's Johnson, isn't it?"

"That's right," Duck confirmed, extending his wing. "And I not only wish to thank you for allowing me to come, I also wish to take the opportunity to say how deeply impressed I was at your manner of conducting the questions and conversation just now, Deacon. That requires not only the greatest sensitivity and talent, but integrity as well. And it seems to me that you possess all that in abundance."

Deacon Chaffinch, who like most of us was not unduly accustomed to praise, did not know what he should say. And when Duck realized that he had placed the deacon in a somewhat uncomfortable situation, he added, "Wolf and I were just talking about this, that the bewildering requires its interpreter. And that Maximilian no doubt requires even more clarifying."

Chaffinch laughed, I laughed too, and Duck laughed with us.

He was quick, I noticed. He had perceived where the limits were, and he had made Chaffinch feel at ease again. And despite the fact that even then I realized that Duck Johnson should not be underestimated, I fell into the trap.

He continued to show up at seminars, and soon he was one of our most visible participants. Always formally dressed, stiff, and with a smile on his beak. Always with a well-aimed compliment and taking care to let the others shine, strongly and clearly, at his own expense.

I realize that I am describing Maximilian as if he were almost otherworldly. This is of course a result of my own priorities. For long periods Maximilian was like any stuffed animal, but this is hardly interesting to a Recorder. It is not my intention to paint a portrait; it is my cause to reproduce words and actions in a way that allows the observant reader to draw his own conclusions.

Let me now make a small exception.

One of Maximilian's commonplaces was that he loved sweets. This is not something I recall from his early youth, but over the years he had developed a clear weakness for pastries and desserts, chocolate and candy. I will not go so far as to maintain that he gorged on sweets, but if the opportunity was there, he took it. Duck Johnson, the sensitive and attentive guest in our group, took unerring note of this weakness.

"What's this?" asked Maximilian one day as we sat in the living room, reading.

He got up and stared at me inquisitively. I looked around in confusion. I did not know what he was talking about.

"What?"

"Don't you smell it?" he asked, sniffing the air. "Wonderful. The aroma . . . I don't know . . . do you have . . . ?"

But I didn't have anything. Maximilian walked slowly out to the hall, sniffing the air the entire time, and I leaned forward in my armchair to see what he was doing. At the next moment there was a knocking at the door. Maximilian threw it open. Outside stood Duck Johnson. Even he looked somewhat surprised at the forceful jerk with which the door was opened.

Duck held out a small brown paper bag.

Without a word Maximilian snatched it. He breathed in the aroma with pleasure.

"It's chocolate," Maximilian observed.

"Chocolate-dipped pieces of mango," Duck Johnson confirmed. "I think it's fun to do something a little extra when I make chocolate."

"Do you make chocolate, Duck?" asked Maximilian, obviously fascinated. "Do you do that often? May I taste?"

"It's yours," said Duck. "It makes me happy that you appreciate it. If you want, I can come by tomorrow again. Because just at this moment I have a pot on the stove at home."

With his mouth full of chocolate-dipped mango bites Maximilian had a hard time producing more than an appreciative noise. Duck raised his wing to the brim of his hat, nodded courteously toward me—I had taken a few steps out into the hall to see what was happening—and left.

Today I know that Duck was no confectioner, that he actually started making sweets only for Maximilian's sake, and I admit that his inventiveness—for a novice—was impressive. He visited a few times a week, and the assortment he brought varied: honey-drenched pear slices rolled in almond brittle, milk-chocolate-coated fruit marshmallows, apple cubes in dark and light chocolate with candied figs on top. He also knew Maximilian's favorite: light cola fudge inside a thin envelope of orange marzipan; white balls small enough to eat whole.

Duck never had any treats for me, but always a friendly smile.

Sometimes Adam Chaffinch was at Leyergasse when Duck came with his treats. Then Duck stayed behind. He flattered the deacon so crudely that even I became embarrassed, and he always seemed to want to talk about religious subjects without having any religious insight of his own. Only a fool could shut his eyes to the fact that Duck Johnson had a design with his visits, but neither Adam nor I could find out what the design was.

After a seminar one late afternoon in October—I no longer recall what we talked about—Adam unexpectedly asked Duck Johnson to stay behind a while. Duck suspected no mischief, but rather accepted with delight. This meant that Maximilian, Chaffinch, Duck, and I remained sitting in the little lounge suite in the living room while the other participants quietly left. I recall this as an uncomfortable moment. Maximilian fiddled with his cake plate. I drank the rest of my cold coffee, seemingly meditatively, pretending like I knew what this was about and staring at the painting above the couch, which depicted a knight on a wall. Only Duck Johnson seemed the same, calm and serious.

"Yes," Chaffinch began when the final participants had closed the outside door behind them, "I would like to know what caused you to come here, Duck. I mean, you have no religious background, do you?"

If Duck suspected anything, he concealed it skillfully.

"No," he said, "no, I don't. How I ended up here? I heard about Maximilian, and . . . Why does a person seek something in life? Why isn't it enough to simply live? To be honest, I don't know. But there are surely explanations . . . there always are."

"And if I say Wright's Lane and King's Cross?" asked Chaffinch.

King's Cross was the prison at the end of Eastern Avenue. I held my breath: Had Johnson been in prison? What had Adam found out, and why had he not said anything to me? Duck did not change his expression, but his reply took time.

"If you say Wright's Lane, Deacon," he repeated at last very slowly, "I can say that you have done your homework."

"You have an extensive criminal record," Chaffinch stated drily.

"I don't deny it," replied Duck Johnson. "But you cannot readily blame me for choosing not to talk about that time of my life. That is behind me."

I turned toward Maximilian to see how he reacted, but could ascertain only that he wasn't listening. That annoyed me. He could sometimes turn off his surroundings and go into himself in a troublesome manner, and that had happened now.

"And today?" asked the deacon. "How does Duck make a living today?"

Duck did not reply. He was staring at the deacon, and for the first time I saw a fire flame up in Duck's eye; a genuine emotion. It was hatred.

"You have nothing to do with this," Duck replied calmly.

"We gladly accept a repentant sinner here in the circle around Maximilian," said Adam, "but not one who still sins."

Duck looked down at his shoes. They were the same ones he had on at the first meeting two months ago, the black ones with holes in the soles.

"Then I would answer," he said slowly, and met the deacon's gaze in a way I perceived as challenging, "that the greater the sin, the greater the reason to listen to Maximilian's wisdom."

With that Duck got up, bowed stiffly in the deacon's direction, nodded to me, and left the apartment. We sat silently and listened to his steps on the stairs. I did not dare look at Maximilian, but I admit that I felt a certain relief. Duck's ingratiation had been irresistible at the beginning, but with the sweets it became obtrusive and unpleasant. If this had anything to do with jealousy, I do not know, but I felt relieved to be rid of him.

We left the place with light steps that evening, Deacon Chaffinch and I. Never could we have sensed that Maximilian would receive Duck Johnson in his home again as soon as the next day, and that we were the ones, the deacon and I, who were put to shame.

It would take another month or two before Duck had maneuvered me out completely and, through his manipulation and his chocolate-coated fruit pieces, won Maximilian over to his side.

The day I came to bark brown Leyergasse and was evicted at the door by the manipulative duck was one of the two or three worst days of my life.

I am not blaming Maximilian. He was a victim; he could not guess the duck's shady intentions, because Maximilian was simply unequipped to believe bad of anyone. Maximilian was above loyalty and friendship with an individual stuffed animal; he was loyal to the collectivity that was Mollisan Town. He loved all of us. I, if anyone, knew all about that.

But it did not hurt any less.

It was night in Lanceheim, and in the blocks around mauve Pfaffendorfer Tor life could finally resume. Every morning dawn arrived and broke up the party; the day was one long wait for darkness, and only at twilight could the neon lights swagger again: their yellow, green, and red sheen fell soundlessly against the sidewalks and in the shadows beyond their glow, where couples aroused one another with promises of what the night would hold. At bars and restaurants the atmosphere was loud; through open doors and windows culinary aromas and the laughter of fellowship invited guests to the tables. The stuffed animals of the night were like migratory birds on their way toward dawn; they flew off in flocks from one bar to the next, deeper and deeper into the night and the narrow blocks around Pfaffendorfer Tor, where gloom and shadows ruled and where anonymity promised happiness and freedom. Here the facades stood dark and silent, here doors and shutters were closed.

At one of these bars, far belowground in a cellar that smelled of mold and dampness during the day, sat Duck Johnson. At least I am imagining that this was how it came about, the background to everything that happened in the time before he showed up at Leyergasse for the first time. He was sitting at a round table; he had a bottle of whiskey before him, and in the overflowing ashtray a cigarette was smoldering.

Across from him a stranger had sat down. Duck was pleasantly drunk, but understood enough that this stranger, an owl, wanted something. No one came to this place voluntarily. The place was neither large nor charming; one lightbulb blinked nervously over a worn billiard table, and on the sticky floor around Duck's table were food scraps and splinters of glass. Behind the bar over by the stairs, the one that led up to the exit, stood a bald ape. How had Johnson become a regular at this miserable dive? He did not know. Perhaps because the alcohol was not diluted, and you could drink more of it here than at other places in the neighborhood?

"Duck Johnson?" the owl on the chair across from him asked.

Duck nodded. At the same time he lit a fresh cigarette, forgetful that the last one was still glowing in the ashtray.

"I'd like to ask you a favor," said the owl. "Are you sober enough to get what I'm saying?"

Duck giggled. "Why the hell should I do you a favor?"

"Because you're going to get something for it," the owl replied. "Let me tell you. The Ministry of Finance has quietly started its collection. This happens every ten years. The bills we use get worn out, they fall apart and start to discolor. Without making a big deal of it, the National Bank gathers them up."

Armand Owl fell silent and observed Duck to see if he was listening and understood. When Owl felt convinced, he continued.

"The collecting goes on for a few months. The bank systematically takes care of all the old money and stores it in a large bank vault until they finally drive it out to the Garbage Dump and throw it into the Hole. The night before, the amount in the vault is . . . enormous. The following day the newly printed money goes out into the whole system."

"And?" wondered Duck.

"There is one individual in this city who can make his way into the vault."

"The bank director," said Duck.

"There is a stuffed animal who can go right through walls of steel and metal," said Armand Owl, undisturbed. "His name is Maximilian, and I want you to become his friend."

Duck took the bottle of whiskey and brought it to his beak. He drank a few gulps, and nodded to himself.

"You're cracked," Duck declared, looking at Armand. "Completely disturbed. What kind of money are you talking about?"

Armand explained. It was not every day that he carried out this type of assignment for Vincent Tortoise, but it happened. Minister Tortoise did not know exactly what Armand was up to or what methods he used; it was the overarching goal that mattered. And Armand felt uncertain after the meeting with Duck whether this would really work. Armand did not himself believe the stories he had heard about Maximilian.

The night of the third Thursday in October, Duck Johnson and Maximilian were standing on cucumber green place St.-Fargeau in northwest Tourquai, looking across the street. The National Bank was on the other side, a heavy stone building of granite and concrete, gray and awe-inspiring with a thick flagpole pointing straight up from the facade like a rhinoceros horn. Behind the rows of pillars on which the bank's projecting roof rested, the entry doors could be glimpsed.

For three weeks I had been up knocking on the door to Maximilian's apartment on Leyergasse every other day without being let in. I tried to convince myself that it served me right, that I had fallen into the classic trap of defining myself through others; that it might actually be useful for me to realize that I was Wolf Diaz, not simply Maximilian's Recorder. But that sort of self-deception is not for me. I cannot describe painfully enough the shame and terror I felt as I went up the steps on Leyergasse, aware that all that awaited me on the second floor was the uncompromising Duck's vacant gaze.

I should have given up, accepted my fate, and resumed some sort of life, but I did not do that. I spent hours every day outside Maximilian's entryway, and I sought support and sympathy from everyone I encountered. I knew I was making a fool of myself, but I did not care.

Excuse me.

This emotional digression has nothing to do with the night when Maximilian and Duck stood on the sidewalk across from the National Bank. Nothing. Back to the matter.

The Midnight Breeze was playing with the mauve, richly embroidered caftan that Maximilian had put on, and Duck nodded brazenly.

"Not much to wait for," he said, stepping out into the street.

Maximilian followed a few steps behind. They were a strange pair. In the glow from the streetlights they crossed the deserted place St.-Fargeau, one in hat and suit with his lightly swaying and at the same time stiff gait, the other close behind, soft and lithe but nonetheless uncomfortable in the peculiar body the factory had allotted him.

"Are we really going to get in?" Duck Johnson asked nervously as they approached the bank.

He had been here a few times the week before to recon-
noiter. On the street level the bank consisted of two halls,
more than twenty meters to the ceiling and large as small
cricket fields. There were cashiers and all the rest of the cus-
tomer operations. The offices were in the building's upper
stories, and in the cellar was the vault. In order to get there,
Duck and Maximilian would be compelled to force three
doors of bulletproof glass and then make their way through
the almost absurdly thick vault.

On recommendations from Armand Owl, Duck had kept
Maximilian ignorant of what the intent of this nighttime
expedition was. Duck did not know, of course, who the owl
was or why he had chosen him. At the same time this was
of no importance.

"We'll go in here, and go down to the cellar," Duck explained. "Do you think you can help me?"

"I can help you," Maximilian replied.

"Because it's locked this time of day," Duck clarified.

They were almost at the bank. Maximilian reached out
his hand and took hold of the duck's wing.

"Close your eyes," said Maximilian.

Duck closed his eyes and reduced his speed, but Maximilian kept walking. When Duck dared open his eyes again,
they were inside the bank's first hall.

"How . . . ?"

"Are we there?" asked Maximilian, looking around.

He had never been in a bank before. After first growing
up in Das Vorschutz and then being shut up at Leyergasse,
there were many things in our ordinary lives that Maximilian did not know about.

"There? Not yet, really," said Duck.

Presumably they had already set off some of the alarms.
There ought to be motion detectors in the bank, perhaps
heat sensors. The opportunity was in acting quickly.

"We'll go down one flight," said Duck. "Follow me."

Duck walked quickly, and when they came down the stairs, they saw the great vault right ahead of them.

"Here," said Duck.

The procedure from the street was repeated: Maximilian took hold of Duck's wing and together they went right through the vault door. Duck was less surprised this time, and the sensational feeling from before was suddenly colored by discomfort. Duck and Maximilian stood silently next to each other in the darkness. The stench in the vault was nauseating; it reeked of excrement and rotten fabric.

"Are we there?" asked Maximilian.

Duck found the electrical panel to the right of the vault door, and turned on the ceiling lights. The reason for the overpowering smell was a few meters away from them. Fifteen, perhaps twenty pallets of old bills, impossible to trace and already deregistered; early tomorrow morning they would be driven away—escorted by the military in armored vehicles—out to the Hole at the Garbage Dump, where they would go up in smoke forever.

Duck gasped for breath. Maximilian looked around and realized where he was.

"We are in a bank vault," he declared without surprise. "What are we doing here?"

Duck had opened his long coat, and from the specially sewn inside pockets he took out four linen bags. They had been carefully folded, and when he unfolded them, they proved to be larger than you might think. He gave two of them to Maximilian, who took them but stood still.

"What are we doing here?" he repeated.

Duck had discussed this situation with Armand Owl. It was unavoidable that Maximilian would ask the question at last, and that it must be answered.

"We're in a bit of a hurry," Duck explained.

The pallets of money were secured with rope and covered with plastic. Duck took out a small pocket knife and made a long cut in the plastic, at the same time as he started gathering bundles of bills and placing them in the first bag.

"I'll tell you later. The money belongs to no one, it's going to be burned, and when I think about the poor stuffed animals in Yok . . . it simply doesn't feel right. We have to save the money. For Yok's sake. And . . . if you want . . . everything you see here can be yours."

Duck dug deeper into the nearest pallet, but Maximilian remained motionless.

"Here," said Duck, pointing with his wing to the cut he had made with the knife. "Go ahead. I'll take another one, take this one here."

Duck went deeper into the vault, and the sound of yet another cut with the knife was heard. While Duck continued working in silence, Maximilian remained mute.

How great was the chance that this coup would succeed? Probably negligible. Armand Owl had devoted great care to assuring Duck Johnson that whatever alarms might be set off, they would have at least fifteen minutes in the vault.

This had been a lie.

Duck had not even had time to fill the first bag with bills before he heard the sound of a series of mechanical clicks from the vault door; it sounded like iron pipes dropped on asphalt. The vault was about to be opened from outside.

After that things went very quickly.

The police stormed in, ten specially trained attack police in riot gear from the renowned Nashville district in Amberville.

As soon as Duck and Maximilian had gone through the hall on the upper level, they had set off the alarm, and the call-out had highest priority. Before the police force arrived, they had received information from command central that the thieves were in the vault; in principle motion detectors covered every square decimeter of the premises. When a few minutes later the police themselves investigated the place, they found that the vault was closed and locked. To open it required authorization from the bank management, and only after repeated confirmations from command central did the police receive this authorization. The sigh that met them when the vault door glided open was tragic and comic at the same time.

A single, grotesque being dressed in a long caftan and with a kind of shawl wrapped around his head was standing before a pallet of bills. On the floor beside him was a bag half filled with money.

No trace of Duck Johnson was seen, but at the same time the police were not searching for anyone else. It was obvious who had committed this crime.

The prosecutor's office found us through the dry cleaners. After Maximilian had spent a few days in jail, one of the guards discovered the pink receipt that the Siamese always clipped to the collar on Maximilian's mauve caftan when I made use of the Siamese's establishment on Hüxterdamm. On the receipt was a telephone number that the guard dialed, and the Siamese recognized the item of clothing from the description; the embroidery on the caftan depicted a swan with a rhinoceros horn on its forehead. In that way the guard got my name and telephone number.

They called late in the afternoon, when the breeze had slackened and the blue of the sky had intensified, and the joy I experienced when the acting prosecutor described the peculiar individual who was jailed for attempted break-in at the National Bank cannot be exaggerated. I struggled not to scream out loud. I confirmed Maximilian's identity, provided information about family situation and address, and then ran the whole way over to Adam Chaffinch to tell him the good news. Fortunately there were no more than five minutes between us; I have never been a very athletic animal.

That same evening I made my way to lemon yellow Kaufhof and the peculiar police station that was the head-quarters for this part of the city's constabulary: a mauve building reminiscent of a fairy-tale castle, complete with towers and pinnacles. The jail—the largest in all of Mol-lisan Town—was directly connected to the police station, and the contrast could not have been more conspicuous. From the outside the jail resembled an aboveground bunker, an almost windowless monolith in which Maximilian was imprisoned.

I had never been in the police station before, but I had still heard a lot about it. Here the legendary Major Fender-gast had command, and he was one of the primary reasons that Lanceheim remained underrepresented in the crime statistics. At least that was what was said, but who knows. Perhaps it was Fendergast himself who spread that rumor?

After having identified myself at the reception desk and been searched in a small room connected to the coatroom, they led me to the prisoner. Maximilian sat waiting on an uncomfortable Windsor-style chair in a cell with poor light-ing that reeked of cigarette butts. I could not keep from smiling when I saw that he had made a headcloth from a pillowcase.

"Maximilian," I exclaimed, sitting down across from him, on the other side of the rusty table that was the room's only furnishing, "I've been so worried."

Maximilian looked at me and nodded absently.

"If you see the world through a soap bubble," he said, "you don't see clearly. But one thing is certain: Sooner or later the bubble will burst."

And I did not get more than that out of him. Maximil-ian had already confessed everything to the police; he had accounted for what had happened during the fateful night, and omitted neither odors nor colors. When I read the interrogation report a few months later, I was surprised by the wealth of detail; it was not like him. But there was not a word about Duck Johnson.

Even when I met Maximilian in the jail that first time I had a hard time controlling my frustration. We sat there on either side of the table for another half hour, and I pressed him with questions that soon proceeded to theories and increasingly aggressive accusations. Not toward him, of course, but toward Duck. Finally Maximilian got up.

"Enough now, Wolf," he said. "If you can't play hopscotch, it's pointless to blame the one who drew the squares."

A police officer opened the door behind my back, and I was thereby forced to leave.

"We'll get you out of here," I called in vain to Maximilian while the police officer escorted me along the claustrophobic corridor toward the exit. "We'll get you out, as soon as tomorrow."

I found it absurd that the most good stuffed animal who has ever lived in Mollisan Town was accused of a crime. However honorably intended, my promise, however, proved as empty as the apartment on Leyergasse. During the month that led to the trial, we hired the best attorneys we could find, given our finances. All of them failed, because Maximilian did not cooperate. He made no credible account of how he had made his way into the bank or the vault, but worse yet, the attorneys could not get a single mitigating circumstance out of him. And when they pressed him harder, he replied with similes that these verbal acrobats of the law could neither understand nor use.

On one occasion, in deep dejection, Adam Chaffinch went to the jail himself to see him. Even for Adam, Maximilian would not place any guilt on Duck Johnson.

"The free will that leads your steps," Maximilian is said

to have explained to Chaffinch in one of the small interrogation rooms with rusty tables, "is your own. And when
your free will leads you astray because you are no more
than a stuffed animal, always remember this: Have confidence. Magnus will lead you right again."

For a deacon like Chaffinch, the citing of Magnus as an
argument was easy to refute.

"The responsibility we have for our lives, as long as we
live them in Mollisan Town," replied Adam, "we cannot
avoid by referring to Magnus. True, our faith rests in his
paws, but our lives are still our own. He is going to forgive
us and have mercy on us however we choose to use our
will."

When Maximilian heard these words, he smiled amiably,
as when you hear a cub counting out loud for the first time.
But he did not reply, and Adam Chaffinch too had to leave
the jail with unfinished business. It was obvious that Maximilian did not intend to tell what had caused him to end up
in the vault of the National Bank, much less disclose Duck
Johnson's participation.

When the trial began—with a public defender because
the attorneys we had hired had all withdrawn—Maximilian immediately declared himself guilty. And we understood that our only chance to exonerate him was to find
Duck Johnson. During an intensive week of searching, we
did all we could. I myself did not have time to be present at
the court proceedings; I neither slept nor ate and spent every
hour of the day following up what proved to be empty tips
about where Duck might possibly be hiding.

The judge who took care of the case was named Hawk
Pius, and he was a certifiably tough bird. His small, peering
eyes stared straight at Maximilian during the entire trial.
Because the question of guilt was established, it was mostly
about the length of the sentence. This sounded ominous.

Even more disheartening was our pursuit of Duck; he had vanished without a trace.

On the fifth day of the proceedings came the sentence. It was conspicuously severe considering the facts that the defendant had no previous record, no damage had occurred, and no money had disappeared.

Maximilian was sentenced to fifteen years in prison.

I wept when I received the news. Adam Chaffinch shut himself up in the sacristy and remained there almost twenty-four hours. Even now the days that followed form a kind of vacuum in my life, an absurd existence of meaninglessness and confusion, a fog of guilt and curses.

Now I know that all of it had a meaning.

Now I know that in his absence, the myth of Maximilian would grow with a force that no living stuffed animal, not even himself, would have been able to live up to.

But this took time to realize, and the year that followed was the darkest in my life.

REUBEN WALRUS 6

His name was Giraffe Heine.

Philip Mouse was waiting with Reuben Walrus outside a shabby restaurant on golden brown rue Ybry in south Yok. The Afternoon Weather was at a late stage, the temperature was falling fast, but the sky was still blue. It had been two days since Reuben had given the private detective the assignment, and he had already achieved some type of result.

"Is it here?" asked Reuben.

Philip Mouse nodded. The brim of his hat concealed the mouse's eyes.

"Just as sure as a female's mysteriousness," said Mouse.

It was the surest thing he could think of.

"Shouldn't we go in?"

"Soon," said Mouse, crushing the glowing cigarette butt with his heel.

Giraffe Heine had gone into the bar a good while ago, and what caused Philip to hold back his client, he himself was not sure of. Perhaps he feared that Reuben would be disappointed. After the rat had been in touch, Mouse had worked up a certain expectancy. He had phoned Reuben and told him the good, and the bad, news. True, he did not know where Maximilian was, but he had every reason to believe that they would get hold of the giraffe.

During the past few days Philip Mouse had received a number of tips about the giraffe. A few were anything but reliable; others bore consideration. It started with Annette Afghan telling the same story to Philip that she had told to Reuben. Then a hamster who maintained that he knew where Giraffe Heine usually bought wine said that he had not had cancer of the throat, as the afghan alleged; instead it was something about his nose.

From a yellow koala who claimed to know where Giraffe lived (which proved to be a lie or a misunderstanding), Philip found out that Maximilian had shown himself to Giraffe in a dream, and not at all in reality. Being in several places at the same time, said the koala, was a prerequisite for Maximilian. How else could he affect the lives of so many animals? The koala then hinted that he himself had seen Maximilian flash by in more than one dream. It was the koala who confirmed that the name of the giraffe was Heine.

A beautiful pelican by the name of Linda—or was it Lina—could relate that Giraffe Heine worked as a proofreader at a publisher that primarily published university dissertations. She was quite certain that Giraffe had never met Maximilian. It was actually the case that Giraffe had a brother who as a youth had lost one of his feet in an escalator. Maximilian had come down from the sky as an angel and conjured forth a new foot for the brother. (Of all the stories that Philip uncovered, this was the most ridiculous. On the other hand, the beautiful pelican was correct in that Giraffe Heine did work at the University Press.)

With every new tip, Mouse got a new version of what had happened. Soon he could see a pattern. Everyone he talked to begrudged the giraffe his experience, and tried to belittle or erase it. All were just as unconditionally possessed by Maximilian's divinity and power.

But the clues also led to skeptics. The receptionist at the University Press explained curtly to Philip that she did not know who Maximilian was, and did not intend to find out either. Neither Heine nor any other proofreader had a permanent position or employment at the publisher, she said, and she dismissed Philip as yet another in a series of religious fools who called to ask questions about the giraffe.

"There's nothing special about Heine," she told him with irritation before he left. "And if he is supposed to have met some kind of shaman, then you can ask him why he always has a cold. Don't miracles work on the sniffles?"

Philip could not answer that question.

It was through Daisy and her unfathomable network of social workers all over Mollisan Town that the tip about the bar on golden brown rue Ybry turned up. A rat at the social services office in south Yok took Daisy's bait, and revealed that Giraffe Heine was one of his cases. There was no fixed address for the giraffe, but when the rat wanted to get hold of him, he would leave messages at the bar on rue Ybry, and most often he heard from Heine afterward.

It was this information that Philip Mouse gave Reuben Walrus on the third day. The composer had been disappointed at first when he realized that Mouse had not gotten any closer to the trail of Maximilian, but then he cheered up and asked whether they could drive down to Yok immediately and look for the giraffe.

"It's your money," Mouse replied.

Walrus picked up Mouse in a taxi outside the detective's office, and in silence they traveled southward to Yok's bewilderingly narrow and incoherent blocks.

"I have a few receipts that are due," Mouse took the opportunity to explain.

"Huh?"

"Extra expenses. Doing investigative work isn't free," said Mouse.

Walrus nodded, and Mouse took that as agreement.

They were let out a few blocks from rue Ybry, because it would take the taxi driver an eternity to come back out on South Avenue if he drove up the whole way. Philip made sure to get out first to avoid paying. He led Reuben Walrus the few blocks up to the golden brown street, and after a short distance they found the bar.

At the very next moment they caught sight of Giraffe Heine.

At least it was a giraffe, and he was going into the restaurant.

It was almost a parody. Philip had not had any plan, hardly even any expectation. And then the giraffe was the first one they ran into. If Mouse had not been such a confirmed fatalist, it would have been hard to dismiss the thought that higher powers had a finger in the game.

"Now?" asked Reuben.

Mouse nodded. "Sure. I'll wait out here on the street. We don't want to scare him."

It seemed wise.

Reuben took a deep breath, gathered his courage, and a minute later crossed the street and went into the bar.

It was the sort of place you would expect in a neighborhood like this.

At first Reuben could not see anything, the place was so submerged in deep darkness. Rock music roared out of cracked speakers, loud enough to conceal the silence. Then Reuben made out ten or so stuffed animals spread out at round tables in a surprisingly large room. Low red kerosene lamps stood flickering on the tables. Reuben went over to the bar, where small lamps above the large mirror caused him to see himself ordering a beer.

Giraffe Heine was sitting alone at a table to the right of the bar. He was sipping a whiskey and soda and seemed deeply submerged in himself. Reuben put the money for the beer on the bar, taking the mug with him to the giraffe's table.

"May I join you, my friend?" he asked with the low voice that the murmur and music seemed to require.

And before he got an answer, he sat down.

The giraffe sat quietly. His gaze was clouded, and despite the fact that a stranger had just joined him, he seemed to have a hard time being involved in the moment.

"Who are you?" he finally forced out. "Are you from Social Services?"

"Reuben Walrus," replied Reuben with exaggerated formality. "I've been looking for you for several days."

"I don't have a cent."

"I'm not interested in—"

"Ask anyone, you know? Not a cent," and the giraffe let his hoof sweep across the room with a kind of leisureliness that did not appear to agree with his narrow, long limbs.

"What?" said Reuben.

He did not want to admit it, but if he did not concentrate on what the giraffe was saying, if he looked in a different direction, he had a hard time hearing.

"I don't have a cent," repeated Heine.

"I'm here to talk about Maximilian," said Reuben.

The giraffe reacted. His gaze cleared; the entire stuffed animal stiffened.

"Maximilian?" said Giraffe Heine. "Don't think, like, I've ever heard of him."

There was something in the suspicious gaze and the immediate denial that convinced Reuben that Giraffe was lying.

"I wish you no harm," said Reuben. "And you don't need to talk. I'm really not in pursuit of you—it's Maximilian I want to meet. But you seem to be the only one who has actually met him."

"I haven't, like, met him, you know?" the giraffe persisted. "And even if I had, I know nothing, like, about him, you know? Where he is or how you get hold of him, and that."

"Do you know anyone who knows?"

"No."

"And you've never seen him again?"

"No."

"But you must have been contacted by lots of animals like me, who wonder what happened and where Maximilian is staying."

"Hundreds."

"What?"

"There have been hundreds like you here, asking."

Reuben pondered this.

"It's completely crazy," sighed Giraffe Heine, sipping his whiskey and soda. "First the . . . impossible happens, you know? Then I can't go home without being jumped, you know? Stuffed animals who think I'm some sort of guru, and the kind that are pissed off and want to punch me in the mouth. It really sucks. It was better before I met him, you know? Better that stomach than those . . ."

The giraffe emptied his glass, and made a sign with his hoof to the bartender for another round.

"You're paying, you know?" he asked the walrus. "You all usually pay."

Reuben nodded.

"Stomach?"

"He healed me," nodded Giraffe.

"You were sick to your stomach," asked Reuben, and hoped that his mustache concealed the smile that he couldn't hold back. "That's what it was about? You had pain in your stomach?"

"It's nothing to laugh at," said Giraffe. "It hurt like hell. Hurt like hell, every day, year out and year in. Colic, like, or whatever it's called."

Reuben held up a fin, as if to ask for forgiveness for his little smile. But Giraffe felt offended.

"I spent half of my childhood at Lucretzia, in intensive care or up in gastronomy, you know? No one could help me, no one got, like, what it was."

Reuben attempted an understanding nod. Lucretzia was the hospital in Tourquai; it had a reputation of being the worst in the city.

"And then he came," declared Giraffe.

"What'd you say?"

"Yes, well, Maximilian came."

"Did he come to the hospital?"

The giraffe stared at the walrus as if he were an idiot. The bartender brought over a large whiskey and soda, taking the empty glass with him.

"No, not to the hospital. I met him a year ago. The hospital was when I was little, you know?" said Heine, sipping the fresh drink.

"Of course."

"I don't know why he came to me in particular," said Heine.

"No. For that is a good question," admitted Reuben.

"But can I tell about what happened?"

"That would be exciting."

Giraffe prepared himself by taking a large gulp of whiskey.

"It was a dark night," he said.

"Tell it like it was," asked Reuben.

"It was dark, anyway," said Heine morosely, "and I was on my way home, you know? And even if I've told this story at least a hundred times, I can't remember where I'd been. But I was on my way home. And then there was a stabbing pain, you know? Like it usually is. A stabbing pain in the abdomen, hurt like hell."

Giraffe pointed with his hoof toward his abdomen to make clear exactly where the pain had arisen. Reuben nodded.

"I fell apart, like," continued Heine. "But before I fell to the sidewalk, there was someone who caught me. A chaffinch."

"What did you say?"

"A chaffinch helped me."

"Maximilian is a chaffinch?"

Reuben was astonished.

"No, no," said Heine, "that's his helper, you know? A chaffinch, his name is Adam, he caught me and helped me to a . . . store, or something. That was where I met him."

"A store?"

"Or something," repeated Heine irritably. "I don't know. It was an entryway right nearby, you know? I think it was a store."

"Excuse me, I was just wondering."

"Do you want to hear, or what?"

"I really want to hear," answered Reuben.

"We walked in there, I was completely doubled over, I was in so much pain, the chaffinch dragged me, like, across the threshold. It was completely dark, I couldn't see more than outlines, you know? But there was a chair in the middle of the room, and there they sat me down. It hurt so much that I was whimpering, the attacks are different, this was one of the worst. The chaffinch stood beside me, he said nothing."

"And you just went along?" asked Reuben, frankly surprised. "A strange animal down here in Yok, who does not explain anything, takes you over his shoulders and you just follow along?"

"When I'm in pain, you know," explained Heine, "then it's like everything else disappears, you know? What I'm telling you, that's how I remembered it afterward. But just then . . . then it just hurt like holy hell. And I was sitting there on the chair in the middle of the room and wasn't thinking about anything other than my belly, and then he spoke to me."

"What did he say?" asked Reuben.

He surprised himself with the intensity of the question. Reuben realized that he really, really wanted to know what Maximilian had said.

"The first thing he said," said Heine, "was that I was not in pain."

"That you were not in pain?"

"And you know, it was like I wasn't in pain anymore, you know? At the same moment as he said it, it didn't hurt anymore. And when I sat up on the chair—I'd been, like, halfway lying down before—then he said that I would never be in pain again. And I have never been in pain again. Never. I tested it. Once I ate two kilos of plums and drank a bottle of rum. I shit like a cow, but it didn't hurt, you know? Then he said that I must never lose hope, and then I could go."

"Go?"

"That's all. I never saw them again, neither the chaffinch nor Maximilian."

"But . . . but how do you know that it was . . . Maximilian?"

"No idea."

"What'd you say?"

"That I don't know. There are others who have said that it must have been Maximilian. He looked shady, and had some kind of coiled cap, you know?"

"And how do you know the chaffinch's name was Adam?"

"Maximilian called him Adam. He said, 'Adam, who have you brought with you?' "

"And what did the chaffinch say?"

"No idea. I was hurting like holy hell."

"And that was it?"

"Yep."

Giraffe drank up without immediately waving for a new glass.

"But that was when it started," he added. "With all you cuckoos who come and ask the same things all the time."

Philip Mouse was standing outside, waiting, but thankfully he demanded no immediate account of the conversation.

They walked together through the random streets in south Yok en route to the avenue and a possible taxi. There was something that felt different, and not until Reuben had been able to walk silently and think about the matter a long while did it occur to him what it was.

Hope.

"Mr. Private Detective," he said. "I have a new lead to give you."

She had never forgiven him. They didn't talk about it; they had put it behind them. Fox von Duisburg was a stuffed animal who seldom dwelled on times that had passed. But where Reuben Walrus was concerned, she could not forgive, only try to forget. That was not to say that she didn't feel for him now. In Fox's opinion Reuben was a poor wretch for all time, and after the news about Drexler's syndrome, she saw the panic shimmering in his round, black eyes of glass. He put on a good face, but was close to a breakdown. He had always been the weaker of the two of them.

"Do you really have time for this?" she asked.

Walrus had begged and pleaded to be allowed to go along and shop. It was absurd, considering that he had always despised going into stores. And it was even more absurd that he still loved her. Despite the fact that she dismissed his constant declarations of love with feigned severity, she knew that he was serious. In his way. And now, under these circumstances, she gave in. She let him go along.

Reuben looked out through the window. Still no sign of clouds. He should be back at the rehearsals in the concert hall before the Afternoon Rain. At most it took half an hour to walk from Grand Divino. The orchestra had been at it for nine days now; soon half the time would have passed. He nodded.

"I have time."

"Good," said Fox, "there's a jacket I would like your opinion on."

This was a lie. She did not care in the least what he would think of the jacket, and he knew that too. She set the money on the black tray where the check already was, and they got up at the same time. Lunch had consisted of a much-too-healthy shrimp salad, and she would be hungry again in an hour.

At the Grand Divino department store there were two lunch restaurants, an exclusive variety with white linen tablecloths and an extensive à la carte menu on the street level, and a simpler café on the sixth floor. Fox preferred the café. Probably it was the ultimate form of snobbery: shopping at the city's most exclusive department store and at the same time choosing the cheapest lunch alternative. Only a stuffed animal with a lot of money could afford to appear thrifty, at least in the circles in which Fox moved.

She had cast covetous glances at the jacket in question for a whole week. It was too expensive and did not go with anything else in her wardrobe.

"It's a Carél av Turtiano," she said.

"That says nothing to me," answered Reuben, shaking his head. "But it sounds expensive."

"Worse than you think." She smiled.

She led him through the department store down to the fourth floor, where Carél had a boutique with gloomy clothing deep within one of the most exclusive departments. Fox parked Reuben on a hard couch and went off to demand the attention of the clerks. It did not take long before she was standing before him dressed in the jacket. Opposite was a full-length mirror in which she critically regarded herself.

"What do you think?" she asked.

"Nice," he said neutrally.

"Is it worth five thousand?" she asked.

"Are you joking?"

He was shocked.

"But it suits me in some way," she added, turning her back on him.

"What does he think? The other male?" asked Reuben.

He sounded so bitter that she instinctively avoided meeting his gaze in the mirror.

"It's you who are the other male, fool," she replied.

"It's not that way at all."

"Oh, yes, it is."

"Not."

"Careful now," she advised. "I have sympathy, but not an unlimited supply. He was there when I needed him."

"You need resistance," he maintained condescendingly.

"You're the one who needs resistance. I need support."

"From someone you respect."

"You're not going to talk your way out of this," answered Fox in an attempt to jokingly redirect a conversation that she knew was heading in the wrong direction, seen from Reuben's perspective. "Shall I take this one or the green one?"

"Take the one you have on," he advised.

"But is it worth the money?"

"Absolutely not."

She sighed but ignored him, and both of them knew that she would buy the jacket.

Reuben and Fox left Grand Divino a few minutes later by way of the exit toward Krönkenhagen. In her paw she was carrying a white paper bag that read "Carél," with expensive strips of leather as a handle. Out of the corner of her eye she saw that he had stopped on the sidewalk.

"I don't know what I should do," he said piteously.

The clouds had gathered at the horizon, and animals passing by them on the narrow sidewalk hastened their steps. Fox waited. She knew him so well.

"I don't even have two weeks left," he said.

He said this as much to himself as to her. He remained standing, frozen stiff by the cruel sentence he had just pronounced. Fox observed him. When she was certain that he did not want to say anything more, she took a step forward. Endlessly careful, so that he would not recoil, she placed her arms around him and enclosed him in an embrace. He let her do this, as so many times before. She gave him her warmth, her confidence, and power. He needed her more than ever.

They remained standing like that until an angry truck honked at a wobbly cyclist farther down the street. Reuben gave a start and again became aware of reality. The clouds were on their way in over the city; the philharmonic was surely back after lunch, ready to attack his unfinished symphony anew.

In silence they again began walking north on Krönkenhagen. The peddlers along the river observed them hopefully, and Reuben's gaze roved involuntarily along the spines of the used books. The rain would be upon them soon, and the stands would close. Not because the goods were unprotected, but because the customers had disappeared.

"Won't it be better if you take a taxi?" she asked.

He nodded. They placed themselves on the sidewalk and turned toward the cars driving from the south.

"Can't you come along?" he asked.

"Absolutely not," she said firmly.

"I need you," he said.

"I know."

"I've always needed you."

"I know."

"We were much too wise when we left each other," said Reuben.

"Careful now," she warned.

"No, it's true," he insisted. "We certainly did the right thing, but—"

Fox raised her paw and waved a taxi over to the sidewalk. She opened the back door, and unwillingly he got into the car. The rain was no more than a few minutes off.

"I never should have let you disappear from my life," he said.

"I never disappeared." She smiled gently, feeling endlessly tired. To the driver she added, "He's going to the concert hall."

Then she closed the car door on him, and walked quickly away.

They had been happy. They had lived in an equal, intense relationship; they had been so different, and yet she felt that they were very close. It had always been hard for her to show her feelings, let herself go, let someone else get inside the protective walls. With him she had given in. In the clarifying paleness of reflection she understood exactly how it had happened. Reuben Walrus was one of the most naive stuffed animals she had met; he showed his feelings spontaneously like a little cub, it was impossible to feel threatened. He was thirty-four years old when they married; it was his second marriage. She was a year younger, and she had no experience with relationships. That was one of her many excuses.

The early years of their marriage were hesitant. Then they found their routines, their roles, positions they were comfortable with, and they lived a few happy years together. As the von Duisburg conventions directed, they put themselves on the Cub List, and after Josephine was delivered . . . Reuben changed. Probably Fox changed too. It was not something that happened overnight, but their daughter took time away from them. Gave life a new meaning. She would have the exact same priorities if she could do it over again today. Besides, his temperament and character had nothing to do with either her or Josephine. Reuben Walrus's reality—this she had always been aware of—orbited exclusively around Reuben Walrus.

Josephine had reached the age of six when it happened. It was by chance, which was obvious: Only chance can expose such things.

Hotel Grandville was on fire red Mount Row in Amberville. Fox von Duisburg knew of the hotel, but had never visited it. It was her brother who suggested they should meet there and have a cup of tea, but as usual he was late. The hotel was of the smaller variety, furnished like a private home from the turn of the century, and she went into the lounge and sat down on a couch that was right out of a fairy-tale book about princes and princesses. Embroidered pillows rested against the pink velvet on the seat and back. The room had a low ceiling, and on the walls hung solemnly framed oil paintings depicting the forest under dramatic skies. Chairs and tables stood close beside each other. She was the only guest. While waiting for her brother, she ordered a cup of coffee with hot milk. She felt stressed and irritated. The cubsitter had said firmly that she had to be back and pick up Josephine before the breeze died down for the evening.

When Fox von Duisburg heard the sound of the little bell on the outside door in the next room, she prepared herself to give her brother a proper telling-off. But it was not her brother. Into the lounge came a beautiful silver fox. The stranger sat down as far from Fox von Duisburg as possible, and they exchanged a hasty nod.

In the following moment the server, a suave sloth dressed in a waiter's uniform, appeared and approached the silver fox.

"Madame is early today," he said in a low voice.

"I went past Jean-Luc, but that was a waste," the silver fox said.

"Really? Shall I bring in the tea?"

"Please," she replied, taking a magazine out of her handbag.

Preoccupied, she began leafing through the periodical. The sloth left the lounge with the order, but nonetheless his words were clearly heard from reception:

"Madame von Duisburg will have her chamomile now."

Time stopped.

Fox von Duisburg kept her eyes riveted on the silver fox on the couch. She did not look up from her magazine; she appeared completely undisturbed. It was impossible that her name was von Duisburg. The family was not so large that Fox did not know all its members. She had not said her name to the sloth, so it could not be a matter of a misunderstanding. Fox von Duisburg was dumbfounded.

The silver fox closed her magazine and got up.

"Alex," she called to the sloth, "I've changed my mind. I'll take tea up in the room instead."

And without wasting any more time she left the lounge. Fox remained sitting. But she did not have time to pursue her thoughts in one direction or the other before the doorbell was heard again. The voice that greeted the reception clerk was familiar.

"Has Mrs. von Duisburg arrived?" asked Reuben Walrus.

Fox von Duisburg was in the lounge and could not see

what was happening at the reception desk. Nor could Reuben Walrus see her.

"Madame went up to the room just a moment ago," Fox heard the reception clerk report.

"Fine. I'll keep her company. You can send up dinner in an hour."

And then footsteps were heard on a stairway.

Fox von Duisburg could not breathe. It was Tuesday, and as usual Reuben was rehearsing with the Conservatory chamber orchestra the whole evening. As usual. On Tuesdays.

Fox von Duisburg was short of breath. She got up from the couch, happened to bump against the table, whereupon coffee splashed out of the cup and down onto the table and rug. She ran out to the reception desk, and at the same moment the little doorbell was heard for the third time, and in came her brother. She fell into his arms and wept bitter tears.

It was not only the flagrant infidelity that she had uncovered, it was the way in which he had done it. It would chafe like a sharp stone in her heart longer than she would ever admit. He had stolen her identity and given it to someone else.

It would be many years before Fox von Duisburg, also by chance but possibly a related one, met Reuben Walrus's first wife Vanja Duck, and realized that Walrus had two lovers at that time who had both been ducks, both of whom for the sake of simplicity he called Vanja.

WOLF DIAZ 6

Whether they wanted to or not, the prisoners were forced to have two outdoor breaks a day, one before lunch and one before dinner. The break area consisted of a patch of woods whose pine trees were shorn of branches the first five meters; the lower part of the trunks looked embarrassingly naked. Some played ball, some did their exercise routines in small groups, but most sat or stood, carrying on quiet conversations, smoking or trying to figure out how they would survive one more day in this realm of monotony. The scene was beautiful, in a way; the prisoners all had on prison clothes, so that thousands of pieces of mauve cloth moved slowly around the stripped tree trunks.

King's Cross was Mollisan Town's only prison, a fact to which Mayor Sara Lion gladly called attention; thanks to her social welfare program, no more than one institution was needed to take care of the city's criminals. At the same time an unceasing expansion of King's Cross went on in silence; when Maximilian was brought in, the facilities housed almost four thousand prisoners. Wing was added to wing, square kilometers of forest were cleared, and new underground passages were constantly being added. Again and again the prisoners' previous exercise yards had been transformed into cells, dining halls, workshops, and space for personnel or modern maximum-security cells.

Security at King's Cross was rigorous. The guards were well trained and armed. Their instructions were to attack rather than wait, and to assist them they had the most sophisticated electronic system imaginable. Surveillance cameras were built into the walls and thereby impossible to detect; there was at least one eavesdropping microphone per square meter, and infrared light doors and enclosures were used around the entire prison area. All information was recorded and analyzed in a computer center that was run by programmers and civil engineers who, with their experience at King's Cross, could get any job whatsoever in the private sector. For every server there was at least one backup located at a secret address in the city; it goes without saying that no one had ever escaped from King's Cross.

There were several firsthand accounts of how Maximilian passed his initial weeks at the prison, and they all testify to the same thing: Maximilian seemed to feel at home. At least he appeared unperturbed by his new situation. He ate, slept, and participated in therapy with an indifference that was reminiscent of acceptance. He prayed quietly in his cell and kept to himself. During breaks outside he would withdraw and sit on one of the stumps just beyond the provisional cricket field. Those who were there at the same time say he looked calm and collected, and most often would direct his gaze up to the sky.

That was how he was sitting when Dennis Coral sought him out the first time.

"Uh . . . sorry, but you're new, aren't you?"

Maximilian turned toward the snake and nodded. For

reptiles there was a variation on the washed-out, mauve prison clothes with broad trousers and large shirt; a closer-fitting extended shirt without sleeves. In addition, Dennis had on a mauve cap that was the internees' only free choice in the question of clothing. The mauve color contrasted beautifully against the red, yellow, and black bands so characteristic of coral snakes, embroidered with a coarse yarn in broad bands across his body, almost up to his eyes. Dennis's black face almost looked marbled; he was a beautiful animal, but the way he wriggled back and forth, he could have been a mamba.

"And . . . mmm . . . sorry, but what's this?" asked Dennis, making a movement with his head.

Maximilian understood the question because he'd gotten it many times in recent weeks. Under the cap he wore his usual cloth. One of the many doctors at the prison had given his approval. Since the first day under lock and key, Maximilian had suffered from a splitting headache. It would not go away as long as he was at King's Cross.

Maximilian noted, however, that the pain diminished somewhat when Coral approached.

"For the headaches," Maximilian answered amiably, as always.

"Mm," nodded the snake.

As with all the stuffed animals who lived in Mollisan Town, there was anxiety deep inside the snake's salt-and-pepper eyes, but despite Maximilian's considerable experience at that point, he could not immediately interpret it.

"I'm Dennis," the snake introduced himself, making a kind of pirouette with the tip of his tail, "and . . . uh . . . I know who you are. That's why . . . uh, there are a few of us who shouldn't be here, right? You, for example, I'm sure of that, you shouldn't be here. And . . . uh . . . me. I shouldn't be here. But nobody knows that. I mean, there's probably not a soul in here who wouldn't say that they're innocent, right? But . . . mm . . . I don't know. It's all the same. We . . . uh . . . are where we are. And that wasn't why . . .""

Coral fell silent and looked down at the ground. Maximilian said nothing.

"Watch out," Dennis said at last, looking up again. "That's all I was thinking, huh? Mm . . . watch out. You're starting to get a reputation. That you don't squeal or quarrel. That can be . . . uh . . . not so nice."

Maximilian still did not reply, but he met the snake's gaze and was again surprised that he could not decide what it was he saw in the mirrors that were the other animal's eyes. The tip of the snake's tail swayed back and forth in front of his face in warning.

"You . . . uh . . . you're in prison now, huh?" said Dennis. "If the others think that you're . . . mm . . . weak . . . if they take you for the kind who goes along . . . who does what's he's told . . ."

Coral shuddered so that his thin body was shaking under the mauve shirt.

"Uh . . . watch out," he said. "It's called . . . uh . . . Slave. You don't want to be that."

"Why are you warning me?" asked Maximilian.

"Uh," said Coral, but he couldn't put what he felt into words, and wriggled away instead.

For me the prison was like a place taken right out of my nightmares. I had grown up in the forest; I was used to a sky that opened over my head and the feeling of infinity right around the corner. I would not describe myself as claustrophobic, but to be put in a cell . . .

Once a month I visited him; I did not dare go more often than that. I still did not know what had preceded Duck Johnson's sudden appearance in our lives, and I did not make the connection with the Ministry of Culture; how could I have? I understood that forces were in motion, powerful forces, but I understood no more than that, and that made me slightly paranoid.

We sat on either side of a thick glass window, Maximilian and I, and talked to each other through telephone receivers. He never said much. I was forced to control myself so as not to say too much. He was pale, horridly dark around the eyes, and the pain that pounded inside his temples caused him to squint in daylight. I suffered when I saw him.

At the same time I could not keep myself away.

From what I understood about Maximilian, it was a

matter of surviving. The prisoners struggled against the destructive monotony. Every day looked like the one before; after the first year at King's Cross, Maximilian had woven a hundred and thirty-four baskets. He had grown tired of the three types of fish that were served at lunch and dinner: fish with rice and carrots, fish with potatoes and broccoli, and fish with pasta and ketchup. He knew the structure of the plaster on the wall of the cell in detail, and he knew exactly how the morning, noon, and evening scolding of the guards sounded; they constantly repeated the same invectives.

In addition, like all prisoners, he was living with a feeling of physical fear that overshadowed everything else. The days seemed to me, both when Maximilian described them and when I listened to conversations among former internees, like a sort of obstacle course where it was a matter of avoiding, to the greatest degree possible, those individuals and gangs who mistreated and degraded others to pass the time. It's not possible to describe the anxiety that the majority experience at King's Cross: Chance directs their fate, there is nowhere to flee, nothing to do to escape.

Despite a charisma that kept stuffed animals at a distance—this applied both outside as well as inside the walls—Maximilian sometimes had difficulties. For him everything changed the day when Conny Hippopotamus offered him protection—on his own initiative and without a promise of anything in return. It was something that happened; Maximilian hardly reacted anymore. With Hippopotamus as a bodyguard, life in prison became easier.

Every time I came to visit, I was reminded that he had exposed himself to a self-inflicted martyrdom. If he only spoke up about Duck Johnson's involvement, his own punishment would be mitigated. This was not a matter of betrayal or informing, I explained patiently, it was only about telling the truth. And every time I tried to get him to listen to reason, Maximilian looked at me as if I didn't understand a thing. In reality, of course, at the time I did not know with certainty that Duck was involved.

It would be almost ten months before Maximilian caught sight of Dennis Coral a second time. This happened during the lunch hour, when the prisoners were in the dining room. Conny Hippopotamus was sitting at Maximilian's right side. Hippopotamus pointed over toward the food line and nodded.

"There's the snake slave," whispered the hippopotamus. "If you need help, you can always take him."

Perhaps this conversation was once again about headaches and the helplessness of the bewildered doctors? There were pain pills that relieved the pain for short periods, but distribution was not in proportion to need.

"Snake slave?"

"Dennis Coral," whispered Hippopotamus. "His cell's not far from mine. He's in here for the rest of his life."

The dining hall was as large as a hangar and lacked windows. There was room for a thousand prisoners to sit; meals were in four shifts, thirty-five minutes per sitting. If anyone got the idea of raising his voice, even to a normal conversational level, the animal in question was punished with a baton across the neck or back of the head. Discipline was absolute.

"Coral fell in love," whispered the hippopotamus, just as a fly sat down to the left of Maximilian, poking at his lukewarm rice with distaste. "A real romance, great passion, but the husband found out about it. He followed one night when his wife went to the hotel where she used to meet Dennis Coral. He made his way into the hotel room; the snake had not yet arrived, and the husband's anger knew no bounds. It ended with him cutting her up, emptying out her cotton, just as Dennis Coral came in the door to his appointed love meeting. How it happened I don't know—if I understood correctly, the husband was some type of mammal—but the snake found his weak spot and beat him unconscious. Then Dennis Coral took his victim with him out to the forest and buried him alive. Disgusting story. Dennis Coral still maintains that he's innocent."

"He is a snake slave?" Maximilian repeated.

"Shh," Hippopotamus hissed, because Maximilian always spoke in a normal conversational tone. "Coral is a Slave. He has lost his soul in here. You can do whatever you want with him, he can't say anything. You can demand whatever you want from him, he can't protest. He may be useful."

"Leave Dennis Coral alone," said Maximilian.

But he said this somewhat too loudly, and behind his head he heard the swoosh of a baton before he collapsed with his face right down in the fish.

Dennis Coral lived with a secret. He had done so as long as he could recall, and this had marked his life. The secret was part of his makeup, and he could think of it as though he were carrying a time bomb sewn into his body, as if someone at the factory had played a deadly joke on him. Why—and this was the question he asked himself over and over again during his youth—was he forced to discover it? Why couldn't the secret simply rest in the dark shadows that could be called his soul?

He knew exactly when it happened, when he discovered it. He had been fifteen years old. He had been standing in the schoolyard in Tourquai talking with one of his classmates, a whale who played on the same curling team as Dennis. The school was in the center of that part of the city, an asphalt landscape where the schoolyard resembled a deep, empty well in a giant's stone-paved garden; the sun never found its way to the bottom.

Dennis had met the whale a few months earlier, but suddenly this day, in the middle of a sentence, he knew. The insight was as inescapable as a wad of gum in your fur; never again would he be able to talk with the whale without getting that hollow feeling in his belly and the fear and the shame that followed so quickly after. Later he thought he must have known about it much longer without admitting it.

What struck Dennis on the schoolyard was love. But the whale was a male, just like Dennis.

His parents could not be called conservative, other than in the sense that they were old-fashioned. They lived a secure, comfortable life rooted in routines and humility. While he was growing up, Dennis Coral had never heard them say a single degrading word about anyone—other than sometimes about Mayor Sara Lion, but then with a clear factual issue as a starting point—and he had never heard them sit in judgment over the lifestyles of others.

What Dennis did know was that no one in his parents' circle of friends was homosexual, but of course you couldn't be sure about such things. Without there being any homosexuals in the school or on TV that Dennis could remember or disapprove of, he nonetheless decided from that first moment of insight never to tell anyone how he felt.

Sometimes in life it is the case—and I am speaking from my own experience—that intuitively you make incorrect decisions. No one chooses, with open eyes, a path in life that leads into incomprehensible labyrinths or dead ends. Dennis Coral became, like so many of us, panic-stricken at not being the stuffed animal he wanted to be. And he chose—you must remember that he was only fifteen years old at the time—not to accept himself.

Ever since that day on the schoolyard there was a shadow over Dennis Coral. He was weighed down by the knowledge that he carried, knowledge that strengthened with the years. In secret he had devoted himself to an experiment or two, and the conclusions were always the same. Females exercised no attraction whatsoever for him; males did.

Living a life of secrets and lies can, I have been able to observe at close hand, create a certain energy. This energy often goes to the more destructive aspects of the same life. But exceedingly few are able to live a life based on denying who they are. Shame was like a wet rag over Dennis's character and personality, and indifference became his attitude.

When, due to circumstances so laughably accidental that I do not even intend to go into them, he landed in a situation that singled him out as involved in a drama of passion, it was as if fate were laughing right in his face. In his own absurd manner, Dennis realized that the punishment to which the court sentenced him was no more than right, even if his crime was a completely different one.

Self-denial.

And why did he search out Maximilian that day on the exercise yard? Obviously he could not explain it, but somewhere in Maximilian's charisma was a promise of atonement, and Dennis Coral must have sensed this.

I t's over," said Adam Chaffinch.

He had been silent since we came, and only now did he look up from the table. He observed each and every one of us searchingly for a long time.

"It's over," he repeated. "But that is my decision. You all have to make your own conclusions. For my part, I know. It's over, but I think it is now that it begins."

We were sitting at Der Lachen Hunde at Krönkenhagen on the Dondau, and darkness had fallen over our city. Along the river there was a whole battery of restaurants, some miserable pizza dives, others seven-star gourmet restaurants. Der Lachen Hunde was neither nor. Fritz Polar Bear ran his little place as if it were a personal neighborhood tavern; the stuffed animals who weren't regulars had to put up with the fact that Fritz knew the majority by name and preferred exchanging a few words to filling orders.

"I've given notice," said Adam. "I do not intend to be a deacon any longer in the service of the church."

We almost always had the same window table. Sitting there, with the water outside and the old-fashioned lanterns on the pier on the other side of the river, was like finding yourself on another planet. The odor of food, smoke, and community. The murmur from the guests, the clinking of glass and porcelain from the bar, created a special sort of coziness. That evening I seem to recall there were five of us, and I know that Missy was along. We used to linger until late, and often Fritz sat down at our table and counted the till after midnight.

I was living with the star-eyed, talented, and seductive Missy Starling at that time. She had a long theater career behind her, and with a blush that mixes pride with shame, I admit that the first time I saw her, she was on a stage. For once I had decided to celebrate my birthday—it was my thirty-third—together with a few friends, and go see a cabaret that had received fantastic reviews. That was why we ended up in a disreputable place in, I must say, the less scrupulous blocks on Pfaffendorfer Tor.

She made her entry after a quarter of an hour, but only seconds later I was enchanted. The harsh, dark, melodic singing voice that came out of the slender, feminine, and captivating body; oh yes, it is such things that males are fascinated by. That Missy Starling, when I knocked on the door to her dressing room afterward, let me enter still seems unbelievable. And it was of course no less remarkable that only a few days later she moved in on Schwartauer Avenue. But her impulsiveness in combination with a faintly despotic feature—which I believe she has in common with many theatrical workers, at least those I have met—was part of her charm.

I will not maintain that day-to-day life with Missy Starling was pain-free or . . . pleasant, but it was a time of passions and catastrophes, of drama and betrayal, of heaven-storming love and unfathomable contempt, and this suited me fine, afraid as I was of solidifying into the conformity of early middle age.

"Gave notice?" Missy now asked with all the drama of which her dark voice was capable. "You're not an official at the ministry . . ."

"Gave notice?" repeated a bream who worked at the telephone company.

"Can you give notice, Adam?" I asked.

The general murmur around the table indicated that we were all equally astounded, as much over the decision as over the fact that a deacon could quit, as if this were any old job.

"I can't do it anymore," Adam explained, and we fell silent. "I preach the words of the Proclamations at the same time as I think about your Book of Similes, Wolf. I talk about Magnus, but I think about Maximilian. There is no other way; the church is no longer my place."

Coming from Adam Chaffinch, these were big words: massive words, even. I was taken by the moment, and it felt strange that the murmur from the stuffed animals at the tables around us went on with unaltered strength. I almost asked them to quiet down.

"This is an end," said Adam, "but it is also a beginning. There is a meaning in everything that Magnus does. It was no accident that Maximilian sought me out in Sagrada Bastante once many years ago. And what has happened now is no accident either. Maximilian has been wrongly convicted. There is a reason for that. But we must not let this happen in vain. I have made my decision; you have to make your own."

"Adam," I replied, "we others made the same decision many years ago. We have just been waiting for you."

And carefully we laughed. Then the chaffinch smiled, raised his glass, and toasted with us. It was a moment I recall with warmth.

"But what will you do now?" asked the bream.

"Now I will evangelize for real," Chaffinch answered with a smile.

"Good!" said Missy with theatrical confidence in her voice. "I will gladly help, if I can!"

No one paid her any mind, this was just the sort of thing Missy said; she was not the helpful type.

We ordered food, and while we ate, Adam told us about his plans. I must admit that he did not impress any of us, but we put on a good face.

It was not about starting a new church, he explained. It was not about a sect. On the contrary, Maximilian's message was that rituals of that type were not required; it was only about believing, hoping, and feeling love, and that would be difficult enough.

He would start at home, at his kitchen table, he explained. And when it got too cramped there, he intended to find somewhere else equally humble. The word of Magnus had been preached far too long among gilded ornaments and expensive embroidery.

"I intend to create a Retinue," said Chaffinch, "which is neither afraid to believe nor to listen. The stuffed animals in this city are suffering. You know that, Wolf, you know it well—the terrified pursuit of success and material happiness that never has an end. Weighed down by the dogmas of the church. The thought of the Chauffeurs, and that they might come any day whatsoever. Stuffed animals are to be pitied. And if we can give them solace, we must do so. If ten stuffed animals can repeat what I say, what Maximilian has taught us, we are ten times more effective."

The evening belonged to Adam, and we were already his Retinue. His decision and his action had been braver than his words, but I sensed that there would be more than ten animals gathered around his kitchen table.

Not even I understood what Adam Chaffinch was starting that evening at Der Lachen Hunde.

After having described the evening when Adam told us about his life-changing decision, which soon enough would transform my life as well, I am forced to back up a few months. I recently mentioned my new apartment on Schwartauer Avenue. At that time you could borrow up to ninety-five percent of the investment, if you purchased a residence in an attractive part of the city. Taking out a loan was a new experience for me, and I had put on my best clothes when I left to go to the bank that morning: dark gray suit, white shirt, and dark blue tie. I had borrowed Father's black leather shoes, and even allowed myself a splash of his eau de cologne.

At the bank I was led into a small room that, in its gloomy seriousness, reminded me somewhat of the classroom in our house at home in Das Vorschutz. Dark paneled walls, dark green carpet, and a table whose varnish glistened in the glow from discreet ceiling lamps.

On the other side of the shiny polished table sat four bank officials in identical black suits. Three of them each had a fiercely knotted tie in various shades of red, while the fourth—a female—wore a reddish scarf around her neck instead. I was so nervous that I did not notice what kind of animals they were. I sat on a chair that was clearly the borrower's place, with my back stiff as an unused pipe cleaner.

Right before I got the first question, for that was what this was about—I was undergoing a regular interrogation in there—I thought it looked as if the bank official with the scarf was crying. Large tears fell as if from her eyes. But neither she nor her three colleagues seemed to notice that, so I thought perhaps I must have imagined it, and when she asked her first question to me, her eyes were just as dry as mine.

"Wolf Diaz," she said, "on the question about occupation you have indicated 'Writer.' What exactly do you mean by that?"

I'd been asked that question many times before, and I had learned to answer it evasively. I knew that no one asked out of genuine interest; there was always an ulterior motive.

Was I famous? Was I a journalist? And in this case, did my writing lead to a steady income? Because Adam Chaffinch was still paying me, I could answer somewhat fuzzily about the writing but more clearly about the monthly payments that were made to my account.

One of the other bank officials took over the lead and began to ask questions about the apartment that I was about to purchase, and it was while we were talking about drainage and pipe replacement that I thought I saw it again from the corner of my eye. The female on the other side of the table, sitting there in her strict suit and her white blouse, observed me with unchanged acuity at the same time as tears again began rolling down to her lap.

This was highly unusual.

I looked at the other three, but none of them reacted. And I kept to the subject, of course; the loan was much too important to risk it by saying something about those tears. Before the meeting was over—we sat for perhaps half an hour in the bank's sober interrogation room—it happened two more times, and when I left I was sure I had not been mistaken. Perhaps, I thought, it was some type of disease? There were so many ailments that you weren't aware of.

One week later I was called to the bank again, to sign the actual loan papers. I had been informed by telephone that they had decided to grant me the loan, and therefore I was more relaxed this time. I was received by one of the four official animals I had met the last time, now in his regular office, and while he instructed me on where I should write my initials and my name, I asked in complete goodwill what the reason was for his colleague's tears the other day. Personally, I admitted, I always cried when I was slicing onions.

"Yes," he replied, "Maria is . . . a little special."

There was a discomfort in his voice that made me immediately regret it. I should not have asked. I hurried to sign where he had made little pencil marks in the loan documents, but he continued talking.

"She is rather new here, Maria," he said. "A real rising star. Won't stay long in our department. Valedictorian, scholarships, all of that. And then there are the tears . . ."

He sounded bitter, and I tried to distract him by asking questions about the interest rates that were in the document, but this did not get him to stop. He obviously needed to talk about his new colleague. He thought she was at least as peculiar as I had thought.

"She maintains that it's about . . . injustices," he explained with an obvious repudiation in his voice. "Or animals to feel sorry for. She weeps when she happens to think about something that . . . something she has seen or read. Do you understand?"

"No," I answered honestly. "I must say that I do not really understand."

"She's nuts," he stated simply. "She says that she cries because she happens to think of someone to feel sorry for. She can't avoid it, she says."

He shook his head. I shook my head too, giving back the signed papers.

"And when might the money be in my account?" I asked.

"She's out of her mind," he continued. "If I understand the matter correctly, all the directors have their eyes on her. Last week I heard that she had three job offers, both here and at Banque Mollisan—all at salaries I am never going to see. And then she sits and cries because it's a shame about some lizard who can't make it across the street. Do you get it?"

"No," I answered. "It sounds unbelievable. Hmm. Back to my loan . . . I was wondering when the money might be in my account?"

"The loan, yes," he answered slowly. "The loan. Tomorrow. You'll have the money tomorrow."

I stood up, thanked him, and left the bank.

It is not strange that I related this story to Adam Chaffinch the same evening when we met. In part I was exhilarated by the loan that I had been granted and the apartment on Schwartauer Avenue that was no longer just a dream; besides, the story was funny. One of the bank's management trainees who sat there in her strict bank clothing and wept over the injustices of the city.

Adam was interested, but I never sensed the extent of his interest.

Adam and I were working day and night on how his Retinue should be built up, but even more on what to focus on from the Book of Similes. Most often we were at my place on lime green Schwartauer Avenue, but sometimes up at his place on orange yellow rue d'Oran. It was there too that to my undeserved surprise I encountered the crying animal from the bank the next time. Adam had not mentioned this to me in advance, so I was completely unprepared. Because she had her black suit on, I recognized her immediately. I entered Adam's bare, boring living room—he was good at many things, but home decor was not one of them—and she quickly got up from the couch.

"Diaz," she said curtly, "we meet again."

I of course went up to greet her.

"You didn't recognize me at the bank," she said, smiling broadly. "And not now either. But I was the stuffed animal that was standing up at the altar that afternoon when the angels in the ceiling at Kerkeling's church wept for Maximilian."

And then I recognized her. Maria Mink.

Unknown to me, Adam Chaffinch had made contact with the weeping bank official, and unknown to me he had—after a single long conversation with her—been able to confirm what he had already suspected when I told him about Maria Mink's tears.

That evening at home with Adam he made it easy for me to understand what a unique stuffed animal Maria was.

"I want us to gather a Retinue for Maria too, Wolf," he said. "She has something to say to Mollisan Town, something that Maximilian has taught her."

It was nothing more than that. No other discussions, no room for consideration or objections. I would be lying if I maintained that Adam's order made me happy. I returned home to Missy Starling that evening, and instead of allowing myself to be drawn into her ongoing drama as usual, a performance without spectators that always ended in effusively heated emotions in some direction, I locked myself in the bathroom and sulked the whole night. I was not so naive that I didn't understand that I felt rejected and abandoned by Chaffinch, and that it was jealousy I felt toward Mink. It would take almost a month before I had an opportunity to have a talk with Maria, and see for myself what Chaffinch had understood immediately.

Her story was of course strange. When she had been standing there in the pouring rain outside the church in Kerkeling being harassed by the ox, she only had a few months left in her studies at the business college in Tourquai. Her grades were the most outstanding in her class; she was studying in parallel at the philosophy department at the University of Amberville, and there too she dumbfounded the professors with her ability to understand and draw conclusions. Her entire life, however, Maria had been plagued by a shyness that severely impeded her, and despite the fact that she was clearly a unique talent, hardly anyone knew the name of the mink who got everything correct on all the tests.

"No one saw me," Maria related, "because I didn't dare see anyone."

Like the other stuffed animals that Maximilian healed

during our sessions, Maria could describe little of what had happened up there at the altar in Kerkeling's church. But when she finally ran away from there, it was "as if a roof had been pushed aside." That was how she described it. As if her feelings had been encapsulated in a narrow hovel, and Maximilian had pushed aside the roof and freed them.

"It was love that frightened me," she said as the tears again ran from her eyes. "It was its strength, and at the same time the lack of it, which I suddenly saw everywhere, and that since then I am never going to be able to close my eyes to. That was what Maximilian showed me, what was already inside me, love was what frightened me."

I did not really understand what she meant, but I preferred not to ask. I pointed to the tears that were falling.

"But you're crying?" I said.

"I happened to think about an ermine that was working the cash register at Monomart yesterday," she replied. "I happened to think about her claws, the most well-manicured claws I had ever seen, red as blood. And it hurts me when I think about why her claws are so perfect, and then I cry. Forget about it, Diaz. I can't close off. It will soon pass. Before I happen to think about something else."

"But . . . ," I said, "if this is what Maximilian did to you . . . ?"

"He showed me love," she answered.

"But love is happy," I said, speaking from my own experience. "Love is happiness and strength, love is—"

"Happiness is wonderful." She smiled. "Love is greater than that."

None of us believed that things would move as quickly as they did, or be so simple. Adam and Maria had originally proposed that we should have meetings with their Retinues in the large kitchen on rue d'Oran, but this was a modesty that quickly proved futile. The rumor about Maximilian had had ten years in which to take root and grow, counting from the day when Maximilian and I started our work of healing the mortally ill and deformed stuffed animals in Lanceheim. And no marketing campaign in the world is more effective than word of mouth. When the searching souls in Mollisan Town now realized that Adam Chaffinch offered an outlet for their curiosity about Maximilian and their longing for a message of love and a gentle religion of forgiveness, they streamed in from near and far.

Everywhere the spaces were filled, in halls for a hundred or for five hundred visitors. I still cannot understand how the animals showed up, especially because we kept the place and time secret as long as we could.

Adam and I worked exclusively with the Retinues, while Maria Mink continued her civilian career in parallel. Her almost unbelievable capacity for empathy made her enormously successful in the business world, and she went from success to success, even though I realize that my limited knowledge of her world makes it difficult for me to really assess her efforts. She earned ever so much money, money she gave us and which we needed. Adam and I were living on gifts and contributions, and Maria was and remained the single greatest contributor.

Our common work had been going on a few years and had almost begun to be routine the day the police came.

By then we had been housed for about a month at the Astor cinema on red-and-white-striped Bahnhofplatz. The auditorium held six hundred animals, and as long as we made sure to be ready before the Afternoon Rain, we could pay the rent with the modest collection we took in. The demand, in combination with Adam's and Maria's high level of ambition, meant that we held lectures on four of the seven days of the week.

The police came one Thursday, during one of Adam's lectures.

Adam usually divided his lectures into three parts. First he spoke about one of the similes in the Book of Similes, then he led his Retinue in a kind of strange song, and finally he invited the animals up to the stage to "testify." This might be about anything whatsoever: The purpose was not to reach any insights but rather simply to create intimacy and closeness between stage and Retinue. It was during this part of the sermon that the police stormed the cinema.

They came from all directions. Ten or so animals from the response force ran to either side of the auditorium up against the stage, and just as many rushed up to the sides of the screen. We had been completely unprepared. Adam's Retinue saw how Adam himself was brusquely taken into custody and led away, while one of the policemen shouted at us to "disperse." The whole thing was over in only a few seconds.

Adam returned home the same evening.

He had not received any explanation. On the contrary we realized, when during the following days we could think through and analyze what had actually happened, that the scare tactics were in the incomprehensibility itself. No explanations, no accusations, only proof of who had the power, and how it could be used.

After this, Adam and Maria started holding their meetings at night and in places that we tried to keep considerably more secret than a cinema in the middle of the city.

REUBEN WALRUS 7

The moon was whole. The breeze was blowing the chill of the night through his ample mustache. Reuben Walrus did not know where he was. Philip Mouse was standing a few steps in front of him; the mouse's silhouette was black and threatening.

"Stay completely still," Mouse hissed.

"What'd you say?"

Mouse turned around. "Completely still," he whispered.

Reuben stood as quietly as he could.

For a long time he thought he knew roughly where they were in Yok's labyrinthine alleys, but after twenty minutes of wandering, he had lost his orientation. They could be anywhere within a radius of a few kilometers. When at last they stopped, they were in front of an area, large as a cricket field, of half-demolished apartment buildings. Crushed facades, fallen-in ceilings, broken windows, and walls of once tolerable apartments stood like sculptures before piles of stone and debris. A landscape of decay and oblivion. Here and there in the ruins, small fires were burning, and Reuben could smell cigarette smoke. Perhaps it was from Mouse's trench coat? Or were there stuffed animals there in the darkness, sitting around the sporadic fires?

"A little ways more," hissed Mouse as he started to move.

Reuben followed without hearing what Mouse had said. They walked slowly down toward the landscape of ruins, moving carefully. After ten meters or so the private detective stopped abruptly and pulled Reuben roughly into a dark entryway. He nodded out toward the night, and Reuben turned around to discover what Mouse had already seen.

There was only one way through this area. It ran fifty-some meters from Reuben and Mouse's entryway, and was edged by debris and desolate buildings. There were still scattered streetlights here and there casting a dull glow over the asphalt. Along the way three figures came walking. Because the sidewalks were full of broken glass, waste, and large, foul-smelling pools of water, the three night wanderers were walking in the middle of the street. Seeing living stuffed animals moving through this dead landscape was fascinating. The three turned off the street after a while and followed a smaller asphalt path over toward a flat, massive building, in whose shadow they disappeared.

Reuben turned toward Mouse.

"That's where we're going," Mouse confirmed with a nod. "And it's best if we hurry."

He took a step out of the entryway, and Reuben followed. He did not know where they were going. When the telephone rang a few hours before, he had been sitting at home on Knobeldorfstrasse, hammering at the grand piano in pursuit of a harmony, or a discord, that might create additional tension in the third movement. Half panic-stricken by the fact that he was not getting anywhere and just as dejected by the fact that he was hearing so poorly, he picked up the receiver.

It had been Mouse.

"Your miracle animal is still out of reach," said Mouse. "But I think I've got hold of someone who is almost as valuable. I can pick you up. I guarantee you won't be disappointed."

The private detective did not say more than that, and he came by in his old Volga half an hour later. In silence they drove down to Yok.

"Where are we going?" asked Walrus.

"If I tell you, it won't be a surprise," said Mouse.

After the meeting with Giraffe, Mouse and Walrus had agreed on payment for an additional week. A lower cost per day, with a larger finder's fee when—or if—Maximilian could be located. Reuben's expectations were low. Mouse behaved strangely, as if he were playing the part of a private detective rather than being one.

When Mouse stopped a second time and pulled Reuben with him into the shadows, Reuben's pulse began to beat faster.

Yet another pair of creatures came walking along the road. Like the earlier group, they turned off onto the smaller path and went straight toward the large, flat building that was in darkness.

"What kind of place is it?" asked Reuben with a nod toward the building into which they all appeared to be going.

"It was once a bathhouse," Mouse whispered back. "Not anymore."

For the moment the street was empty, and Mouse and Walrus advanced quickly. When only a few meters remained, Mouse sneaked in behind an arch that appeared to be the remnant of a stairwell. The private detective was as usual wearing his long trench coat and a dark hat pulled down onto his forehead. Reuben shook his head. The clothes were hardly suitable for the occasion.

Away from civilization new stuffed animals came walking in the night, and the composer and his hired help waited while one group after another passed by.

When the interval between groups became shorter, Mouse finally emerged from the hiding place with Walrus close behind him. They fell into what more and more resembled a procession and ended up behind a pair of bears and a few steps ahead of some sort of bird and his wife. They were all en route to the abandoned bathhouse.

The first thing that struck Reuben was the massive proportions.

The bathhouse was high enough for the large diving tower and wide enough for a swimming pool where the city championships had once taken place. Through a series of inexplicable holes in the facade high up in the far wall, the moonlight made its way in. The building was in miserable condition; insulation was hanging down from the inside ceiling, and there were treacherous holes in the floor.

Then there were all the wax candles. Hundreds and hundreds of them. Small yellow flames burned steadily from every corner and cranny. They were sitting right on the floor, they were sitting on tables and chairs. The chandeliers that hung from the ceiling were so discreet that the light seemed to hover freely in the air. They spread their warmth, and the night chill outside was suddenly distant. Mouse had taken off his hat.

Then Reuben realized that the bathhouse was empty. Not a glimpse could be seen of any of the stuffed animals he had watched go in. He walked beside Philip Mouse, after the bears, and looked discreetly around. But there was only one massive room without doors.

First it was heard at a distance, and Reuben assumed that it was the customary buzz in his ears. But the sound became more and more evident. There was a roar in the room, the toneless murmur that arose when hundreds of stuffed animals whispered to one another. In the next moment Reuben came far enough up to the empty swimming pool that he could see over the edge.

There they were. In the glow of the candlelight he saw how the stuffed animals who had gone into the bathhouse now filled the bottom of the drained pool. It was already crowded. The bears ahead of Walrus and Mouse went down the steps, and the uninvited guests followed. In the shallow end of the pool there was room, but Mouse cleared a way down the slope to the deeper end. Involuntarily Reuben directed his gaze down to the bottom of the pool. Fellowship lay like a thick fog over the assembled animals. Reuben was ashamed, without really understanding why.

"We'll stand here," said Mouse.

They were somewhere in the middle of the deepest part. The murmur rolled along the smooth walls of the pool, drowning any conversations that were going on.

"What happens now?" whispered Walrus.

"No idea," answered Mouse. "This is the first time for me too."

The murmur changed character. It must have happened at some signal that Reuben and Philip had missed. The hundreds of stuffed animals in the pool were suddenly united in one key, and the chattering Retinue was transformed into a two-voiced chorus. The moment itself, from chaos to discipline, made a deep impression on Reuben. Multiplicity was transformed to accord.

The stuffed animals sang a simple melody. It was created by the two original voices executing a kind of braid pattern, changing between high and low in a way that was simultaneously ancient and ultramodern, a counterpoint disguised as a beat. Just when Reuben began to understand the structure of the piece, the choir transitioned to the conclusion through a short andante followed by a drawn-out fortissimo.

Then it was silent.

Dead silent.

And the silence dragged out in time.

When the voice from above resounded with its powerful pathos, Reuben gave a start. He had been unprepared, and he looked around in confusion. All gazes were aimed in one direction, and he twisted his neck. It was the first time he had noticed the diving tower. Highest up on the three-meter board stood a chaffinch in the beam of a white spotlight. The chaffinch had on a dark, ankle-length mantle. No microphone was visible, but the chaffinch's voice sounded strong and clear throughout the massive space.

"Tonight," he said with a sound that connected to the key of the Retinue, "I will tell the story of Igor Salmon. I will tell about an animal who did what he thought was right, without thinking about himself a single time. An animal whose faith was stronger than his will to please, stronger than his need to live comfortably, a faith stronger than life itself."

The chaffinch fell silent, and then asked humbly, "Do you want to hear this story?"

The Retinue replied in two voices.

Philip Mouse was fascinated. The private detective was not a religious animal. He had not been in church since he was a cub, and his fear of death was of the panic-stricken variety. He did not want to think about what would happen after the Chauffeurs had picked him up, neither on Sundays nor otherwise. But it was an essentially overwhelming experience to stand in an empty swimming pool in a massive bathhouse lit by wax candles in the middle of the night, and listen to the more and more frenetic Retinue's sung responses to the chaffinch's rhetorical questions.

Seeing the hope that was awakened and shone stronger

and stronger in Reuben Walrus's eyes was, thought Philip Mouse, tragic and beautiful at the same time.

It had proved to be simpler than he had thought to find the chaffinch. Everything around Maximilian was guarded and concealed, but as far as Adam Chaffinch was concerned, the situation was different. According to the phone book, Adam Chaffinch lived on orange yellow rue d'Oran in Tourquai, where Mouse did not need to wait more than an hour or two outside the entryway before the chaffinch himself came out—it was right after lunch—and let himself be followed. Mouse trailed him the following day as well.

The hope was that Chaffinch would lead him to Maximilian. Giraffe had seen the two together, and besides, Mouse had no other ideas. The results were, however, gloomy.

Chaffinch seemed to live a quiet life. From what Mouse understood when he asked around, Adam Chaffinch was an animal of habit who performed voluntary aid work at both the general library in Yok and the Lucretzia hospital. The chaffinch was taciturn and friendly, but there was not much more to say.

If Daisy had not made Philip aware that the chaffinch seemed to start up his imposing work only toward lunchtime, the idea probably never would have struck him. Such a righteous animal, with such late-morning habits? It was not in the daytime that Mouse should keep an eye on him, but at night.

Yesterday at midnight Mouse had been standing outside the bathhouse, peeking in through one of the holes in the far wall. Tonight he was standing in the middle of the empty swimming pool, letting himself be swallowed up by the atmosphere.

"The story of Igor Salmon is a story about what faith can do," said Adam Chaffinch in a reverent whisper.

The words of the chaffinch, every nuance and subtle

modulation, were heard just as clearly as if he had been right next to the walrus. Reuben was fascinated. He realized that it had to do with the sound system, but he had not heard anyone speak as clearly as this for several days. This was so fulfilling that he even forgot his otherwise skeptical attitude to preachers in general and this type of spectacle in particular. He listened devoutly.

"Igor Salmon was a wretch," continued Adam Chaffinch in his forbidding voice. "But he was called many other things besides. It was said that he was the most easily fooled animal in the city. They laughed at him.

"He was born to a prosperous family. Their large mansion was in west Amberville; their beautiful orchard ended where the forest began. Igor's parents loved him. His childhood was not remarkable, his youth was like many others, so what actually happened with Igor Salmon?"

A two-voiced sigh of wonder passed through the Retinue.

"He was afflicted by his faith," Chaffinch answered his own question. "Yes, I use the word 'afflicted.' For that was what happened. Life was never the same again. Igor Salmon had a vision, an insight; he awoke one day and knew that the Savior would come."

The two-voiced congregation let out a shout, a song, and Chaffinch waited until silence had again settled in the pool.

"Everything was different, although nothing had changed. In Igor Salmon's restless teenage breast faith had taken hold, and he understood that the grace he had been granted, the divine grace that faith entails, would not let him avoid trials. Igor's faith was such that it bordered on certainty that the Savior would come and that the Savior held his watchful hand over the city. This certainty gave him strength that not everyone possessed, and Igor realized that his duty was to use it well. The envy he encountered was unavoidable, the happiness he radiated aroused jealousy, sometimes anger, because what cannot be understood is frightening.

For Salmon himself jealousy was not possible, because he knew that all of us stood under the guardianship of the Savior and that He assigned us our roles. We must dare to believe that.

"Do you dare to believe?"

The Retinue obviously felt some uncertainty about what they were expected to answer. Adam Chaffinch continued inexorably.

"We are all doubters!" he cried out. "All of us, except Igor Salmon!

"One day one of Igor's neighbors knocked on his door. The neighbor maintained that Igor's dog had dug up his rhododendrons. The neighbor demanded compensation. It would cost at least a month's salary to plant new bushes. Igor let the neighbor wait at the door while he got his wallet and paid him the money. Without questioning the story. Without doubting his neighbor's goodwill.

"To doubt your neighbor is to doubt the Savior. Behind the false is the true, behind the malicious is the good. Anyone who believes knows that is how things are. Igor was happy for the opportunity to demonstrate his faith. When the neighbor related the episode down at the neighborhood bar that same evening, he made fun of stupid Igor. The high point of the story was the fact that Igor Salmon did not even own a dog."

This time the Retinue murmured spontaneously and not in key.

"The rumor of the wealthy 'idiot' quickly spread," continued Chaffinch from up on the diving board. "Animals from near and far knocked on Igor's door and alleged one thing more unbelievable than the other. Some of them suspected that if they had asked flat out for money, the result would have been the same. But the deception itself, and afterward telling the story about what they had pulled off at Igor's door, was perhaps even more important than the money.

"A nurse who had worked her entire life at Lakestead

House, and therefore was accustomed to lunatics, heard the story of Igor Salmon one day. She felt sorry for the poor fish who not only let himself be fooled, but was reviled so crudely besides. She decided to have mercy on him. She looked for his house, knocked on his door, and asked if he needed any help. Judging by her tone of voice, it was clear that he should say yes, and so he did. The nurse moved in, and they lived together for almost four months. After that she moved out again in a fury.

"During the time they lived together, she realized that Salmon was not mentally defective at all. He was on the contrary a sensitive, talented stuffed animal. And despite the fact that he daily and sometimes hourly let himself be fooled by idiotic, transparent lies, he was happier than the nurse was ever going to be. Angrily she left the house. Things she did not understand had always aroused her indignation."

The Retinue let a concurring murmur be heard.

"The years passed," continued Adam Chaffinch, "and one fine day Igor's money ran out. The animals' visits to his door ceased, and he was allowed to live in peace. He lived a happy life. Sometimes he grieved that he had to be so alone, but he understood that this was the trial he was forced to undergo. His faith frightened the world around him; the animals assumed that there were hidden motives behind his goodness. They could not, however, understand what they were. At regular intervals Igor Salmon sold some of the beautiful furniture that was in his parental home, and in that way he kept himself alive.

"At last came the day that comes to all of us. The Chauffeurs steered their red pickup through Amberville and parked outside Igor Salmon's house. The believing fish's days in Mollisan Town were at an end. The Chauffeurs got out of their truck and with heavy, determined steps went up to Salmon's house and knocked.

"No one opened.

"They knocked again.

"Salmon did not open.

"Salmon had been ready to meet the Chauffeurs his entire life. Nothing bad awaited him; his faith was unshakable. The reason that he did not open the door was that he had gone out the back door of the house two minutes earlier."

A sigh of confused disbelief passed through the Retinue. This was a strange sermon; it was hard to understand in what direction the chaffinch's story would go. One of the stuffed animals in the pool fidgeted nervously, and this started a chain reaction. Suddenly there was an uneasiness in the pool that had not been there before.

"But he didn't go alone!" cried Adam Chaffinch to his congregation. "Igor Salmon did not go alone through his orchard, he did not go alone into the forest, into which he had never dared go before even though he had lived at its edge his whole life. Igor Salmon did not go alone, because a few minutes before the Chauffeurs parked outside his house, Maximilian had knocked on Igor Salmon's kitchen door. And together they disappeared into the forest, the believer and the believed."

"Amen," sang the Retinue in its two voices. "Amen, amen."

Again and again they sang. The uneasiness that only moments before had been in all of them and was now dissolved made the song stronger, more liberating.

"Amen, amen," they sang.

Adam Chaffinch remained standing on the diving board for a long time. The spotlight that had been aimed toward him gradually dimmed. When the preacher was finally embraced by the same warm darkness as all the others—the light from the thousands of wax candles was yellow and flattering—he slowly withdrew. The Retinue continued to sing, and when the first stuffed animals unwillingly went up the steps in the pool, they were still singing.

Reuben Walrus went along with the others. The performance was over, and he was strangely moved. But Reuben did not manage to go more than a few steps before Philip Mouse pulled on his arm.

"Slowly," Philip whispered in his ear. "I was thinking we could exchange a few words with the preacher before we leave."

Philip Mouse led Reuben Walrus to the right of the lobby, where the shadows were deeper and darker than anywhere else in the bathhouse. There they stood quietly and waited for the stuffed animals to disappear out into the night. When silence at last returned, it took a moment, but then they saw.

There he was, the preacher, in the farther left corner of the bathhouse. He was still wearing his long gown, but without the strong spotlight it looked almost seedy. He walked slowly from candlestick to candlestick, blowing out the candles. He held his wing behind the flame, even if the concern seemed misdirected—it was a long time since the abandoned bathhouse's worn-out, pitted concrete floor had been worth protecting.

When Mouse was certain that they were alone, he carefully pulled Reuben Walrus with him out to the pool. Chaffinch did not raise his gaze, but he must have felt their presence nonetheless. Suddenly he said, "I understand that you have something on your mind."

Only then did he look up and meet their surprised gazes. The mouse and the walrus halted.

Chaffinch smiled.

"I know my Retinue," he said, observing them thoroughly. "And I noticed a couple of new animals in the pool. We all did, even if perhaps it didn't seem like it."

Mouse shrugged his shoulders. He had no desire to end up at a disadvantage.

"Perhaps you'd like to help me?" Chaffinch asked quietly. "Blowing out all these candles takes a while."

"Of course," replied Reuben.

Mouse shrugged his shoulders again. He took a few steps over toward one of the swaying chandeliers that made such a powerful impression from the bottom of the pool, and started blowing. During the afternoon he had decided to maintain a certain distance. Walrus would certainly like to talk to Chaffinch in peace. Therefore Mouse selected a chandelier a little ways away.

"I'm looking for Maximilian," said Reuben Walrus, blowing out a candle.

"So I've heard," answered Adam Chaffinch amiably.

He had nothing more to say. He continued calmly blowing out the candles, and Reuben Walrus did the same. This went on for a few minutes. They worked from the left corner of the bathhouse in toward the middle, the whole time with Philip Mouse at a respectful distance.

"Maximilian needs protection," said Adam Chaffinch when they arrived at the pool. "He doesn't think so, of course, but that's how it is."

All the questions Reuben had, and the hopes he harbored, made it hard to know how he should approach this conversation. He tugged absentmindedly at his mustache.

"Protection?" he asked. "What does Maximilian need to be protected from?"

"Above all, from himself," Chaffinch replied.

The answer came immediately.

"The external threats," repeated Chaffinch, returning to his own train of thought, "can never frighten us. But against his own . . . goodness . . . Maximilian cannot struggle. Without protection, the surrounding world will destroy him."

"What did you say?" asked Reuben. "Forgive me, but I didn't hear—"

"If we aren't there for Maximilian," Chaffinch repeated gruffly, "his goodness is going to destroy him."

The preacher nodded to himself, and then concentrated on the candles around the pool. A few silent minutes passed as Chaffinch took care of the right-hand long side while Reuben Walrus helpfully worked his way methodically down the left. They met at the short end of the pool. As the wax candles were successively extinguished, the moonlight gained the upper hand. The soft, warm yellow-red glow that had filled the bathhouse was replaced by a cold, white light, which made its way in through the holes in the decaying exterior walls.

"I want to meet Maximilian," said Reuben.

"You don't want to meet Maximilian," replied Adam Chaffinch sternly. "You want him to grant you a miracle. For you Maximilian could be anyone at all."

Reuben was ashamed. Chaffinch was right.

"Forgive me," he asked. "It's true. It's nothing less than a miracle I ask for. I'm a composer, that's what they call me. I'm in the process of losing my hearing, and the doctors say there's nothing that can be done. Time passes, and . . . I don't know where I should turn. I spoke with someone who said . . . there were several who said that my only hope was Maximilian."

Chaffinch nodded.

"And how do you think the miracle itself comes about?" asked Chaffinch.

Reuben shook his head. He did not know; he hadn't thought about it.

"That he would receive you in an apartment and give you a miracle? That it could be bought? Or that you could beg your way to it? Did you think this was something he stored in a desk drawer and doled out to animals that came to visit? I don't want to hurt you, but I'm sincerely interested."

"I don't know," Reuben answered quietly. "I . . . met a giraffe who . . . he had just been walking on a street and—"

"Heine," Chaffinch nodded quietly. "Didn't it strike you that Heine had never asked for a miracle? That he actually has a hard time believing that it happened?"

Reuben still had no answer.

"I don't know what I thought," he said at last.

"That honors you," answered Chaffinch.

"What?"

"That honors you. That you didn't worry about the matter honors you. It speaks for you."

"Really?"

Adam Chaffinch blew out the last candle.

The moon was still whole and the gentle wind cold against the cloth when Reuben Walrus and Adam Chaffinch left the dilapidated bathhouse. Philip Mouse walked a few meters behind them. His mission was not yet complete; he had been contracted to find Maximilian, and every lead was valuable. Therefore he made sure to hear everything the finch and the walrus said, without intruding.

"You must prove yourself worthy," said Chaffinch.

"What'd you say?"

Reuben had a harder time understanding what the chaffinch said when the treacherous breeze carried each and every word with it westward.

"You must prove yourself worthy," repeated Chaffinch.

"Yes, yes, I understand that," answered Reuben politely.

"Maximilian himself will certainly meet you; he wants to meet as many as possible. The problem is that . . . there are getting to be too many. . . . We must make a selection."

"We? Meaning who?"

"It becomes unmanageable otherwise. We select which

ones get to meet him, but that is not the same as having your dreams fulfilled. He is a Savior, not a spirit in a bottle."

"What?"

"He's not the spirit in the bottle that fulfills wishes."

"I realize that."

They had come halfway through the deserted landscape of ruins that surrounded the bathhouse. It was just as silent and still as it had been a little more than an hour ago, but the shadows that the moonlight produced seemed longer and sharper now.

"What should I do?" asked Reuben.

"Do?"

"To be . . . worthy?"

Adam Chaffinch stopped and looked intensively at the old walrus.

"You will be tested," he said.

Philip Mouse stopped too, a few meters away. They stood at a crossroads. A narrow asphalt path led back up onto the street, another slithered away toward the outer area of the ruins. It was obvious that Adam Chaffinch intended to take leave of them here.

"I know that you are short of time. If we can, we will take that into account. I promise nothing."

Chaffinch extended his wing, and the walrus shook it as well as he could. After that he turned for the first and only time directly to Philip Mouse. The chaffinch spoke very clearly, as if it were Mouse that was deaf.

"It's no use searching, Mr. Mouse. Better animals than you have tried and failed."

The words hung in the air a few moments before they fell to the ground. Chaffinch turned around and continued quickly down the long path toward the ruins. Walrus and Mouse remained standing and watched him.

"And now?" asked Reuben at last.

"I wouldn't say no to a whiskey," said Mouse.

The moment Philip Mouse opened the door to his office, they attacked him. The Morning Rain had just ceased, and his trench coat was still wet. He took a heavy blow to the neck, and they were over him before he realized what had happened. They dragged him through Daisy's office, and the sight that met him inside was macabre.

With a rope that he had never seen before, they had hung one of the Windsor chairs up in the ceiling fan. In the chair sat Daisy. Her dress was torn to shreds, and they had taped her mouth shut. Her hands were secured behind her back, her legs tied to the legs of the chair. With a mechanical screech the fan still managed to turn, so that Daisy was twisting around and around.

Mouse tried to take in the situation. There were three of them. They had pulled nylon stockings over their heads. They were dressed in black from top to toe, and judging by bodies and movement patterns, he guessed that they were mammals. More than that, it was hard to say.

They pulled Philip up from the floor and pressed him down on the desk chair. Two of them remained standing behind him, holding him in place, while the third placed himself at an angle in front of the desk, screaming something that at first was impossible to hear. The voice was shrill. "It goes like this! It goes like this! It goes like this!"

He got a hard blow to the face. It came without warning, from the right. Two days had passed since Philip Mouse and Reuben Walrus had visited Adam Chaffinch, and this was the result of too many questions in too short a time. A reward for quickness, thought Philip, taking the next blow.

The animal that had screamed went up to Daisy and the whirling chair. This caused Mouse to stiffen. There was no reason to mix Daisy up in this.

"She knows nothing," he protested. "She hasn't asked any questions."

The masked stuffed animal went over to the bookshelf and reached for a table lamp that Philip had bought many years ago from a poet who changed professions and nowadays sold spices.

Sparks came out of the wall outlet as the masked animal tore the lamp loose and used it as a weapon. He struck wildly around himself. Books and decorative objects fell to the floor. He attacked the paintings and the armchair.

"Bloody hell bloody hell bloody hell bloody hell bloody hell bloody hell bloody hell!" he screamed. "Bloody hell bloody hell bloody hell!"

He turned around and attacked the desk, tossing aside papers that whirled as if the Evening Storm was blowing right through the room. The pistol that had been concealed under a folder on the table slid down onto the floor right next to Philip's left paw. The masked stuffed animal then began hitting the lamp against the floor, striking like a maniac, and he was not content until the desk gave way and with a crack broke in two.

Then he turned around, taking a few steps toward Daisy. He raised the lamp that he was holding in his paw, aiming a violent blow. He hit her cheek, and she screamed loudly in pain. The adrenaline was pumping in Philip's body. The hoodlum struck Daisy a second time, and she jerked back so violently that the chair on which she was sitting fell to the floor, the fan fell down over her, and Philip tore himself out of his attackers' grasp.

After that, everything happened very fast.

Philip Mouse threw himself down under the desk and got hold of his pistol. With the weapon in hand he rolled away from the animals that had been standing at his side and who now threw themselves after him. He managed to kick one of them with his shoe; it landed right over the head. The other could not catch up with him. The private detective quickly got up on his knees and fired the pistol at the animal that had struck Daisy.

The bullet went through the hoodlum's leg. With a howl he fell down on what remained of the fan. Right next to him Daisy lay on her side, still tied to the chair.

The pistol in Philip's hand changed the situation. Instead of taking up the battle, the three attackers reacted as if they had been talking about it and come to agreement in advance. They fled.

The one with the hole in his leg was limping, and the one who got Philip's foot in the head was dazed, but they were running anyway. As well as they were able.

Mouse set aside the weapon and bent over Daisy. He carefully pulled the tape from her mouth. And when he had stroked her across the forehead and assured himself that she was all right, he went out to her office to find a knife to free her from the rope and tape.

What the hell was that? he thought. What the hell was that?

Fassbunden Church is in central Lanceheim, built in the bombastic eighteenth-century style that would be so scoffed at during the centuries that followed. While many buildings in the same style were torn down during the late nineteenth century, the church remained. Today it is the foremost example of the grandiose, not to say megalomaniac, idea of good architecture of that bygone age.

A stone's throw from the church is the monastery, the only one of its type in Mollisan Town. There is a convent in south Yok, not far from the retirement home, but it was to the monks that Philip Mouse embarked that same afternoon. He had been there to visit Brother Tom before, but it must have been more than fifteen years ago. That visit was, as Philip recalled, very brief. On the other hand he recalled, strangely enough, a detail that had etched itself into his memory in the mysterious manner that details have a way of doing. If the cowl Brother Tom had worn was gray or dark red, Philip had already forgotten that same day. But in contrast, the detective could, even fifteen years later, see Tom's shoes in front of him, the red leather sandals that he had never seen either before or since.

Not until today.

One of the three intruders that attacked Daisy and him had just that kind of sandals on.

Now Philip Mouse stepped up to the impressive monastery gate and used the door knocker. The monastery was built like a regular fortress of red brick. No one came in through the gate without being invited, and—looking at it a different way—it was not easy to get out.

A rooster appeared. It looked funny when the little stuffed animal stuck his head out through the enormous gate.

Rust red, thought Philip. The tunic was rust red.

The rooster looked kindly at the private detective, who explained that he had come to see Brother Tom. With a nod he was let in.

The monastery received visitors in a gloomy stone hall from which three stairways led, one in each direction. The daylight filtered in through a series of small openings up under the ceiling, which meant that the floor of the hall was in darkness. The rooster went off, and Philip was left alone. There was no furniture, not even a bench to sit on, and there was a damp chill in the air.

The mouse leaned nonchalantly against the wall and prepared to wait. He was just about to sit down on one of the stair steps when Brother Tom came down the middle staircase.

"Tom!" exclaimed Philip. "I thought someone would come and get me? Last time I got—"

"We both remember what happened last time," replied Tom.

With the rust-colored tunic Brother Tom looked less like a spider than he usually did. He radiated a kind of calm, there was a gentle friendliness in his gaze that had not been there before, but at the same time one of the reasons for Tom's considerable success as a poker player had been that he was difficult to read.

"I'm sorry about last time," said Philip Mouse. "It was simply not—"

"That was ages ago," answered Brother Tom. "Nothing to talk about now."

The last time Philip Mouse had come to visit was to find out how Tom became a believer and monk overnight. About how it was that this had happened the night when the largest winnings of the century had been paid out at VolgaBet. No one knew who had won, or if the betting that night had been manipulated, but Mouse had a feeling that Tom was involved in some way.

They had thrown the private detective out of the monastery that time. To his great surprise, Philip had ascertained later that Brother Tom had remained within the monastery walls.

"No, I have a completely different type of errand today, Tom," the mouse confirmed.

When Brother Tom showed no signs of going anywhere,

Philip assumed that the meeting would take place here, in the darkness of the hall. And that it was just as well to make the best of the situation. He breathed in the damp, close air and shrugged his shoulders.

"Nowadays I . . . investigate things," said Mouse. "It can be a dirty job sometimes, but I do it anyway. And now I am searching for a stuffed animal—"

"Is it someone in the monastery?"

There was no worry in Brother Tom's voice, but no surprise either.

"No, I don't believe so."

"For it has happened before. That stuffed animals have hidden in here. . . ."

Philip felt uncomfortable standing there, in the middle of a massive hall, and he decided to get to the point.

"I only know the name," he said. "The stuffed animal I am seeking is named Maximilian."

Despite the darkness the reaction was apparent. Brother Tom's eyes widened, his chin fell down, and his mouth opened. Several of his many arms stuck out of the tunic.

"Shh," whispered Tom. "Not here. We'll go . . . to the garden."

And without further ado the monk led the mouse up the left stairway, through a series of smaller, vaultlike rooms and along a colonnade alongside the magnificent courtyard that was surrounded by a dense, high hedge. It was a walk of a few minutes. Brother Tom said nothing in the meantime, but he got more and more out of breath.

"Here," he said at last with a nod.

In the hedge next to the colonnade a small arch opened. The garden that was concealed behind it caused Mouse to involuntarily sigh. To the right hovered a heaven of pink and white cherry blossoms; to the left was a labyrinth of boxwood-lined gravel pathways between which mimosa trees and a jungle of pink and red rosebushes had burst into full bloom. The scent of flowers and the explosive display of color, intermingled in the midst of the stern monastery building, were overwhelming. Even for someone dressed in a beige trench coat and a dark hat.

"Unbelievable," exclaimed Philip Mouse.

Brother Tom conveyed the mouse with unaltered haste along the winding gravel paths, and he did not stop until they had reached a bower of grapevines over a green wrought-iron bench. There he signaled to Mouse to sit down, and he himself sat down close beside.

"That name," whispered Brother Tom breathlessly, "may not be said out loud in this monastery."

"Maximilian?" asked Mouse, startled.

"Shh!" admonished Tom. "I'm begging you."

"But . . . ," Mouse began without arriving at which of all the questions he should ask first. "But—"

"There are those who maintain that he is the Savior, the Messiah."

"Messiah?" echoed Mouse. "Maximilian?"

"Dear friend, stop that immediately!"

Brother Tom's cheeks were red. He believed that Mouse was provoking him. Now that they had sat down on the bench, the birds resumed their concert, and Philip sensed that was why they had sat just here. Their words were drowned in an extravagant chirping and twittering.

"Where is he?" asked Philip, not beating around the bush.

"I don't know," replied Tom. "No one knows. If we knew, we would take him prisoner and put him on trial."

"Take him prisoner?"

"He pretends to be the Messiah!"

"Does he?"

"He has never denied it."

"But the police can't arrest someone who—"

"Not the police," interrupted Tom with a contemptuous

snort. "We're the ones who will hold him accountable. The church. This is a matter for us."

Philip Mouse nodded thoughtfully, as if what Brother Tom had said was reasonable and sensible. He dug in the inner pocket of his trench coat and took out a pack of half-smoked cigarettes; a kind of reserve pack for when he forgot to buy a new one. He found one of the longest butts, lit it, and took a deep puff.

"Have you seen him?"

Brother Tom shook his head. "Never. But we've been talking about him for many years. At the beginning no one listened. And when we finally understood that . . . others were listening . . . it was too late."

"Too late?"

"Then he had already . . . been heard of. If you try to stop it now, in the wrong way, he becomes a martyr. That is probably the worst thing that can happen. Now you have to . . . consider."

"In the wrong way?"

"He has several friends. A chaffinch and a snake. They're not saying anything new. Talk about faith and hope and love. There was a mink too, who was especially trouble-some. We tried to make her see reason a few times. I mean, not here, but . . . yes . . . our animals talked with her. She refused to listen. I thought we ought to have been . . . more definite."

"You haven't got hold of Maximilian?" asked Philip with surprise. "I thought you had enormous resources."

"We do. That's what has made certain parties . . . ex-tremely worried. And we have devoted a number of years to this."

Philip put out his cigarette in the gravel under the bench. The church had tried for several years; he thought he could manage it in a few days.

There was not much more to say. The mouse and the

monk wound up the conversation, and went back together.

On the way through the colonnade they encountered an elderly deacon who blocked their path and looked searchingly at Philip.

"Brother Tom," he said without releasing his gaze from Philip. "A visit, I see?"

"I'm following my old friend to the exit," explained Brother Tom, doing nothing to conceal his restlessness. "He's in a bit of a hurry."

The deacon extended his claw.

"Nice to meet you," he said, smiling gently. "Your name?"

Philip extended his paw and thought about saying just what his name was, when the elderly deacon held up a claw.

"Wait, don't tell me. It's Philip Mouse, isn't it?" he said.

All of Brother Tom's arms and legs were gesticulating wildly at the same time as he tried to draw Mouse away from there.

"We're in a hurry, Philip," he said.

"Philip Mouse," repeated the deacon. "You are a stuffed animal of normal intelligence, aren't you? You don't need a clearer warning, do you?"

For once the flabbergasted mouse was speechless. The deacon, a large eagle, looked at the mouse for a moment as if he were prey, and then left.

"Who was that?" asked Philip.

"You don't want to know," answered Tom. "But get out of here now, Mouse. I think you've already stayed much too long as it is."

WOLF DIAZ 7

The day Eva Whippoorwill climbed down from her tree and ran up to Das Vorschutz to receive Maximilian had been the thirteenth of October.

While Maximilian was growing up, therefore, the thirteenth was celebrated as his birthday, and we maintained the tradition during the years he was in prison. We invited Sven Beaver and Eva Whippoorwill and tried to make something special out of the day, tried to remember and celebrate Maximilian the individual, Maximilian the stuffed animal, rather than Maximilian the Savior. Most often this happened in more intimate gatherings, and the two Retinues were left out for practical reasons. But this year, the eighth after the unjust conviction of Maximilian, Maria Mink had conceived a larger event. During the fall she had hinted at this several times for her Retinue, which by this time was truly curious. For that reason we had booked one of our largest meeting places long before, a library that was above one of the retirement homes in Yok and which we had used on a few prior occasions. Changing places often, not starting the meetings before midnight, and not revealing the

time or place more than a few days in advance were routines we no longer thought about; they were obvious. We
did not have any further incidents with the authorities, but
I did sometimes feel watched, and I know that the church
made sure to remind Adam at regular intervals—sometimes
not very subtly—that they were still following his life and
activities.

"Cake isn't vulgar, it's just rewarding," said Maria with
a certain degree of irritation.

"And good," I pointed out quietly.

We were discussing the birthday celebration, and Adam
Chaffinch had expressed his hesitation about serving cream
cake during the break. Seldom if ever did they get involved
in each other's arrangements. Adam performed his ser-
mons in a rather traditional manner; Maria saw to it that
her meetings had a warmer setting. Between them, however, there was always mutual respect. Adam had thought
about taking part in Maria's Retinue on the night of the
thirteenth, and so Maria wanted to hear what he thought
about the cake.

"I don't know if cream and Maximilian go together,"
said Chaffinch in an attempt to conclude the discussion.

He knew that Maria would do as she wanted in any
event, and he regretted even opening his beak.

We were sitting in one of the rooms on the lower floor in
what I and many others called "Maria's House." Through
transactions the details of which I do not know, Maria Mink
purchased an entire apartment building in east Lanceheim,
and for tax purposes donated it to a foundation run by herself. After that, she had turned the house over to us without
restrictions, and it was now in Maria's House that I spent
most of my time during the day. But more about that later.

"Cream goes with most things," Maria smiled.

"Do you want me to make a note of that?" I asked
jokingly.

Maria gave her consent and said that such pearls of wisdom should not only be written down, they should be embroidered besides.

This too I noted, and in the corner of my eye I saw that even Adam had a hint of a smile.

The atmosphere was jovial, and when we left the place half an hour later we all had the feeling that the evening's meeting would be unusually exciting and vigorous.

I escorted Maria; we took her car to drive over to the bakery on mustard yellow Krönkenhagen, where she had already ordered her cream cakes. On the way we continued the discussion about how the evening would take shape.

"Do you know how many are coming?" she asked.

Maria was always convinced that no one would show up at her lectures, and when the meeting place was filled time and again to the last seat, she was always equally overwhelmed.

"It will be a full house, Maria," I answered. "As usual."

"But are you sure?"

I nodded.

Tears were running from her eyes as she turned right onto Eastern Avenue, but nowadays I did not even think about that. Everyone who associated with Maria was used to this constant weeping, and even if it might sometimes be perceived as disruptive—or downright provocative—it was a natural aspect of who she was. The first months I had curiously asked her each time what she was thinking about, but after getting answers that varied from "a limping chimpanzee on the crosswalk over there" to the discussion of our generation's debt to our parents' generation, I stopped asking.

"I was thinking about talking about unrequited love, Wolf. Do you think I can do that?"

This was one of the lectures that was always most appreciated. Maria described unrequited love in a new way each time, but her fundamental message of course remained the same. And at no time did her Retinue go home in the cool night across Mollisan Town as sorrowfully satisfied as after one of these lectures.

"Or have I done it once too often?" she asked while she passed a Volga truck from Springergaast. "Should I do something different?"

"Never," I replied with certainty. "Never. Talk about unrequited love."

She shook her right hand lightly so that the bracelet with little hanging silver pigs slipped down on her arm a little.

"Don't they get tired of it?"

If it had been anyone else, I would have maintained with certainty that this was coquetry, fishing for praise. But Maria was always honestly worried. It had to do with her level of ambition. She knew her value, but she always wanted to be better. Her reward was in the Retinue's appreciation.

"No," I said. "It is never tiresome."

It went as I had predicted. In the twilight the library on the sixth floor of the Wrest retirement home was packed with stuffed animals. No new faces, only old familiar ones, but there was an unusual sense of exhilaration. The birthday celebration was something new. It was unusual that both Maria and Adam would be at the same place at the same occasion, and due to this, the assembly felt chosen and special.

Cream cakes were lined up on a side table, and Maria had decided that the event should start with the celebration itself, cake and coffee, before the more ordinary part of the night began. It was not possible for Eva Whippoorwill to come—it was something about her throat—but Maximilian's discoverer and father Sven Beaver stood conversing with Adam. Sven tried to disregard the many curious looks that were thrown in his direction, but I could see how hard it was for him not to feel watched. I smiled to myself as I observed him, and knew how he would prefer to return home to the calm and silence of Das Vorschutz.

It happened just when we were about to take our places in the library and listen to Maria's sermon.

It began with the tall windows breaking, and thousands of small pieces of glass raining down over us.

It was unbelievable. No one understood what was happening, but the screaming contributed to the panic. The cold evening air streamed into the library, and there were voices outside that we still barely heard.

We had not seen the arrows.

Seconds later, when the next salvo was sent into the library through the windows that were still unbroken— closely followed by a hailstorm of glass—I understood what was going on. They were standing down on the lawn in front of the building with bows and shooting toward us. The assembled stuffed animals ran around like intoxicated bumblebees among the bookshelves, looking for shelter. The screams meant that no one noticed that no more arrows were coming, that there were no more windows to break.

It was right when the animals had calmed down somewhat that the door to the library was thrown open, and there they stood. Most turned around to see who they were, and the three animals with black nylon stockings over their heads gave rise to many terrified shouts. But only Mr. and Mrs. Kwai screamed in recognition: "Not you!"

"Let's see if your damn Maximilian can fix this!" the hoodlums yelled, throwing a burning bundle of straw right in the midst of us.

Perhaps it sounds ludicrous to state that this was dangerous. If the fire happened to brush against any of the stuffed animals in the library, if a spark traveled through the air and landed against nylon or rayon, against cotton or polyester, it would have been a catastrophe. Instead, with combined efforts, Adam Chaffinch and a few others poured all that was left of the juice and coffee over the flaming threat and extinguished the fire. Sven Beaver was already on his way toward the exit and the hoodlums, who of course were running away.

I went up and consoled Mrs. Kwai. Sobbing, she was sitting on a chair near her husband. She held her face buried in her paws and wept.

"We'll never escape them," she sobbed. "And now we've drawn them here!"

"Who are you talking about, Mrs. Kwai?" I asked.

"The hoodlums. It's Bull's son, I think. We never should have come."

"Bull's son?"

But her explanations were drowned in sobbing and tears, and I got no more out of her right then. The stuffed animals in the library were slowly calming down. Adam organized a small group that began to clean up the chaos, while Maria helped the elderly find their coats. There would be no sermon tonight; we would all remember this birthday for the wrong reason.

I found Mr. Kwai at the checkout desk, where he was standing together with three rats who were helping each other get rid of glass splinters in their fur.

"Mr. Kwai," I said, "may I speak with you a moment?"

We moved to the side to talk.

"Mr. Kwai," I said, "if I understood your wife correctly, you know who they were?"

He stared at me in surprise and shook his head.

"Did she say that?"

"She said that," I confirmed.

He stood silently for a few moments, but soon made up his mind.

"It's true," he said gloomily. "It's true. Oh, I'm so sorry. I beg your pardon. I should have realized—"

"Realized what, Mr. Kwai?"

"That they would follow us here. We've had them on our heels for months. I know who they are. We have a bull that lives on our street. He's always been surly. He knows that we belong to Maria's Retinue, we've never made a secret of that. And he mocks us openly. Says terrible things about Maximilian. Bull's son was one of those hoodlums this evening."

"But," I said, "why . . . ?"

"Why?" Mr. Kwai repeated my question. "Why? Look around you, Diaz. This is not just happening to us. I have to speak with Chaffinch."

Mr. Kwai hurried off, and I stood like a question mark watching him go.

When we went home that night—it took several hours to clean the room, and when we left the broken windows were still there with their spiky openings, screaming out what had happened—I realized for the first time something that everyone else already knew. Parts of our Retinues were being persecuted for their faith and conviction. Perhaps not as aggressively and dramatically as what I had just been a part of, but it came as a shock to me that many testified to similar experiences.

We passed through deserted Yok along deep blue Avinguda de Pedrables, en route to the bus stop. The street looked almost black at night, and in their conversations the animals described the same thing over and over again. It was about taunts and jeers; someone spoke about anonymous threats in the mail, and someone else maintained that he had lost a job because of the Retinue.

"You're living in a bubble, Wolf," Chaffinch said irritably when I expressed my astonishment and alarm. "And maybe that's a good thing."

I did not reply. I was sincerely moved.

Many times I have thought that Maximilian's birthday ought to have prepared me better for what was waiting further along on my life's path. Unfortunately that is not the way life works. Perhaps I ought to say, fortunately.

I had sensed the hatred that was all around us; one day I would be staring it right in the eyes.

The third time Maximilian met Dennis Coral, they had both been confined to King's Cross so long that they had lost track of days and weeks and months and years. Time seemed to go slower for anyone who ignored it. I do not know if time had ever meant anything to Maximilian. As a twelve-year-old he had been more aware than an adult, and as an adult, more innocent than a twelve-year-old.

Once a month I still went out to the jail to see him. Maximilian knew nothing about Adam Chaffinch or the Retinue we had created. I assumed that the guards routinely eavesdropped on all conversations between visitors and prisoners, and the less they knew, the better.

But Maximilian never asked about life outside the walls or about the time that passed. He listened when I babbled on about what I was doing; he observed me with his gentle indulgence when I continued to nag about Duck Johnson. Sometimes he said something that I made note of and later entered into the Book of Similes, but often we simply sat there, on each side of the glass, and with my own eyes I could see that the hope that burned within him was not affected by the time that passed, or by the headaches that pounded behind his eyes, or by the monotony that sucked the life out of most of the others in there. It was hope, his stark, unshakable hope, that meant that he endured.

The third time Maximilian encountered Dennis Coral was in the library. By then Maximilian had been in King's Cross for over nine years. The prisoners who conducted themselves especially well might enjoy certain privileges over the years. Visiting the library once every other month was one of these.

The library was a cramped barracks with a few thousand books piled helter-skelter on shelves that had previously been in the kitchen to hold jars of preserves. In the spartan checkout area were couches and armchairs that had been used in the personnel quarters until the feathers were gone or the fabric worn out. There the prisoners could spend a few hours sampling the books they had just taken down from the shelves, before they decided. You were only allowed to borrow one book at a time, so it was important to choose the right one.

As Maximilian was standing in the library barracks that day, Dennis Coral was deeply submerged in a light blue armchair that was halfway turned away from the entrance. He did not hear anyone coming; nothing could have disturbed his concentration. The book he was reading was *Fantasia*, Ben Puma's pioneering work of homosexual literature, and Coral followed the sentences across the pages with the tip of his tail, engrossed in the words. There was something moving about this scene, and Maximilian remained standing a few steps inside the door, observing him.

Few may be granted eyes in the back of their head, but we have all experienced the feeling of being observed. Suddenly the snake realized that he was no longer alone, and he twisted his neck at lightning speed and discovered Maximilian. The following second he slammed the book shut and managed to poke it halfway down under the cushion. Shame broke out on his narrow cheeks like raspberry stains on a linen tablecloth, and he stammered something that was impossible to make out. Maximilian looked at him with a gaze that was at once understanding and penetrating. Dennis Coral lost his composure.

"You . . . uh . . . don't say it, what?" hissed Coral, and his appearance became so dark that the marbling over his face was hardly visible anymore. "Anything at all . . . mm . . . but you can't say it!"

Maximilian made no reply. He sat down across from Coral on a couch that had once been beige. Tears were now coming out of the unhappy snake's eyes.

"I . . . uh . . . do what you want," Coral pleaded. "What you want, huh? But . . . mm . . . don't say it."

Maximilian cast a glance at the book that lay beside the snake in the armchair. He understood that Coral's entreaty had something to do with the book, but he understood no more than that. He raised his eyebrow to indicate a question; Dennis perceived it as condemnation.

"No one knows," whimpered Coral as he pressed the book farther under the cushion. "No one . . . uh . . . in the whole world knows. No one must know, huh? My mom would . . . mm . . . my dad . . . Damn, promise, huh? You have to!"

The panic in Coral's voice was heartbreaking. The tip of his tail lay placid and still on the couch instead of executing its usual amusing twists and turns. Maximilian, however, still did not understand what the snake was talking about. His gaze was gentle; he placed his hands in his lap and waited for an explanation.

"It's . . . uh . . . something with you, huh?" Dennis continued. "It . . . doesn't add up? I don't know, you've uncovered me, huh, and still I can't—"

"Uncovered?" asked Maximilian.

"Shit. I know who I am, huh? Mm . . . I've known it a long time," Dennis admitted. "But it would crush Mom and Dad. They are simple . . . uh . . . they, I don't know how to say this, they would die."

The tip of his tail came back to life, and after a brief circular motion it swept across the bookshelves behind Maximilian.

"Mom has never read a single page, huh? If they knew that I . . . uh . . . was . . . mm . . . that I didn't like females . . . that I . . . wouldn't get married . . . that I was, you know, the word. Homosexual, huh? They would freak out. It would . . . uh . . . be the end."

"Homosexual?" Maximilian repeated.

He pronounced the word neutrally, almost without understanding.

"To ME . . . uh . . . it's a big deal!" said Coral, and after a short dance he let the tip of his tail point right at his own head. "Others may . . . others . . . mm . . . there are those who can write 'GAY' on their forehead and go around and be . . . uh . . . proud, huh? But to ME it's not like that. And . . . uh . . . I DON'T know why!"

Maximilian did not reply.

Dennis Coral had been overcome by his own emotions, emotions he had never before let out; it was like opening a dam of terror and shame. In a low voice—quickly and yet in the special, halting manner that was typical of Dennis Coral—he told his story, accompanied by his lively tail. About school days and about high school, when he dated a female for almost a whole semester for the sake of appearances, and despite the fact that it tormented him. About the period after that, professional life, years of adaptation and self-denial. And about nights of agony and anxiety, sometimes outside clubs in Yok, clubs for the similarly oriented, when he stood in dark entryways without ever daring to cross the street. And the shame afterward, which grew with every new fiasco.

Dennis Coral's confession began in early childhood and ended twenty minutes later with a depiction of life as a Slave in King's Cross. When he fell silent, tears were running from his narrow eyes and his body was still shaking with anxiety as he sat in the armchair with the book by Ben Puma literally beneath him.

Maximilian let the echo of the words that had fallen die away before he spoke.

"A kite playing in the sky," he said calmly, "gets life from the wind, not from the hand that holds its string."

Those were his exact words. Dennis Coral would repeat them many times. I readily admit that I do not really understand what Maximilian meant. Coral remained uncertain as well, and he asked the question.

"Huh?"

"On a cart on its way to market," said Maximilian, "sat a donkey, counting the clouds floating along in the sky. He divided them into categories, soft and hard clouds, happy and sad clouds. The donkey was on his way to the Autumn Festival in Yok, and on the cart he had cartons full of candied apples and honey-dipped pears.

"There were mostly soft and sad clouds. This made the donkey sorrowful. Finally he stopped adding any sad clouds when he saw one, and instead searched across the sky for a happy cloud. He did the same with the soft clouds: Even if they were in the majority, he seemed to constantly be discovering hard clouds on the horizon. In this way he arrived at the market without feeling depressed.

"It took the donkey a few hours to sell all his sweets to the cubs who were running around between the stands, and soon he was again sitting on his cart on his way home. But then the sun had gone down, and the sky was black. So black that there were no longer any clouds visible."

Maximilian fell silent, and looked at Dennis Coral. Tears were running from the snake's eyes, but they were tears of relief and joy. On the intellectual level, Dennis still understood nothing, but intuitively he seemed to have perceived a truth: an alleviating, liberating truth.

"You have never lusted after another male's female, have you?" said Maximilian.

Dennis shook his head.

"You have never buried anyone alive, have you?" said Maximilian.

Dennis shook his head.

"Take my hand," said Maximilian, getting up.

Dennis Coral got up, took Maximilian's hand, and let himself be led out from the small barracks that served as the prison library.

"Now I want you to close your eyes," said Maximilian, "and let me take you out of here."

Dennis Coral closed his eyes. His trust lacked limits. They walked next to each other for an hour, and Dennis felt no unease. He was still bewildered by his own confession, finally having said it.

When they stopped, Dennis had no idea where they were, but he guessed it was somewhere near the exercise yard.

"I am leaving you here," said Maximilian. "You can open your eyes now. Take good care of yourself."

Dennis looked up, and the light was so strong that he was forced to squint. He looked around. He was standing in the middle of Mollisan Town, in—it would prove to be—the heart of Yok, but before he really dared believe it, Maximilian was gone.

. . . .

The excitement when Maximilian returned to King's Cross
lacks a counterpart in the prison's modern history. Enough
prisoners and guards had seen Maximilian and Dennis
Coral walking hand in hand through the walls for the
entire prison to know about it little more than an hour later.
They discussed the supernatural phenomenon; this was unavoidable: the power of thought and the fifth dimension.
Others giggled contemptuously at such ideas and instead
emphasized the possibilities of technology, hidden doors,
and projected holograms. A third group maintained that
both versions were baseless legends: Maximilian had dug
a tunnel, and now the prison administration was trying to
cover up its shortcomings by spreading preposterous stories.
The prison administration, for its part, formed an investiga-
tion in utmost secrecy to immediately look for the answer
to the question of what had really happened. Regardless of
theory and tone of voice, everyone was talking about it, and
when a prison guard crow en route to going off his shift
passed Maximilian's cell and saw the headcloth-adorned
prisoner calmly and quietly sitting on his bed as if nothing
had happened, he immediately sounded the alarm.

And a tumult broke out.

A few minutes later a troop of guards appeared, tore
Maximilian from the cell, and dragged him away. The
prison warden himself caught up to the procession en route
to Section G, where the isolation cells were located the past
few years, and could conduct a short interrogation of the
returned prisoner en route.

They crossed the cricket field and passed through the corridors in Sections L and F, which, if the matter had been
handled with greater forethought, it would have been wise
to avoid. But the situation was unique, and emotions had
been stirred up. The prison warden came back again and

again to his two main questions: How had Maximilian succeeded in escaping, and why had he come back? The prisoner repeated his answer just as many times: He had not escaped, he had helped the innocent Dennis Coral out of the prison, and he came back because he was serving a sentence that society had rendered on good grounds.

This answer, the warden explained with as much desperation as anger, was not satisfactory.

At King's Cross there were no more than about fifty solitary confinement cells. They were notorious and feared, and awareness of them maintained reasonable order and discipline in the prison. The claustrophobic cells lacked windows, the ceiling height made it impossible for a normal stuffed animal to stand upright, and with the exception of the distilled daylight that made its way through the cracks in the cell door, it was coal black inside, night and day. An internee could be in solitary confinement for seven days at the most, and during this time seven meals were served. The capriciousness of when the food was placed in the cell was carefully calculated: One meal might follow only a few minutes after the previous one, while two full days might then pass without even a glass of water. The cells were punishment for the already penalized, and no mercy was shown.

Maximilian was literally thrown into cell 22, and there he would be for twelve days. I tried to visit him. It was a few days later that I drove out to King's Cross, knowing nothing about what had happened. This was my usual monthly visit. The personnel let me stand on one side of a closed wooden door and call out to Maximilian, whom they maintained was on the other side—I still do not know whether that was true—and then I had to leave.

"Tell them about Duck!" I called in despair. "Don't do this to yourself, tell them about Duck!"

This was futile, of course.

. . . .

There are several eyewitness accounts of what happened after the twelve days in solitary. Many tell about how extremely drawn and worn Maximilian looked when they hauled him back to his regular cell. It sounds paradoxical, but more than one eyewitness states that Maximilian's fabric had turned pale in the darkness and was almost white. The certified energy that he usually radiated was reduced to a thin mist, and not once on the way back from Section G did he raise his gaze from the ground. The guards threw him on the floor in his old cell and left him there, like a remnant of a stuffed animal, a spirit conquered at last.

Fifteen minutes later the chaos was a fact.

During the twelve days that had passed since Maximilian left, and came back to, King's Cross, the knowledge of what had happened deepened to an insight: There was a stuffed animal in the prison who could help anyone whatsoever get out.

Before Maximilian had even recovered his senses and gotten up from the floor, a small collection of animals had formed outside the cell in the corridor. They all had something to offer; no one cared whether the guards came running to push them away. Only Maximilian, knocked out on the floor of the cell, was unaware of what was happening.

It got worse.

Already during the first break it was clear that Maximilian could not be let out among the other prisoners. He was run down, jumped on; he was at the bottom of a tumultuous pile of stuffed animals, and the guards barely managed to pull him loose.

But he could not be inside either. There were enough prisoners who realized that when the majority of guard resources were required to maintain order outside or in the dining hall, an opportunity arose at Maximilian's cell. The dream of being channeled to the outside by a miracle animal—Dennis Coral's escape had taken on mythical proportions—made the prisoners bold beyond the bounds of reason; not even fear of solitary confinement seemed able to dampen their eagerness any longer. The prison administration held an emergency meeting, and the decision they made was the only one possible.

Maximilian had to return to solitary. On the question of how long he would stay there, a question I placed directly to the prison warden by telephone when my normal visiting time was canceled for the second time in two months, the answer was: "For the time being." And because I knew how hard the first twelve days had been on Maximilian, I protested wildly. The warden, however, had already hung up before I got going.

In this context and from the perspective of the authorities, I was of course easy to disregard, but I forced the equally indignant and worried Adam Chaffinch—he was still a former deacon—to go out to the prison and discuss the situation with the stuffed animals responsible. Adam got nowhere either. He was allowed to meet with a dromedary who called himself "Head of Planning" and who pretended to be ignorant of Maximilian's case. The only thing he could offer Adam was, as I had done, to stand outside a door and try to talk with Maximilian.

Standing and shouting at a closed door in front of the eyes of two sneering guards was a humiliating experience. Adam appealed to Maximilian to listen to reason and tell the whole truth about the night in the vault of the National Bank.

Not a sound came from the closed door.

The last thing to leave a stuffed animal is hope, it is often said. We were certain that nothing could budge Maximilian's hope, but when the defeated Adam Chaffinch came back that day, I heartily wished that the same applied to us.

REUBEN WALRUS 8

Excuse me, but Minister Tortoise is wondering if you have time to meet with him for a little while."

Reuben Walrus winced. Darkness had fallen over Pfaffendorfer Tor, and the mauve street was a shade of black. The philharmonic musicians had left the concert hall several hours ago, and Reuben had stayed behind with Dag Chihuahua and discussed . . . possibilities. But Dag did not let himself be provoked either by Reuben's indignation or sarcasm, nor did he let himself be persuaded by flattery or promises. They sat and talked in the auditorium, the stage lights for the orchestra still on and the mighty concert hall silent and deserted.

Walrus was panic-stricken, and he admitted it. Panic paralyzed him. Chihuahua showed no compassion. Walrus told him how it was: So far he had been incapable of completing the composition of his Symphony in A Minor. Chihuahua found this regrettable. Reuben asked for help, but was intentionally vague; he had not said anything he would have to regret. At the same time Chihuahua had to play dumb so as not to understand where Reuben was heading.

"I'm getting nowhere," admitted the great composer. "And the days are running away. I think that someone else, who knows me and knows the symphony, might even have greater possibilities of bringing this project to a successful close."

And Dag Chihuahua answered, at the same time sorrowfully shaking his little head and angling his small, pointed ears forward.

"This is very regrettable, Mr. Walrus. But don't give up the ship."

At last Chihuahua left the walrus to agonize alone by the stage that had seen him triumph many times, but would now experience the opposite.

Reuben climbed up the steep stage stairs and sat at the piano. With one fin he plunked out his theme, over and over again, but without ambitions. It had gone too far. He had played the same series of notes so many times that all he heard was the echo of his own failure in every imaginable continuation, loud or soft, major or minor.

And his hearing was getting worse and worse.

He had started the day with a short follow-up visit at St. Andrews. His hearing had become measurably worse during the past week. When he left the hospital grounds, he decided not to return. Never again. It was equally pointless and demoralizing. And now as he sat playing the piano and knew that his keystroke was louder than he could hear it, he still refused to understand what was happening. He kept it at a distance. It was as if the disease were encapsulated in a closed box with transparent walls. He could see and understand what was going on inside, he could talk about it and feel sorry for himself, but it was still as if someone were playing the part of Reuben Walrus, and he himself was sitting in the audience. If it got too unpleasant, he could get up and go.

The real anxiety, the night-black unendurable anxiety,

came over him for brief moments. And such a moment suddenly occurred as he played the sequence B, F sharp, D on the piano. Reuben pulled back his fins as if he had burned himself, and stared spitefully at the keys. They were his enemies. He got up, quickly left the spotlight, and gathered his coat and things in the large dressing room next to the performers' dressing rooms behind the stage.

Reuben knew that Denise was expecting him to stop by. Not that he would stay the night, but that he would come up for a drink before he went home to Knobeldorfstrasse. He had no desire. Not this evening. He disappointed her, but in the midst of all this misfortune and grief he could only take responsibility for himself. Hardly even that. When he left the concert hall through the unmarked door to the performers' entrance on the back side, the darkness struck him by surprise. Perhaps, he thought, he could stop by Fox von Duisburg's and see what she was up to.

Then he felt a grip on his fin. A stately owl whose facial features were concealed in the shadows loomed up at his side.

"Excuse me, but Minister Tortoise is wondering if you have time to meet with him for a little while."

The owl spoke directly into Walrus's ear. The voice was harsh and deep, but still distinct. This was a stuffed animal who was used to getting what he wanted.

Walrus wriggled instinctively out of the owl's grasp and took a step to one side in order to better see who he was talking with. The owl had a military appearance, his back was as straight as if he had steel wire for a skeleton, and his stuffing was ready to burst.

"Who are you?"

"My name is Armand Owl," replied the owl, making a kind of salute that looked strange in relation to his long, black coat and the civilian suit that could be glimpsed beneath it. "I have worked for Minister Tortoise for many years."

"Really? How is it that I've never encountered you? I'm a good friend of Vincent, and I haven't—"

"We have never had reason to . . . take you seriously before," said Owl, without trying to soften the tenor of his words by his expression. "I have a car waiting over here. If you would be so kind . . . ?"

"Reuben, I beg your pardon a thousand times for this," said Vincent Tortoise, with a gesture inviting the walrus to sit down on one of the many chairs around the conference table. "You must not construe this as anything other than a practical solution, evidence that I'm really looking after you."

Reuben Walrus knew the minister of culture well enough to know that nothing Vincent Tortoise did was by chance. The abruptness, the autocratic attitude behind sending the owl to fetch Reuben outside the concert hall, had been clearly evident.

Reuben informed his old friend of this.

"No, no," Tortoise dismissed, "that's not true at all."

But the denial lacked feeling.

Reuben was sitting as far away from Tortoise as he could get.

"Now I'm here," he said. "What did you want?"

"I'll get right to the point," Tortoise began.

"What'd you say?"

"I will get right to the point," repeated Tortoise in a louder voice. "You've been seen as part of what is called 'Adam's Retinue.' I got the report this morning, and I understood how things stand. You ignored my advice the other day. You're in pursuit of Maximilian."

" 'Adam's Retinue'?"

"Don't put on airs," said Tortoise dismissively. "The last time we talked about this matter, I asked you to give this up. Now I'm asking you again, albeit more firmly. I do not want to see you together with . . . those stuffed animals."

"You have nothing to do with who I meet," said Walrus.

The anger caused him to breathe through his mouth. He took short, quick breaths but controlled himself, experienced enough not to show Tortoise what he was feeling. The fact remained. They were keeping him under surveillance. Or else it was Adam Chaffinch they were spying on. In either case this was at odds with the democratic freedom that Walrus had always believed prevailed in Mollisan Town.

"I have nothing to do with your private life, Reuben," said Tortoise in a friendly tone. "But you are a public animal. That means that what you do is not only your private concern. And what you are doing now . . . affects security in the city."

Reuben swallowed. The wisest thing, he thought, was probably to get up and leave without saying another word. Nonetheless he could not refrain.

"This, Vincent," he replied quietly, "shows that I am on the right track. I have had my doubts regarding Maximilian and what he can do . . . but this . . . that even you . . . send lackeys . . . are afraid—"

"I am not afraid!" roared Tortoise. "You . . . you still believe that this is a game, don't you?"

"I'm not playing—I'm in the process of losing my hearing."

"Reuben, for once take me seriously. I don't intend to ask you again. And I don't intend to threaten you. Give up this thing with Maximilian."

Reuben Walrus sat awhile and observed the minister. Then he got up and left the office without another word.

. . . .

He woke up early the next morning. It was the silence that woke him, and it had been like that the last few days. No longer hearing the creaking of the floorboards, the breeze that set the curtains in the bedroom window in motion, and the water running through the building's old pipes: This silence was more effective than the sound of the loudest alarm clock.

And in the solitude on Knobeldorfstrasse, when the black night sky outside did not offer an ounce of hope, he got up and shuffled out to the kitchen, where he measured out coffee, sat down at the kitchen table, and watched the vapors rising from the coffeemaker without being able to hear its suppressed snorting. During the time it took for the approaching dawn to color the sky red and then blue, he held sorrow and fear in check by concentrating on household chores and planning for the approaching day. He succeeded only partially.

The telephone rang when he was through with his morning toilet, and he considered not answering. He assumed that it was Denise Ant, since he had avoided her the whole day before. He nonetheless felt obliged, and sullenly he picked up the receiver.

"Good morning, Daddy," said Josephine.

"What'd you say? Josephine?"

She called so seldom that Reuben was surprised every time by how light and young her voice sounded on the copper wires.

"Josephine?" he repeated, even though he knew.

"You have to wish me good luck today, Daddy," she said. "I need a good start to the day."

He had to concentrate to hear her.

"Good luck?"

"Not like that," his daughter laughed. "For real."

Then he remembered. It was today that admissions to the

fall courses at the Music Academy began. He was on the jury, which he had been for the past twelve years; it was a task that confirmed his authority in a way that elevated him above daily criticism and trends.

Josephine had reminded him, most recently the other day in the studio, but he had forgotten it again. She had been called to the first day. That was both good and bad. The jury was interested and positive the first day—at the end of the week it was not possible to maintain the same enthusiasm—but at the same time they were stricter, in the hope that greater talents were expected on subsequent days.

"Good luck, my cub," said Reuben.

Then he added, as if he were talking to one of all the hopeful, and then disappointed, students he had met through the years, "It will work out the way it works out, and that doesn't make you either a better or a worse stuffed animal."

"Oh, don't be silly, Daddy." Josephine giggled happily.

She was more than hopeful, she was certain of being accepted. They hung up. No one, he thought as he returned to the kitchen and his coffee, could take her ambition away from her. He readily admitted that she was technically proficient.

It had become an agreeable ritual, the members of the jury meeting in the teachers' lounge before the sometimes painful, sometimes stimulating work of admissions week began. They had tea, the Shetland pony brought cookies every year that he had baked the evening before, and they gossiped about the academy in general and its rector in particular. Reuben had announced early on that he would not serve as dutifully as usual this year, because he was in the middle of his rehearsals. But the academy gave him great scope; he was now one of the oldest members of the jury and therefore had a senior position.

When they met right before the Morning Rain, it took a few minutes before the right mood was established. Despite the fact that Reuben had still not announced his diagnosis of Drexler's syndrome in any official way, they were all aware of his condition and eager to express their sympathy. But he quickly lured them onto another track by bringing up the rector's latest misstep—a failed attempt to breathe life into the old academy tradition of a rowing team on the Dondau—and merry laughter and abuse took the place of gloom.

Cookies were eaten, the coffeepot was emptied, the gossip ebbed out, and outside the rain was about to recede. In other words, it was about time, and the members of the jury got up, brushed the cookie crumbs from their clothes, and went into the large auditorium, where according to tradition they sat down at the table up on the stage.

"Well, then," said Reuben with the natural authority that came from many years' experience, "you can start sending them in now."

The academy caretaker, a koala who had worked in the building as long as anyone could remember and who was rumored to live down in the cellar, nodded seriously. He backed out of the auditorium and went around the corner out into the corridor, where the tension was like a dense fog over the stuffed animals already there, some wet from the pouring rain. The moisture was the least of their worries on a day like this.

"Anaconda, Gabriel," the caretaker read from the list of names that was set up in alphabetical order, and with a certain trembling Gabriel Anaconda, with his flute on his back, wriggled after the koala into the auditorium.

The snake glanced up toward the stage, where the terror-inspiring admissions jury sat, and sweat broke out on his forehead.

"Come, come," the Shetland pony called amiably, "we're not dangerous."

But the pony was not fooling anyone.

. . . .

It was Josephine's turn right before lunch. Reuben had been afraid that as her free choice she would choose a piece he had written, but thankfully she refrained. Instead she played some passages from a cantata by Rachmolotov, and this indicated good taste. There were friendly nods from the jury table, and Josephine herself looked content when, with a nod, she left the auditorium after her ten minutes.

"Lunch and deliberations!" said Reuben as the door closed behind his daughter, and he got up from the table and stretched.

This was completely in line with the procedures. They listened through twenty or so applications, broke for lunch or afternoon coffee, and went over what they had heard while impressions were still fresh. Lunch was taken next to the teachers' lounge in a small cafeteria that was seldom used. During audition week the menu was always the same, and the first day cabbage with pork was served. The discussion followed the order of performance, and therefore it took a while before, over coffee, they came to Josephine Lamb. The food was consumed, and the jury was ready to break up.

"I didn't think she did badly at all, Reuben," began Shetland Pony McCain.

Reuben had not said that Josephine was his daughter, but it was of course a vain hope that he could keep it secret. He sighed.

"I don't know," he said. "There was something mechanical about her playing. Perhaps not so much in the touch as in the phrasing?"

"I think you're judging too strictly now, Reuben," objected Daniel Poodle.

"What'd you say?"

"You don't have to be so strict," repeated Poodle.

"I am afraid that you will be overly kind," countered Reuben. "She is my daughter, but the tuba is her idea, and she must build her career on her own merits. This becomes that much more important, because not only the outside world is going to suspect that she got into the academy thanks to me, but she as well. There will always be a seed of uncertainty. It's really important that she knows she's capable."

The jury sat silently, considering this.

"I think," said the Shetland Pony, "that this must be your decision, Reuben. No one else will feel comfortable deciding Josephine's fate. You make the decision, and we will back you up, whatever you decide."

"McCain is right," agreed Poodle. "That's how it must be."

"Then . . . ," said Reuben Walrus, drawing out the words, "then . . . Josephine will just have to accept being kept out this time."

There was dead silence around the table.

WOLF DIAZ 8

Would you like another beer?" asked Mary-Jo Antelope.
I nodded. The sound level in the restaurant was so
high that there was no point in trying to say anything when
you could nod. Mary-Jo forced her way over to the bar,
and she would be coming back sooner than most; personally, I would probably never have even managed to force my
way up to the counter. Two times a week the foremost of
Mollisan Town's so-called Discontented Singers appeared
at Veronica's in Tourquai, but I had never been there before.
The Discontented Singers were artists who, equipped with
a guitar or an accordion or sitting at the piano, performed
simple songs with complicated—and long—lyrics. Often
the point was aimed at our mayor, Sara Lion, but of course
all kinds of authority needed to be criticized. I cannot say
that I thought what I heard was either especially good or
bad; I am not a musical stuffed animal.

Mary-Jo Antelope had been in my life a few months,
and I was deeply impressed by her sincerity and patience.
Usually I remained unaffected—if I may express myself
carelessly—by the splashing of bleeding hearts, my own

included, but my experiences with Missy Starling had left certain traces. Anyone could have figured out that of course Missy would leave me for another, but when it happened at last I was nonetheless unprepared. This contributed to my being crushed.

Even six months later I was not prepared to move in with a new female, my nerves being to some extent still in disarray. Mary-Jo, however, demanded nothing of the sort. She was comfortably unaffected, with all her hooves on the ground. With Mary-Jo there was no calculation or dissimulation, only a straightforward manner that possibly might get a little . . . boring . . . in the long run. For me, however, this was both unusual and refreshing.

Neither of us had room to move in with the other. Missy Starling found a way to buy me out. I was staying temporarily in the guestroom at the home of my childhood friend Weasel Tukovsky, who had unexpectedly become the advice columnist at the *Daily News* and was making a good living at that.

Mary-Jo understood that I needed time and care, and that was partly why she dragged me along to Veronica's— a little distraction from an existence that consisted of duties to Adam and Maria and their Retinues, as well as my gloominess at all the lies that Missy Starling had left behind her.

I was looking preoccupied toward the stage while I waited for my antelope and the beers. A snake was performing; his voice was nasal, and the tip of his tail was strangely involved in the performance, simultaneously a conductor's baton and a drumstick that rhythmically beat the tambourine on the chair beside him. Some sort of insect accompanied him on the piano, but I only heard fragments of the text itself. The audience closest to the stage was polite and listened quietly, but the farther into the place you went, the higher the volume of conversation was. At the bar I am sure that no one cared about the snake's intense song.

"Let's sit down," called Mary-Jo when she came with our glasses, and we made our way to a little table that was vacant.

With Missy Starling every silence had been a threat, an insult of some kind, if the silence was not a "stage pause" on her terms. With Mary-Jo it was different. We could sit there at our table and drink a little beer and listen a little to the snake on the stage without having it feel uncomfortable in any way. A quarter of an hour passed, twenty minutes, and I do not know if I even thought about the fact that a new Discontented Singer had taken the stage before I gave a frightened start at hearing a sudden hissing in my ear.

"Uh . . . I'd like to talk a little, is that . . . mm . . . okay?"

The snake who had recently been onstage had slithered up along the back of the chair beside me, and his eyes were only centimeters from mine when I turned around.

Of course he did not wait for my answer. He glided down the table without letting me out of his sight for a moment. This meant that he carelessly turned his tail toward Mary-Jo Antelope. Like me, she recognized him from the stage, and perhaps she was impressed that I kept such a low profile. Judging by this, I must know a Discontented Singer.

But I wasn't the one who knew the snake; he was the one who knew me.

"You are . . . uh . . . Diaz, right?"

I nodded.

Up to that day I had not had any snake friends, and therefore I did not know how I should behave. Should I lean forward and talk with him, or should I simply raise my voice? Even if there were no animals right next to our table, another Discontented Singer was making considerable noise through the speakers.

"Super-sorry to intrude . . . mm . . . huh?" said Dennis. "But I know that you . . . uh . . . work with . . . mm . . . Maximilian."

After the police effort against the cinema—and despite the fact that a few years had passed since then—my conspiracy theories had gotten extra nourishment, and I was extremely suspicious of questions of this type. Therefore I neither confirmed nor denied the snake's assertion.

"I, uh, am his friend, huh?" Dennis Coral announced solemnly, but corrected himself immediately. "He is my Savior."

I was forced to agree.

"He is the Savior of us all," I replied.

"And I know who, mm, you are. You're the Recorder, huh?"

I felt both disturbed and flattered. He must have seen it in my eyes, for he quickly added, "It's, uh, Maximilian himself who told me that, huh? He told me about the Recorder Diaz."

"You've met Maximilian?" I asked with surprise.

The snake nodded. "In the slammer," he said.

I took a breath. Since they had locked Maximilian up in solitary confinement, I had hardly gotten any information at all. Here in the flesh before me was an ex-convict with his own account of Maximilian's experience in jail. The surroundings suddenly became intrusive and unworthy. No one there—the drunks over at the bar, the singer on the stage, not even Mary-Jo Antelope—fit into this solemn context. I got up.

"Mary-Jo," I said. "I have to go. I'll call you later and explain."

And it was her strength of character to accept my action with a noble calm. She nodded, raising her beer mug in an undramatic farewell, but the snake and I were already on our way out.

. . . .

We found nowhere else to go, so for a few hours we strolled around Tourquai's empty, broad sidewalks from which the massive skyscrapers grew up, concealing the night sky. He had a mission, but I was still the one who got the most out of our walk, I think. Dennis told me everything he knew about Maximilian's time in prison, and concluded by recounting their spectacular flight. For someone else this might have been unbelievable, but not for me.

In Dennis Coral's eyes, Maximilian represented unshakable hope. Dennis had had time to think about the matter since he had slipped out of King's Cross, and this was what he had arrived at: Maximilian had shown that the impossible was possible, that however dark the future might appear, hope—naive and ridiculous, of course, but at the same time heartening in a fundamental way—must be kept alive. Dennis had lived a life without hope, but that would not be repeated. That was Maximilian's teaching. Never let hope die.

Dennis revealed what Maximilian had said when they left the prison.

"If you set an arrow to your bow, uh, you can still only shoot it as far as the eye can see through force and will. That's what he said, huh?"

"And?" I asked. "What more did he say?"

"Nothing more." Dennis smiled.

"But what does it mean?" I asked.

"I, um, thought about it a long time," Dennis admitted. "And I think he meant that if you want to shoot the arrow even farther, you have to dare to hope. Thus it is, uh, only in the great idea that you can take yourself anywhere, uh, that we are limited by our reality, and that it, mm, isn't always enough?"

Dennis continued his explanation, and I cannot say that

I understood everything exactly, but one thing was sure: He spoke with an infectious fervor.

"That's what I am, uh, singing about, huh?" he said. "But I think I'm, uh, through singing at Veronica's. I want to be with you all instead, huh?"

"With us?"

I remember the moment. We were standing outside a shop that sold expensive watches. We were by a street with six lanes, ten or so traffic lights, but not a car. It had started to get light, and my legs suddenly felt tired. I had carried the snake on my arm most of the way, because it was easiest to talk that way.

"Mm, with you all, huh?" he said. "I've heard about, mm, your Retinues. I'm the one you've been waiting for, huh? Do you get it?"

"Well, I—"

"Faith, hope, and love, like."

"Indeed. Yes, I—"

"If Chaffinch talks about faith, if Mink talks about love—mm, I have actually been at one of, uh, her lectures. Then I'm left, huh? The voice of hope."

We got no further that evening than me promising to introduce him to Adam Chaffinch, but I tried to offer as little encouragement as I could. That a Discontented Singer would have one of Maximilian's Retinues was not an idea I especially liked.

Naturally I could not sleep that night. The encounter with Coral had been overwhelming. I had been given a view into Maximilian's life in prison that shook me, and the idea of Dennis Coral as the third apostle gave me no rest.

A month earlier Adam Chaffinch had more or less gone to pieces. I had talked a good deal with Maria Mink about this, because I had expected it to happen. Adam was running himself into the ground; he was working too hard, and he disregarded my warnings. After he became ill and was in bed with a high fever for four weeks, I humbly presented the idea that he ought to ramp down.

He took too much on himself, I said. The need among stuffed animals was great, of that there was no doubt, but if he could find another who could speak to those in need? That was exactly what I said, and now Coral showed up.

Adam had not immediately dismissed the idea, but I could not be more specific than that. Besides, medicine should be taken in small doses.

I am not a stuffed animal who wants to promote myself in an unjust manner, but there is no reason for feigned humility either. The first meetings between Coral and Chaffinch did not go well—they did not go well at all. Chaffinch was, and is, a stern and serious bird who, despite everything had a number of unshakable ideas about right and wrong. Dennis Coral—this homosexual jailbird who had escaped from King's Cross, appeared as a Discontented Singer, and spoke in a manner that was difficult to imagine in connection with the word of Magnus—did not fit into Chaffinch's templates. It took time before Adam gave in—which to his credit he never regretted—and I definitely had something to do with it.

Duck Johnson heard the bolts in the great vault door and realized what was about to happen. They must have set off an alarm, as he expected; in reality the question had always been how much time they would have.

Now that time had run out.

Duck increased his pace. He had been working on one of the pallets of bills farther inside the vault, and what he did now had been his alternative plan the whole time, something to try if everything else went wrong. He emptied the pallet of bundles of bills so that a deep hollow space was formed. Just as the police opened the vault, Duck pressed himself down into the little grotto, and from there he could hear everything that happened.

When they took Maximilian, Duck did not dare breathe. But he did not dare move later either, when the darkness and silence almost suffocated him, for fear that there were heat or motion detectors in the vault.

The next morning they came early and loaded the pallets. They used a small truck that drove between the vault and the securities transport that was waiting by the bank's underground loading dock. No one saw Duck or his hiding place in the fifth pallet of bills; no one looked.

On board the truck, he had plenty of time to prepare himself. He knew that they were on their way to the Hole at the Garbage Dump, and he knew that his only chance to get away was when the back of the truck opened and dumping began. Even if the guard who was driving the truck were to see him running away, there was no reasonable connection between the National Bank, the transport, and a duck running at the Garbage Dump.

The duck crept out of the bills, no longer even thinking about the stench, and at the moment the truckbed began to tip and open, Duck squeezed out on the side and ran away faster than he had ever run.

Duck hid in an overturned bathtub a short distance from the Hole, and there he waited until it got dark. He had heard the stories about the Garbage Dump and the psychopathic overseer named Bataille, and he did not intend to stay longer than he had to.

When night came, he snuck away, following one of the broad roads through the refuse toward the exit, and then continued along Eastern Avenue for a few kilometers. After that he turned south, to Yok, where his aunt had an overnight apartment that she never used. It was on mold green rue d'Uzés, and for many years Duck had had a key to it without his aunt knowing about it.

From the beginning his strategy had been to lie low a while and keep out of the way. But after a week, Duck was completely paranoid. He imagined that animals were looking at him when he went shopping, and he seemed to recognize an otter who went past his doorway every morning from the

Seminars on Faith, Hope, and Love. It was a bad spiral: The more time he spent inside his aunt's apartment, the less he dared go out.

Just over a year later, still tormented by his persecution complex, Duck Johnson booked time with an unscrupulous plastic surgeon who had his practice in a former garage two blocks from rue d'Uzés. Duck had to pay for the operation on credit, but nothing in life was free. The plastic surgeon executed a beak exchange and a neck lengthening that meant that when Duck left the place, he could call himself Sam Goose. This granted him a certain respect, but only a few days later the plastic surgeon, who now had a perfect hold on Duck, called and demanded payback—everything from stealing prosthetics from the city hospitals to collecting money from delinquent former patients.

Duck carried out these unpaid assignments for four years, until one morning, the Chauffeurs fetched the plastic surgeon. It was a relief, but also left a vacuum in his life. That he did not feel any great happiness when the blackmail ceased awakened a further existential emptiness in Duck's soul. The sudden idleness brought with it fundamental questions about who he really was and what his purpose was in Mollisan Town, and inconsolable brooding led to a long, deep depression.

One morning a few months later, Duck's aunt found him under the bed in the apartment in Yok in a pose for healing meditation that caused his eyes to roll back in his skull while he hyperventilated. She forced him to seek professional help immediately. It could not go on like this.

The therapist must have rubbed his hands: On the couch lay a real challenge. After a few weeks of treatment, he convinced Duck Johnson to try to write out his anxiety.

"Confess," said the therapist, "get your inhibitions and secrets out. Unscrew the lid. You've kept your misdeeds secret so long that they are eating you up from inside."

But at this point Duck Johnson was too complicated a stuffed animal for this simple advice. Simply buying himself a notebook and a pen and starting to write was not enough for him. True, he bought the notebook and pen, but he also bought a large pocketknife and—when he passed by a lumberyard on his way home—a couple of good-sized pieces of wood. After this, a period in Duck's life began that was marked by manic activity. The door to the apartment on rue d'Uzés remained locked, and his aunt's key no longer worked.

Time passed, and Duck's aunt became more and more worried about her nephew. She made it a habit to go past the apartment a few times each day, and soon lost count of how many weeks and months this went on. She knocked on the door, opened the mail slot, and called his name, but except for an increasingly rotten stench, there were no signs of life.

When the door was suddenly thrown open one day in March, the aunt took a few astonished steps backward. The duck—transformed to a goose—who came out of the apartment reminded her only vaguely of the nephew she had once had. He was a wreck, he did not seem to recognize her, and with a cry of pain and sorrow she saw him stagger down the steps, never again to return.

Where he disappeared to, as far as I understand, no one yet knows.

Hesitantly Duck's aunt went into the apartment—it was hers, after all—to find, on the spice rack above the stove, twenty-three small but carefully carved globes lined up next to each other. They were no larger than the spice jars beside them. She took one of them down, twisting and turning it in the daylight that fell through the window. It depicted a planet: All the globes depicted planets, in what was possibly an alternate universe. Duck had carved entire miniature worlds, with contours of continents, mountain ranges, and seas in beautiful patterns. The traces of his work were everywhere; wood chips and sawdust lay like a film over bed and floor.

Duck's aunt weighed the globe in her paw with admiration. This was a remarkable thing that her nephew had achieved; would it be possible perhaps to make a buck from his unknown talent? By the end of that same week the aunt had received offers from three different art galleries in Lanceheim. Without batting an eye, she then sold the globes to the highest bidder. She got seven thousand, and would thereafter always remember her nephew with warmth.

What neither the art dealer nor Duck's aunt knew was that inside each and every one of the twenty-three planets was a handwritten confession of the twenty-three sins Duck counted as his worst. On the other hand, the art dealer would not have cared; he knew he had a bargain. His prosperous clientele was made up of collectors whose taste he knew well, and by the following week he had already sold two of the planets at impressive prices.

On Thursday evening, when his poker-playing friends had gathered in the gallery right before the Evening Storm, the art dealer cockily displayed his treasures. It was thereby natural that when, with a full house in his hand during the last deal long after midnight, he raised Judge Hawk Pius—the table's leading bluffer—and took one of the planets down from the shelf and put it in the pot.

Judge Pius was holding a straight. He smiled his cunning smile, put the planet in his pocket and the money in his wallet, and went home shortly thereafter as the biggest winner of the evening. Tomorrow would be a good day in Pius's court, but something even more astounding was to happen.

The judge always slept uneasily, and this short night was no exception. He had set his trophy on the night table, and woke up when, in his sleep, his wing happened to strike his newly won planet, knocking it to the ground. With a distinct crash it split in two, and from inside fell Duck Johnson's confession.

Hawk Pius was one of the strictest judges in Mollisan Town, but he had always prided himself on being just. The morning he read Duck Johnson's confession of how he had lured Maximilian to the break-in at the National Bank, it took him less than a few hours to decree what Maximilian's sentence should have been, provided that the whole truth had been known at the time of the trial. By then Maximilian had been at King's Cross for nine years and ten months, and the last four months he had been in solitary. Regardless of the fact that Maximilian's punishment had been increased over time due to complicity to flight—something Judge Pius felt was questionable in any event when he read the account of the circumstances—the prisoner had more than paid for the crime he had committed against the state. Pius and his animal officials filled out the required forms, stamped and sent the certified letters that were demanded, and when the red tape was done, a date for Maximilian's release was agreed on: Thursday the twenty-seventh of December. On that day Maximilian would have been deprived of freedom for nine years, eleven months, and three days.

The decision didn't raise any eyebrows among the prison administration. True, it was good to be rid of the troublesome prisoner—he made use of valuable resources—but in general the prison had no opinions on the work of the courts.

In accordance with procedure, the prison administrators sent a concise memorandum to the Police Authority and Ministry of Finance. This was done before every release: It was a matter of seeing to it that the individual in question returned to society's customary orbit, not least in terms of tax registration.

The next day, when the Ministry of Finance databases had been updated by cross-tabulation against the registries of the other departments, Maximilian's name also showed up at the Ministry of Culture. An unpaid student loan meant that the Ministry of Culture was automatically informed of the release, so that they could once again demand the long-outstanding payment.

As chance would have it, Maximilian's name was not unknown to the official who administered this procedure. This official, an insignificant individual in our context—I have never even cared to search out his correct name—put in motion a series of conversations at the ministry. By late afternoon the information had made it all the way up to Vincent Tortoise.

Vincent Tortoise, head of the Ministry of Culture, sat in a swivel-type leather armchair at the end of the table. In front of him were piles and bundles of papers, in envelopes and plastic folders, handwritten or typed, all asking for his attention. The sun was shining through the windows, the clouds had just dispersed after the Afternoon Rain, and the polished surface of the black walnut table sparkled with satisfaction.

Armand Owl was sitting on one of the chairs on the long side of the conference table. Only the two of them were in the room. Owl's back was straight, the knot of his tie small and hard, and he had hung his jacket over the back of the leather armchair so that it wouldn't wrinkle. His short beak opened only when required, and this was the case now.

"Bullshit!" he said.

"I am still not certain that this is even a bad thing," Tortoise continued sarcastically. "I don't suppose you could say that you've managed to keep a lid on things as long as he's been in prison?"

"That is certified bullshit," repeated Owl. "What we see now is only a whisper of what would have been the case if we had remained passive."

"Whisper . . . or hissing," answered Tortoise. "Or growling?"

"Whatever . . ." Armand sighed. "Whatever—"

"In any event, he is being released on the twenty-seventh. There is not much we can do about that. What do you propose?"

"They have already started planning," said Armand Owl, worriedly wrinkling his eyebrows. "Chaffinch and the others. They intend some type of public demonstration."

"We don't want that," declared Tortoise.

"No, we don't. So my specific proposal is—and I have already talked with all the parties—that we release him two days earlier."

Tortoise nodded, thought about the matter awhile, and smiled when he understood.

"Cancel their party?"

Owl nodded.

"And you haven't . . . ," Tortoise began with a familiar worry in his voice.

"There are no connections to the Ministry of Culture," Owl hurried to assure him. "I have a few . . . friends . . . who owe me some favors. This is not a big deal, if we don't make it a big deal. He'll be released two days earlier, it's no more than that."

"Good," said Tortoise.

He picked up some papers that were in a bundle to the right and set them aside to the left, to indicate that the matter was finished.

(I realize now that the attentive reader will not be content without an explanation of how it came to be that Dennis

Coral could join our group and start a Retinue without the police authorities arresting him. From a legal perspective he had without a doubt escaped from King's Cross, and he had a long prison sentence still to serve. My original idea was to remain somewhat unclear about what happened after the "escape," but of course that generates more questions. The explanation is not complicated. When he was growing up, and as a prisoner at King's Cross, Dennis Coral had a different name. He was a different type of snake as well. The red, yellow, and black bands that I described previously he still wears today. The embroidery was Adam's idea, and afterward there was no doubt: Dennis had been transformed into a coral snake. That's the story, and more than that I do not, for understandable reasons, intend to tell.)

REUBEN WALRUS 9

Reuben Walrus counted backward from the fifteenth of April, when the concert hall would be filled with the cultural elite of Mollisan Town. He imagined them before him, stuffed animals with superior smiles flocking into the foyer, airing their expectations, dressed in tuxedos and glittering sequin gowns, with champagne glasses offered by the Music Academy. In his head Reuben heard snippets of conversation that had not yet played out. Someone would remark, "They say that this simply doesn't add up." Someone else would whisper, "The walrus should have quit when he was on top." And perhaps the most wounding, "This makes you wonder about his earlier works. Were they really that ingenious?"

The orchestra would need at least two days of intensive rehearsal to prepare the final movement. This meant that Reuben must have a finished symphony sitting on his desk on the evening of the twelfth of April for copying the following morning. Which in turn meant that there were no more than four days remaining.

He twisted and turned in bed. He had been awake since

midnight, staring furtively at the cold moonlight trickling in through the curtains. After a few hours of cold sweat and anxiety, he got up. There was no use. He pulled on his heavy terry-cloth robe that smelled of cigar and honey, and went to the grand piano.

In the darkness the open lid resembled a mouth laughing out loud. Reuben sat down on the uncomfortable piano stool, but he let the silence in the room remain undisturbed. He stared down at the keys, but was thinking about Fox von Duisburg's telephone call last evening.

"You can't be serious" had been her first words, without even saying hello or identifying herself.

He didn't understand what she was talking about.

"Hi, honey," he had said.

"During all those years," she said, "I still believed, deep inside, that when it really came to the point . . . that beneath the attitude, beneath that instinct to always look for the easiest way, always try to do things as painlessly as possible, you were—"

"Excuse me," interrupted Reuben, "but what are you talking about?"

"What am I talking about?"

"What'd you say?"

All the phones at home had been reset, but he still had difficulty hearing what Fox said. Yet there was no mistaking the weary disappointment in her voice, and he could scarcely recall having heard her sound so dejected before.

"Did you ask what I was talking about?" she repeated.

"Yes. I don't know what you . . ."

Reuben did not finish the sentence, but she remained silent on the other end.

"Hello?" he said. "Did you say something?"

"Reuben, I . . . ," she began, not knowing how she would continue. "You rejected Josephine."

"Is that why you're calling?" he asked.

"The decision was yours, and you didn't let her start at the school?"

"For one thing," he began, "the decision was not mine at all, and you know that. Besides, this is not a school, the Music Academy is—"

"She's crushed," interrupted Fox. "I don't think I've ever seen her like this. Not even when she was little. She's locked herself in her room, won't open the door, she's unplugged the phone."

"Time will—" Reuben began.

"This is not about the fact that she didn't get into the school," said Fox. "This is about the fact that her father did not give her the acknowledgment she's been waiting for her whole life."

There was a whirring in his ears. It sounded like when the top is popped off a soft drink bottle, with the difference being that the sound was constant.

"Hello?" he said.

"Hello," she confirmed.

But there was no force in her voice, not the usual energy.

"My life," said Reuben, feeling a tear forcing its way out of the corner of his eye, "is numbered. There is less than a week until Drexler's syndrome has put an end to my auditory nerves, and then I'll be deaf. For the rest of my life. If I have much life left, that is. My professional life is over in any event, my calling is—"

"You crushed her, Reuben," she said and hung up.

The pain in his chest.

He lifted his fin and played in the darkness, a few passages from an early work, a string quintet in G minor, a tragic story. Outside the windows he stared toward the building facade opposite, illuminated by the streetlights. It looked scuffed and gray and sad.

He was a worthless stuffed animal, he thought. He always had been. A worthless husband and an equally worthless father. He was a dishonest, unscrupulous specimen. And for that Magnus had punished him with Drexler's syndrome.

All attempts to compose were fruitless. He was too tired. He lacked talent. And he was far too panic-stricken.

After sitting on the hard stool, staring at the keys for almost an hour, Reuben was about to fall asleep. Could he carry this fatigue with him into the bedroom? Perhaps it was possible if he walked slowly and didn't waken his body through unnecessary movements. He slid off the stool and shuffled across the floor. His eyes were half closed, he breathed slowly, and he exerted himself to empty his brain of thoughts. Possibly this would have succeeded if he had not happened to twist his head to the right as he passed by the narrow corridor out to the hall.

He stopped.

Inside the door, on the floor, was a white envelope. Reuben was certain that it had not been there when he turned off the lights last night. Fatigue was instantly replaced by curiosity and—even if he dared not admit it—hope. Could it have been Josephine who had left a message? All he could expect was her anger and disappointment, but he could defend himself against that. He wanted to defend himself against that.

On his way out to the hall, he no longer remembered that he intended to go back to bed. He leaned over to take a look. His name was on the outside, but nothing else. No postmark or stamp.

The envelope was of normal letter size and sealed shut. He held it up, twisting and turning it as if he could figure out what it contained. Then he placed it under his fin and went into the bedroom, where he sat down at the little desk and turned on the lamp. Painstakingly he slit open the mysterious envelope and took out a piece of paper with typewritten text. He read the short message twice:

Dear Reuben Walrus,
I understand that you are interested in meeting me,
and I understand that the circumstances do not give us
much time. Therefore it is my suggestion that we meet
at Charlie's Bowling this evening, at the commencement
of the Evening Weather. If you take a seat at the upper
blue bar and order a Strike, I will make contact. However, I must ask you to come alone.

Sincerely,
Dennis Coral

It was still early in the morning, but as the clouds drew together and colored the sky gray-black, Reuben Walrus dialed the number of private detective Philip Mouse.

"I got a letter," said Reuben.

"Sooner or later this happens to all of us." Mouse yawned from his side of Lanceheim.

"From Coral. He suggests that we meet. This evening."

"Okay. Don't do anything," Mouse ordered, suddenly wide awake. "I'll come over in twenty minutes."

"Good."

Philip Mouse knew about Charlie's Bowling, and was therefore not surprised that Walrus had never heard of the place.

On flax yellow Piazza di Bormio was a shabby Monomart alongside an unassuming storefront that sold fishing poles, and which had been closed as long as anyone could recall. The outdated fishing tackle was still in the shop window. Otherwise the buildings on the piazza were not noticeably different from the average gloomy and half-dilapidated buildings in the depressing district of Yok. Appearances, however, were deceiving.

Charles Gull had embarked on a military career early in life, but the day he turned forty and had still not attained the rank of lieutenant, he could no longer overlook the truth. The military was holding him back. He left the army and used all of his severance pay to make the down payment on a bowling alley of a seldom-seen type. It would be in the middle of Yok and exceed everything that had hitherto been seen. Charles was a visionary and a skilled orator, and he convinced the banks to contribute capital, despite the fact that the stuffed animals in Yok were not a sought-after clientele.

The largest building by far built on Piazza di Bormio was meant to be an old people's home, but that never happened. The old people's home was instead relocated to south Yok, and the building stood empty a few years and was then rented out for a time to the Ministry of Finance, just as the Lucretzia hospital was undergoing extensive renovation work.

When Charles Gull bought the building, however, it had stood empty for almost ten years, and calculated per square meter he got it ridiculously cheap. The bowling alleys constructed in the basement became the base of the operation, but Charles's plans were more extensive than that. He saw before him a building where divisions were bridged, where there was both a haven for the poor and a luxury hotel for the wealthy on the same floor; he dreamed of seven-star restaurants alongside soup kitchens; he intended to let the prosperous stuffed animals in other parts of the city share their excess with the poor residents of Yok under one roof. For Charles, the bowling alleys were the symbol of brotherhood; here rich and poor could meet on equal terms.

Now Charles Gull was only able to realize half of this

amazing business concept. The stuffed animals from Yok came, but after initial interest—and not even that was markedly great—customers from Lanceheim, Amberville, and Tourquai stayed away. The homeless who sought shelter with Charlie were soon staying in the hotel suites as well, and after a few months the white tablecloths from the exclusive restaurant were used as bibs in the soup kitchens. The entire massive building was transformed into a kind of refuge for homeless stuffed animals and those who did not have the energy or desire to go home. They wandered around in the corridors and large halls for months, and at regular intervals Charles encountered animals who had not been outside the building for several years.

The only part of the operation that actually worked was, ironically enough, the bowling alley itself, and the associated blue bar.

Philip Mouse parked on the piazza. Cars were parked every which way in Yok, and as long as they looked worn-out and cheap, most often they were secure. Mouse's car was both worn-out and cheap.

"I'll follow you," he said to Walrus. "You don't need to be worried. Even if you don't see me, I'll see you. We'll do as we decided this morning."

"What'd you say?"

"Don't worry, I'll be watching you the whole time," Mouse repeated patiently.

"Why should I be worried?" asked Walrus. "I was the one who wanted to meet Coral, wasn't I? On the other hand, I don't understand why you're here. He wrote—"

"It's not Coral we're looking for," Mouse reminded him again.

"Keep at a distance," Reuben answered.

He did not know what he was most worried about, that

the private detective's presence would sabotage the meeting with Coral or that Mouse's absence would mean that they did not take the next step toward Maximilian.

"Keep at a distance," repeated Reuben.

He got out of the car and quickly headed toward the modest entryway that Philip Mouse had pointed out a few minutes before. The square was filthy and deserted, and the building that Mouse had described that morning looked insignificant. Reuben came up to the entry, and there stood a small copper sign that had acquired a greenish patina over the years.

It read "Charlie Bowling," as if this were a first and last name.

The door was open, and Reuben stepped into an ordinary but worn stairwell. It smelled faintly of mold, and the ceiling light did not work. He glimpsed someone climbing up the stairs, but knew that he was to go one floor down. And there, behind an iron cellar door, he entered a world that he never would have suspected.

Not even Reuben Walrus's ears, with their few remaining auditory hair cells, could be immune to the thunder from the forty-five parallel bowling lanes, all occupied by playing stuffed animals. The size of this underground hall was immense, as was the number of animals who were there.

"Thousands," thought Reuben Walrus to himself. "There must be thousands of animals here."

He would never meet any of them again.

These were the stuffed animals of Yok, and it was only after a few minutes that Reuben realized why he thought the atmosphere was unique. No one was looking at him. No one recognized him. It had been many years since this had happened in a public place in any of the other parts of the city.

Reuben wandered around for a while in a chaos of sound and light, colliding with stuffed animals going one way or another, or the sort who were not on their way anywhere, instead standing apathetically behind the waist-high barrier, observing the bowlers on the other side. Successful throws resulted in scattered applause and shouts, but with so many playing there was screaming and applause the whole time. Philip Mouse was nowhere to be seen, just as he had promised, but Reuben felt reluctantly happy that the private detective was in the vicinity.

After a while he noticed the staircases. They were wide as six bowling lanes—the comparison was unavoidable—and were roughly in the middle of the hall, with stairs from three different directions. The stairs ran together after twenty or so steps in a massive landing with room for at least ten tables, where animals were sitting and drinking and eating. Then you could continue approximately twenty more steps to the upper story.

Reuben noticed a blue neon sign that told him the way to the bar was up. He nodded to himself.

Now it was time.

The bar stool was more comfortable than Reuben expected. He was sitting on a thick, bright blue leather cushion attached to a strong metal pole that in turn was bolted to the floor. Four stools away sat Philip Mouse. Reuben had ordered a Strike—this proved to be a gin and tonic in which ten thin pieces of carrot cut like bowling pins were swimming. He sat sipping the alcohol and tried not to look for the snake. His gaze had locked on the private detective instead when it happened.

Everything went very fast, and only afterward did Reuben realize how it had happened. He felt a powerful jolt through his body, and then the floor opened up beneath him. Literally. Reuben Walrus and the barstool disappeared down into a hole that closed after a few seconds. Philip Mouse reacted with lightning speed, but he was still too late. The last thing Reuben saw before everything went black was the private detective's astonished expression.

The hydraulics were gentle and quick. He sank four or five meters, and then felt solid ground under himself and the stool again. He found himself in coal black darkness, and when the lamp was lit, right in his face, he instinctively closed his eyes.

"Walrus?"

"Yes?"

"You are . . . mm . . . Reuben Walrus?" the voice asked again.

Reuben squinted. The lamp had been lowered. The light kept him from seeing who was speaking, but he could keep his eyes open without being blinded.

"Yes."

"It's because . . . uh . . . your faith is not sufficient . . . that you're with me, huh?" explained Dennis Coral. "If your faith had been sufficient . . . mm . . . Adam Chaffinch would already have let you meet him, huh? Now there's me . . . uh . . . and Maria left, huh?"

"I see."

"You . . . mm . . . feel hope?" asked the snake.

Reuben did not know how he should answer.

He had feared and looked forward to this meeting since this morning. He had practiced certain formulations, a few lines, should he lose the thread, but after experiencing Charlie's Bowling and its remarkable atmosphere, all these preparations had been blown away. Besides, he had not yet recovered from the shock of the bar-stool trap.

Did he feel hope? He felt despair and confusion.

"I will feel whatever I need to feel to get to meet Maximilian," he replied.

"That was . . . hm . . . not really what we wanted to hear, huh?" said Coral.

Reuben felt a certain respect for the chaffinch. In part this had to do with the situation, but also with the chaffinch's calm and dignity. Now he noticed that he was starting to get angry. What was the idea of this parodic mysteriousness? Was the idea that he should be afraid? Was it some kind of test?

"Why can't I see you?" he asked. "I already know who you are. This is ridiculous. Ridiculous."

Coral let out a quiet but friendly laugh.

"Hmm . . . we'll stick to you, Walrus," he said calmly. "For that's how you usually like to have it, huh?"

"And what is that supposed to mean?" asked Walrus with irritation, snorting so that his mustache wiggled.

It was hard to sit up straight on the bar stool, and the situation was laughable.

"Back to . . . hm . . . hope," reminded Coral.

"Do you think I would subject myself to this if I didn't have hope?"

"Did have hope?"

"I'm doing exactly everything I can to try and meet a stuffed animal that no one can even categorize. The doctors have already sentenced me to deafness, and I have put my trust in a miracle. And you ask me if I feel hope? I want nothing better than to—"

"Your wants . . . hm . . . I don't doubt, on the contrary," answered Coral in a normal conversational tone. "It's whether you can feel hope that I . . . uh . . . am wondering, huh?"

"So you can distinguish them, want and hope?" asked Reuben.

"Can't you?" asked Coral.

"To want . . . to believe, and to hope, it would take a preacher to hold those concepts apart," muttered Reuben.

"And if I . . . uh . . . give you a hint?" suggested Coral. "If I . . . uh . . . say that the one thing has to do with you, and . . . hm . . . the other has to do with others, huh?"

"Others?" Coral nodded, although Reuben could not see him in the darkness. "I don't understand," he said.

"To hope for its own sake, it's that . . . what's it called? But . . . hm . . . Walrus . . . isn't that . . . to wish for something?"

"Are you asking whether I'm hoping for my own sake? Whether it's for my own sake that I want to hear again? You can bet your sweet ass on that," snapped Reuben.

At the same moment the lamp went out, and the room again became black. An instant later someone placed a damp cloth over his nostrils, and Reuben Walrus went out as quickly as the lamp.

Dag Chihuahua lived in a three-room apartment on the sixth floor of one of the white turn-of-the-century buildings on mustard yellow Krönkenhagen. In the bay window in the living room was Chihuahua's music stand, and in front of that, a tall stool that was wonderful to lean against when rehearsals dragged on. Through the thin white linen curtains Dag could look out toward the Dondau. The river flowed in a soft curve under his windows, and if he leaned out a little he could see all the way to Eastern Avenue. On weekends the stuffed animals liked to take walks on the paths along the river. Sometimes one of them would turn their head when they heard the notes of a violin, like a melodic buzzing in the air, but they could not see him. He liked observing the stuffed animals as they passed by. It was one of his many ways of cultivating solitude, this physically tangible complaint that had tormented him for many years.

Why had it become like this? In the gentle twilight of the Evening Weather, Dag Chihuahua might let the question pass like a glissando over the neck of the violin. He had no answers. He had not chosen to live alone. On the other hand, he had chosen to say no to . . . certain invitations. And he had firmly said no to advertising his desperation. To him it had always seemed . . . unworthy . . . to go out in pursuit of . . . someone. It was a terrifying thought to sit alone at a bar, casting discreet glances in all directions in the hope of getting a glance in return. And even if he did read the personal ads in the Sunday newspaper with delight mixed with terror, he would never sink so low that he would take out an ad himself. He would never be that desperate.

Better hopeless than humiliated, he thought, raising the bow in the air.

But the moment he let the tense horsehair of the bow land softly against the string of the violin, there was a banging on the door.

With his nose anxiously wrinkled Dag put down his instrument on the little stool, carefully set the bow on the music stand, and went with hesitant steps out toward the hall. Who could it be, this late in the evening? The only one he could think of was his father, who as of three years ago was also living alone, a few blocks farther east in Lanceheim. They had never had any relationship to speak of. His beloved mother had been the cement that held the family together, and when she was no longer alive, nothing held them together. Dag did not believe that his father minded. He had always been something of a lone wolf, never amused by social life. Dag Chihuahua knew that this might just as well be a description of himself, and this made him worried and melancholy.

He opened the door with the safety chain on, peeked out into the stairwell, and was frightened by the stench of alcohol.

"Well, now, let me in, then!" exclaimed Reuben Walrus. "Do you intend to let me stand here?"

Dag Chihuahua quickly closed the door, unhooked the safety chain, and opened again. He took a step to one side so that the great composer could come in, but despite that, Walrus only narrowly avoided hitting the doorpost.

"My friend!" bellowed Walrus. "The time has come at last for a candid conversation!"

The walrus continued into the apartment, and Chihuahua followed. It was apparent that Reuben was drunk beyond the bounds of decency.

"Would you like anything, Mr. Walrus?" asked Chihuahua. "I could make some strong coffee?"

"What?"

"Should I make some coffee?"

"What?"

"Coffee!" shouted Chihuahua.

"Coffee? Absolutely not! Coffee? I want alcohol! I want vodka! Do you have any vodka at home?"

Dag Chihuahua had no vodka at home; he had no alcohol whatsoever. Walrus did not believe him, and decided to investigate for himself. He veered off to the right, out into the kitchen, and rummaged around on shelves and in cupboards while the violinist stood in one corner and watched. When at last Walrus got tired and gave up, Dag confessed that he had a few bottles of vintage wine, from Yunger, in the sideboard in the hall.

"There's better," asserted Walrus. "But I'm not stingy."

Chihuahua took out the wine, uncorked it, and then watched as Walrus filled an ordinary drinking glass to the brim.

"Good," he said. "Let's sit here in the kitchen. It feels better. You have one heck of a nice place here."

Chihuahua shook his head. It was fine with him. Reuben nodded, took a large gulp of the wine, and grimaced a little.

"Don't you think you—"

But Walrus did not finish the sentence because he did not care where it was going.

It seemed as though Reuben could not concentrate on the

violinist at all as long as the wine bottle was on the table, but soon he had emptied it and remembered his business again.

Dag Chihuahua waited patiently in silence. He suspected that Walrus would once again air his anxiety and his impotence over the situation in general and the unfinished symphony in particular, and Dag was not a good consoler. On the contrary, he thought it was crazy to begin rehearsals without having the finished composition. For a long time he had harbored a well-concealed contempt for Walrus; in Chihuahua's eyes Walrus had always been a populist. It was lamentable that the old geezer was losing his hearing, but that this was a matter of civic grief—as the newspapers claimed—Chihuahua could not agree.

"You are my friend," said Reuben, thereby causing Dag to feel ill at ease. "You are my friend, you have always been. And now . . . now . . ."

Reuben lost the thread. For being so intoxicated, he still spoke clearly and distinctly. He must have practiced, thought Dag acidly.

"Chihuahua, you are my only hope," said Reuben. "I am now planning to ask you for something that is going to surprise you, but you must not . . . must not . . ."

Once again Walrus lost the thread. He looked stupidly at the empty wine bottle on the table, and then looked up at Chihuahua.

"You have several, did you say?"

But Chihuahua shook his head; that would have to be enough for now.

"Do you remember Bill?" asked Walrus. "Blazes, he could drink. He always said he drank for the camels. For the camels!"

Walrus snorted a laugh, and his mustache quivered. Chihuahua had not thought about Buffalo Bill for many years. Now he remembered, but vaguely, that Bill had been one of

Reuben's best friends. But that was long ago, before Walrus's breakthrough.

"I remember Bill," he said. "He was a pianist, wasn't he? But he . . . disappeared?"

"One time," Reuben continued without having heard Chihuahua's comments, "we had been out on the town . . . you did that at that time . . . went out on the town . . . and on the way home we were thirsty. Then it appeared that Bill had the key to Monomart's warehouse up in Tourquai on him, and we took a taxi up there and drank up all the—"

"There was no Monomart at that time," said Chihuahua, but Reuben did not hear this objection. "The Chauffeurs must have taken Buffalo Bill, but I don't remember when it was. For he was never at the Music Academy."

"Are you sure you don't have another bottle?" asked Reuben. "That was sour as hell, but if there's nothing else—"

"Mr. Walrus, tomorrow is also another day. When you rang, I was just going through the passage before the andante in the second movement—"

"Dag Chihuahua!" Walrus suddenly roared. "Let me talk! You . . . you play my harmonies . . . my melodies . . . for yourself in the evening. That is why I . . . Now I intend to ask you for something, do you understand. Something that is going to surprise you."

Reuben thought.

"Are you ready?" he asked.

Chihuahua nodded, without curiosity, without enthusiasm.

"I want you to finish my symphony," said Reuben. "For you . . . to finish . . . my symphony. But when you've done that . . . it's still mine. Mine! It will always be mine. Do you understand?"

Dag Chihuahua refused to believe his ears. It was the alcohol talking. It was the desperation talking.

"Mr. Walrus, this is foolishness."

"What'd you say?"

"This is foolishness!"

"Oh, get down off your high horse! This is not foolishness. Why should it be foolishness? It will be a little . . . secret. Between you and me. Nothing more. You get the money, I get a little honor. It is my symphony, after all, my composition. You . . . are simply helping out a little. For the sake of friendship. And money, of course."

Dag got up from the kitchen table.

"It's time for you to go home now, Mr. Walrus," he said.

"But don't you understand? This is the first time in ten years . . . It must be all right? You can, Dag. Of course you can!"

"Mr. Walrus, this is foolishness. Go home and sleep. Forgive me for saying this, but you are not sober. You don't know what you're saying."

Reuben got up. He did it so forcefully that the chair he had been sitting on fell to the floor, but he didn't notice.

"You are worried because you can't," he mumbled. "My friend Dag. Worried. You shouldn't be worried, Dag. Of course you can."

Chihuahua shook his head.

Reuben took a few steps toward the dog with the intention of hugging his old friend. Chihuahua recoiled in terror. He had difficulty with all forms of physical touch, and the old composer, reeking of alcohol, disgusted him.

"Go home now, Walrus," he repeated firmly, keeping the disgust out of his voice. "Then I will forget that you were ever here."

It took him almost half an hour to coax Walrus out into the hall. He did it with flattery and threats, and one thing was quite certain: He would not forget what Walrus had proposed. He would never forget it.

. . . .

The sun was shining in through the windows on sea blue
Knobeldorfstrasse the next morning, and when the sharp
rays reached Reuben's eyelids, a pain cut through his head
that caused him to waken with a gasp.

He understood why Dennis Coral had rejected him. Just
as he knew why Adam Chaffinch had done the same thing.
When he woke up in the middle of the night after the visit to
Charlie's Bowling, sweaty and nauseous from the ether they
used to chloroform him, he had hobbled out to the kitchen
to get some water. He knew exactly what had happened. He
lacked the right faith. He lacked hope, at least in the sense
that he suspected Coral was looking for.

I am a worthless stuffed animal, he thought gloomily.

And love?

He had loved. Was it not true that he loved Fox von
Duisburg? Could he use that love as an entry ticket to
Maximilian? The third guard must be the "Maria" that
Coral mentioned, and Adam Chaffinch had said that it
was a matter of faith, hope, and love.

Reuben drank tap water in greedy gulps and tried to
think through his possibilities. There was a chance, he
thought hopefully. But in his heart he felt less certain. He
did not even pretend to himself that the feelings he'd had for
other females had anything to do with love. And the love
he harbored for Fox, the longing and the need he still felt
for her, was that perhaps not love? Were they the usual feelings? He needed her. He missed her. She made him strong.
She gave him a connection. Was that love?

He looked around.

He was lying on his back on the floor beside the piano.
He had on the same clothes he had when he left Dag Chihuahua's, but he had no memory of how he'd gotten home.

With effort he climbed up onto the piano stool and looked out. It would soon be time for lunch. The thought made him inexpressibly hungry; the alcohol was in the process of leaving his body, and as always on such occasions he had to eat. Sweaty and shaking he made his way out to the kitchen, but the refrigerator proved to be a disappointment. On the other hand, in the cupboard above the sink there was a carton of alphabet crackers and another with honey-puffed breakfast cereal, the latter half-eaten. Taking both packages with him, Reuben left the apartment.

There were no traces of the anxiety that he ought to feel after the meeting with Dag Chihuahua. When he came out on Knobeldorfstrasse, he could hardly perceive the sound of the city. He had stayed away from his examination at St. Andrews yesterday, but he knew how things stood. His hair cells were dying at an ever-faster rate. The change over the last two days was more tangible than before.

As if blown away, his bad conscience about Fox and Josephine had left him. The ant, the female who thought she owned him, he hardly remembered. He had a single matter before his eyes. Today was the eleventh of April; tomorrow evening his symphony must be finished, and that was all that mattered. He could care less about Dag Chihuahua and the little snob's stuck-up manner. Reuben Walrus had a single way out, a single possibility left, and despite the fact that it was like grasping for stars, he had to try. He had to.

Walrus had only driven the golden Volga Deluxe with the crème-colored leather seats and shining, star-shaped rims that was in the garage on sand yellow Lychener Strasse on two occasions. One time from the ceremony where he got the car, a TV gala that for a long time he was ashamed at having attended, and the other time to an all-night pharmacy one evening when he really needed to sleep. But because he did not have a driver's license and was a public stuffed animal, he avoided the car. At the same time his vanity meant that he did not get rid of it.

Now he threw the cartons of crackers and cereal onto the passenger seat and sat down behind the wheel. He turned the key and was surprised that the engine actually started. With a jerk he backed out of the garage, and with a hop, after having popped the clutch, he drove off along Lychener Strasse down toward Eastern Avenue. It was easiest to take the avenues out of the city.

Reuben Walrus arrived at Lakestead House right before the Afternoon Rain. The sky was dark over the horizon as he parked his golden car in the lot outside the main entry, and on the sea waves foamed white in the wind. He thought he could hear the rush of the hard wind, but perhaps that was imagination. He had been a part of Hillevie when he was young, but the sea, the beaches, and the open landscape had always frightened him. He was a confirmed city dweller, and was not comfortable with unbroken views.

He did not recognize any of the aides who were standing in reception, but they recognized him. He did not hear what they said, but he thought he could read on their lips that they said his name. From their body language he understood that they wanted to help.

"I'm looking for Buffalo Bill," he said.

He hoped that his tone of voice was firm but friendly.

There was nodding and strutting, and finally an elderly heifer came and asked him to follow her. They went through the corridors, and to his surprise Reuben realized that he could find his way, despite the fact that it had been ten years since he was last here.

The heifer stopped outside the door, and gave him a questioning look.

"Thanks," he said. "I think I'll manage from here."

"He can be violent," said the nurse.

"What'd you say?"

The heifer repeated loudly and clearly what she had just said, and Reuben nodded.

"I remember that," he confirmed. "It comes and goes, doesn't it? I'll have to take the risk. There was an alarm by the electrical panel inside the door—is it still there?"

The heifer nodded.

"I'll buzz if things get crazy."

Without asking for permission, Reuben then opened the door and stepped in.

Buffalo Bill was sitting in front of the window in a bamboo armchair looking out at the rain that had just started to fall. The chair stood with its back toward the door, and Bill was accustomed to nurses coming and going. Therefore he didn't react. In peace and quiet Reuben could observe the room that for most of Bill's life had been his universe. The patient became uneasy when he had to leave it, and therefore he was allowed to stay there.

Reuben walked slowly up to the bookshelf, and ascertained that the few books were the same ones that had been there last time. The worn blue dressing gown hanging over a bedpost even seemed to be hanging just as crooked as it had when Reuben last left Bill in a fit of fury and impotence.

Time had stood still.

"Bill?"

He did not want to frighten him.

"Bill?"

And now he could see that the buffalo had heard. He slowly turned around. His lips were moving, even if Reuben did not hear what he said.

"Reuben?"

"What'd you say? Bill, I'm almost deaf. I hear almost

nothing. You have to speak loudly. And slowly. Can you do that? Talk loud and slowly?"

Buffalo Bill nodded, but turned his head back so that he was again looking out over the beach and the sea.

"Reuben? Did you bring any pictures with you?"

"Pictures?"

"I need pictures," said Buffalo.

He spoke loudly, and he spoke slowly. Despite the fact that Reuben only saw his neck, he heard fine.

"Without pictures I can't write," he said. "Have you brought pen and paper with you?"

"Write?" asked Reuben. "Do you want to write?"

"Not without pictures," said Bill.

"I don't understand," said Reuben. "What pictures?"

"I don't want to write anymore, Reuben. I can't. I will tell you what I have written. The opera *Sarcophagus*. A string quintet in G minor. Twenty-three opera arias for sopranos and tenors. Twelve symphonies. Five chamber pieces for tuba and—"

"I know what you've written, Bill," said Reuben. "You are a genius."

"And you've let Mollisan Town hear it," said Bill. "You have let the stuffed animals hear what I've written, haven't you? Of course you've done that. But now I can't write anymore. Not without pictures."

Reuben stood in the middle of the room and listened. He heard what Bill was saying, heard every word. He dared not move, dared not go up and position himself so that he could see the buffalo's face. They were talking with each other.

"Your unfinished symphony, Bill," said Reuben. "Do you remember it? The one in A minor?"

"I need pictures," said Bill.

"Bill, if I give you pictures, do you think you can complete the Symphony in A Minor then?"

"Do you intend to give me pictures, Reuben? Can you do that?"

"I can give you pictures, Bill. Can you . . . write again? Would you be able to?"

Buffalo sat silently.

"What'd you say?" asked Reuben.

But Buffalo sat silently.

Reuben stood completely still for several minutes, but at last he went up and around the chair. Buffalo Bill had fallen asleep.

"Bill?"

Reuben carefully shook his old friend. Bill opened his eyes.

"Reuben?"

"Bill, I—"

"Reuben? Is it you?"

"What'd you say?"

"I don't hear anything anymore, Reuben. I don't hear notes anymore. I can't help you anymore, Reuben. Don't be angry at me. Don't be angry."

"And the pictures, Bill? If I can arrange . . . pictures?"

"Pictures?"

"You said something about pictures?"

"Pictures? I don't know anything about pictures, Reuben."

"What'd you say?"

"I don't hear anything anymore, Reuben. Forgive me. You have to forgive me."

WOLF DIAZ 9

Witnesses say that when they unlocked the cell door and Maximilian crept out on aching joints, blinking his eyes at the blinding daylight, he said: "Hope does not die when the prayer is answered, hope only takes on a new form." It sounds like something Maximilian may have said, and there is no reason to doubt it.

Right after the Afternoon Rain on the twenty-fifth of December, a newly hired guard opened the little door in the great archway that was the main entry to King's Cross, and Maximilian could leave the prison. He wore the embroidered caftan he'd had on when they arrested him; the wide collars betrayed the years that had passed. The street he came out on was a deserted stretch of road to which the Highway Department seldom drives its garbage buses, and Maximilian walked slowly along a sidewalk of refuse: cigarette butts and broken bottles, old leeks and crumpled-up beer cans.

He had received permission to buy a pillowcase from the prison's impressive linen supply, and from this he had tied a cloth to put on his head. In a plastic bag he carried his belongings: a pair of underwear and a small bamboo zebra that Conny Hippopotamus had carved as a going-away present.

I imagine that at no time during his lonely wandering back to Mollisan Town did Maximilian stop, either to observe something in particular or to ask himself where he was going. He was thirty-four years old, but it seems to me as though his life had not really begun. True, at my place there were shelves full of notes, partially written out lectures, and conclusions from the quantities of courses that we had held through the years, all based on the Book of Similes and the deeds Maximilian had performed. Yet when I thought about it, his life seemed incomplete. Therefore the goal of his wandering was understandable.

Maximilian was on his way home to Das Vorschutz.

He arrived home late in the evening, after the Storm, to our glade in the forest. In the darkness it was hard to make out how the cherry trees had grown or that the beds where the roses bloomed were now full of scilla; the houses stood just as heavy and artless as always, and from the four chimneys each pillar of smoke testified to preparations for night. Possibly it is first here, just as Maximilian passes between Karl and Anders Beaver's house and purposefully crosses the round lawn on his way home, that he stops, turns his face up to the sky, sees the stars glittering in infinity, and senses the branches of the trees as dark shadows still swaying after the wild ravages of the Storm.

What does he see?

What is he thinking?

I do not know. I am the Recorder, I tell what there is, interesting or less interesting; what it is that slumbers in the womb of the future.

. . . .

Maximilian knocked carefully on the door to his parental
home, and when his mother, Eva Whippoorwill, uneasily
opened the door and saw him standing there on the stoop,
tired and miserable after months in solitary, she began to
weep. Like all the others, Eva had been told that Maximilian would be released two days later, and the surprise—
in combination with joy and relief and terror at how he
looked—overwhelmed her. She threw herself forward and
embraced him, and they stood like that a long, long time.
She felt the warmth from his body and the beating of his
heart. He was alive.

They had the evening meal together; Eva set the table in
the kitchen. After the time in solitary, Maximilian had contracted—his body was still full of surprises and transforma-
tions—and it was apparent that he needed food. Despite the
fact that he maintained he was hungry and although the
delicacies that Eva Whippoorwill set out in haste—vegetable timbale with cold sliced roast beef, baguettes and coun-
try pâté from lunch, and what was left of the garlic soufflé
and red beet quiche from dinner—would have caused anyone's mouth to start watering, Maximilian managed almost
nothing. He was not used to eating, and after a few bites he
pushed it away.

The conversation was hesitant. Eva told him about the
friends from before who still lived there, and what they were
doing. Weasel Tukovsky, for example, one of my closest acquaintances when we were little, had just the year before
become the first stuffed animal ever to run a marathon in
less than three hours. Sven told about what had happened
in the forest, and how he had fixed the drain and well last
week.

After that, silence fell. It was neither unnatural nor uncomfortable. Sven and Eva were still shocked and happy at having Maximilian at home, but the almost ten years that had passed were like a deep, wide moat between parents and cub.

"Was it hard?" Eva asked at last.

Maximilian set aside his silverware and looked at his mother. In his gaze was something heavy, even unpleasant.

"You can tell us," said Sven Beaver, "we're your family."

Maximilian nodded, and there was a careful smile on his lips.

"You are my family," he said thoughtfully. "Just as all stuffed animals in Mollisan Town are my family. You are my mother and my father and I am your cub, in the same way as all stuffed animals in Mollisan Town are my cubs, my mothers, and my fathers."

Eva, at a loss, looked at her husband, who in turn looked down at his plate. What was the meaning of this? All her love, all her sacrifices, did they mean nothing?

"But," she said, "you can't say that, Maximilian. I am your mother, I have taken care of you, your father and I brought you up and watched you mature, we're not . . . just anyone . . ."

"You are my family," answered Maximilian, "you are a part of the whole, you are a part of all that is good and all that is less good in Mollisan Town, and I have come to lead you from the bad to the good. I love you."

With these words he got up and climbed straight to the upper floor, to the room where he had not slept in almost twenty years. He undressed, lay down on the bed, and fell asleep within the course of a minute. His parents remained sitting in the kitchen. They dared not look each other in the eyes; they said nothing, but I believe they shared the same thought: The months in the claustrophobic solitary confinement cell must have made their son temporarily insane.

. . . .

The following morning Eva Whippoorwill woke up with a start. She sat up in bed, and confirmed that Sven was sleeping beside her. The bedroom on the first floor was in a dense darkness, it was still night, but through the gaps in the shades she could sense that the first rays of the sun were making their way over the horizon. She did not remember what she had dreamed, but it was not the dream that woke her; it was something else. Without trying to put words to her feeling, she swung her legs over the edge of the bed and stuck her claws in a pair of slippers. Her dressing gown was hanging on the bedroom door, and she wrapped it around herself as she went out into the living room.

There was a presence outside the house that she clearly sensed without being able to explain how or why, in the same way as when you wake from someone watching you for a long enough time. Eva continued out into the hall, but as she put her wing against the outside door to open it and see who was out there, she suddenly hesitated. Was there reason to be afraid? Was she in danger? This was the first time she had ever had the feeling of a strange presence in their distant forest glade. Should she wake Sven?

But that would be ridiculous. It was only a feeling, the remnants of a dream that she no longer recalled. It would be best to go back to bed, and back to sleep.

Yet she didn't. Instead she opened the outside door and stepped out onto the stoop. What she saw was—surreal.

On the round lawn in front of the house, but also along the pathways between the neighbors' houses and the whole way up to the forest edge, there were stuffed animals. They stood completely quiet in the early morning, while veils from the damp chill of the night still lay like transparent clouds across the ground. The stuffed animals had gathered in Das Vorschutz by the hundreds; perhaps there were a thousand: elephants and wasps, giraffes and dolphins, dogs and insects, reptiles and birds. Eva got the impression that they were lined up in defined formations, as if a choreographer had divided them into smaller and larger groups, but this was probably only a matter of trying to make room.

The whole thing was overwhelming. The stillness did its part: the fact that no one moved, no one said anything. The air in Das Vorschutz was full of suppressed expectation.

Eva Whippoorwill slowly backed into the house and soundlessly closed the door behind her. Her pulse was racing, but her breathing was calm. She no longer had a thought about Sven; much less did she recall that Maximilian was sleeping in his room for the first time in many, many years. Eva waited, hesitated, but then opened the door again. Perhaps she thought that the stuffed animals outside had vanished?

But they were still there.

We were still there.

The first daylight of the Morning Weather painted us in its yellowish light. We saw Eva Whippoorwill come out on the stoop a second time, and she behaved in the same way as before. Slowly she let her gaze sweep across us, as if she were counting us. Not even a hint of astonishment on her face. We stood motionless as cloth statues in this beautiful forest glade where I had grown up; we must have frightened her, even if she pretended that we hadn't.

I had stationed myself at my parents' house together with a group of stuffed animals that had come from west Tourquai. I did not know any of them; that is how large the three Retinues were nowadays.

We had planned for Maximilian's release as long as we had known the date. We had prepared a demonstration that would have dumbfounded Mollisan Town. We had counted on thousands of animals outside King's Cross. We had talked about how the church would react; we still knew nothing about Vincent Tortoise and his involvement. But we got no further than speculation; in reality we could not see how our Retinues could challenge anyone or anything; we were much too peaceful and introspective for that.

Then came the news that they had fooled us, that Maximilian had already been set free. Therefore we were now standing here, a decimated band, and our only spectators were the trees, the forest, and Eva Whippoorwill.

Eva still said nothing, and I realized that she did not intend to say anything either. We were the ones who encroached on her reverie; we were the ones who needed to explain ourselves. I was just about to take a step forward and make myself known when Adam Chaffinch broke free from a larger group of stuffed animals that had been standing in the middle of the round lawn.

The movement was, in the midst of the compact stillness, almost offensive.

"We have come to meet Maximilian."

His tone was low, soft, full of veneration. Eva nodded. She turned around, but before she had even managed to enter the house, Maximilian came out. He wore the bed-sheet around him, a white cover that dragged behind him like a bridal veil. And he had brought the pillowcase to tie into a headcloth over his head and ears.

Not a word was spoken. Yet what followed happened as if we had rehearsed it.

Maximilian seemed just as surprised as his mother. He went past her without hesitating—without granting her a glance, which afterward I would have a hard time accepting—and down the few steps to the gravel path. The stuffed animals who had stood unmoving took a few steps forward, those who stood nearby and those who stood far away; we all closed up. Who came up with the idea of raising Maximilian from the ground, I do not know. Perhaps it was Adam? In any event, up into the air he was lifted, and the stuffed animals not only formed a king's throne beneath him; we became his ground, his earth.

In this way we carried him out of there, in the same silence in which we came. I never turned around; I did not want to know how Eva Whippoorwill looked when we disappeared with her only son.

Ten years is a long time. Had something happened to Maximilian in prison, something I don't know about, or was it my mental image that had re-formed reality? I do not know, but the stuffed animal who returned was not the same as the one the court had taken from us. The first weeks I consciously avoided making comparisons, and I did not speak with others about the matter when I became certain. But I am positive that at least Adam Chaffinch saw it as I did. It was an older, more serious Maximilian who had come back to us; his youthful energy was gone.

We installed Maximilian in Maria's House on eggplant purple Damm Weg. For me Maria Mink's financial successes remained just as unfathomable as Maximilian's similes. Despite the fact that she worked hard with her Retinue, and despite the fact that I saw her spend just as much time as Dennis and Adam with Maximilian, her financial position only seemed to get stronger.

Damm Weg 62 was a typical three-story brick house built during the fifties. We had arranged a pleasant two-room apartment with a pantry and bathroom for Maximilian on the top floor. On the second floor were three classrooms, smaller than a traditional classroom but somewhat larger than an ordinary living room. Our expressed intent was to avoid institutionalizing the training or the need for such; we offered time to stuffed animals who sought us out. Over the years certain distinctive features of Maximilian's teachings had nonetheless crystallized—even if you, reader and doubter, have already understood the main ideas because I have anticipated our later conclusions in this text—and animals who wanted to do more than simply take part in one of our three Retinues had to be taken care of in some way.

`"This is not about an education with a special degree," Adam Chaffinch emphasized. "More like a deepening in Maximilian's teachings in an organized form."

Our worry was partly political. Starting an educational institution required permission, and one of the referees would in all likelihood be the theological department at the university in Mollisan Town. We already knew what they would say.

On the bottom floor of Maria's House were a large kitchen, some storage areas, and the Planning Room, where Adam, Dennis, Maria, and I usually met. There was also the Chancellery, where Beetle Box and some of his temporary helpers worked. The Chancellery was our heart—or perhaps more accurately, it was the central hub, from which the nervous system of the three Retinues sprang. At that time Adam, Dennis, and Maria each held two lectures per week. Finding new places, and not least spreading information about where the lectures would be held, was an extensive process. Beetle Box was not only responsible for making this work, he was also forced to maintain a low profile, use decoys, and write contracts under assumed names, all to avoid incidents like the one on Maximilian's birthday.

. . . .

The Planning Room was windowless, narrow, and filled with
the type of soft, colorful, plush-covered furniture that was
modern in the seventies. I used to sit in a green-and-yellow-
striped armchair that was very comfortable, and which could
be tipped back. We needed a constant supply of fresh lilies in
the room, however, to cover up the odor of unwashed fabric.

"Is this just the top?" I asked my friends. "That's what I am
worried about. That I haven't even seen the vegetable itself."

I was again speaking about the threat that the Kwai
family was still subjected to, and I readily admit that the
comparison was not the most brilliant. What I meant, and
I think I understood, was that perhaps we weren't taking
the threat against the Retinues seriously, that we only saw
the harmless outgrowths of an invisible, far more imposing
organism.

"I wouldn't worry," said Dennis. "We have, mm, talked
about this before, Diaz. Apart from, uh, that this bull is
crazy, I can't really take him seriously."

"Sometimes I think you isolate yourself too much," said
Maria. "I think it would do you good to go out with me
sometimes, Diaz. I don't mean to the Retinues, but out into
the real world . . ."

She did not finish the sentence, but Adam was thinking
along the same lines.

"What we are trying to say, Wolf, is that even if they turn
against Maximilian, it's not him, but the society, that is
the problem. We respect your instinct, but there are things
going on in this town far more dangerous than youthful
hoodlums."

I shrugged. This was not the first time they had dismissed
me; in fact, by now I was used to it. It was my own fault. I
had not been able to make the threat real to them.

I peeked out the window, but saw that I had time. Every day I went up to Maximilian a while and sat. Ever since his release he had, as I mentioned, been different. We let him stay highest up in Maria's House, but yet we did not see much of him. He mostly kept to himself, in his minimalistic room. Above all, those first months after he came back we made serious attempts to get him to take a greater share in the work. We told each other that that was what was needed; it would entice him out of his shell. But the more we failed, the less we tried. Slowly we were forced to realize that we had built the operation and the three Retinues in a way that did not require Maximilian's presence. This caused us to feel ashamed—we spoke about it often, but secretly we felt a great relief, since Maximilian was not himself.

I was still occupied with my Recording, even if it took no more than a few hours a day; neither Maximilian nor I could concentrate any longer than that. Several days might go by without Maximilian saying anything really important. Of course I asked the question: Did he want to break off these sessions?

"The cat's playing with the ball of yarn does not knit any sweaters," he replied.

I interpreted this as meaning that he wanted to continue.

"Hmm," said Chaffinch.

I was lost in reverie; like mischievous lambs, my thoughts had wandered off in every direction, and now I was forced to gather them together.

"On Friday," I answered to the question I knew he had asked.

Dennis nodded.

"Perhaps we can be down at the Wrest again?" Adam proposed.

"Are you joking?" I said. "We can't be at the Wrest. Never again."

"Simply because it happened once, that doesn't mean it's going to happen there again." Maria smiled gently.

"You can call me paranoid," I said, "but we all know how afraid certain animals have become over the years when Maximilian has . . . healed them. And we all know where that fear can lead. If anyone, such as Rothman, starts systematically spreading lies about Maximilian, it can . . . I don't know . . . We live in our little bubble, Adam. Imagine if there are—"

"Diaz," interrupted Adam when I could not find the words, "I'm not certain that we, you and I, are living in the same bubble. Because I feel, and have felt for more than fifteen years, ever since you were holding forth in the church in Kerkeling, that in the presence of Maximilian there has always been a threat. Rothman or not, what we do . . . We grant faith, hope, and love to those who need it. We have gathered so many; we are a force, Diaz, we have long been a force that threatens established structures. Why do you think that Dennis, Maria, and I do not preach in Maria's House? Why do you think that we steal away to the most unlikely places to hold our meetings? Why do you think we have so few students? I am certainly living in a bubble, but I have never imagined that we are secure."

"But Rothman—"

"He is only one of the many who believe they have reason to get back at us, one of many who are afraid of what they do not understand, and transform their fear into anger."

I did not answer. This was only one of many dialogues that were repeated to the point of exhaustion. The meeting proceeded to practical matters, and when it was over, my frustration was, as usual, as great as my doubt.

I wish with all of my heart that I had been wrong.

REUBEN WALRUS 10

Reuben Walrus lay hidden in one of the covered boxes on the second tier as the orchestra musicians came back to the rehearsals on the morning of the thirteenth of April. The murmur from the arriving musicians suggested a certain expectation; they were looking forward to seeing how Walrus had finally finished his symphony. Yesterday evening he had promised that there would be new scores at their places this morning.

Reuben Walrus himself heard nothing from up in the balcony. He had stayed behind yesterday evening when they had all gone home. Perhaps he thought that a miracle would occur in the concert hall during the night? But more or less deaf as he was, he could not even try to produce one. The promise of new scores was empty and stupid, and when he gave it he had consciously avoided looking at Dag Chihuahua.

Did Chihuahua understand what was going on? That Reuben was a sham? Under other circumstances this question would have tormented him, but as things were now, he didn't care.

When they were younger, Buffalo Bill had been a friendly type, labile and headstrong but also loyal and tenderhearted. He had discussed music with Reuben as if they were equals, despite the fact that the opposite was already apparent even in their teenage years. Reuben's talent went far enough to understand the genius that Buffalo was supplied with, but not much farther. In comparison with Bill, Walrus's efforts as an instrumentalist, composer, and director were no more than mediocre.

They were both accepted at the Music Academy, Reuben as one of many ambitious stuffed animals and Bill as a shining talent. Stimulating personal creation was a significant aspect of instruction at the school, and for the walrus it was painful to see at close quarters how the music was born inside Bill without the least effort. What he himself produced was only affected, stolen, or bad. Bill could hear music inside himself, and wrote it down without even touching an instrument. It was fascinating.

And it became not only Bill's music, but also his process, that Reuben borrowed and made his own when Bill was taken into Lakestead House.

Reuben by then had pretended to be the great composer genius for so many years that he almost believed that it was he who had created these amazing works. He had lived for so long with his false role that he had stopped feeling like a deceiver. So deep was his self-deception that in some small part of his heart he actually believed that during the night he would be able to create the end of the Symphony in A Minor, Bill's last composition before madness finally conquered him.

Reuben Walrus had slept in the box during the night, and his body ached when he woke up. He had slept remarkably calmly, but as soon as he opened his eyes, he realized that he had failed, that it was too late. Nonetheless he did not flee. Instead he sat in the darkness and watched the orchestra members arrive, one by one. He saw them come onto the stage, go up to their places, and search in vain for the music he had promised but which was not there.

Reuben had never been inclined toward self-torment. On the contrary, through his entire life he had chosen to handle problems by closing his eyes to them. Yet he stayed to observe his own defeat. Only when almost the entire orchestra was gathered down on the stage did Reuben get up and steal away.

Reuben went home to Knobeldorfstrasse in the Morning Rain, and was soaking wet when he arrived. On the answering machine there were six messages. From the numbers on the display he could see that five were from Philip Mouse. Instead of calling back, Reuben continued toward the bathroom, undressing on the way. One after another pieces of clothing fell to the floor—his jacket in the hall, trousers, underwear, and socks in the corridor, and at last the damp shirt in the washbasin in the bathroom. Then he climbed into the drying cabinet, turned the heat to maximum, and closed his eyes. He remained in the warm, dark cabinet until long after he had dried.

He heard almost nothing. He tried to stop himself from thinking about it, stop himself from listening, which was actually easier than it ought to be. Only when a sound reached one of his few living hair cells did panic strike him.

He turned off the drying cabinet and got out, positioned himself in front of the full-length mirror on the inside of the bathroom door, and gave himself a crooked smile. It would be known as his unfinished symphony. Perhaps that wasn't so bad? If he forestalled his critics, he could pretend that it was Drexler's syndrome that had kept him from completing this final work. The connection between the illness and the symphony was indisputable. It was better than indisputable; it was true.

The thought gave him a certain consolation and strength, and he went naked out into the kitchen and picked up the phone, dialed the number for private detective Mouse, and waited until he thought he heard someone at the other end.

"Mouse?" he said, and continued without waiting for a reply. "It's Reuben. Mouse, I saw that you'd called. I know what you want. But it's over now, Mouse. I don't need any more help. If you want to find him, you can try on your own. I'm not paying another cent."

Reuben waited a few moments. He thought he heard Mouse say something, but he was not sure. He knew that the private detective wanted to prolong the assignment, wanted to work on, but at some point you had to bring it to an end. Mouse had played out his role.

"So that's the way it is," Reuben resumed when he thought that sufficient time had passed. "Your final payment will come in the mail, no later than Monday. Thanks for your help, and say hello to Daisy."

He was rather sure that Philip Mouse was still talking when he hung up.

When the doorbell rang, Reuben Walrus was on his way from the kitchen back to the bedroom, where his dressing gown waited. It was starting to get cold without clothes. He faintly perceived the sound of the doorbell as he went past the hall, and wondered how long someone had been standing outside and ringing.

His first thought was that it was Mouse, but that was impossible, of course. Reuben shuffled out into the hall. Just as he was about to open the door, he remembered his nakedness and pulled on a coat that was hanging among the outdoor clothes. It was black and made from wool, and he hardly recognized it; it must have been hanging there for many years.

"Yes?"

Outside stood a female in a black suit, a business female in a tailor-made jacket under which she was wearing a white blouse and a discreet, burgundy-colored tie. She was holding an attaché case in her hand, and when she set it down, she produced a little grimace that suggested that the bag had been heavy to carry. For a moment he was uncertain whether this really was a female, but something in her charm made this indisputable. And of course he considered himself a connoisseur.

"Yes?" he repeated.

Then he realized that she was actually talking to him. He held up one fin, the sign for waiting, and went back into the apartment to fetch a pen and some paper. Equipped in this way, he returned to the hall, where the suit-clad stuffed animal politely hesitated outside on the threshold.

"Yes?" he asked again, then handed over the writing implements.

"My name is Maria Mink," wrote the suit-clad female. "Dennis Coral suggested that I should visit you."

Reuben read what was there, and looked up again at the mink. It had been impossible to overlook the suit, but now he took note of her beautifully gleaming fur, her long, pointed nose of yarn, and her small, brown eyes that observed him with curiosity. Was this the apostle of love of which Adam Chaffinch had spoken? This surprised Reuben greatly, and he was uncertain whether the surprise was positive or negative.

She took the paper from him and wrote, "Excuse my apparel, I've come straight from a board meeting at one of the real estate companies."

He stroked his mustache, took a step to one side so that she could come in, and only then realized that he was standing there dressed only in an overcoat. He took the pen from her, and wrote on the same page:

"We both need new clothes."

When he did not hear his voice, he had become uncertain whether he pronounced the words correctly. That was ridiculous, of course—he had been talking his whole life—but it still felt more secure to write.

"Then I suggest that neither of us change. Then it's equal," wrote Mink.

Reuben Walrus went before her into his little study, which was right next to the studio where the piano was. The room had originally been a maid's room, but now it was dominated by a large red antique rug. They each sat down in an armchair. The chairs were turned at an angle to each other, heavy pieces with high backs and generous arm support. Between them stood a little round table with a marble top, and at an angle behind Reuben's armchair an old-fashioned lampshade in aged leather peeked out. The heavy curtains had been half closed, and a pleasant calm rested over this small room.

"I want to meet Maximilian," said Reuben.

But again this feeling of uncertainty, so to be on the safe side he wrote the same thing: "I want to meet Maximilian. I want to get my hearing back."

Under Maria Mink's curious gaze, he felt neither afraid nor impatient. He realized that this was his last chance, but he no longer had anything to lose.

Maria Mink pointed at the notepad and pen that were on his lap, and he gave them to her.

"What is love?" she wrote on the blank page of the notepad.

She was just as direct as Coral, and just as absurdly naive. There was no answer to what love was, thought Reuben. But he didn't intend to make the same mistake he had made last time. So he decided to put arrogance and irony aside, and he took the pad that she had set on the little table and put it on his lap.

Love?

"I think," he wrote slowly when he had thought about it a long time, "that love is the feeling of pain when you think about someone that you're not seeing right then."

He handed her the pad, as if she was going to correct his answer.

"Pain?" was all she wrote, handing back the pen and paper.

He remained sitting, brooding, not in a hurry. She sat quietly too, with time to wait. When he was through thinking, he began to write. But meditatively, word by word.

"To miss someone. To miss someone so desperately that it causes pain in your heart, pain in your fabric, and in your whole body. To be filled by a longing and an emptiness so strong and deep that it paralyzes you and threatens to destroy you. That the only thing you want and can think about is to see the one you long for again, and before that happens you are no one. Half. Only a fragment."

Reuben gave her the pad and closed his eyes. That was how he missed both of them, Fox von Duisburg and Josephine. He longed for them, not only physically, to see them and touch them, but also spiritually. That was how he had always missed them. Like an anxious cry for help that echoed in his heart, whether he had them here or had not seen them in a long time.

"And when you are together with them?" wrote Maria Mink.

Carefully she set the pad on Walrus's lap, and he opened his eyes again and looked down at the single sentence.

When he was together with them? How could he describe that? How would he dare explain it?

"Then," he wrote, "it is like . . ."

"And love, how would you describe that?"

But he continued to owe her a reply. Somehow he knew that he would not be able to lie to her; it was too late for lies. It had been so easy for him to say untrue words over the years, words that simplified his life. But to sit here and write them down on a pad of paper—was impossible. He thought a long time, but wrote at last, "I don't know."

"Has it always been the case," wrote Maria Mink, "that you have only been able to love in solitude? That is not unusual, Reuben. Love requires courage, and not everyone has the means or the opportunity to acquire it."

But again he owed her a reply. He shook his head, not knowing what he should say. Then he thought of something, grasped the pen, and wrote, "It must not be about them. I can love in solitude. I can sit at my piano and place my fins on the keys, and when I hear harmonies arise out of combinations of individual notes, when I see a pattern form through measures and phrasings, I can—often but not always—be filled with joy, at the same time a kind of deepest satisfaction and exhilarated happiness. That I would call . . . love. And then I'm not talking about the ability to create music, or even to play it. When I hear it, when I am sitting in a concert hall and an orchestra of distinction and ability performs one of the old masters' pieces . . ."

He put the pen on the pad and was absorbed in thought. Maria did not move, let him be, let him think about it. How long they sat like that, neither of them could say, but he did not lose his concentration. On the contrary, inside him sounded—note for note and voice for voice—some of the works that he admired the most. Among them Buffalo Bill's unfinished Symphony in A Minor.

At last he grasped the pen and wrote, "Then, in the music, I am complete."

Maria Mink took the pad and read. When she did not write an answer, he took back the writing implements and added, "Let me meet Maximilian."

He showed her, and regretted it at the same moment. He should not have written that last thing. He should not have felt sorry for himself, or demanded anything from her.

Maria got up from the chair, and signaled to him to do the same.

WOLF DIAZ 10

It began in north Lanceheim and at the same time in the central neighborhoods of Amberville. Emerald green Haspelgasse and pink Gruba Street had this in common, that neither of them had been mentioned before in a historical context. I, and many with me, devoted far too much time to discussing and trying to determine how these streets had actually been chosen, or if it was only the finger of chance that had pointed at them. Personally I promoted the latter thesis. It became one of the most unpleasant nights in the history of Mollisan Town, and therefore I understand the need to find a guilty party.

I do not know who threw the first stone, but I know that it either broke the window to the Glen Vulture family bakery on Haspelgasse or Sloth McArthur's watchmaker's shop on Gruba Street. If I may once again make a middling attempt at depicting a course of events, I choose to concentrate on Glen Vulture and his family, and will thereby—in advance—beg pardon of the McArthur family. This was a narrative consideration, not a political stance.

. . . .

Glen Vulture and his family—a wife and three cubs all under the age of ten—were sleeping on the upper floor when the sound of broken glass woke them. The weather was calm, the moon half, and the hour late.

"What was that?" asked Mrs. Vulture, who always slept lightly and woke at the slightest sound.

"It wasn't here," mumbled Mr. Vulture, who wanted to go back to sleep.

But in the following moment the three cubs came into their parents' bedroom, and their worried voices forced Glen Vulture unwillingly out of his lovely, warm bed. He sat drowsily on the edge of the mattress and promised to go down and see what had happened. He pulled on a worn terry-cloth bathrobe, stuck his claws in a pair of old felt slippers, and left the bedroom with a heavy sigh.

The cluster of stuffed animals outside the bakery froze when the light came on inside. It was impossible to imagine that this enraged mob was made up of the greater part of a cricket team in Amberville, but that was the case. Ordinary, simple stuffed animals, changed beyond recognition by their own terror. Soon scattered cries and threats were again heard from the group.

"Renounce him!" screamed a young hen.

"Right-winger!" screamed an elderly horse.

A chimpanzee crouching on the sidewalk managed to pry an emerald green cobblestone loose, which he heaved toward the part of the shop window that was still intact. It was purely a stroke of luck; the glass crashed loudly, and the rabble on the street cheered spontaneously.

When the next stone flew in through the window, Glen Vulture could no longer stand passively watching. He ran down into the bakery and up to the window. Outside, Haspelgasse was dark and quiet as usual. The street was short and narrow, there were no other shops, and only one of the five streetlights worked. Vulture had consciously opened his bakery on a side street; those who appreciated good bread nonetheless found their way there. Now he wondered why none of the families who lived across the street turned on their lights and came out; didn't they have cubs too who were afraid?

"Reactionary!" shouted the mob when they caught sight of him.

"Right-winger!" the horse screamed again.

Glen Vulture assumed that this was a misunderstanding. How or why he did not know. He took a few more steps up toward his broken shop windows, which the mob perceived as a provocation. Several shouts and screams were heard, among them one that finally mentioned the name.

Maximilian.

"Your false Maximilian can't protect you against this!" screamed the chimpanzee, and a third emerald green cobblestone flew through the air and struck Glen Vulture in the head so that he fell down and remained prostrate.

The mob cheered and screamed, perhaps to lessen their shame and their anxiety, and quickly moved on.

This was how it began, on Haspelgasse in Lanceheim.

How do you start an insurrection? I can only guess. By innuendo. A whisper in a long ear. Gratuitous dementia. Keeping track of who, on every block and in every house, is most afraid, and then strengthening that fear. Acting without being seen. Contributing to an organization, and making sure the money is used for something else. Patience, of course. The insight that a seed that is planted must get nourishment and time to grow. Resources are required. Motivation and persistence are required.

What happened that night was well orchestrated, but

behind the years of planning and consistent spreading of rumors that preceded the event itself there was a master of intrigue. For a long time he had made sure that the threat from false saviors was whispered in ears faithful to the Proclamations. For many years the city's reactionary circles had heard about a liberal apostle of love. For just as long liberal stuffed animals had been supplied with news of a fundamentalist prophet who was constantly winning new adherents.

Once again: How do you start an insurrection? Who has those kinds of resources? Who has the motivation, and what aims are being served? These questions lead to one and the same answer. I have no evidence, at least not enough for a court of law. Not because that would lead anywhere. Justice is part of the state. And I write this: In all ages, governments have known the art of manipulating the citizenry. Someone who has been in power as long as a certain tortoise must have learned how things were done. I'm not saying anything else.

When the moon became full, they met on Marktplatz. Various eyewitness accounts state that there were anywhere from a thousand animals to tens of thousands. According to the police, as many as thirty-five thousand stuffed animals were involved, but this figure may have political overtones, as the police always describe themselves as understaffed.

They came from all parts of the city, even if the majority came from Lanceheim. On the way there they had broken shop windows and sprayed graffiti on facades; the bravest—or the most cowardly—had entered buildings and apartments and vandalized and beaten. When every small group had joined the overwhelming mass of animals that was waiting on Marktplatz, the excitement increased further. That there were so many of them! What they had dared until now was nothing compared to what they would dare during the hours that followed.

It was the Night of the Flood; the night when the city

would be rinsed clean. The concept had probably been coined at the ministry, but that would never be explained. The Night of the Flood: a night of cleansing, when mighty forces, natural forces, would be let loose to crush the unnatural and re-create harmony in our city.

Why just this night? Why just this week, this month, this year? I do not know. No one has been able to explain it to me. But judging by the results, the instigators chose the right night, week, month, and year.

When small groups were no longer joining up with the great mass on Marktplatz, the departure began. It took time; it took almost twenty minutes from the first ones starting to go until the last ones set off. They chose the broadest street heading east, mixed-gray Bardowicker Strasse; they took up both sidewalks and both driving lanes. Individual stuffed animals who encountered them fled into the cross streets. It could be seen in the eyes of the mob: If you weren't with them, you were against them.

There was no talking among the agitated animals. Instead they screamed out their terror and their hatred. One by one, without caring whether anyone listened, or in groups, they shouted disgusting rhymes that someone must have created in advance. I do not remember them all; a few I am never going to forget. I will not reproduce them, I do not want to contribute to their distribution, but the message was basically the same: Maximilian and his Retinues must be crushed once and for all.

I have never confirmed this, but lists with names and addresses must have been circulated. The authorities must have registered us over a long period, taken pictures of stuffed animals who took part in Adam's, Dennis's, and Maria's lectures, and then identified them in some way. Found out where they lived.

Homes were destroyed that night. It is possible that this affected more than members of the Retinues, but this was never talked about. With an unfailing scent the mob made their way into the right entryways, doors were kicked in and cut apart, homes were wrecked, and the families who lived there severely shocked. Nothing was stolen—this was obviously important; they were vandalized and destroyed, but no one could be accused of theft.

Boutiques whose owners had longingly listened to Adam Chaffinch's words about faith had their store windows broken and window displays trampled, fathers who had seriously heard Dennis Coral talk about unquenchable hope were forced out of their night sleep while the fired-up mob tore the sheets from their beds and locked their children and wives in the bathroom drying cabinets. Elderly stuffed animals with hardly any sight or hearing left, but who could still be moved to tears by Maria Mink's words about love, saw their memories in the form of photographs hanging on the walls in halls and dining rooms brutally crushed against parquet and stone floors.

And like the mighty flood that they wanted to resemble, the drive continued indefatigably eastward, toward the goal that had been selected long ago: Maria's House on Damm Weg.

For my part, the phone rang in the middle of the night, and someone screamed and cried at the same time. I still do not know who it was who called. I misunderstood the message in parts, but it was nonetheless clear to me that it was about Maximilian, and that he was in danger. I quickly put on my clothes and ran down to Damm Weg, where the others already were assembled. I must have come there about the same time as the masses of stuffed animals up at Markt-platz started moving, but so far it was silent and dark and quiet in east Lanceheim.

Via the telephone in Beetle Box's room we got reports, each more unbelievable than the next. The networks that Box had used to spread information were now used to tell us what was happening. The descriptions made us weep. When we thought we understood what was brewing— something we of course did not fathom and the magnitude of which not even I, who had fantasized about conspiracies for a long time, could understand—we tried to forestall it. We quickly prepared a list of animals that we ought to call and warn, and then went to various rooms in the building and phoned.

We realized that they were on their way toward us.

And none of us woke Maximilian, who was sleeping on the top floor, ignorant of what was on its way.

Or possibly he wasn't?

The first thing we heard were the screams. I imagine that we all heard them at the same time; at least it did not take long before we were all standing in the hall. Someone opened the doors out toward the street. Maria's House was the last building on a dead end, which meant that we now stood looking out toward long, narrow Damm Weg, which in only a short while would be transformed into a chaotic, howling sea of variously colored stuffed animals whose fears were turned into energy and whose hatred was aimed in one direction.

We did not say anything to each other.

Once again: No one ran up to waken Maximilian.

We stood as if frozen into ice, staring out toward the empty, dark street even as we heard the ululating screams coming ever closer, becoming clearer and clearer. It was Adam, Dennis, Maria, Beetle, and I plus five or six other stuffed animals.

I was afraid. I was more afraid than ever before. And

when they came—first far away, like a movement in the night, then filling the narrow street to the brim, first ten, twenty identifiable individuals, then as an anonymous collective—it was as if everything happened in slow motion. I had time to think about every consequence, every possibility, and yet I did nothing, like in nightmares, where your body refuses to obey your brain's orders.

They came closer and closer, and yet it never ended: The line at the crest of Damm Weg remained constant. I have no idea how many there were. A thousand or ten thousand, it was all the same. We who were standing on the stairway outside Maria's House could see them from slightly above; the five stair steps were enough to make the terrifying picture clear to us.

There was a back door. If we had wanted, we could have run into the house, through the hall, past the Planning Room, and out the back.

I'll stay here as long as Adam stays here, I thought. The others must have thought the same.

We stood there, like an honor guard without weapons or discipline, and watched our fate come toward us. We had no defense against clenched paws, drawn-up shoulders, claws that pointed, and eyes that burned.

They stopped only when there were ten or so meters remaining to the stairs. It was a careless, rowdy, unrehearsed stop. The first animals did not want to come closer, as if they were afraid of a deadly infection. For a few short moments they jostled a few meters ahead of the line, which did not understand that there was a halt, but then everything became calm. The screams stopped. I do not maintain that it became silent, but it was considerably quieter.

At that moment Maximilian came out of the door.

He raised his arms.

He had on his white dressing gown and a solid-colored light blue headcloth that he had worn the past month, of which he was especially fond. None of us on the stairs had seen or heard him arrive; we had been paralyzed by the mass of animals surging along Damm Weg.

"Go in," I heard Adam Chaffinch hiss at him.

Adam was standing on Maximilian's other side, and I can imagine the look Maximilian gave him.

"Go in," repeated Adam.

"It is for my sake they have come," replied Maximilian.

He misunderstood the situation. He thought that these stuffed animals were his followers, that they had come to seek his help or ask for his advice. And before any of us realized what he was thinking, he started to go down the steps toward the unruly mob.

They made room for him.

"My cubs," said Maximilian as he stepped down onto the street and went right in among them, "my cubs, I love you all."

It should have been impossible, but in some way they managed to create a path for him. They squeezed out along the edges, and they swallowed him up. Seconds later the shouts started up again.

The whole thing happened so quickly that it was barely comprehensible to me. The terror made me ice cold. I took a few rapid steps down the stairs.

"I love you all!" I heard Maximilian shout from inside the crowd of stuffed animals.

After that, only a breath later: "It is the Night of the Flood!"

A scream, a signal, and chaos broke out.

They stormed up toward us. I had been on my way down the stairs, and was forced to turn in midstep. There was no alternative. I hardly need to explain or prove my love for Maximilian, but with hundreds of stuffed animals who were more or less attacking, there was nothing else to do. I fled, I had no choice. I tried to see where the others were going, but it was impossible to understand what was happening. There were stuffed animals everywhere, screaming and, in some way, exhilarated. The aggression that was let loose that night had long waited for release. It was disappointment over promises betrayed, unfulfilled careers, unrequited love, over the fact that the Chauffeurs carried off the near and dear and over life lies laid bare that could finally be screamed out of soul and heart.

I ran. Sometimes I thought I was running along with the animals of the mob; sometimes I knew that I was running ahead of them. I ran through Maria's House and straight toward the door at the back. I do not know for sure if anyone was pursuing me or if they mistook me for one of them. I did not care which. I ran until someone stopped me. But no one stopped me.

Out behind the building was a well-tended garden that I quickly passed. The next day, when we returned, our garden, like everything else, was completely massacred. There was a gate in the garden fence, and it was the first time I had used it when I threw it open and ran away from there. No one followed me, yet I continued to run for a good ten minutes. And it was only when my lungs hurt so badly that they almost burst that I sank down into a dark entryway and caught my breath. Then I realized that I had left Maximilian.

The silence was suddenly unbroken.

No one followed me, nothing was heard of the animals over on Damm Weg, and after a few minutes I was even uncertain whether what had happened had really happened. It had been so unreal and gone so quickly that now, afterward, it was like a dream. Yet I dared not return. As soon as I shut my eyes it all came back: the screams and the glowing eyes, the hatred, and the fear without end.

I knew that I ought to have made an attempt to return and search for Maximilian, but I also knew that it was meaningless. My own terror slowly caught up with me. I could not go home; they knew where I lived. I could not go to Adam, Dennis, or Maria; I did not even know what had happened to them.

The only place I longed for, where security prevailed, was also where I imagined Maximilian would make his way, if he could.

I got up, and in the approaching hours of dawn began walking the long way home to Das Vorschutz.

I do not know exactly how deep into the agitated mob of stuffed animals Maximilian managed to get before he realized what it was about. Perhaps—and on this point he himself is unclear—he knew exactly what it was about even from the start? He went at a brisk pace and doled out his blessings to right and left; he lightly touched the stuffed animals that he passed and explained that he loved them, that love was all. And the mass of stuffed animals closed around him where he had just proceeded.

Did they recognize him? Did they realize that this was the animal with the headcloth they had come to hate? But the way he behaved, they must have understood. They must have recognized him, they must have known that they were preparing a way for the one they hated and feared the most.

What caused them to draw aside and let him go ahead? This is one of those incomprehensible stuffed-animal phenomena that is difficult to explain. Perhaps it was just as much about Maximilian himself? I have mentioned the charisma that surrounded him many times, the integrity he possessed. Had this kept them at a distance?

Or else were his actions so surprising that they could not attack? He walked right in among his enemies to give them love.

When Maximilian had made it two or three cross streets

up along Damm Weg, the mood of the crowd of stuffed animals changed. Screams again began to ring out. But now they were screaming out their hatred right in Maximilian's face. And the louder they screamed, the braver they became.

He continued walking. He continued to touch them, to talk about love, but more and more often they pushed aside his contact. He looked into their terrified eyes, and he saw how they tried to make themselves blind to conceal who they were. They screamed that they hated him; he replied that he loved them.

The first blow meant nothing. It missed widely, it was no more than a caress across his shoulder. The second blow was decisive, because it was followed by a third and a fourth. Maximilian fell to the ground, and the crowd was over him in a few seconds. In the chaos that followed, other stuffed animals fell as well, and the kicks that were delivered struck Maximilian as well as the others on the ground.

It is impossible to clearly account for what happened next. Maximilian must have been scared and in great pain, even if he would never admit it. And if it was the kicks that moved him out toward the sidewalk after he found himself in the middle of the street, or if he himself had tried to make his way there by crawling, I do not know. But he maintains that he had gotten so far out toward the side that he saw the facade of one of the buildings when he took the last two kicks that made the world spin. A heavy boot struck, once across the mouth and once across the ear, and Maximilian collapsed on the asphalt.

Someone took hold of his arms. Although he was almost unconscious, he perceived how he was being dragged across the sidewalk. A mystical experience, because he did not understand how it was happening. The stuffed animals screamed, hit, and kicked, without him. A spark had been lit, and few cared any more about the fallen Messiah.

"Get up," someone whispered in his ear.

An enormous exertion, and Maximilian managed to get up on one knee. The pain in his head, in his ribs, exploded like lightning behind his eyes, but still he managed to get up with the help of the animal that had dragged him out of the chaos.

"Here," whispered the voice. "In here."

And with one arm on his rescuer's neck, Maximilian let himself be dragged into an entryway. When the door closed and the silence and darkness suddenly encircled him, he began to weep.

"I have a car on the other side," said the voice. "Can you drive?"

Maximilian nodded. He had never driven a car in his entire life, but still he nodded.

"Let's go there," said the voice.

And by more or less carrying Maximilian through the dark entryway this still-unknown rescuer helped Maximilian escape the crowd of stuffed animals.

Only when they came out at the back of the building was Maximilian able to turn his gaze from the ground and see what his rescuer looked like.

"You?" was all he managed to say.

"Will you manage to drive yourself?"

"You have not done this in vain," said Maximilian, nodding as if at the question.

"Nothing in my life is in vain," answered Eagle Rothman.

Rothman dragged Maximilian in behind the steering wheel, started the car for him, and watched him drive away, slowly and bumpily.

It was after the Night of the Flood that we realized that Mollisan Town was no place for Maximilian. Our mission was to spread his word, but also to protect his life. After the Night of the Flood we saw to it that no one who had not first been approved either by Adam, Dennis, or Maria was allowed to meet Maximilian. The building on Damm Weg was closed up; Maria sold it later. That was almost twenty years ago now. The last I heard, the apartments were being turned into condominiums.

EPILOGUE: TWENTY YEARS LATER
WOLF DIAZ

I do not have a confessional nature, but this I confess to you, my reader: Without Maximilian, my own life would hardly have been worth anything. As his biographer, his permanent secretary and clerk, I have found meaning in an existence that otherwise would have remained a mystery to me. Therefore it is infinitely difficult to write these lines, presumably the last I am ever going to write.

As I cannot make what has happened comprehensible to myself, how am I going to make it comprehensible to my reader? No, I am going to betray you, because I have betrayed Maximilian. I know that when you—dare I call you my friend, my temporary companion?—have turned the final page in a little while and vacantly stare out into the emptiness that is sometimes called life, you are going to be both furious and frustrated. For this I beg your pardon. If life were as logical as a fairy tale, everything would be easier.

This is about expectations. We live in a reality where effects demand causes. You have followed my path through the years, I have recounted my actions, sometimes my feelings and thoughts, while I have told the story of Maximilian. This has led up to an image of who I am and how I act, an image that I have no doubt unintentionally idealized. No more about that now.

I have done what was not expected of me. Not least for this I ought to be punished, even if my crime is worse than that. Infinitely worse than that.

Today is the fourteenth of April.

The first time Maximilian said it was four hundred thirty-two days ago.

The second time was the day before yesterday.

Maximilian and I are living in our cabin not far from Das Vorschutz, and life has been good to us. Today I would of course be able to tell exactly where the cabin is located, but after all these years I have secretiveness ingrained in me. We live where no one is going to find us.

After the Night of the Flood we lost our last innocence. We realized that Mollisan Town was no place for Maximilian, and we fled into the forest. We built him a little house, and at no time did anyone ask whether I was prepared to sacrifice everything and settle here, isolated from family and friends. It was taken for granted. In a way, it was a compliment. We built a house that no one could find, and there we have lived ever since.

Adam, Dennis, and Maria are the only ones who know the way here. They have supplied us with everything we needed over the years, and at some point every month they have brought along a strange stuffed animal for a visit. These visitors come blindfolded, let into our little library at the back of the house, and after a conversation with Maximilian, sometimes long but often brief, they leave the house with the blindfold on.

These visits amuse both of us, because our existence otherwise lacks variety and surprises.

I am not complaining. No one forced me into this, and if I were able to live my life over, I would have made the same choice. Nonetheless life has at times been monotonous. We get up in the morning and go to bed at night. I have devoted a few hours every day to my notes, to what has been my life's work: reproducing Maximilian's words and actions. In solitude and concentration under these mighty trees I have found new connections and been able to set some to rights; I have arranged the text for the generations to come, long after we have disappeared, and I have realized that I have an amazing opportunity.

If and when I have been uncertain about interpretations—something that has happened more than once—I have been able to ask Maximilian. Very seldom have I gotten any unambiguous answers, but I have been granted additional images. One day, I am sure of it, these too will be interpreted by stuffed animals more talented and learned than I am.

So life has passed, and I hardly dare think about how long we have lived here together. I have written and thought, cleaned and laundered, prepared food and kept an eye on myself and my life companion, the unparalleled Maximilian. Not once has he expressed that he lacked anything, either physically or spiritually. This I ask you, my reader, to keep in mind. Not once in almost twenty years have I disappointed him.

It happened four hundred thirty-two days ago, in the morning, without my having asked or even brought up the subject. Maximilian raised his eyes from the daily paper he always read when he got it, a few days after the day of publication, and said, "I am weeping inside, about those who do not understand that the love between a he and a she is a promise for life. For each and every one of you stuffed animals, there is one other. Woe to the one who does not understand this."

This is exactly what he said.

I was doing the dishes, he was sitting at the kitchen table. As usual I sensed that he was about to say something, right before he said it, and I immediately turned off the running dishwater. It was unusual for Maximilian to speak without being addressed, and over the years we had both gotten older and thereby less prone to believe we had anything new and urgent on our minds. His way of expressing himself had become more and more old-fashioned; my way of listening had become more sensitive.

Thus I turned off the running water, grasped the pen that I always had at hand in case just this should happen— the opportunity to write down what Maximilian said.

I wrote on the roll of paper towels; it was the only paper I could find at that moment. The words that I read destroyed everything. It erased my future, it betrayed everything that had been.

(Does this sound melodramatic? Does it sound absurd? Does it sound ridiculous? Drop it. I realized immediately, intuitively, that what he had said was as irrevocable as it was destructive. Still I did not want to understand, I wanted to struggle against it.)

There and then, at the kitchen sink, I reasoned with myself. Had Maximilian changed his conception? What was the meaning? The story of the miller and his daughters, the parable that I had made one of the main features of the Book of Similes, possibly because it was so close to my own conceptions and my own life, I had always interpreted opposite to what Maximilian had just expressed.

Was there something in the newspaper that caused him to react, was there a context I did not understand?

"The love between he and she," I asked, surprising myself by the disappointment that was in my voice, "should not be lavished? Shouldn't it be given to as many as possible?"

"Only a fool believes that," replied Maximilian, returning to his newspaper.

"But the story about the miller and his daughters . . . ?"

Maximilian did not answer. Seldom or never did he recall his own parables, and when I read them to him afterward he was always unwilling to comment on them. Most often he did exactly as he did four hundred thirty-two days ago: He pretended that he hadn't heard the question.

When I got no answer, I set aside the pen and paper towels and left the kitchen without another word. To maintain that I was shocked would be putting it mildly. The emotion that filled me made its way slowly to my reason. I was crushed.

I wandered around in the forest for several hours that day, asking myself the same question again and again. Had Maximilian aimed his words directly at me? Was it my life he was condemning?

I had lived with many females. I had lavished my love on first the one, then the other. I was so inclined, and I believed that was how Maximilian wanted it.

When I finally returned home to the cottage, I could not understand it in any way other than that I had lived with a lifelong misunderstanding, a life-lie. The message was crystal clear.

"For each and every one of you stuffed animals, there is one other. Woe to the one who does not understand this," Maximilian had said.

It was those like me he was complaining about and judging.

When I stepped inside the door, the Afternoon Rain was already gathering, and Maximilian had as usual lain down in the bedroom one flight up to sleep. Perhaps he prayed, like the deacons in the church during the afternoon sabbath? But I think he was sleeping. I went out to the kitchen as if in a trance and stared down at the paper towel that lay wrinkled and damp next to the dishes as I had left it. The words written there reduced all of my life, my being, to something Maximilian obviously condemned and despised.

It was naturally my own fault. It was suddenly completely clear. How I had seized on the story of the miller and his daughters and made it into something it had never been. How I had distorted it to suit my own purposes.

Up until that day I had been Maximilian's confidant, his Recorder, an animal who lived in goodness. As of that day I was . . . a sinner.

I am telling what there is, without circumlocutions.

I dried the dishes with the paper towel that carried the despicable words, and threw it into the garbage.

For the first time in more than forty years—for that was how long it had been since I had met the newly confirmed Maximilian and begun my life's mission—for the first time in forty years I denied the world, and posterity, his wisdom.

This is an action that over the days that have passed has been just as hard to live with as the idea that Maximilian expressed.

. . . .

In this simple action—throwing away a paper towel—I had demonstrated an unparalleled power, and at the same time a misuse of that power. Concealing the truth was a passive way to manipulate Maximilian's message. But perhaps worse: It was an attempt to manipulate myself. In this I saw a pattern. It was not the first time. I had done similar things when, in the Book of Similes and during seminars and discussions, I guided the interpretation of the story of the miller and his daughters in the direction I wanted. I had used his words to justify my weaknesses.

These thoughts left me no peace. Existence in the forest was transformed. My patience broke down, time and again. During days that over the years had been devoted to meditation, I was now pursued by restlessness and doubt.

Living out here in the forest with him was one thing, but living here with myself . . .

And perhaps worst of all: I believed that I would get away with what I had done.

You now understand, disappointed reader, that my capacity for self-deception is greater than you could have believed. I thought I would get away with this, that when the paper towel was thrown away, I again had interpretive priority. I did away with the evidence to the contrary, and again my reflections about the lavishing of love were undisputed.

I have been a fool.

I am a fool.

Today is the fourteenth of April.

The first time was four hundred thirty-two days ago.

The second time was the day before yesterday.

I did not write down the words; they were not identical

to those he had uttered a little more than a year ago, but the essence could not be missed. He was airing viewpoints that were as venerable as the city church itself. It was almost unpleasant to hear him. Marriage was sacred, fidelity fundamental. . . . I do not know where this new, reactionary vein comes from.

Was it age?

The question is justified. Maximilian had turned fifty-four, we have lived in isolation out in the forest the last twenty years, and ideas can petrify under less extreme conditions than that.

Is this conservatism—musty, without a doubt—possibly the result of something new, rather than an elucidation of something old? I mean, my interpretation of the story of the miller back then may still have been correct, and now, in old age, Maximilian may have changed his conception?

Just this thought—this possibility, I would say—I twisted and turned yesterday, and the conclusion makes me worried, to say the least. If it is true, if Maximilian has been influenced by time in his isolation, considerably more is at stake than the simile about the miller. If Maximilian, for reasons of which I am not aware, has backed up into a conventionalism . . . We've been together every day, year in and year out, and this type of change occurs so slowly that it is impossible to discover before it is . . . too late . . .

Can he take back what he once said?

The three Retinues—which still exist, but work under far more sophisticated forms than was the case during our early, tentative years—base their meetings on texts from the Book of Similes, and in the interpretations that we have agreed on after many hours of strenuous studies and, sometimes, quarrels.

Can Maximilian take back what he has said?

What would happen to all the stuffed animals who—like myself—got support and power from those words about faith, hope, and love that were Maximilian's? We who have not let ourselves be frightened by the church's threatening images of the judging Magnus and the enticing Malitte, we who therefore had become indifferent, until we heard Maximilian?

Or all the timid ones huddling under the dogmas and rituals of the church in expectation of the day when the Chauffeurs would come to get them, all those who, thanks to Maximilian, could finally straighten their backs and live in the present?

May Maximilian betray us?

So went my thoughts yesterday, and during the evening and the whole night I continued in the same way. I lost myself in details, ever smaller and more irrelevant the more tired I became. I could not let it go. And however many questions I still came up with, there was only one answer. An answer I did not want to hear.

I am Nobody.

I am Maximilian's Recorder.

I have lived my life in relation to him.

He caused me to feel like a good animal.

When I heard Maria come walking along the path, the weather was still only forenoon, but I had not slept the whole night—I had hardly slept the night before either—and I could not think clearly. My instinct was to run and hide, leave the house and go off into the forest and never return. But I did not run.

I went down and opened the door as always. Maria had a walrus with her. As usual I led the guest into the library before I took off the blindfold. After that I went out to the kitchen to arrange the customary tray with tea. I pretended that everything was as usual. That I was as usual. During the few seconds that I succeeded in making the illusion real, I felt an unparalleled relief. It is difficult to explain.

I heard Maria upstairs. She had gone up to bring Maximilian down.

Maximilian always drank his tea out of the same cup. It was large, green, and chipped on the rim. I have never understood why he liked it so much, but he was a creature of habit; we both were. The poison that I put in Maximilian's cup—this was twenty, thirty minutes ago—I actually know nothing about. I got it from my father when the forest rats were trying to chew their way into the cottage. I know that it is strong, and that is all I need to know. A few sips of tea, and then he doesn't wake up until the Chauffeurs arrive. Even if it takes awhile, even if it takes months.

When I set the teacups on the table in the library, I did not even care to say hello to the walrus. I left the room before they had come down from upstairs. My paws were not shaking. One cup for the guest, one for Maria, and the big green cup for Maximilian.

Then I sat down in the kitchen and waited. I do not believe I was thinking about anything. Mute. Numbed by what I had done. It felt unreal. At last I sneaked over to the closed door and put my ear to it.

I heard a strange voice, it must be the walrus.

"Did I think I heard birds?" he said from inside the library.

As always, when the Afternoon Rain approached, the forest birds became restless and excited by the oncoming storm.

"Can it be right, Maximilian?" said the walrus within, and he sounded agitated. "Did I hear forest birds?"

I went back and sat down at the kitchen table. I closed my eyes. Maria just screamed.

But I intend to remain sitting here.

ALSO AVAILABLE
IN THE MOLLISAN TOWN SERIES

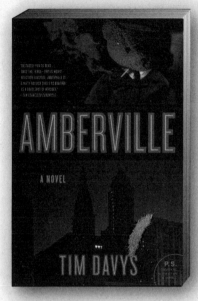

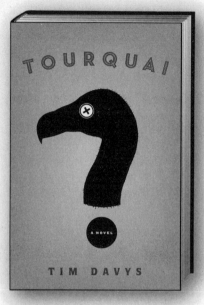

AMBERVILLE
A Novel

ISBN 978-0-06-162513-8 (paperback)

With a nod to the best of noir and the wisest of allegories, *Amberville* depicts an alternate world, mirroring our own realities and moral concerns and reminding us of the inextricable links between good and evil.

"These are stuffed animals like you've never seen: deep, dark, and, somehow, utterly believable. Lucky us—a mystery that's completely original."

—Brad Meltzer

TOURQUAI
A Novel

ISBN 978-0-06-179745-3 (hardcover)

In this third book in the Mollisan Town quartet, Tim Davys weaves together an intricate plot in which Oswald Vulture, a rich and powerful finance mogul, is found beheaded in his office, setting off a chain of events for the stuffed animal citizens that questions whether they are free or whether they are ruled by destiny. As Superintendent Larry Bloodhound uncovers the secrets behind the world of the wealthy stuffed animals, so too does Davys reveal greater truths about the world of humans.